Praise for *B*

"Mbue writes with great confidence and warmth, effortlessly inhabiting the minds of both Jende and his wife. . . . As the story progresses, the plot, which is premised on a class divide, unfolds to reveal many more fissures crackling beneath the surface—immigration proceedings don't go well, marriages falter, friendships fail, children stray. There are a lot of spinning plates, and Mbue balances them skillfully, keeping everything in motion. . . . *Behold the Dreamers* is a capacious, big-hearted novel." —*The New York Times Book Review*

"Mbue's writing is warm and captivating."
—*People* (Book of the Week)

"As a dissection of the American dream, Imbolo Mbue's first novel is savage and compassionate in all the right places. . . . Awe-inspiring."
—*The New York Times*

"*Behold the Dreamers*' heart . . . belongs to the struggles and small triumphs of the Jongas, which Mbue traces in clean, quick-moving paragraphs. . . . A fresh, engaging entry in the eternally evolving narrative of what it means to be an American—and how human beings, not laws or dogma, define liberty." —*Entertainment Weekly*

"A debut novel by a young woman from Cameroon that illuminates the immigrant experience in America with the tenderhearted wisdom so lacking in our political discourse . . . Mbue is a bright and captivating storyteller." —*The Washington Post*

"In the near decade since the onset of the Great Recession, few works of fiction have examined what those years felt like for everyday people, how so many continued to hope and plan and love amid pervasive uncertainty. Enter *Behold the Dreamers* by Imbolo Mbue, a Cameroonian American who situates her characters on U.S. shores just as prosperity is beginning to seem like a thing of the past. . . . *Behold the Dreamers* challenges us all to consider what it takes to make us genuinely content, and how long is too long to live with our dreams deferred."

—ANGELA FLOURNOY, *O: The Oprah Magazine*

"[Mbue's] book isn't the first work of fiction to grapple with the global financial crisis of 2007–2008, but it's surely one of the best. . . . It's a novel that depicts a country both blessed and doomed, on top of the world, but always at risk of losing its balance. It is, in other words, quintessentially American." —NPR

"Even as *Behold the Dreamers* takes some dark, vicious turns, it never feels cheaply cynical, grounded as it is in the problems of well-imagined characters who try, through whatever means possible, to protect their families and better their lives." —*USA Today*

"The eloquent beauty of *Behold the Dreamers* lies in the steady revelation of its characters' behavior under duress. . . . It is not the bedeviling American dream that demands our affection and understanding here. Instead, Mbue insists, it is the humans who dream it." —*Newsday*

"Mbue's story sheds light on so many different corners of the emotional struggle of not only getting ahead, but simply existing. . . . An incredible effort." —*Elle*

"*The Help* meets *House of Cards* meets the read that'll make you forget all about your morning commute." —*theSkimm*

"Imbolo Mbue's masterful debut about an immigrant family struggling to obtain the elusive American dream in Harlem will have you feeling for each character from the moment you crack it open." —*InStyle*

"Mbue proves herself a clear-eyed, unflinching storyteller, and *Behold the Dreamers* is a fearless, head-on journey into the thorny contemporary issues of American exceptionalism."   —*Interview*

"A witty, compassionate, swiftly paced novel that takes on race, immigration, family and the dangers of capitalist excess . . . a compelling view of 21st-century America . . . This is *The Grapes of Wrath* sans Dust Bowl."   —*St. Louis Post-Dispatch*

"Mbue [is] a deft, often lyrical observer. . . . [Her] meticulous storytelling announces a writer in command of her gifts, plumbing the desires and disappointments of our emerging global culture."
                              —Minneapolis *Star Tribune*

"Mbue does an admirable job of developing characters whose lives seem so heartbreakingly real that the pages of this book often seem like something of a confinement. When you close the book, you will hear their pain. You might feel them calling for you."
                              —*Los Angeles Review of Books*

"A witty, empathetic, fast-paced novel that takes on race, immigration, family and the dangers of capitalist excess. In luminous prose, Imbolo Mbue has produced a powerful view of 21st-century America and an important meditation on the true collateral costs of that all-American pastime—the pursuit of happiness."   —*Coastal Illustrated*

"*Behold the Dreamers* is about the consequences of dreaming too long, too recklessly, and too credulously, but even more, it's about waking up from that dream, and living, about the empty space that follows a story that runs out of gas. There might be no second acts in American lives—as F. Scott Fitzgerald once claimed—but if so, it's the brittle resistance to change and the refusal of the new that brings the whole thing crashing down. In the warm comedy of an immigrant family, we find a different story, a story that, in its very irresolution, continues to have a future."   —*Literary Hub*

"Mbue's book feels especially relevant in our present moment, as xenophobia dominates the news cycle and meritocracy can often feel like a fading promise."   —*Refinery29*

"*Behold the Dreamers* reveals the dark side of the American dream."
                                                                                —*Vox*

"This debut is entirely unique, poignant and striking. It's simply excellent fiction, with a tight plot that avoids convention and always surprises, and characters and dynamics that breathe right off the page . . . a refreshing, phenomenal and crucial work."   —*Bookreporter*

"By now we've read quite a number of novels whose action is set in motion by the economic crisis of 2009. Imbolo Mbue's impressive debut takes a singular place among them. . . . Realistic, tragic, and still remarkably kind to all its characters, this diversely peopled and crisply narrated novel is notable for its blend of dark irony and buoyant good humor."
                                                                    —*Critical Mass*,
                  the blog of the National Book Critics Circle board of directors

"At once a sad indictment of the American Dream and a gorgeous testament to the enduring bonds of family, Mbue's powerful first novel will grip and move you right up to its heartfelt ending."
                                                              —*Shelf Awareness*

"Among the spate of novels forged in the crucible of the previous decade, Mbue's impressive debut deserves a singular place. . . . Realistic, tragic, and still remarkably kind to all its characters, this is a special book."
                                                        —*Kirkus Reviews* (starred review)

"The Jongas are . . . vivid, and the book's unexpected ending—and its sharp-eyed focus on issues of immigration, race, and class—speak to a sad truth in today's cutthroat world: the American dream isn't what it seems." —*Publishers Weekly*

"An utterly unique novel about immigration, race and class—and an important one, as well." —*BookPage*

"The book itself is excellent: a beautifully written story about family, dreams, what home means, the different interpretations of the American dream. . . . I will read anything Imbolo Mbue writes." —*Book Riot*

"A fast-paced, engaging read with an interesting cross-cultural background." —*Library Journal*

"Mbue's first novel is a weighty meditation on the true collateral costs of that all-American pastime, the pursuit of happiness." —*Booklist*

"Imbolo Mbue would be a formidable storyteller anywhere, in any language. It's our good luck that she and her stories are American." —Jonathan Franzen

"At once an ode to New York City and an elegy for the American dream, *Behold the Dreamers* reads like a film, shuttling effortlessly between a Cameroonian chauffeur's Harlem and an investment banker's Upper East Side. This is a novel populated by characters so textured they feel like friends: an immigrant with big dreams and limited options; a banker desperate to do better than he's done; a mother, a student and wife determined to express her humanity fully in the world. There are no heroes in this marvelous debut, only nuanced human beings. A classic tale with a surprise ending, as deeply insightful as it is entertaining." —Taiye Selasi, author of *Ghana Must Go*

It ruined the next day for me—I wasn't much good for anything but a nap—but it was worth every lost hour."

—AYELET WALDMAN,
New York Times bestselling author of *Love and Treasure*

"Who is this Imbolo Mbue and where has she been hiding? Her writing is startlingly beautiful, thoughtful and both timely and timeless. She's taking on everything from family to the Great Recession to immigration while deftly reminding us what it means to truly believe in 'the American dream.'"

—JACQUELINE WOODSON,
National Book Award–winning author of *Brown Girl Dreaming*

"A beautiful book about one African couple starting a new life in a new land, *Behold the Dreamers* will teach you as much about the promise and pitfalls of life in the United States as about the immigrants who come here in search of the so-called American dream."

—SONIA NAZARIO,
author of *Enrique's Journey* and winner of the Pulitzer Prize

Behold the Dreamers

Behold the Dreamers

A NOVEL

Imbolo Mbue

RANDOM HOUSE | NEW YORK

Published in the United States by Random House, an imprint and division of
Penguin Random House LLC, New York.

RANDOM HOUSE and the HOUSE colophon are registered trademarks of
Penguin Random House LLC.

RANDOM HOUSE READER'S CIRCLE & Design is a registered trademark of
Penguin Random House LLC.

Originally published in hardcover in the United States by Random House,
an imprint and division of Penguin Random House LLC, in 2016.

Library of Congress Cataloging-in-Publication Data
Mbue, Imbolo.
Behold the dreamers : a novel / Imbolo Mbue.
pages   cm
ISBN 978-0-525-50971-4
Ebook ISBN 978-0-8129-9849-8
1. Cameroonians—United States—Fiction. 2. Immigrants—United States—Fiction.
3. Upper class—United States—Fiction. 4. Family life—Fiction. 5. Family secrets—Fiction.
6. Global Financial Crisis, 2008–2009—Fiction. I. Title.
PS3613.B84L66 2015
813'.6—dc23
2015011560

International edition ISBN 978-0-525-51011-6

Printed in the United States of America on acid-free paper

randomhousebooks.com
randomhousereaderscircle.com

4 6 8 9 7 5 3

Book design by Susan Turner

For my beautiful AMR
with gratitude
for walking with me into the Mystery

For the Lord your God is bringing you into a good land—
a land with streams and pools of water, with springs flowing
in the valleys and hills; a land with wheat and barley, vines
and fig-trees, pomegranates, olive oil and honey; a land where
bread will not be scarce and you will lack nothing; a land where
the rocks are iron and you can dig copper out of the hills.

Deuteronomy 8:7–9

Behold the Dreamers

One

HE'D NEVER BEEN ASKED TO WEAR A SUIT TO A JOB INTERVIEW. NEVER been told to bring along a copy of his résumé. He hadn't even owned a résumé until the previous week when he'd gone to the library on Thirty-fourth and Madison and a volunteer career counselor had written one for him, detailed his work history to suggest he was a man of grand accomplishments: farmer responsible for tilling land and growing healthy crops; street cleaner responsible for making sure the town of Limbe looked beautiful and pristine; dishwasher in Manhattan restaurant, in charge of ensuring patrons ate from clean and germ-free plates; livery cabdriver in the Bronx, responsible for taking passengers safely from place to place.

He'd never had to worry about whether his experience would be appropriate, whether his English would be perfect, whether he would succeed in coming across as intelligent enough. But today, dressed in the green double-breasted pinstripe suit he'd worn the day he entered America, his ability to impress a man he'd never met was all he could think about. Try as he might, he could do nothing but think about the questions he might be asked, the answers he would need to give, the

way he would have to walk and talk and sit, the times he would need
to speak or listen and nod, the things he would have to say or not say,
the response he would need to give if asked about his legal status in the
country. His throat went dry. His palms moistened. Unable to reach
for his handkerchief in the packed downtown subway, he wiped both
palms on his pants.

"Good morning, please," he said to the security guard in the lobby
when he arrived at Lehman Brothers. "My name is Jende Jonga. I am
here for Mr. Edwards. Mr. Clark Edwards."

The guard, goateed and freckled, asked for his ID, which he quickly
pulled out of his brown bifold wallet. The man took it, examined it
front and back, looked up at his face, looked down at his suit, smiled,
and asked if he was trying to become a stockbroker or something.

Jende shook his head. "No," he replied without smiling back. "A
chauffeur."

"Right on," the guard said as he handed him a visitor pass. "Good
luck with that."

This time Jende smiled. "Thank you, my brother," he said. "I really
need all that good luck today."

Alone in the elevator to the twenty-eighth floor, he inspected his
fingernails (no dirt, thankfully). He adjusted his clip-on tie using the
security mirror above his head; reexamined his teeth and found no visible remnants of the fried ripe plantains and beans he'd eaten for breakfast. He cleared his throat and wiped off whatever saliva had crusted on
the sides of his lips. When the doors opened he straightened his shoulders and introduced himself to the receptionist, who, after responding
with a nod and a display of extraordinarily white teeth, made a phone
call and asked him to follow her. They walked through an open space
where young men in blue shirts sat in cubicles with multiple screens,
down a corridor, past another open space of cluttered cubicles and into
a sunny office with a four-paneled glass window running from wall
to wall and floor to ceiling, the thousand autumn-drenched trees and

proud towers of Manhattan standing outside. For a second his mouth fell open, at the view outside—the likes of which he'd never seen—and the exquisiteness inside. There was a lounging section (black leather sofa, two black leather chairs, glass coffee table) to his right, an executive desk (oval, cherry, black leather reclining chair for the executive, two green leather armchairs for visitors) in the center, and a wall unit (cherry, glass doors, white folders in neat rows) to his left, in front of which Clark Edwards, in a dark suit, was standing and feeding sheets of paper into a pullout shredder.

"Please, sir, good morning," Jende said, turning toward him and half-bowing.

"Have a seat," Clark said without lifting his eyes from the shredder.

Jende hurried to the armchair on the left. He pulled a résumé from his folder and placed it in front of Clark's seat, careful not to disturb the layers of white papers and *Wall Street Journal*s strewn across the desk in a jumble. One of the *Journal* pages, peeking from beneath sheets of numbers and graphs, had the headline: WHITES' GREAT HOPE? BARACK OBAMA AND THE DREAM OF A COLOR-BLIND AMERICA. Jende leaned forward to read the story, fascinated as he was by the young ambitious senator, but immediately sat upright when he remembered where he was, why he was there, what was about to happen.

"Do you have any outstanding tickets you need to resolve?" Clark asked as he sat down.

"No, sir," Jende replied.

"And you haven't been in any serious accidents, right?"

"No, Mr. Edwards."

Clark picked up the résumé from his desk, wrinkled and moist like the man whose history it held. His eyes remained on it for several seconds while Jende's darted back and forth, from the Central Park treetops far beyond the window to the office walls lined with abstract paintings and portraits of white men wearing bow ties. He could feel beads of sweat rising out of his forehead.

"Well, Jende," Clark said, putting the résumé down and leaning back in his chair. "Tell me about yourself."

Jende perked up. This was the question he and his wife, Neni, had discussed the previous night; the one they'd read about when they Googled "the one question they ask at every job interview." They had spent an hour hunched over the cranky desktop, searching for the best answer, reading much-too-similar pieces of advice on the first ten sites Google delivered, before deciding it would be best if Jende spoke of his strong character and dependability, and of how he had everything a busy executive like Mr. Edwards needed in a chauffeur. Neni had suggested he also highlight his wonderful sense of humor, perhaps with a joke. After all, she had said, which Wall Street executive, after spending hours racking his brain on how to make more money, wouldn't appreciate entering his car to find his chauffeur ready with a good joke? Jende had agreed and prepared an answer, a brief monologue which concluded with a joke about a cow at a supermarket. That should work very well, Neni had said. And he had believed so, too. But when he began to speak, he forgot his prepared answer.

"Okay, sir," he said instead. "I live in Harlem with my wife and with my six-years-old son. And I am from Cameroon, in Central Africa, or West Africa. Depends on who you ask, sir. I am from a little town on the Atlantic Ocean called Limbe."

"I see."

"Thank you, Mr. Edwards," he said, his voice quivering, unsure of what he was thankful for.

"And what kind of papers do you have in this country?"

"I have papers, sir," he blurted out, leaning forward and nodding repeatedly, goose bumps shooting up all over his body like black balls out of a cannon.

"I said what *kind* of papers?"

"Oh, I am sorry, sir. I have EAD. EAD, sir . . . that is what I have right now."

"What's that supposed—" The BlackBerry on the desk buzzed.

Clark quickly picked it up. "What does that mean?" he asked, looking down at the phone.

"It means Employment Authorization Document, sir," Jende replied, shifting in his seat. Clark neither responded nor gestured. He kept his head down, his eyes on the smartphone, his soft-looking fingers jumping all over the keypad, lithely and speedily—up, left, right, down.

"It is a work permit, sir," Jende added. He looked at Clark's fingers, then his forehead, and his fingers again, uncertain of how else to obey the rules of eye contact when eyes were not available for contact. "It means I am allowed to work, sir. Until I get my green card."

Clark half-nodded and continued typing.

Jende looked out the window, hoping he wasn't sweating too profusely.

"And how long will it take for you to get this green card?" Clark asked as he put down the BlackBerry.

"I just really don't know, sir. Immigration is slow, sir; very funny how they work."

"But you're in the country legally for the long term, correct?"

"Oh, yes, sir," Jende said. He nodded repeatedly again, a pained smile on his face, his eyes unblinking. "I am very legal, sir. I just am still waiting for my green card."

For a long second Clark stared at Jende, his vacant green eyes giving no clue to his thoughts. Hot sweat was flowing down Jende's back, soaking the white shirt Neni had bought for him from a street vendor on 125th Street. The desk phone rang.

"Very well, then," Clark said, picking up the phone. "As long as you're legal."

Jende Jonga exhaled.

The terror that had gripped his chest when Clark Edwards mentioned the word "papers" slowly loosened. He closed his eyes and offered thanks to a merciful Being, grateful half the truth had been sufficient. What would he have said if Mr. Edwards had asked more questions? How would he have explained that his work permit and driver's license were valid *only* for as long as his asylum application was pending or approved, and that if his application were to be denied, all his documents would become invalid and there would be no green card? How could he have possibly explained his asylum application? Would there have been a way to convince Mr. Edwards that he was an honest man, a very honest man, actually, but one who was now telling a thousand tales to Immigration just so he could one day become an American citizen and live in this great nation forever?

"And you've been here for how long?" Clark asked after putting down the receiver.

"Three years, sir. I came in 2004, in the month—"

He paused, startled by Clark's thunderous sneeze.

"May God bless you, sir," he said as the executive placed his wrist under his nose and let loose another sneeze, louder than the first. "*Ashia*, sir," he added. "May God bless you again."

Clark leaned forward and picked up a bottle of water on the right side of his desk. Behind him, far beyond the spotless glass window, a red helicopter flew above the park, going from west to east under the cloudless morning sky. Jende returned his gaze to Clark and watched as he took a few sips from the bottle. He yearned for a sip of water, too, to erase the dryness in his throat, but dared not change the trajectory of the interview by asking for some. No, he couldn't dare. Certainly not right now. His throat could be the driest spot in the Kalahari and it wouldn't matter right now—he was doing well. Okay, maybe not too well. But he wasn't doing too badly, either.

"All right," Clark said, putting down the bottle. "Let me tell you what I want in a driver." Jende swallowed and nodded. "I demand loyalty. I demand dependability. I demand punctuality, and I demand that you do as I say and ask no questions. Works for you?"

"Yes, sir, of course, Mr. Edwards."

"You're going to sign a confidentiality agreement that you'll never say anything about what you hear me say or see me do. Never. To anyone. Absolutely no one. Do you understand?"

"I understand you very clearly, sir."

"Good. I'll treat you right, but you must treat me right first. I'll be your main priority, and when I don't need you, you'll take care of my family. I'm a busy man, so don't expect me to supervise you. You've come to me very highly recommended."

"I give you my word, sir. I promise. My full word."

"Very good, Jende," Clark said. He smirked, nodded, and said again, "Very good."

Jende pulled his handkerchief from his pants pocket and dabbed his forehead. He took a deep breath and waited for Clark to scan his résumé one more time.

"Do you have any questions for me?" Clark asked, moving the résumé to a pile of papers on the left side of his desk.

"No, Mr. Edwards. You have told me what I need to know very well, sir."

"I've got one more interview tomorrow morning, then I'll make my decision. You'll hear from me, maybe later tomorrow. My secretary will call you."

"Thank you so much, sir. You are very kind."

Clark stood up.

Jende quickly pushed back his chair and stood up, too. He straightened his tie, which over the course of the interview had become as tilted as a willowy tree in a wild storm.

"By the way," Clark said, looking at the tie, "if you hope to further your career, you'll get a better suit. Black, blue, or gray. And a real tie."

"Not a problem at all, sir," Jende replied. "I can find a new suit, sir. I surely can."

He nodded and smiled awkwardly, revealing his crowded teeth and promptly shutting his mouth. Clark, without smiling back, offered a hand, which Jende took with both of his and shook with great care, his head bowed. Thank you so much in advance, sir, he wanted to say again. I will be the best chauffeur ever if you give me this job, he almost said.

He didn't say it; he had to keep his desperation from bursting through the thin layer of dignity it had been wrapped in throughout the interview. Clark smiled and patted him on the arm.

Two

"One and a half years today," Neni said to Fatou as they walked through Chinatown looking for make-believe Gucci and Versace bags. "That's how long it's been since I came to America."

"One and half years?" Fatou said, shaking her head and rolling her eyes. "You count half-years, too? And you say it, no shame." She laughed. "Lemme tell you something. When you in America *vingt-quatre ans*, and you still poor, you no gonno count no more. You no gonno even say no more. No. You gonno shame to say anything, I tell you."

Neni chuckled as she picked up a Gucci tote so determined to pass as real it glimmered. "You're ashamed to tell people you have been here for twenty-four years?"

"No, I no shame. Why I shame? I tell people I just come here. They hear me talk, they say ah, she don't know English. She musto just come from Africa."

The Chinese store owner rushed toward them. Take the bag for sixty dollars, he said to Neni. Why? Neni asked, contorting her face. I give you twenty. The man shook his head. Neni and Fatou started walking away. Forty, forty, the man shouted at them as they pushed through a throng of European tourists. Okay, come take for thirty, he shouted. They went back and bought it for twenty-five.

"Now you look lika Angeli Joeli," Fatou said as Neni walked with the bag on her arm, her curly weave flowing behind her.

"Really?" Neni said, tossing her hair.

"What you mean, really? You wanno look lika Angeli Joeli, no?"

Neni threw her head back and giggled.

How she loved New York City. She still couldn't believe she was here. Couldn't believe she was walking around shopping for Gucci, no longer a jobless, unwed mother, sitting in her father's house in Limbe, sunrise to sunset, dry season to rainy season, waiting for Jende to rescue her.

It didn't seem like eighteen months already, perhaps because she still remembered much about the day she and Liomi arrived at JFK. She still remembered how Jende had stood at the terminal waiting for them, dressed in a red shirt and blue clip-on tie, a bouquet of yellow hydrangeas in his hands. She still remembered how they had embraced and held each other for almost a minute in silence, their eyes tightly shut to banish the agony of the past two years in which he had worked three jobs to save the money needed for her student visa, Liomi's visitor visa, and their airline tickets. She remembered how Liomi had joined in their embrace, grabbing both of their legs before Jende had paused from holding her to pick him up. She remembered how the apartment—which Jende had recently found after almost two years of sharing a two-bedroom basement apartment with six Puerto Rican men in the Bronx—was that night filled with Jende's laughter and her voice delighting him with stories from back home, alongside Liomi's squeals as father and son roughhoused and tickled each other on the carpet. She remembered how they had moved Liomi from their bed to the cot in the middle of the night so they could lie side by side, do all the things they had promised to do to each other in emails and phone calls and text messages. And she still clearly remembered lying in bed next to Jende after they were done, listening to the sounds of America outside the window, the chatter and laughter of African-American men and women on the streets of Harlem, and telling herself: I am in America, I am truly in America.

She could never forget that day.

Or the day, two weeks after their arrival, when they were married at city hall with Liomi as their ring bearer and Jende's cousin Winston as their witness. On that day in May 2006, she finally became a respectable woman, a woman declared worthy of love and protection.

Limbe was now some faraway town, a place she had loved less with every new day Jende was not there. Without him to go for a walk on the beach with, go dancing with, or sit with at a drinking spot and enjoy a cold Malta Guinness on a hot Sunday afternoon, the town was no longer her beloved hometown but a desolate place she couldn't wait to get out of. In every phone call during the time they were apart she had reminded him of this, of her inability to stop daydreaming about the day she would leave Limbe and be with him in America.

"I dream, too, *bébé*," he always said to her. "Day and night I dream all kinds of dreams."

On the day she and Liomi got their visas, she had gone to bed with their passports under her pillow. On the night they left Cameroon, she felt nothing. As the bus her father had rented to drive them—and the two dozen family and friends who came along to escort them—pulled out from in front of their house to begin the two-hour trip to Douala International Airport, she had smiled and waved at the neighbors and extended-family members who had gathered on the front lawn to enviously bid them farewell. She had taken a panoramic mental photograph of them, knowing she wouldn't be missing them for too long, wishing them the same happiness she knew she was going to find in America.

A year and a half later now and New York City was her home, a place with all the pleasures she desired. She woke up next to the man she loved and turned her face to see their child. For the first time in her life, she had a job, as a home health aide through an agency that paid her in cash, since she had no working papers. She was a matriculated student for the first time in sixteen years, studying chemistry at Borough of Manhattan Community College, never worrying about her tuition because she knew Jende would always pay the three-thousand-dollars-a-semester fee without grumbling, unlike her father, who unceasingly complained about his financial headaches and delivered a lecture about CFA francs not growing on mango trees whenever one of his eight children asked for money for school fees or new uniforms. For the first time in much too long, she didn't wake up in the morning with no plans except to clean the house, go to the market, cook for her parents and siblings, take care of Liomi, meet with her friends and listen to them bash their mothers-in-law, go to bed and look forward to more of the same the next day because her life was going neither forward nor backward. And for the very first time in her life, she had a dream besides marriage and motherhood: to become a pharmacist like the ones everyone respected in Limbe because they handed out health and happiness in pill bottles. To achieve this dream, she had to do well in school, and she was doing just that—maintaining a B-plus average. Three days a week she went to school and, after classes, walked the school's hallways with her bulky algebra, chemistry, biology, and philosophy textbooks, glowing because she was growing into a learned woman. As often as she could, she sat in the library to do her homework, or went to office hours to hound professors for advice on what she needed to do to get better grades so she could get into a great pharmacy school. She was going to make herself proud, make Jende proud of his wife, make Liomi proud of his mother. She'd waited too long to become something, and now, at thirty-three, she finally had, or was close enough to having, everything she'd ever wanted in life.

Three

HE WAS ON WHITE PLAINS ROAD WHEN THE CALL CAME IN. FOUR MIN-utes later, he closed his flip phone and laughed. He pounded the steer-ing wheel and laughed even louder: jubilant, bemused, incredulous. If he had been driving in New Town, Limbe, he would have gotten out of the car and hugged someone on the street, telling them, Bo, you won't even believe the news I just got. In New Town, he would have known at least one person on the street with whom to share his good news, but here, on these streets of old brick houses and faded lawns in the Bronx, he knew no one he could run to and repeat what Clark's secretary had just told him. There was a young black man walking with headphones on, banging his head to some kind of good music; three teenage Asian girls covering their mouths and giggling, none of them with a school bag; a woman rushing somewhere, pushing a fat baby in a pink um-brella stroller. There was an African man, too, but judging from his dark angular face and flowing *grand boubou*, he had to be Senegalese or Burkinabé or from one of the other French-speaking West African countries. Jende could not run out to him just because they were both

West Africans—he needed to rejoice with someone who knew his name and his story.

"Oh, Papa God, Jends," Neni said when he called her with the news. "I cannot believe it! Can you?"

He smiled and shook his head, knowing her question needed no response—she was merely as happy as he was. From the sounds coming alongside her voice, he could tell she was dancing, jumping, skipping around the apartment like a child bearing a handful of sweets.

"Did she say exactly how much they're going to pay you?"

"Thirty-five thousand."

"Mamami, eh! Papa God, oh! I'm dancing right now, Jends. I'm doing gymnastics, oh!"

She wanted to stay on the phone, rejoice together for at least ten more minutes, but she had to leave for her chemistry class. He kept on smiling after she hung up, amused by her joy, which flowed mightier than Victoria Falls.

He called his cousin Winston next.

"Congrats, my man," Winston said. "Wonders shall never end."

"I'm telling you," Jende said.

"So, you, this bush boy from New Town, Limbe, you're going to drive a Wall Street exec, eh? You'll now be driving a shiny Lexus, instead of that *chakara* Hyundai?"

Jende laughed. "I don't know how to thank you," he said. "I just can't even begin to—"

His passenger in the backseat said something.

"Hold on, Bo," he said to Winston. He turned around and realized the woman was on her cell phone, too, speaking in a language he'd never heard while he was speaking in pidgin English interspersed with French and Bakweri—neither of them understanding the other, both of them inadvertently creating a quasi-Babel in a New York City livery cab.

"What did you tell these people about me?" he asked Winston. "The man said I came to him highly recommended."

"Nothing," Winston replied. "I only told Frank you drive a limo sometimes, and that you used to chauffeur a family in New Jersey."

"What!"

"I lie, I die," Winston said, snickering. "You think a black man gets a good job in this country by sitting in front of white people and telling the truth? Please, don't make me laugh. I just didn't want to tell you beforehand and get you even more nervous."

"Bo, you serious? But I didn't have any of that on my résumé! How come—?"

"Ah, you and your shocks. The man's a busy man. I knew he wasn't going to sit there asking you every kind of question. Frank's his best friend. What? You're not happy I told him?"

"Happy?" Jende said in a near-scream, shaking his head and throwing it back. "I want to jump out of this car right now and come kiss your feet!"

"No, thank you," Winston said. "I'm interviewing some *ngah*s to do that for me."

"Yes, you are!" Jende said, guffawing. "I won't get jealous, because Neni will kill me."

Winston laughed so hard, he snorted. "The one last night, Bo, let me tell you—"

"But what are we going to do about this background check thing?" Jende asked. "The secretary says I have to give this thing, this rev . . . em . . . reve . . . reverencies?"

"Don't worry about that. We'll fill out the forms together when I come over. I have some people for the references."

"I owe you, Bo . . . In short, I don't even know how I'll ever thank you."

"Just stop this thank you business right now, eh?" Winston said. "You're my brother. If I don't do it for you who will I do it for? Tell Neni to cook for me her special pepper soup recipe, the one with cow feet and chicken gizzards. That's all I want. I'm coming over tomorrow evening."

"You don't even have to ask. The food will be waiting for you, plus frozen palm wine and fresh *soya*."

Winston congratulated him again and said he had to get back to a brief he was working on. Jende continued driving around the Bronx, picking up passengers, dropping them off, listening to Lite fm, unable to discard the grin on his face. His cell phone beeped to announce a new text message. *You just get your papers now*, Neni wrote, *and we'll be all set!*

Isn't that the truth, he thought. First a good job. Then papers. How good would that feel?

He sighed.

Three years: That's how long he'd been fighting for papers in America. He'd been in the country for only four weeks when Winston took him to meet with an immigration lawyer—they needed to find a way for him to stay in the country permanently after his visitor visa expired. That had been their plan all along, though it wasn't what Jende had said when he went to the American embassy in Yaoundé to apply for the visa.

"How long do you plan on staying in New York City?" the consulate had asked him.

"Only three months, sir," he had replied. "Just three months, and I promise I will return."

And he had submitted evidence to back his claim: his work supervisor's letter describing him as a diligent employee who loved his job so much he would never abandon it to go roam around aimlessly in America; his son's birth certificate, to show he would never remain in America and desert his child; the title on a piece of land his father had given him, to show he intended to return and build on the land; a letter from the town planning office, which he'd paid a distant uncle who worked in the office to get for him, stating that he had applied for a permit to build a house; a letter from a friend who swore under oath that Jende wasn't going to remain in America because they were going to open a drinking spot together when he returned.

The consular officer had been convinced.

The next day Jende had walked out of the consular office with his visa. Yes, he was going to America. He, Jende Dikaki Jonga, son of Ikola Jonga, grandson of Dikaki Manyaka ma Jonga, was going to America! He skipped out of the embassy and onto the dusty streets of Yaoundé, pumping his fist and grinning so wide an Ewondo woman carrying a basket of plantains on her head stopped mid-stride to stare at him. *Quel est son problème?* he heard her say to a friend. He laughed. He didn't have a problem. He was leaving Cameroon in a month! Leaving to certainly not return after three months. Who traveled to America only to return to a future of nothingness in Cameroon after a mere three months? Not young men like him, not people facing a future of poverty and despondency in their own country. No, people like him did not visit America. They got there and stayed there until they could return home as conquerors—as green card– or American passport–bearing conquerors with pockets full of dollars and photos of a happy life. Which was why on the day he boarded an Air France flight from Douala to Newark with a connection in Paris, he was certain he wouldn't see Cameroon again until he had claimed his share of the milk, honey, and liberty flowing in the paradise-for-strivers called America.

"Asylum is the best way to get *papier* and remain in the country," Winston told him after he had gotten over his jet lag and spent half a day walking around Times Square in astonishment. "Either that or you marry an old white woman in Mississippi with no teeth."

"Please, God forbid bad things," he had replied. "Better you give me a bottle of kerosene to drink and die right now." Asylum was the only way for him to go, he decided. Winston agreed. It could take years, he said, but it would be worthwhile.

Winston hired a lawyer for him, a fast-talking Nigerian in Flatbush, Brooklyn, named Bubakar, who was as short as his speech was fast. Bubakar, Winston had been told, was not only a great immigration lawyer with hundreds of African clients all over the country but also an expert in the art of giving clients the best stories of persecution to gain asylum.

"How d'you think all these people who gain asylum do it?" he asked the cousins when they met with him for a free consultation. "You think they're all really running away from something? Puh-leez. Let me tell you something: I just won asylum only last month for the daughter of the prime minister of some country in East Africa."

"Really?" Winston asked.

"Yes, really," Bubakar replied, snarling. "What d'you mean, really?"

"I'm just surprised. What country?"

"I'd rather not mention, okay? It doesn't really matter. My point is that this girl's father is a prime minister, eh? She has three people wiping her ass after she shits and three more people dragging the boogers out of her nose. And here she is, saying she's afraid for her life back home." He scoffed. "We all do what we gotta do to become American, *abi*?"

Jende nodded.

Winston shrugged; a friend of his in Atlanta was the one who had referred him to Bubakar and spoken highly of the man. The friend had no doubt that Bubakar was the reason he was still in America, why he now had a green card and was only two years away from being eligible to apply for citizenship. Still, from Winston's downturned lips, Jende could tell his cousin was having a hard time believing that the small man with extra-long hair flying out of his perpetually flared nostrils was an expert in anything, never mind the complex legal field of asylum-based immigration. The diploma on his wall said he'd gone to some law school in Nebraska, but to Winston his mannerisms must have said he'd gotten his real education via online immigration forums, the sites where many with aspirations for American passports gathered to find ways to triumph over the American immigration system.

"My brother," Bubakar said to Jende, looking at him across the bare desk in his ultraclean and perfectly organized office, "why don't we start by you telling me more about you so I can see how I can help you?"

Jende sat up in his chair, clasped his hands on his lap, and began telling his story. He spoke of his father the farmer, his mother the trader and pig breeder, his four brothers, and their two-bedroom *caraboat* house in New Town, Limbe. He spoke of attending primary school at CBC Main School, and the interruption of his secondary education at National Comprehensive Secondary School after he impregnated Neni.

"Eh? You stopped because you pregnant a girl?" Bubakar said, jotting down something.

"Yes," Jende replied. "Her father put me in prison because of it."

"Boom! That's it!" Bubakar said as he lifted his head from his writing pad, his eyes glowing with excitement.

"What is it?" Winston asked.

"His asylum. The story we'll tell Immigration."

Winston and Jende looked at each other. Jende was thinking Bubakar must know what he was talking about. Winston looked like he was thinking Bubakar must know nothing about what he was talking about.

"What're you talking about?" Winston asked. "The imprisonment happened in 1990, fourteen years ago. How are you going to convince a judge that my cousin's afraid of persecution back in Cameroon because he impregnated a girl and got sent to prison a long time ago? Mind you, in our country, and maybe even in your country, it's perfectly within the law for a father to have a young man arrested for complicating his daughter's future."

Bubakar looked at Winston with scorn, his lip curled down on one side. "Mr. Winston," he said after a long pause, during which he wrote something down and deliberately placed his pen on his writing pad.

"Yes?"

"I understand we're both lawyers, and you're Wall Street smart. Is that not so?"

Winston did not respond.

"Let me guarantee you something, my friend," Bubakar continued.

"You wouldn't know the first thing to do if you were put before an immigration judge and asked to fight for the likes of your cousin. Okay? So, why don't you allow me to do what I know, and if I ever need a lawyer to help me find a way to hide taxes from the government, I'll let you do what you know."

"My job is not to help people find ways to hide taxes," Winston replied, keeping his voice low even though Jende could tell from his unblinking eyes that he yearned to reach across the table and punch out all the teeth from Bubakar's mouth.

"You don't do that, eh?" Bubakar asked with mock interest. "So, tell me, what is it that you do at Wall Street?"

Winston scoffed. Jende said nothing, equally as angered as his cousin.

Perhaps afraid he'd gone too far, Bubakar tried to rein in his comments and appease the cousins.

"My brothers, make we no vex," he said, switching to a blend of Cameroonian and Nigerian pidgin English. "Now no be time for vex. We get work for do, *abi*? Now na time for go before. No be so?"

"Na so," Winston replied. "Let's just stick to the matter at hand."

Jende sighed and waited for the conversation to return to his asylum application.

"But just so you know," Winston added, "my job as a corporate lawyer does not involve any lying or manipulation."

"Of course," Bubakar replied. "I'm sorry, my brother. I must have mistaken it with another kind of law."

The two men laughed.

"What happened to the young lady you impregnated?" Bubakar said, turning to Jende.

"She is back in Limbe."

"And the child you had with her?"

"She died."

"I'm so sorry, oh, my brother. So sorry."

Jende averted his gaze. He needed no sympathies. He certainly did not need condolences coming fourteen years later.

"You went to prison before or after she died?"

"Before she was born, when my girl's parents found out I was the one who pregnant her."

"That's how it normally works," Winston said. "Parents call the police, boyfriend gets arrested."

Bubakar nodded, double-underlining a word on his writing pad.

"I was in prison for four months. I came out, the baby was one month old. Three months later, she died of yellow fever."

"Sorry, oh, my brother," Bubakar said again. "Truly sorry."

Jende took a sip from a glass of water on the table and cleared his throat. "But I have another child in Cameroon," he said. "I have a three-years-old son."

"With the same woman that you had the daughter with?"

"Yes. She is the mother of my son. She is still my girlfriend. We would be married now and be a family with our son if only her father would let me marry her."

"And what's his reason for disapproving of the marriage?"

"He says he needs time to think about it, but I know it's because I'm a poor man."

"It's a class thing," Winston said. "Jende's from a poor family. This young lady's family has a bit more money."

"Or maybe it's because this young lady's father hasn't gotten over what happened to his daughter?" Bubakar said. "I mean, as a father, to see your young daughter get pregnant, drop out of school, and then lose the child, it's all very hard, *abi*? I don't think I'll ever like the person who did this to my daughter, whether he is from a rich family or poor family."

Neither cousin responded.

"But it doesn't really matter what his reason is," Bubakar continued. "I think the story is our best chance for your asylum. We claim persecution based on belonging to a particular social group. We weave a story about how you're afraid of going back home because you're afraid your girlfriend's family wants to kill you so you two don't get married."

"That sounds like something that would happen in India," Winston said. "No one does anything like that in Cameroon."

"Are you trying to say Cameroon is better than India?" Bubakar retorted.

"I'm trying to say Cameroon is not like India."

"Leave that up to me, my brother."

Winston sighed.

"When can we send the application?" Jende asked.

"As soon as you provide me with all the evidence."

"Evidence? Like what?"

"Like what? Like your prison record. Birth certificates of your children. Both of them. Death certificate of the little girl. Letters. Lots of letters, from people who'll say that they've heard this man say he's going to kill you if he ever sees you again. People who've heard his brothers, his cousins, anyone in that family talk about destroying you. Pictures, too. In fact, anything and everything about you and this gal and her father. Can you get it for me?"

"I'll try," Jende said hesitantly. "But what if I cannot get enough evidence?"

Bubakar looked at him with a dash of amusement and shook his head. "Ah, my brother," he said, putting down his pen and leaning forward. "Do I have to spell it out for you? You got to use your common sense and produce for me something I can show these people. Eh? It's like that man Jerry Maguire says, show me the money. These people at USCIS are going to say, show me the evidence. Show me the evidence! You get me?"

He laughed at his own joke. Winston puffed. Jende did not react—he'd never heard of a man named Jerry Maguire.

"We got to show a lot of stuff to convince them, you understand me? One way or another, we produce a lot of evidence."

"We'll see what we can do," Winston said.

Jende nodded in agreement, although he knew getting the kind of letters Bubakar wanted would be difficult. Neni's father didn't like him—that he'd known for years—but the old man had never once threatened to kill him. No one in Limbe could attest to that. But filing for asylum was his best chance at staying in the country, so he had to do something. He would have to talk it out with Winston and see what could be done; Winston would have ideas on how to do it.

"And you're confident this will work?" Winston asked.

"I'll make a strong case," Bubakar said. "Your cousin will get his papers, Inshallah."

Four

SHE COULDN'T GO TO BED UNTIL HE GOT HOME; SHE HAD TO HEAR EVERY-thing about his first day at work. When she had called him around noon to find out how his day was going, he had hurriedly said it was going good, he couldn't talk, but everything was good. So she'd had no choice but to wait, and now, at almost midnight, she could finally hear him at the door, panting after having climbed the five flights of stairs it took to get to their apartment.

"So?" she asked, grinning as he sat down on the threadbare living room sofa.

"I cannot complain," he said, smiling. "It went well."

She went into the kitchen and got him a glass of cold water, helped him take off his jacket and, after he'd rested on the sofa with his head thrown back for about a minute, brought out his dinner and pulled out a chair so he could make himself comfortable at the dinette set.

Then she began asking him questions: What exactly did he do for the family? Where did he drive them to? What did the Edwardses' apartment look like? Was Mrs. Edwards a nice lady? Was their son well behaved? Was he going to be working this late every day?

He was tired, but she was persistent, scattering the questions all over him like confetti on a victorious warrior. She had to know how rich people lived. How they behaved. What they said. If they could hire someone to drive them around, then their lives must really be something, eh?

"Come on," she said. "Tell me."

So he told her everything he could in between mouthfuls of his dinner. The Edwardses' apartment was big and beautiful, he said, millions of dollars more beautiful than their sunless one-bedroom apartment. One could see the whole city through the window in their living room—his mouth had dropped open when he saw it.

"*Chai!*" she said. "What would it be like to have a place like that? I'll jump and touch the sky every day."

The place looked like one of those rich-people apartments you see on television, he went on. Everything was white or silver, very clean, very shiny. He'd spent only a few minutes there while waiting to take Mighty to school after he returned from dropping Mr. Edwards at work. Mrs. Edwards had asked him to come upstairs because nine-year-old Mighty wanted to be properly introduced before being chauffeured to school. "A very nice child and a well-brought-up one, too, that Mighty," he said.

"That's good to hear," she said. "A rich child who is well brought up." She wanted to ask if Mighty was as well brought up as their Liomi, but she didn't—she thought it best to follow the advice her mother had given her years ago about abstaining from comparing her child to another woman's child. "They only have this one child?" she asked instead.

He shook his head. "Mighty told me he has a big brother. He lives uptown in another apartment they own and goes to Columbia University. The School of Law."

"You're going to be driving him around, too?"

"Maybe, I don't know. If I have to drive him, too, it's no problem, but from the way Mighty was talking it looks like the brother doesn't come to visit them often, and Mrs. Edwards is not happy about it. I didn't ask him any more questions."

She filled up his half-empty glass of water and allowed him to eat in silence for a few minutes before resuming her questions. "And Mrs. Edwards," she went on, "what does she look like?"

"Good-looking," he replied. "Just like a woman with a rich husband should look. Winston said she's one of those food people."

"What food people?"

"The people who teach other people how to eat ... so they can look one way or not look another way." He picked up the can of Mountain Dew she'd set on the table, opened it, and took a long sip. "People in this country, always worrying about how to eat, they pay someone good money to tell them: Eat this, don't eat that. If you don't know how to eat, what else can you know how to do in this world?"

"So she must be slim and really good-looking."

He nodded distractedly, sweat pouring down his face from the extra pepper she'd tossed into the chicken and tomato sauce. Ignoring the sweat, he picked up a drumstick, ripped the meat off the bone with his front teeth, and sucked the juice inside the bone.

"But what exactly does she look like?" she pressed on. "Ah, *bébé*, details, please."

He sighed and said he couldn't remember too much about what she looked like. The one thing he remembered, he said, was that when he first saw her, he thought she looked something like the wife in *American Beauty*—a movie they both loved and watched whenever they wanted to remind themselves that life in American suburbs could be very strange and maybe it was best to live in peaceful American cities, like New York City.

"What's the real name of that woman again?" he asked with a full mouth, tomato sauce running down his fingers. "You're the one who knows these things."

"Annette Bening?"

"Yes, yes. That's who she looks like."

"With the same eyes and everything? She must be beautiful, eh?"

He said he could not remember if Cindy Edwards had Annette Bening's eyes.

"It's not like you can even know what her real eyes are like," she said. "Some of them wear colored contacts; they can change their eyes whenever they feel like it. A woman like Mrs. Edwards, she was probably born into a rich family and started wearing colored contacts even as a child."

"I don't know . . ."

"Rich father, rich mother, rich husband. I'm sure her whole life she's never known what it's like to worry about money."

Licking his lips, he picked up a piece of plantain from the plate, broke it with his fingers, dunked half of it into the tomato sauce bowl, and hurriedly pushed it into his mouth for processing.

She watched him, amused at the speed with which he was devouring his food. "And then what happened after you dropped Mighty off at school?" she asked.

He came back and picked up Mrs. Edwards, he said, took her to her office and then to an appointment in Battery Park City and to another appointment in SoHo, before taking her home and picking up Mighty from school and driving him and his nanny to a building on the Upper West Side where he got his piano lessons. He took Mighty and his nanny home after the lesson and then picked up Mr. Edwards from his office and drove him to a steak house on Long Island and back to the city around ten. He refilled the gas, parked the car in the garage, and took the crosstown bus from the east side to the west side. Then he caught the uptown 3 subway home.

"*Weh!*" she exclaimed. "Isn't that a lot of work for one person in one day?"

Sure, it might be, he told her. But for the kind of money he was being paid, wasn't it to be expected? She shouldn't forget, he said, that two weeks ago he was making only half of what Mr. Edwards was paying him, driving the livery cab twelve hours every day.

She nodded in agreement and said, "We can only thank God."

He lifted his glass of water and took a sip.

"I calculated your thirty-five thousand salary, plus my ten thousand," she said as she refilled his glass again. "After we pay your taxes and my school fees and rent and send money back home and everything else, we can still save like three or four hundred dollars a month."

"Four hundred dollars a month!"

She nodded, smiling, amazed, too, at how so much can change in so little time. "We save like that, *bébé*," she said, "we try really hard, we can save five thousand a year. Ten years, we could have enough money for down payment for a two-bedroom in Mount Vernon or Yonkers." She moved her head closer to his. "Or even New Rochelle."

He shook his head. "We're going to start paying more for rent one day. How long do you think before the government finds out Mr. Charles is qualifying for cheap housing even though he drives a Hummer? They find out we're paying him to live here, they kick us out—"

"So?"

"So? Someday we're going to start paying more than five hundred for rent, and forty-five thousand to live in Harlem will be nothing."

She shrugged: just like him to think of all the bad things that could happen. "Someday is not today," she countered. "Before they find out, we would have saved some money. I'll be a pharmacist by then." She smiled again, her eyes narrowing as if she were dreaming of that day. "We'll have our own apartment, two bedrooms. You'll make more money as a chauffeur. I'll make a good pharmacist salary. We won't live in this place full of cockroaches anymore."

He looked at her and smiled back, and she imagined he believed, too, that someday she would be a pharmacist. Hopefully five years, maybe seven years, but still someday.

She watched him take the last piece of plantain from the plate, use it to clean the tomato sauce bowl, and rush it, together with the last piece of chicken, into his mouth. Looking at him lovingly, she giggled as he finished up the Mountain Dew and burped. "You're a tanker," she said to him, poking him in the ribs.

He giggled, too, wearily. Tired as he was, she could see how pleased he was. Nothing pleased him like a delicious dinner after a long day of work. Nothing pleased her like knowing she had pleased him.

After a long pause, during which he leaned back in his seat and stared at the wall with a faint smile, he washed his hands in the bowl of water she had placed on the table and stood up. "Is Liomi in our bed or his bed?" he whispered from the hallway.

"His bed," she said, smiling, knowing he would be happy for them to have the bed to celebrate on. She picked up his dirty dishes and took them to the sink. *E weni Lowa la manyaka*, she sang softly, smiling still and swinging her hips as she cleaned the dishes. *E weni Lowa la manyaka, Lowa la nginya, Na weta miseli, E weni Lowa la manyaka.*

These days she sang more than she had in her entire life. She sang when she ironed Jende's shirts and when she walked home after dropping Liomi off at school. She sang as she applied lipstick to head out with Jende and Liomi to an African party: a naming ceremony in Brooklyn; a traditional wedding in the Bronx; a death celebration in Yonkers for someone who had died in Africa and whom practically none of the guests knew; a party for one reason or another that she'd been invited to by a friend from school or work, someone who knew the host and who'd assured her that it was okay to attend, since most African people didn't care about fancy white-people ideas like attendance by invitation only. She sang walking to the subway and even sang in Pathmark, caring nothing about the looks she got from people who couldn't understand why someone could be so happy grocery shopping. *God na helele, God na waya oh, God na helele, God na waya oh, nobody dey like am oh, nobody dey like am oh, ewoo nwanem, God na helele.*

When she finished cleaning the dishes she picked up Jende's jacket, the new black suit she had bought from T. J. Maxx for a hundred and twenty-five dollars, a third of their savings. She cleaned it with a lint brush, sprayed perfume on it, and laid it on the sofa for the next day. She looked at the jacket and smiled, glad she had bought it. She'd wanted to buy a cheaper one at the discount department store on 125th Street, but Fatou had dissuaded her. Why you gonno buy cheap suit for him to drive big man, she had asked. You musto buy from good store lika T. J. Maxx. Buy him fine suit for wear to drive fine car for rich man. And then one day, when he become rich man himself, you gonno buy from better store. You gonno buy his clothes, you gonno buy all you clothes from better, better store. Fine white people store lika Target.

Five

CINDY EDWARDS HAD BEEN NOTHING BUT CORDIAL TOWARD HIM (RE-sponding promptly to his greeting every time he held the car door open for her; asking, albeit disinterestedly, how his day was going; saying please and thank you as often as she needed to), and yet whenever she was in the car, he stiffened up. Was he breathing too loudly? Driving five miles per hour too fast or too slow? Had he cleaned the backseat well enough so a lingering speck of dust wouldn't dirty her pantsuit? He knew she'd have to be a precision-obsessed woman with the sensitivity of a champion watchdog to notice such minor transgressions, but that wasn't enough to allow him to sit at ease—he was still new at the job and thus had to be perfect. Thankfully, she was on her cell phone most days, like the Tuesday two weeks after he began driving her and her family. That afternoon, upon reentering the car in front of a restaurant near Union Square, she had immediately gotten on her phone. "Vince won't be coming to Aspen," she'd said slowly and sadly, almost in shock, as if reading aloud the headline of a bizarrely tragic news story from the paper.

Two hours earlier, a much happier Cindy had exited the car, and it

had been clear to Jende that the young man she was meeting in front
of the restaurant was her son Vince—he was a replica of his father,
bearing the same six-foot frame, slender build, and wavy hair. Cindy
had all but sprinted out of the car to get to him, to hug him and stroke
his cheeks and give him three kisses. It seemed she hadn't seen him
in months, which, based on what Mighty had said, was entirely likely.
For minutes they had stood on the sidewalk chatting, Vince rubbing
his hands and moving them in and out of his blue Columbia hoodie,
Cindy motioning toward Union Square Park and smiling broadly, as if
reminding Vince of a special moment they'd once shared there.

"I just had lunch with him," she went on. "He didn't say why . . .
No, he says he's definitely not coming . . . I said he said he's not coming! . . . He's going to some silent retreat in Costa Rica, something
about his Spirit badly needing to get away from the noise . . . What
do you mean it's okay? Don't tell me it's okay, Clark. Your son's deciding to not spend the holidays with his family and you're telling me it's
fine? . . . No, I don't expect you to do anything. I know there's nothing
you can do . . . I know there's nothing I can do, but doesn't it bother
you? I mean, do you not care how he has no sense of family? He doesn't
come for Mighty's birthday, doesn't even care to ask me before deciding to go away for Christmas . . . I'm not rescheduling it . . . Sure, it
might all be for the best. You're now free to work on Christmas Eve and
Christmas Day, and why don't you just work nonstop till next year? . . .
Don't tell me I'm being ridiculous! . . . If you cared more, Clark, just
a little bit more, about how the boys are doing, if they're happy . . . I
don't want you to do anything else, because you're incapable of looking past yourself and putting the needs of others above yours . . . Yeah,
of course, but someday you're going to have to realize that you can't
keep on doing what you're doing and hope that somehow, by chance,
the kids are going to be all right. It doesn't work like that . . . It'll *never*
work like that."

Jende heard her toss her phone onto the seat. For a minute the car
was silent except for the sound of her heavy breathing.

"Are you coming to Mighty's recital?" she said after picking up the phone and apparently calling her husband again. "Yes, call me right back, please . . . I need to know ASAP."

His hands firmly at the nine and three o'clock positions—as he'd been taught to drive in Cameroon—Jende made a turn onto Madison Avenue. The sun had already left the city on the frigid late afternoon, but Manhattan shone brightly as always and, beneath its streetlamps and in the white lights spilling from glowing stores, he saw faces of many colors going north and south at varied speeds. Some along the crowded avenue looked happy, some looked sad, but none seemed to be as sad as Cindy Edwards at that moment. Her voice was so drenched in agony Jende wished someone would call her with good news, funny news, any kind of news to make her smile.

Her phone rang, and she promptly picked it up.

"What do you mean you'll make it up to him?" she shouted. "You promised him you'd be at the recital! You can't keep telling a child . . . I don't care what's going on at Lehman! I don't care how awful things might get if Lehman doesn't . . . And what about the Accordion Gala? I need to RSVP by the end of the week . . . Oh, no, please go on the trip, Clark. Just . . ."

She tossed the phone aside again and sat with her left elbow against the car door, resting her head in her hand. She sat like that for minutes, and Jende thought he heard the sniff of a downcast woman fighting back tears.

Somewhere in the East Forties, she picked up the phone again.

"Hey, Cheri, it's me," she said after the voicemail prompt, her voice placid but the anguish therein still evident. "Just calling, nothing much. I finally got the tickets, so we're good. Call me back if you're free. I should be home in about . . . Never mind, you don't need to call me back. I'm good, just having a real crappy day. You're probably still out with your clients . . . Oh well. By the way, let me know if you'd like some company when you go visit your mom next week, okay? I'll be glad to come with you."

She dialed another number, and this time the person appeared to pick up.

"Are you home?" she asked. "Oh, right, I forgot . . . Yeah, we can talk later. Tell Mike I say hello . . . Nothing . . . I mean nothing new, just the same old things. I'm just so upset, and on top of everything else that's going on . . . No, no, I'm sorry, please go . . . No, you don't have to call me back tonight . . . Yes, really, I'm fine . . . I'll be fine, June, promise. Go. Have fun."

For the remaining ten minutes of the ride she made no phone calls. She sat quietly, looking out the window, watching happy people marching up and down Madison.

Six

THEY HAD CROSSED THE DELAWARE MEMORIAL BRIDGE AND WERE MORE than halfway back from Washington, D.C., cruising through New Jersey with turnpike signs appearing every few miles.

"Tell me about Limbe," Clark said. "I want to hear about this place where you grew up."

Jende smiled. "Oh, sir," he said, his voice rising with nostalgia, "Limbe is such a nice town. You have to go there one day, sir. In fact, sir, you really must go. When you go, you will see a sign welcoming you as you enter. The sign is special, sir. I have never seen a sign like that welcome anybody to any place before. You see it just as you are coming down the road on the way from Douala, after you pass Mile Four. Nobody can miss it above their heads. It is there in big letters, supported by two iron red pillars, going from one side of the road to the other side. It says 'Welcome to Limbe, The Town of Friendship.' When you see that sign, sir, ah! No matter who you are, whether you are coming to Limbe just for one day or to stay for ten years, whether you are big or small, you will feel happy that you have made it to Limbe. You will smell the ocean breeze coming from plenty of miles away to salute you.

That sweet breeze. It will make you feel like, truly, there is no place in the world like this town by the ocean called Limbe."

"Interesting," Clark said, closing his laptop.

"It is, sir," Jende replied, eager to tell more. He knew Mr. Edwards was open to hearing more. After three months of driving around together, he'd come to realize that whenever the boss needed a short break from his computer or his phone or the papers scattered on the backseat, he asked him questions about his childhood, his life in Harlem, his weekend plans with his wife.

"And then after the welcome sign, sir," he continued, "as you pass through Mile Two, you will see the lights of the town at night as they are shining all around you. The lights are not too bright or too many. They are just enough to say that this is a town made of magic, an OPEC city, national refinery on one side of the shore, fishermen with their nets on the other side. Then when you enter Mile One, sir, you begin to really feel Limbe proper. It's something else, sir."

"Sounds like it."

"Ah, yes, sir. Limbe is very special, Mr. Edwards. In Limbe, we live simple lives, but we enjoy our lives well. You will see it when you visit, sir. As you keep on driving through Mile One, you will see young men buying grilled corn on street corners and old men playing draughts. The young women have all kinds of fake hair weaved into their hair. Some of them look like *mami wata*, those mermaids in the ocean. The older women tie two *wrappers*, one on top of the other. That is how mature women like to dress. Soon after, you will be at Half Mile Junction. There, you will have to decide whether to turn right, toward Bota and the plantations; left, toward New Town, where I am from; or continue straight, toward Down Beach, where you will see the Atlantic Ocean."

"Fascinating," Clark said, reopening his laptop.

"I swear to you, sir, it is the best town in Africa. Even Vince says it's the type of town he wants to live in."

"Of course he did," Clark said. He looked up at Jende in the rearview mirror. "When did he say this?"

"Two nights ago, sir. When I was driving him back uptown after dinner."

"What dinner?"

"He was home to have dinner with Mighty and Mrs. Edwards, sir."

"Right," Clark said. He moved his laptop to his left and picked up a folder of documents held together by jumbo paper clips.

"He's a very funny guy, Vince," Jende said, smiling. "He thinks Obama is not going to do anything about—"

"So why are you here?"

"I am sorry, sir?"

"Why did you come to America if your town is so beautiful?"

Jende laughed, a brief uneasy laugh. "But sir," he said. "America is America."

"I don't know what that's supposed to mean."

"Everyone wants to come to America, sir. Everyone. To be in this country, sir. To live in this country. Ah! It is the greatest thing in the world, Mr. Edwards."

"That still doesn't tell me why you're here."

Jende thought for a second; he thought about what to say without saying too much. "Because my country is no good, sir," he said. "It is nothing like America. I stay in my country, I would have become nothing. I would have remained nothing. My son will grow up and be poor like me, just like I was poor like my father. But in America, sir? I can become something. I can even become a respectable man. My son can become a respectable man."

"And that could never happen in your country?"

"Never, Mr. Edwards."

"Why?" Clark asked, picking up his buzzing phone. Jende waited for him to finish his conversation, a ten-second discussion during which he only said, "Yes . . . No . . . No, I don't think he should be fired for that." The phone buzzed again and he told whoever was on the line to call HR and tell them he was going to take care of it. He hung up and asked Jende to continue.

"Because . . . because in my country, sir," Jende said, his voice ten decibels lower, far less unbound and animated than it had been before he heard that someone was in danger of being fired, "for you to become somebody, you have to be born somebody first. You do not come from a family with money, forget it. You do not come from a family with a name, forget it. That is just how it is, sir. Someone like me, what can I ever become in a country like Cameroon? I came from nothing. No name. No money. My father is a poor man. Cameroon has nothing—"

"And you think America has something for you?"

"Ah, yes, sir, very much, sir!" he said, his voice escalating once more. "America has something for everyone, sir. Look at Obama, sir. Who is his mother? Who is his father? They are not big people in the government. They are not governors or senators. In fact, sir, I hear they are dead. And look at Obama today. The man is a black man with no father or mother, trying to be president over a country!"

Clark did not respond, picking up his buzzing phone instead. "Yeah, I saw his email," he said to the person on the line. "Why? . . . I don't know what to say. I'm not sure what Tom's thinking . . . No, Phil, no! I completely disagree. We can't keep on doing the same things and expect that the results will be different . . . Right, let's stick with the strategy, even though for three years we've been making one poor choice after another. I mean, the level of shortsightedness here . . ." He scoffed and shook his head. "I've spoken up as much as I can . . . No, I won't . . . What baffles me is how no one else, I mean no one, except for maybe Andy, sees how ridiculous it is that we've been doing the same things over and over and expecting that somehow we'll survive. We've got to change course. Now. Completely rethink our strategy . . . Repo 105 isn't going to keep us sailing forever . . . I don't believe that will, either, and I've told Tom that . . . Everyone's in denial! I don't get how no one's thinking about the fact that superficial short-term fixes are only going to come back to haunt us . . . Of course they will . . . How? Are you really asking me that? Have you thought for a second about the fact that everything's on the line if this shit blows up? Our lives, our careers, our families, reputations . . . Trust me, it will. And I can guarantee you that the feds will be ready to hang Tom the way they hung Skilling, and the rest of us . . ."

For a few seconds he said nothing, listening to his colleague. "You think it's going to be that nice and clean, huh?" he said. "Somehow everyone's just going to walk away nice and clean from the burning building . . . No! How long we've been at it isn't going to mean anything pretty soon. Hell, it doesn't mean anything right now, Phil. We're drowning."

He took a deep breath as he listened again, then laughed.

"Fine," he said. "I could use that. Maybe one round. Haven't been on a course in a while . . . No, save that for yourself; one round of golf sometime soon will be enough . . . No, thank you very much, Phil. Not my cup of tea . . . Yes, I promise—I'm going to desperately beg you for her number as soon as I find myself on the verge of an explosion."

He hung up, reopened his laptop smiling and shaking his head, and began typing. After thirty minutes of silence, he put his laptop aside and made three phone calls: to his secretary; to a person named Roger about the report he hadn't yet received; to someone else, to whom he spoke in mediocre French.

"Always fun getting a chance to practice my French with the team in Paris," he said after he'd hung up.

"It is very good French, Mr. Edwards," Jende said. "You lived in Paris?"

"Yeah, for one year, while I was studying at Stanford."

Jende nodded but did not reply.

"It's a college," Clark said. "In California."

"Ah, Stanford! I remember them now, sir. They play good football. But I have never been to California. Is that where you are from, sir?"

"No, my parents retired there. I grew up in Illinois. Evanston. My dad was a professor at Northwestern, another college."

"My cousin Winston, sir, when he first came to America, he lived in Illinois for a few months, but he called us all the time saying he was ready to leave because of the cold. I think that is why he joined the army, so that he could move to a warm place."

"I don't see the logic there," Clark said, chuckling, "but yes, it's very cold. I can't tell you Evanston's anything as wonderful as your Limbe, but we had a great childhood there, my sister, Ceci, and I. Riding our bikes around the block with the other neighborhood kids, going with Dad downtown to Chicago, to museums and concerts, picnicking by the lake; it was a really wonderful place to be a kid. Ceci's thinking she might move back there one day."

"Oh, yes, your sister, sir. I did not know you are a twin. It was only a few days ago that Mighty told me your sister is your twin sister. I really like twins, sir. In fact, if God gives me one—"

"Speaking of which, I need to check up on her," Clark said as he pressed a few keys on his phone. "Hey, it's me," he said after the voice-mail greeting. "Sorry I didn't call back last week. Ridiculously busy at work, so much going on. Anyway, I spoke to Mom last night, and she told me you and the girls aren't coming to Mexico? Cec, listen. Put everything on my credit card. Okay? I'm sorry if I haven't made it clear enough, but I want you to put everything you can't afford on that credit card. Everything. The flight, the hotel, the rental car, Keila's braces, whatever you need, just put it on the card. You know how much all of us being there means to them. It's Dad's eightieth, Cec. And I want to see the girls. It's been so crazy at work, I'm barely breathing, but I'll try to pick up the next time you call. Or email. You know email or text is always better for me."

He threw his head back after hanging up, his eyes closed.

"So, you didn't have a job back home?" he asked Jende, opening his eyes and picking up his laptop.

"Oh, no, sir, I had a job," Jende replied. "I worked for the Limbe Urban Council."

"And it wasn't a good job?"

Jende laughed, taken aback by Clark's question, which he found naïve. "Sir," he said, "there is no good or bad job in my country."

"Because?"

"Because any job is a good job in Cameroon, Mr. Edwards. Just to have somewhere that you can wake up in the morning and go to is a good thing. But what about the future? That is the problem, sir. I could not even marry my wife. I did—"

"What do you mean, you couldn't marry? Poor people get married every day."

"Yes, they can, sir. Everyone can marry, sir. But not everyone can marry the person that they want. My wife's father, Mr. Edwards, he is a greedy man. He refused for me to marry his daughter because he wanted my wife to marry someone with more money. Someone who can give him money whenever he asks for it. But I didn't have. What was I supposed to do?"

Clark snickered. "I guess people don't elope in Cameroon, huh?"

"A rope, sir?"

"No, elope. You know, when you run away and get married without involving your crazy family?"

"Oh, no, no, no, sir, we do it. People do it. We also do *'come we stay.'* Which means a man says to a woman, 'Come let us live together,' but he does not marry her first. But I could never do that, sir. Never."

"Why?"

"It does not show respect for a woman, sir. A man has to go to a woman's family and pay bride-price for her head, sir. And then take her out through the front door. I had to show I am a real man, sir. Not take her for free as if she is . . . as if she is something I picked on the street."

"Right," Clark said, snickering again. "So you've paid for your wife?"

"Oh, yes, sir," Jende said, beaming with pride. "Once I come to America and send my father-in-law a nice transfer through Western Union, he sees that maybe I am going to be a rich man one day, he changed his mind."

Clark laughed.

"I know it is funny, sir. But I had to get my wife. By two years after I came to New York, I had saved good money to pay the bride-price and bring her and my son over here. I sent money to my mother and father, and they bought everything my father-in-law wanted as the bride-price. The goats. The pigs. The chickens. The palm oil, bags of rice. The salt. The cloth, bottles of wine. They bought it all. I even give an envelope of cash double what he asked for, sir."

"No kidding."

"No, sir. Before my wife comes to America, my family goes to her family, and they hand the bride-price and sing and dance together. And then we were married."

Clark's phone buzzed. "Fascinating story," he said, picking it up and putting it back down.

"And the truth, sir," Jende went on, unable to stop himself, "is that the paper I signed as marriage certificate at city hall is not what makes me feel like I marry my wife. That does not mean too much. It is the bride-price I paid. I give her family honor."

"Well," Clark said, clicking on his laptop, "I hope she's been worth it."

"Oh, yes, sir! She is. I have the best wife in the whole world, sir."

They drove in silence for the next forty-five minutes. Traffic was sparse in the lower part of New Jersey except for tractor-trailers, which seemed to appear out of nowhere.

"So you think America is better than Cameroon?" Clark asked, still looking at his laptop.

"One million times, sir," Jende said. "One million times. Look at me today, Mr. Edwards. Driving you in this nice car. You are talking to me as if I am somebody, and I am sitting in this seat, feeling as if I am somebody."

Clark put aside the laptop and picked up another folder, one with loose sheets. He flipped through the sheets, scribbling on a writing pad. "What I'm curious about still," he said, without pausing to look up at Jende, "is how you could buy a ticket to come to America if you said you were that poor."

Once more Jende thought of the best answer. There was no shame in telling the truth, so he told it. "My cousin, sir," he said. "Winston."

"The associate at Dustin, Connors, and Solomon?"

"Yes, sir. He is the one who bought me a ticket. He felt sorry for me. My cousin, he is a better brother to me than some of my brothers from the same mother, same father."

"And how did he get here?"

"He won the green card lottery, sir. Then he joined the army. He used the money—"

"I know," Clark said. "Frank told me."

His phone buzzed. He looked down at it and turned his face toward the window. The phone buzzed several more times before he picked it up. "No, I haven't," he said to the caller. "Why?" The car in the left lane honked and cut in front of them. "Arizona?" he said. "When did he tell you this? . . . Never mind, I'll call him right now . . . No, I'm not mad. He's got to have a pretty good reason, which I'd like to hear . . . Of course I don't think it's a good idea . . . Yes, yes, I'll talk to him."

He quickly dialed a number.

"Hi, it's Dad," he said. "Give me a call when you can, will you? Mom just told me you turned down the Skadden internship offer, and she's very upset. Why are you doing this? She says you want to spend a month at a reservation in Arizona? I'm just . . . I'm not sure what your thinking is—Skadden's a great opportunity for you, Vince. You can't just throw it away because you'd rather go sit around in Arizona. Can't you go there before or after the internship? Please call me back as soon as you get this. Or come to my office tomorrow. Call Leah and check my calendar. Just wish you'd talk to me before making a decision like this. I wish you didn't go about making major decisions without talking to Mom and me. It's the very least you can do."

He hung up and sighed, a sigh as deep and audible as it was hopeless and defeated. "Unbelievable," he muttered to himself. "Un-be-lieve-able."

In the front seat, Jende drove in silence, though he yearned to tell

Mr. Edwards he was sorry Vince had upset him, that nothing could be harder than a disobedient son.

For twenty minutes they rode up the turnpike in silence, from exit nine toward Rutgers University, to exit ten for Perth Amboy, behind tractor-trailers and beside sedans with napping babies and dogs sticking out their heads for air; above a sky that bore the same cumulus clouds that had been following them like spies for three hours. Clark made a call to Frank, asked if he could arrange an internship for Vince at Dustin, in case Skadden's was no longer available; in case Vince realized that he had to start acting like a grown man.

"I'm glad you understand what an opportunity you've been given," Clark said to Jende after getting off the phone with Frank. The tallest skyscrapers of Manhattan had just begun appearing as they entered northern New Jersey. "I'm glad someone understands when they've been given a great opportunity."

Jende nodded with every word. He thought about the best thing to say to make Clark feel better, the right thing to say to his boss at a time like this. He decided to say what he believed. "I thank God every day for this opportunity, sir," he said as he switched from the center to the left lane. "I thank God, and I believe I work hard, and one day I will have a good life here. My parents, they, too, will have a good life in Cameroon. And my son will grow up to be somebody, whatever he wants to be. I believe that anything is possible for anyone who is American. Truly do, sir. And in fact, sir, I hope that one day my son will grow up to be a great man like you."

Seven

ON A SUNNY DAY IT WAS HARD TO SEE HOW FAR THE LEHMAN BROTHERS office tower extended into the sky. Its walls seemed to soar on forever, like an infinite spear, and though Jende sometimes pushed his head far back and squinted, he couldn't see beyond the sunlight banging against the polished glass. But on a cloudy day, like the day he finally met Clark's secretary, Leah, in person, he could see all the way to the top. Even without the sun's rays falling on it, the building glimmered and Lehman Brothers stood regal and proud, like a prince of the Street.

Leah had called him around noon, saying he needed to drive back to Lehman from wherever he was: Clark had forgotten an important folder in the car and needed it for a three o'clock meeting. "No, I'll meet you downstairs," she said after Jende offered to bring it upstairs. "Clark's going crazy today and I could use some air," she whispered.

She arrived downstairs while he was leaning against the car with the folder in his hands. He had expected her to be small—tiny, even—based on her high-pitched honeyed voice and the girly manner in which she sometimes giggled at banal things he said, but she was wide and round, like some of the people he'd seen when he landed at Newark; thick and fleshy humans who had made him wonder if America was a country of large people. In Limbe there were perhaps two people of that size in a neighborhood of hundreds, but at the airport, walking from the plane through immigration and customs to baggage claim, he had counted at least twenty. Leah wasn't as plump as the largest of the women he'd seen that day, but she was tall, a head above most of the women standing in front of the building. She walked toward him waving and smiling, dressed in a lime-green sweater and red pants, sporting a curly bob that reminded him of the crazy wig Neni wore whenever Fatou didn't have time to braid her hair.

"So good to finally meet you!" Leah chanted, her voice even more sugary than on the phone. Her lipstick matched her pants, and her round face had at least a half dozen layers of makeup, which were woefully failing in concealing the deep lines circling her mouth.

"Me, too, Leah," Jende said, smiling back and handing her the folder. "I was wondering if you were going to know it was me."

"Of course I was going to know it was you," Leah said. "You look very African, and I mean that in the nicest way, honey. Most Americans can't tell Africans from Islanders, but I can pick out an African from a Jamaican any day. I just know these things."

Jende chuckled nervously and said nothing, waiting for Leah to say goodbye and leave, which she didn't. What was she going to say next? he thought. She seemed nice, but she was most likely one of those American women whose knowledge of Africa was based largely on movies and *National Geographic* and thirdhand information from someone who knew someone who had been to somewhere on the continent, usually Kenya or South Africa. Whenever Jende met such women (at Liomi's school; at Marcus Garvey Park; in the livery cab he used to drive), they often said something like, oh my God, I saw this really crazy show about such-and-such in Africa. Or, my cousin/friend/neighbor used to date an African man, and he was a really nice guy. Or, even worse, if they asked him where in Africa he was from and he said Cameroon, they proceeded to tell him that a friend's daughter once went to Tanzania or Uganda. This comment used to irk him until Winston gave him the perfect response: Tell them your friend's uncle lives in Toronto. Which was what he now did every time someone mentioned some other African country in response to him saying he was from Cameroon. Oh yeah, he would say in response to something said about Senegal, I watched a show the other day about San Antonio. Or, one day I hope to visit Montreal. Or, I hear Miami is a nice city. And every time he did this, he cracked up inside as the Americans' faces scrunched up in confusion because they couldn't understand what Toronto/San Antonio/Montreal/Miami had to do with New York.

"So, how do you like working for Clark?" Leah asked, wisely skipping all the questions about Africa.

"I like it very much," Jende replied. "He is a good man."

Leah nodded, pulling out a pack of cigarettes from her purse and moving to lean against the car next to Jende. "Mind if I smoke?"

Jende shook his head.

"He's a good man to work for," Leah said, puffing out a straight line of smoke. "He's got his bad days, when he gets on my nerves and I just wanna throw him out the window. Otherwise, I've got no complaints. He's treated me very well. Never thought about leaving him."

"You have been his secretary for a long time?"

"Fifteen years, honey," Leah said, "though I can't say I've got too many left, with the way this company is going . . . The whole place is a big stinky mess."

Jende nodded and looked toward the building's entrance, at the twentysomething-year-old young man in a black suit who was pacing to the right of the doors, his anxiety apparent in the way he paused every few steps to stare at the ground. Jende imagined he was on his way to a job interview. Or spending his first day at the company. Or his last.

"Ever since the subprime unit fell apart," Leah went on, flicking the ashes off her cigarette, "everyone's been nervous like crazy. And I hate being nervous. Life's much too short."

Jende thought about asking her what the subprime unit was and why it had fallen apart but decided it was best not to ask about things he most certainly wouldn't understand, even if someone illustrated it to him with pictures. "I see how busy Mr. Edwards is," he said instead.

"Oh, everyone's busy," Leah said. "But Clark and his friends up there, they don't have any reason to be nervous. When it's time to lay off people, do you think they're the ones who'll be going? No, honey, it'll be us, the little people. That's why some people are already sending out résumés; I don't blame them. You can't ever trust these people."

"I do not think Mr. Edwards will let you go anywhere, Leah. You are his right-hand woman."

Leah laughed. "You're sweet," she said, smiling and revealing neatly arranged smoke-stained teeth. "But no, I don't think it'll be his decision. And you know what? I don't give a damn. I can't lose sleep over this company. Everyone's gossiping, talking about stock prices going down, profits going down, all kinds of stinky things happening in the boardroom, but the top guys won't tell us squat. They're lying to us that everything's gonna be fine, but I see Clark's emails sometimes, and well, pardon *mon français*, but there's a lot of dirty shit they're hiding."

"I am sorry to hear, Leah."

"Oh, I'm sorry, too, honey," she said, shrugging and pulling another cigarette from her purse. "And you know the worst part," she went on, moving closer to Jende and lowering her voice, "one of the VPs I'm friendly with told me there's talk that there may be some Enron-type stuff going on, too."

"Enron?" Jende asked, shifting his head to let Leah's smoke sail by.

"Yeah, Enron."

"Er . . . who was that, Leah?"

"Who?"

"This person, Enron . . . I don't know who he was."

Leah burst out laughing. She laughed so hard Jende feared she was going to choke on her smoke. "Oh, honey!" she said, still laughing. "You really just came to this country, huh?"

Jende laughed back, embarrassed and amused all at once.

"Maybe it's best you don't know what Enron was or what they did," Leah said.

"But I would like to know," Jende said. "I think I have heard the name somewhere, but I do not know what they did."

Leah pulled out her phone, looked at the time, and dropped the phone back in her purse.

"They cooked books, honey," she said to Jende.

"They cooked books?"

"Yeah," she said, her lips quivering in an attempt to suppress her laughter. "They cooked their books."

Jende nodded for a few seconds, opened his mouth to say something, shut it, opened it again, shut it again, and then shook his head. "I do not think I should ask any more questions, Leah," he finally said, and they both burst out laughing in unison.

Eight

MIDNIGHT, AND SHE STILL HADN'T STARTED. FIRST IT WAS JENDE'S WORK clothes she had to iron. Then it was Liomi's homework she had to help with. After that she had to cook dinner for the next day because, between work and evening classes, there would be no time to cook and clean the kitchen. She had to do everything tonight. She had thought she'd be done with the chores by ten o'clock, but when she looked at the living room clock it was eleven and she hadn't washed her hair, which badly needed washing. By the time she came out of the shower, the only thing she could think about as she dressed in her sleeping *kaba* was her bed, but there would be no sleep for her just yet.

She went into the kitchen and took the instant coffee out of the cabinet above the stove, turning her nose away as she opened the can to put two teaspoons of the ground beans in a mug. Nothing about coffee's forceful smell and dry, bitter taste pleased her, but she drank it, because it worked. Always did. One cup and she could stay up for two more hours. Two cups and she could be up till dawn. Which wouldn't be such a bad idea tonight: She needed at least three hours of studying if she were to finish all her homework and start preparing for her upcoming precalculus test. Maybe she'd spend two hours on the home-work and one hour on precalculus. Or stay up four hours, do two hours on homework and two hours on precalculus. She needed an A on the precalculus test. An A-minus wouldn't be good enough. A B-plus defi-nitely wouldn't do. Not if she hoped to finish the semester with at least a 3.5 GPA.

She tiptoed into the bedroom and picked up her backpack, which was lying next to Liomi's cot. He was sleeping on his side, breathing silently (unlike his father), curled under a Batman comforter, his mouth open an inch, his right palm on his right cheek as if he were pondering matters of great import in his dream. Quietly, she moved closer to him, pulled the comforter to his chest, smiled as she watched him sleep, before returning to the living room.

For three hours she studied, first reading at the dinette in prepara-tion for her next history class, afterward moving to the desktop by the window to finish the English Composition essay she had started in the library, then returning to the dinette to study precalculus, referencing her class notes, her textbook, and practice problems and solutions she had printed from the Internet. The silence in the apartment was like a celestial choir, the perfect background music to her study time—no one to disturb her, interrupt her, ask her to help do this or please come over right now. No sound but the faint noises of Harlem in the night-time.

Drinking a despicable beverage was a little price to pay for this joy of quiet. Two students in her precalculus class had formed a study group and invited others to join, but she hadn't bothered replying to their emails—she couldn't give up this pleasure of being alone just to be able to study with others. It wasn't even as if there was much to gain from a study group. She had joined one earlier in the semester, for her Introduction to Statistics class, and it had been nothing but an improper use of time. Barely thirty minutes into the group's first study session (in the students' lounge), one of the members had suggested they or-der Chinese, as if their hunger couldn't be put on hold for two hours.

Neni had been sure the other members would say they weren't inter-ested, but all of them—two young white women, an African-American youngish woman, a teenage-looking young man of indeterminable ethnicity—were in agreement that it was a great idea. She'd had no choice but to order moo shu pork and spend ten dollars she didn't want to spend, because she knew the sight of the others eating would make her hungry and ultimately chew into her concentration for the dura-tion of the session. The group had stopped studying to order, stopped studying again to eat. While they ate, they chatted about *American Idol*. Who was better than whom. Who was most likely going to win. Who was definitely not going to win. Their conversation didn't return to the upcoming test for a whole hour. Perhaps losing an hour of study time was nothing to them. It was something to her.

Around three-thirty, she went to the kitchen for another cup of coffee. Opening the can of instant coffee the second time was better, but the ground beans were still a foul-smelling thing, and no one could convince her otherwise.

She returned to the dinette, took a sip of the coffee. She rested her head in her right hand, closed her eyes, and exhaled. For a minute she kept her eyes closed, staring at the billions of tiny bright spots floating in the blackness. How good would it be to stay in this stillness for much longer, she thought; with nothing to do, nowhere to go. Her mind was always active, it seemed—what needed to be done, by when, how long it would take to get done. Even when she sang during her chores, she was mindful of the next chore. And the one after that. Life in America had made her into someone who was always thinking and planning the next step.

She opened her eyes.

She'd had enough studying for now, she decided. The precalculus test wasn't for another two weeks. She was in a good place with her preparation. She'd do a round of practice problems on Sunday, another round the night before the test and, come test day, she'd be ready.

Nine

HE KNEW BAD NEWS COULD COME EVEN ON THE HAPPIEST OF DAYS. HE knew it could arrive even when sadness was as far from the heart as Ras ben Sakka is from Cape Agulhas.

He knew any given day could be like the day his brother sent a text message asking him to call back as soon as possible. That had been a good day, a warm sunny Saturday. He was at the Red Lobster in Times Square with Neni and Liomi, eating with his favorite people at his favorite restaurant. He had immediately called his brother back and listened to him say, in a panicked voice, that their father had come down with an ugly case of malaria and could barely talk. Pa Jonga's eyes had rolled to the back of his head, Jende learned, and he was now in a conversation with his long-dead father. He needed to be rushed to a private hospital in Douala; money for the hospital could be borrowed from a businessman in Sokolo if Jende could talk to the lender and promise to send the funds for repayment as soon as possible. I beg you, Jende, his brother had said, you get for promise for send the money now-now-so, or Papa go die by daybreak.

Jende had not been able to finish his food after that call. Neni had asked the waiter to wrap up the sautéed shrimp while Jende ran, first to an ATM, to withdraw money from their savings account, and then to a bodega bearing a Western Union logo on its window, to transfer the funds to Cameroon. He ran along Eighth Avenue like a deranged man, pushing aside tourists so he could send the money as soon as he could even though the time would make no difference since his brother would not be able to retrieve the money till Monday.

His father had survived, and Jende had been reminded that, indeed, bad news has a way of slithering into good days and making a mockery of complacent joys. But the day Bubakar called, that Tuesday in April 2008, was not a special day. Jende was at work, the weather was cold, the streets of Manhattan as brutal to drive on as any other day.

He was parked on a street corner, reading Clark's discarded *Wall Street Journal*, when he saw Bubakar's name flashing on his phone. He picked up the phone warily, knowing it had to be big news, good or bad: Immigration lawyers, like doctors, did not call to say hello.

Bubakar said hello, asked about his day. His voice was somber and serious, lacking the *eh*s and *abi*s he often added at the end of sentences, and from that Jende could tell something was amiss. Even when Bubakar asked about Neni and Liomi and tried to make small talk about life as a chauffeur, Jende could tell the man was merely sterilizing a spot on his heart so he could inject painful words.

"I finally received the letter," Bubakar said.

"What did they say?"

The asylum application was not approved, the lawyer told him. The case was being referred to an immigration judge. Jende would need to appear in court because the government was going to begin removal proceedings against him. "I tried my very best, my brother," he said. "I truly did. I'm sorry."

Jende said nothing—his heart was pounding too fast for his mouth to open.

"I know it's not good news, my brother, but don't worry," he went on. "We'll keep fighting. There is a lot we can do to keep you in the country."

Still, Jende could muster no words.

"It's very hard, I know, but we must try to be strong, okay?"

The silence remained.

"Stay strong, my brother. You've got to stay very strong. I know it's a mighty shock. Really, the decision is shocking me, too, very much right now. But what can we do? The only thing we can do right now is to keep fighting."

Finally, Jende muttered a barely audible something.

"Huh?"

"I say, this means I have to leave America?"

"They say that, yes. They don't believe your story that you'll be killed by Neni's family if you go back to Cameroon."

"I thought you said it was a good story, Mr. Bubakar. In fact, you yourself told me that they would believe me. We left the interview happy. You told me I had answered the questions very well and that the Immigration woman looked like she believed me!"

"Yes, but like I told you the last time we spoke, I didn't think it was a good sign when she told us to go home and wait for the decision in the mail instead of asking us to come back to the asylum office in a couple of weeks to pick it up. I didn't want to read too much into it—"

"You told me not to worry too much about the fact that it was taking them too much time to mail us the decision, because Immigration is very slow. That's what you said!"

"They don't even have the decency to apologize and explain why it took them a whole eternity to make one decision—"

"You didn't make it sound that bad, Mr. Bubakar! You told me that the woman was very satisfied with my answers!"

"I thought so, my brother. I thought she was. But who knows how those bastards at Immigration really think? We give them a story and hope they believe it. But some of them are wicked people, very wicked. Some people in this country don't want people like me and you here."

"What is going to happen to me now? Are they going to arrest me and force me inside a plane? Will I get a chance to say goodbye . . ."

"Oh, no, God forbid! Inshallah, it'll never get to that. No, for now you're going to get a date when you have to stand in front of an Immigration judge. ICE lawyer will be there, pushing for the judge to throw you out of the country. I will be there, standing next to you, pushing for you to remain. I'm going to do everything I can to convince the judge that the people at USCIS are wrong and that you belong in America. The judge will either side with ICE lawyer and deny your asylum application or he'll side with us and approve the application so you can remain in the country and get a green card. Inshallah, the judge will side with us."

"So you are saying it's going to be you versus the lawyer from the government?"

"That's correct. Me versus their lawyer. Better man go win all."

"Oh, Papa God!"

"I know, my brother, I know, believe me. But you have to put your faith in me. You must, okay? We're going to do this together. Have we not made it this far together?"

Jende took in a deep breath. The car seat had turned into a bed of needles.

"Did I not help you make it this far?" Bubakar said. "Did I not petition USCIS to give you a work permit when they were taking too long to get to your case? Eh? Is it not because of that work permit that you were able to get a driver's license and now have a better job?"

"What am I going to do?"

"You've got to trust me."

"It's not that I don't trust—"

"Did I not help you apply for a student visa for your wife to come here and go to school? I got your whole family together in New York, my brother. Got you this close. The least you can do is trust me that, Inshallah, we will win this case and you'll get a green card."

Jende's mouth dried up.

Bubakar asked if he had any other question.

"When do I have to be in court?" he asked softly, dreading the response.

Bubakar said he didn't know—he'd received only a letter of explanation today but Jende should be getting the Notice to Appear, with a court date, soon enough.

"You have any more questions, my brother?"

Jende said no; he could think of nothing more to say or ask.

"Call me anytime with any questions, okay? Even if you just want to talk."

Jende hung up.

He dropped his phone on his lap.

He did not move.

He could not move.

Not even his mind could move; the ability to create thoughts deserted him.

What he'd lived in fear of the past three years had happened, and the powerlessness was worse than he'd imagined. If not for his pride, he would have cried, but tears, of course, would have been useless. His days in America were numbered, and there was nothing salty water running out of his eyes could do.

Upper West Siders strolled by. MTA buses stopped by. A chaos of kids on scooters rushed by, followed by three women—their mommies or grandmas or aunties or nannies—cautioning them to slow down, please be careful. Mighty would soon be done with his piano lesson. The nanny would be calling in about twelve minutes to ask Jende to bring the car to the front of the teacher's building. What should he do in those twelve minutes? Call Neni? No. She was probably on her way to pick Liomi up from his after-school program. Call Winston? No. He was working. It wouldn't be right to call him with bad news at work; besides, there was nothing he could do. There was nothing anyone could do. No one could save him from American Immigration. He would have to go back home. He would have to return to a country where visions of a better life were the birthright of a blessed few, to a town from which dreamers like him were fleeing daily. He and his family would have to return to New Town empty-handed, with nothing but tales about what they'd seen and done in America, and when people asked why they'd returned and moved back into his parents' crumbling *caraboat* house, they would have to tell a lie, a very good lie, because that would be the only way to escape the shame and the indignity. The shame he could live with, but his failings as a husband and father . . .

He looked out the window at the people walking on Amsterdam Avenue. None of them seemed concerned that the day might be one of his last in America. Some of them were laughing.

That night, after he'd told Neni, he watched her cry the first tears of sadness she'd ever cried in America.

"What are we going to do?" she asked him. "What do we have to do?"

"I don't know," he replied. "Please dry your eyes, Neni. Tears are not going to help us right now."

"Oh, Papa God, what are we going to do now?" she cried, ignoring his plea. "How can we keep on fighting? How much more money do we need to spend now that it's going to be a court case?"

"I don't know," he said again. "I'm going to call Bubakar soon to discuss more. The news hit me so bad . . . it was as if someone was pressing a pillow against my face."

They would have to use the money they had saved, they agreed. All of it: the couple thousand dollars they had put away by sticking to a monthly budget and which they hoped to one day put toward a renovation of his parents' house, a down payment on a condo in Westchester County, and Liomi's college education. If they had to get rid of their cable and Internet and take second jobs, they'd do that. If they had to go to bed hungry, they'd do that, too. They would do everything they could to remain in America. To give Liomi a chance to grow up in America.

"Should we tell Liomi now, so he can be prepared if we have to leave?" Neni asked.

Jende shook his head and said, "No, let him stay happy."

Ten

She dragged herself through the city, from work to school to home, because she needed to carry on as if nothing had changed, as if their lives hadn't just been opened up to unravelment. She couldn't summon a smile, sing a song, or string together two thoughts without the word "deportation" finding its way in there, and yet she propelled herself forward the morning after the news, dressed in pink scrubs and white sneakers for a long day of work, an overloaded backpack strapped on her shoulders so she could study at work while the client slept. Fatigued but unbowed, she traveled every day that week from Harlem to Park Slope to Chambers Street, even though she had a headache so vicious she groaned on subway platforms whenever trains screeched toward her. Once, on her way to work, she considered getting off the train to run into a Starbucks bathroom and have a good cry but she resisted the urge, because what good had all the tears done? What she needed to do was start sleeping better, stop staying up all night dreading the most horrid things that had not yet happened. We'll take it as it comes, Jende said to her every day, but she didn't want to take it as it came. She wanted to be in control of her own life, and now, clearly, she wasn't, and simply thinking about the fact that someone else was going to decide the direction of her future was enough to intensify her headache, leave her feeling as if a thousand hammers were banging on her skull. This helplessness crushed her, the fact that she had traveled to America only to be reminded of how powerless she was, how unfair life could be.

Six days after the news, her headache abated—not because her fears had diminished but because time has a way of abating these things— but new symptoms cropped up: loss of appetite; frequent urination; nausea. The symptoms could mean only one thing, she knew, and it wasn't something to cry over. And yet when she told Jende about them, she burst into tears, her joy and despair so mingled she seemed to be crying tears of joy out of one eye and tears of despair out of the other. She couldn't join him in laughing in amazement at the fact that it had finally happened, just when they had stopped worrying about whether it was ever going to happen after almost two years of trying. She couldn't marvel at how wonderful it was to get good news at a time like this, but she hoped she would be happy soon, as soon as she could eat without throwing up and get through a day without feeling like a movable lump of hormones.

"Mama," Liomi said to her one morning as she packed his lunch, "please don't forget we have the parent-teacher conference today."

Tell your teacher I cannot come, she wanted to say, but she looked at him sitting at the dinette eating his breakfast cereal, peaceful in his ignorance in the way only a child could be, and she knew she had to go to the meeting, because Jende was right—they had to keep him happy.

"Liomi's a good student," the teacher said to her by way of opening the conference, after she arrived fifteen minutes late from work. Neni nodded absentmindedly. Liomi was a good student, yes, she knew—she sat with him most evenings to do his homework. She didn't need to attend a meeting to hear this, not after having spent ten hours attending to a bedridden man while her stomach churned from not having eaten lunch because of a lack of appetite. It had been about as awful a day as any other to be a home health aide: Every time the man had coughed and asked for his spit cup to deposit yellow globs of phlegm, her nausea had returned and she had rushed into the bathroom to throw up the water and crackers she'd had for breakfast.

"The only thing that concerns me about him," the teacher went on, "is that—"

"What concerns you about him?" Neni asked, suddenly alert.

"Oh, nothing too bad," the teacher said with a short laugh, a faint accent (Hispanic? Italian?) seeping through her warm voice and causing Neni to wonder if she was an immigrant or a child of immigrants. If she was an immigrant, she didn't appear to be a poor one, not with the dazzling diamond ring on her finger and the Coach bag on the table. She was new to the school and seemed no older than twenty-four, probably only a year or two into teaching, and it was clear to Neni, from the young woman's cheerful demeanor and easy smile, that she was enjoying her job, and that regardless of why she initially took the job, she believed in what she was doing, in the difference she was making in the lives of her students. It was evident she was nowhere close to being as disillusioned as Liomi's teacher from the previous year, who repeatedly shook her head and sighed at least ten times during parent-teacher conferences.

"Liomi's a good student, Mrs. Jonga," she said, "but he could be more attentive in class."

"Attentive, eh?"

The teacher nodded. "Just a little bit more, yes. It could make a world of difference."

"And by not attentive, what do you mean? Is he sleeping when you are talking?"

"Oh, no, not at all," the teacher said, smiling again, apparently to put Neni at ease. Her makeup and pink lipstick were fresh, as if she had applied them between the end of classes and the start of her meetings with the parents; every strand of her hair was pulled into a neat bun at the back of her head. As far as Neni was concerned, she looked as if she was all set to go out to dinner with her fiancé, or to one of those lounges where young women without family responsibilities went to drink and laugh after work.

"I didn't say he's not attentive," she said. "He is. He's a good listener. But every so often, he lets himself get distracted in class. He and his friend Billy—"

"They do what?" Neni asked. She was aware of the anger in her voice but didn't care to tell the teacher that the anger wasn't directed at her.

"Billy's the clown, but Liomi can't stop himself from laughing at every silly thing Billy says or does. Liomi's a great kid, Mrs. Jonga. He's obedient, he's sharp, he's just an all-around good boy. I'm sure I don't need to tell you this—I can tell from his performance how involved you are in his schooling."

"But he makes noise in class?"

"He loves to laugh. Which is fine, of course. It's a good thing to be happy, don't get me wrong, but when he's in class, it would help for him to be less . . . giggly?"

"And you spoke to him? He does not listen to you?"

"He listens sometimes. I've moved him and Billy to extreme ends of the classroom. It's not just Liomi. Other kids get a kick out of Billy and his little brand of comedy—we're working on him. But in the meantime, it'll be good if we can help Liomi so he doesn't continue to—"

"Oh, don't worry about anything continuing," Neni said, widening her eyes as she stood up to button her jacket. "None of this nonsense will continue after today."

The teacher nodded and was about to add something, but Neni was already out the door. She ordered Liomi to stand up and he complied, jumping up from a bench in the hallway and strapping on his backpack. She said nothing more to him until they got home, though she held his hand firmly as they walked down Frederick Douglass Boulevard, tightening her grip as they hurried past a housing project where two young men had been gunned down the week before.

At home, she gave him crackers and orange juice. She could see his fear as he gingerly moved the crackers into his mouth.

"Lio," she said to him softly, after he had finished his snack and she had asked him to sit next to her on the sofa. She hadn't envisioned herself speaking to him this gently when she'd walked out of the parent-teacher conference, but something about walking past a place where young men had died, then watching him eat his crackers so sadly, had softened her heart.

"Lio, do you know why we send you to school?" she said.

He nodded, looking down to avoid her eyes.

"Do we send you to school to play, Liomi?"

He shook his head.

"Tell me why we send you to school."

"So I can learn," he said slowly, almost shamefully.

"To learn and do what else?"

"You send me to . . . nothing, Mama. Just to learn."

"Then why do you play in class? Eh? Why do you not listen to your teacher?"

He looked at her, then the floor, then the wall, but said nothing.

"Answer me!" she said. "Who is Billy?"

"He is my friend."

"Your friend, eh?"

He nodded, still looking away.

"Because he's your friend, you have to let him distract you? Have I not told you that when it comes to school, you cannot let yourself be distracted?"

"But Mama, I did not do anything—"

"Listen to me, Liomi! Open your ears and listen to me, because I will say this once and then I'll *never* say it again. You do not go to school to play. You do not go to school to make friends. You go to school to sit quietly in class and open your ears like *gongo leaf* and listen to your teacher. Are you hearing me?"

The child nodded.

"Open your mouth and say 'Yes, Mama'!"

"Yes, Mama."

"Do you think Papa goes to work every day so you can play in school? Without school, you will be nothing. You will never be anybody. Me and Papa, we wake up every day and do everything we can so you can have a good life and become somebody one day, and you repay us by going to school and playing in class? You know what's going to happen if I tell Papa what the teacher told me? Do you think he'll be happy to hear that you think school is a place to play?"

"Mama, please . . ."

"Why should I not tell him?"

"I won't do it—"

"Wipe your eyes," she said. "I won't tell him. But if I hear that you did one stupid thing in class again . . ."

He nodded, drying his eyes with the backs of his hands.

"I hope so, because you don't know how it hurt me today, what the teacher said."

His lips started trembling, and with one look at them, and his tear-stained face, her heart softened again. She moved closer to him, wiped his cheeks with her palm.

"You're going to do well in school, Liomi," she said, drying her palm on her scrubs. "You're going to graduate high school with A grades and go to a good college and become a doctor or a lawyer. You want to become a lawyer like Uncle Winston or a doctor like Dr. Tobias, don't you?"

The child shook his head.

"What are you shaking your head for? Don't you want to be a lawyer or a doctor?"

"I want to be a chauffeur."

"A chauffeur!" Neni exclaimed. "You want to be a chauffeur?"

Liomi nodded, looking at her confusedly, his brow furrowed and lips slightly parted.

"Oh, Lio," she said, laughing, enjoying the first light moment of her day. "Nobody chooses to be a chauffeur. You think Papa would choose to be a chauffeur if he could choose to be anything in the world? Papa is a chauffeur not because it is the best thing he can be. Papa's a chauffeur because he didn't finish school. And he'll never be able to finish school now, because he has to work so me and you can finish school. A chauffeur job is a good job for Papa, but it won't be for you."

Liomi forced a smile.

"I've told you this, and I'll keep on telling you: School is everything for people like us. We don't do well in school, we don't have any chance in this world. You know that, right?"

He nodded.

"Me and Papa, we don't want you to ever be a chauffeur. Never. We want you to have a chauffeur. Maybe you'll become a big man on Wall Street like Mr. Edwards, eh? That'll make us so happy. But first you must do well in school, okay?"

Liomi nodded again and she smiled at him, then rubbed his head. For the first time since Bubakar told Jende about the possible deportation, she was hopeful. Until the day she left the country, she was going to keep believing that she and her family had a chance.

When Jende returned home from work around six o'clock (thanks to Mr. Edwards being out of the country for work and Mrs. Edwards canceling her evening plans because of a cold), she served him his dinner and left for her eight o'clock precalculus class without telling him what Liomi's teacher had said. In class she sat in the front row, as she did in every class, believing physical proximity to the teacher was directly related to class grades. Except that night, her theory was once more proven wrong: When the instructor returned the previous week's test, she had a B-minus.

"I just . . . I don't understand this grade, Professor," she said to the instructor after she'd lingered around him long enough for all the other students to leave.

"Do you disagree with the grade?" the instructor asked as he moved a folder into his burgundy man bag.

"No, I don't think I disagree," she said. "It's just that I stayed up all night the night before this test to study. I did many practice problems, Professor."

"I'm not sure what you're asking me to do."

"All this studying and I end up . . . I hate it when I work so hard for something and I get a result like this. I just hate it! No matter what I do, I just cannot do well in precalculus, and now my whole GPA is going to go down . . ."

"I'm sorry," the instructor said as she began walking toward the door.

"It's okay, Professor," she said, turning around. "I'm not angry at you."

"Why don't you email me? I'll be glad to meet to see what you're struggling with."

She sighed and nodded, fatigue blended with frustration making it hard for her to utter words.

"And cheer up," the instructor said. "Lots of students would be happy with a B-minus."

Eleven

Around him tourists and New Yorkers chatted or ignored each other, everyone enfolded in their joys and sorrows and apathies. Someone laughed at one end of the subway car, a sweet laugh that on any other day would have made him look around because he loved to see the faces from which happy sounds came. Not tonight—he couldn't care about the merriment of others. He kept his head down, immersed in his misery. This is what it had come down to, he thought. This is what all his suffering had amounted to. Where did he go wrong? He rubbed his face with his palms. What would he do in Limbe if he returned there? Maybe the Council would have a job for him, but it would probably be a laborer job. No way in heaven and on earth was he going back to sweeping streets and picking up dead cats and dogs. Maybe he'd move to Yaoundé or Douala, get a job as chauffeur for a big man there. That might work . . . but such a job would never come by without a connection, and he knew no one with a solid link to a minister or CEO or any of the big men who ran the country and always kept at their service chauffeurs/bodyguards to tail them from dawn to dusk and run errands for their wives and mistresses and make their children feel like little princes and princesses. If by chance he could get such a good job, he might be able to rebuild his life in . . . No, he wasn't going to think about what he would do in Cameroon. He wasn't returning. That was *never* the plan. He'd done everything the way he had planned to. He was in America. Neni was here with him. Liomi was an American boy now. They weren't going back to Limbe. Oh, God, don't let them deport me, he prayed. Please, Papa God. Please.

"Can I sit here?" a pleasant voice asked him. He lifted his head and saw a young black man pointing to the seat next to him, where he had placed his bag.

"Oh, yes," he said, taking the bag and putting it between his feet. "So sorry."

He bowed his head again. He exhaled. What were his choices? What could he do to stay in America? Nothing, except ask for the judge's mercy, Bubakar had said. Or maybe he could talk to Mr. Edwards. Yes, he could tell Mr. Edwards the truth about his immigration situation. Mr. Edwards might help him. He might give him money to hire a better lawyer. But Winston had said it was better he stayed with Bubakar. Bubakar may be a useless *mbutuku*, Winston had said, but he was the architect of the case, and he would know best how to handle it in front of a judge. Winston was sure the judge would not deport Jende—New York immigration judges were known for their leniency, he'd found out.

It was of no consolation.

Jende heard the automated system tell riders to stand clear of the closing doors, please. He lifted his head. The white people were nearly all gone. Mostly black people remained. More black people got in. That was how he knew it was Harlem, 125th Street. He picked up his bag and stood by the door. When he exited at 135th Street, he went into the bodega at the corner of Malcolm X Boulevard and bought a Diet Coke to change his mood, to help him force out a smile when he walked into the apartment and saw Neni sitting at the table waiting for him with a face as crestfallen as a basset hound's.

The next evening he called Bubakar from the car while waiting for Cindy, who was treating her friend June to a facial on Prince Street. It had been a week since Bubakar called him and in that time he had wanted to call the lawyer to get a better understanding of his case, but every time he picked up his phone he couldn't dial the number because . . . what if Bubakar had more bad news for him?

"Listen, my brother," Bubakar said. "These things take time, eh? Immigration courts are backlogged these days like nothing I've ever seen before—there's just too many people the government wants to deport and not enough judges eager to deport them. You should have received your Notice to Appear long ago, but the way your asylum case has been going, I don't even know when you're going to get it because I'm calling the asylum office and nobody is telling me anything useful. So you may not even have to stand in front of a judge for up to six months, maybe even one year. And then after the judge sees you, he's going to want to see you again, and the next court date may not be for Allah alone knows how long. And even if the judge denies your asylum case, my brother, we can still appeal the decision. We can even do more than one appeal."

"Eh?" Jende said. "You mean to say I'm not going to court any day now to hear that I have to leave the country as soon as possible?"

"No! It's not that bad, at all! There is still a long process ahead."

"So I could still have a few years in this country?"

"A few years?" Bubakar asked in mock shock. "How about thirty years? I know people who've been fighting Immigration forever. In that time, they've gone to school, married, had children, started businesses, made money, and enjoyed their lives. The only thing they cannot do is go outside the country. But if you're in America, what is there to see outside America, *abi*?"

Jende laughed. Truly, he thought, there was nothing much to see outside America. Anything a man wanted to see—mountains, valleys, wonderful cities—could be seen here, and God willing, after he'd saved enough money, he would take his family to see other parts of the country. Maybe he would take them to see the Pacific Ocean, which Vince Edwards had told him was where he'd seen a most beautiful sunset that had brought tears to his eyes and left him humbled by the beauty of the Universe, the magnificent gift that is Presence on Earth, the vanity that is the pursuit of anything but Truth and Love.

Jende began to feel lighter, a leaf released from beneath a rock. His situation wasn't half as bad as he'd feared. How much would it cost to fight all the way to the end, he asked Bubakar. A few thousand, the lawyer told him. But no need to worry about that just yet. "You and your cousin have already spent a good amount of money to get you this far. Take a break and save for the battle ahead. When the court sends the Notice to Appear, we'll discuss a payment plan.

"You are in a better situation than many others," Bubakar added. "You have a wife who has a job, even though she does not have working papers. Immigration didn't get back to us within a hundred and fifty days after we filed your application so I forced them to give you a work permit. At least you have been able to work legally. At least there are two of you, my brother. You can both work and pay whatever bills you have. Some families don't even have one job."

"But what about my work permit?" Jende asked. "Will I be able to renew it after it expires now that Immigration wants to deport me?"

"Did your employer ask to see your work permit when he hired you?" Bubakar said.

"No."

"Good. Then stay with him."

"But what will happen if I cannot renew it and the police stops me and—"

"Don't worry about things that might never happen, my brother."

"So if my work permit expires and I cannot renew it and the police stops me on the road, I won't get into trouble for working as a driver?"

"Listen to me," Bubakar said, somewhat impatiently. "As far as Immigration is concerned, there are many things that are illegal and many that are gray, and by 'gray' I mean the things that are illegal but which the government doesn't want to spend time worrying about. You understand me, *abi*? My advice to someone like you is to always stay close to the gray area and keep yourself and your family safe. Stay away from any place where you can run into police—that's the advice I give to you and to all young black men in this country. The police is for the protection of white people, my brother. Maybe black women and black children sometimes, but not black men. Never black men. Black men and police are palm oil and water. You understand me, eh?"

Jende said he did.

"Live your life wisely and put aside all the money you can," Bubakar said. "Maybe one day, Inshallah, an immigration bill like the one Kennedy and McCain were fighting for will pass Congress and the government will give everyone papers. Then your *wahala* will be over."

"But Mr. Bubakar, after that thing did not pass, I just lose all hope."

"No, don't lose all hope. Maybe one day, Obama, Hillary, if one of them wins president, they'll give everyone papers. Who knows? Hillary likes immigrant people. And Obama, he must know some Kenyan people without papers that he'll like to help."

"But can such a thing ever really happen?"

"Oh, yes. It happened before, one time, I think 1983. It can surely happen again, but we cannot hope for it. We'll keep on trying our own way, and you keep on sleeping with one eye open, eh? Because until the day you become American citizen, Immigration will always be right on your ass, every single day, following you everywhere, and you'll need money to fight them if they decide they hate the way your fart smells. But Inshallah, one day you'll become a citizen, and when that happens, no one can *ever* touch you. You and your family will finally be able to relax. You'll at last be able to sleep well, and you'll begin to really enjoy your life in this country. That will be good, eh, my brother?"

Twelve

She met him at a café across from the public library on Forty-second Street, the same place where she had met him the past two times. After she'd emailed him the morning after he suggested they meet to talk about improving her precalculus grade, he had replied within an hour and proposed they meet in the café because he didn't have an office since he wasn't really a professor, just a mathematics Ph.D. student at the Graduate Center who was teaching for extra income and experience. He went to the café every Sunday to study, he told her during their first meeting, and he was glad to meet students there, though he didn't understand why more students didn't take his offer to help them. I am very grateful for your offer, Professor, she'd said to him, leading him to remind her once more that she didn't have to keep on calling him Professor. Call me Jerry, just like everyone in class does, he'd said, but she couldn't because he was her teacher and she had to address him properly, as she'd been taught to do in primary school.

"This is my son, Liomi, Professor," she said upon arrival for the third meeting, pulling a seat from the adjacent table for Liomi. "I am sorry I have to bring him, but my husband is working, and we have plans after this with my friend."

"No, not at all. Hi, Lomein, how are you?"

Liomi smiled.

"Open your mouth and talk to the professor," Neni said.

"I am fine," Liomi said.

"How old are you?" she heard the instructor say as she walked toward the counter to order two cups of hot chocolate. She heard Liomi say six going on seven, then giggle at something the instructor said. By the time she got to the front of the line Liomi and her instructor were chatting like old friends, the instructor drawing something on a notepad and making hand maneuvers which thoroughly amused Liomi.

"You have children, Professor?" she asked as she set the cups of hot chocolate on the table.

The instructor shook his head and, with a feeble smile, said, "I wish."

"You can borrow mine if you want."

"Oh, I'll take him," he said. "Just don't be surprised if I refuse to give him back."

"We can make arrangements for that," she said, smiling as she pulled out her precalculus textbook. She was glad she was feeling more at ease with the instructor, to the extent that she was making jokes. On their first meeting, she'd been immensely uncomfortable spending one-on-one time in a café with a man she barely knew: The whole hour she had mostly nodded while the instructor spoke, scarcely asking questions, because she was afraid of asking a stupid question and embarrassing herself. Before the second meeting, though, she told herself it was no use going downtown if she couldn't take full advantage of the instructor's offer and ultimately improve her grade. So, though nervous, she had pushed herself to ask multiple questions, and the instructor had answered even the most stupid of them. By the third meeting—

despite still being anxious enough that she'd told Liomi before they entered the café not to say a word to the professor lest he get upset by a child disturbing him and leave—she was feeling far more comfortable, so much that, toward the end of their session, she and the instructor began chatting about where they'd each grown up. The instructor's father was in the military, she learned, and he'd lived in many parts of America and Europe. Germany was his favorite place to live, he said, because, even as a child, he could tell how much the Germans loved Americans, and it felt great to be loved for his nationality. She wanted to know more about what such a life was like, how wonderful or awful it must have been not to have the same friends for all of his childhood, but she didn't know which questions were appropriate to ask of an instructor and which ones weren't, so she told him about her life in Cameroon instead, about how she'd never traveled farther than forty miles from Limbe, laughing at how pathetic it now sounded. He was curious about her pharmacist dreams, but Fatou arrived early, with her two youngest children in tow, to put an end to their conversation.

"We gonno drop the childrens to play games," Fatou announced to the instructor as she sat down in Liomi's seat after Neni had introduced them and sent the kids off to get cookies. "Then we gonno do we eyebrow and we do we nails and we gonno go to all-we-can-eat Chinese restaurant because today is day for mothers and we musto be very, very special."

"Ugh," the instructor said. "Totally forgot about Mother's Day. I should call my mom and do something nice for her, right?"

"And you wife," Fatou said.

"I'm not married."

"Girlfriend?"

Neni kicked Fatou's leg under the table.

"Boyfriend," the instructor said.

"Boyfriend?" the women asked in unison.

The instructor laughed. "I take it you ladies don't know many men with boyfriends?"

Fatou shook her head. Neni's mouth remained ajar.

"I don't know no gay man from my country," Fatou said. "But my village we used to got one man who walk lika woman. He hang his hand for air and shake his *derrière* very nice when he dance."

"That's funny."

"Everybody say he musto be woman inside, but nobody call him gay because he got a wife and childrens. And we no got no word for gay. So, I am happy to meet you!"

"But I thought you said you like children, Professor," Neni said, the shock still apparent in her voice.

"Oh, I love children."

"But how can you . . . I thought . . ."

"I've always wanted kids. As soon as I'm done with school, my boyfriend and I, we really hope we can adopt."

"Take one of my childrens," Fatou said, giggling. "I got seven."

"Seven!"

Fatou nodded.

"Wow."

"Yes, me, too, I say the same thing every day. Wow, I got seven childrens? *Un, deux, trois, quatre, cinq, six, sept, mon Dieu!*"

"How many do you want?" Neni asked the instructor.

"One or two," he said, "but definitely not seven."

Fatou and the instructor laughed together, but Neni couldn't find a way to get past her confusion. How could he be gay? Why was he gay? I can't believe he's gay, she said to Fatou over and over as they walked toward the subway with their sons.

"Oh, no, you no musto tell me," Fatou said. "I see you face when he say it."

"It's just that—"

"Just that you like tall Porto Rican boy with long hair. I see for you eyes how you like him."

"Why does everybody who looks Hispanic have to be Puerto Rican to you?"

"He like you, you like him."

"What are you talking about? I don't like him."

"What you mean, you don't like him? I see how you look at him when I enter café. You laugh at everything he say, ha, ha, ha, too funny. *Ah, oui, Professeur; vraiment, Professeur.*"

"I did not say anything like that!"

"Then why you lie?"

"Lie about what?"

"Why you no tell Jende you gonno meet *professeur* inside café?"

"I already told you. I don't want him to worry."

"Worry for what?"

"Worry about the things men worry about when their wife has a rendezvous on a Sunday afternoon with a young professor. If you were him, would you like it?"

"I no worry if Ousmane gonno meet anybody . . . but what if Liomi tell him?"

"I told Liomi to say I went to study, which is true. What is the difference between me telling Jende I'm going to study versus I'm going to meet my professor to help me with my schoolwork? It all has to do with my school."

"Aha," Fatou said as they descended the stairs to the downtown D train.

"Aha, what?"

"That be the same reason why my cousin husband beat her one day back home."

"Because she went to meet with her professor?"

"No, no," Fatou said, shaking her head and wagging her index finger at Neni. "Because she do what you just do. Husband think she somewhere, then he pass somewhere different and see her drinking beer with other man. Husband drag her back to house and beat her well. He say, why you gonno disgrace me, lie to me, and then go sit drink beer with other man? She say, oh, no, he just my friend, but husband say, then why you lie to me?"

"So what did your cousin do?"

"What she gonno do? She do stupid thing, husband beat her. That all. She learn lesson, marriage continue, everybody happy."

Thirteen

Though he loved New York City, every winter he told himself he was going to leave it for another American city as soon as he got his papers. The city was great, but why spend four months of the year shivering like a wet chicken? Why go around wearing layers upon layers of clothing like the madmen and -women who roamed the streets of New Town, Limbe? If Bubakar hadn't cautioned him that it was best he remained in the city (it might complicate matters if they tried to move his case to another jurisdiction, the lawyer had said), Jende would have been long gone, because there was no reason why a man should willfully spend so many days of his life in a cold, costly, congested place. His friends, Arkamo in Phoenix and Sapeur in Houston, agreed with him. They begged him to move to their warm, inexpensive cities. You come over here, Arkamo told him, and you'll taste real American enjoyment. Life in Houston, Sapeur said, is sweeter than sugarcane juice. At least half a dozen times every winter, they told him he would forget all about that *worwor* New York the moment he arrived at their city's airport and strolled on its clean streets and moved around freely in February without a winter jacket. So convincing were they that on the coldest days of the winter, he and Neni Googled Phoenix and Houston to learn more about the cities. They looked at the pictures Arkamo and Sapeur sent of their spacious houses and gargantuan SUVs and, try as he might, Jende found it impossible to not envy them. These boys, and others he knew in those cities, came from Limbe around the same time as him. They made the same kind of money he made (or less, working as certified nursing assistants or stockroom associates at department stores), and yet they were buying houses—three-bedroom ranch-style houses; four-bedroom townhouses with backyards where their children played and where they hosted Fourth of July barbecues teeming with grilled corn and *soya*. Arkamo told Jende how easy it was to get a mortgage these days, and promised that as soon as Jende was ready, he would connect him with a loan officer who could get him a zero-down-payment mortgage on a sweet mini-mansion. It all sounded wonderful to Jende (one of the many things that made America a truly great country), but he knew such an option wouldn't be available to him without papers. Arkamo and Sapeur already had papers—Arkamo through a sister who became a citizen and filed for him; Sapeur through marrying an American single mother he met when he showed up at a nightclub dressed in a three-piece orange suit and red fedora. They could afford to get high-interest loans that would take thirty or more years to pay off because they were green card holders. Jende would buy a nice house in one of those cities, too, if he had papers. As soon as he could, he would move, most likely to Phoenix, where Arkamo lived in a gated community. There would be no more freezing days for him; no more mornings of vapor spewing out of his open mouth as if he were a kettle of boiling water. Neni had her dreams of a condo in Yonkers or New Rochelle because she didn't want to leave her friends, and she loved New York too much, cold or warm, but he knew he would leave behind the city and its hopeless predicaments if he weren't stuck in an immigration purgatory.

Every winter, he was certain of this.

But then the spring came, and his dreams of Phoenix evaporated like the dew in Marcus Garvey Park. He couldn't imagine a city more beautiful, more delightful, more perfect for him than New York. Once the temperature rose above fifty-five, it was as if the city had awakened from a deep slumber and the buildings and trees and statues were singing as one. Heavy black jackets flew away and colorful clothes rushed in. All over Manhattan, people seemed on the verge of a song or a dance. No longer pressed down by the cold air, their shoulders opened up and their arms flung freely and their smiles shone brightly because they felt no need to cover their mouths while talking. Sad, Jende often thought, how winter takes away so many of life's ordinary pleasures.

On the third Thursday in May—as he was driving Cindy across Fifty-seventh Street to lunch with her best friends, Cheri and June, at Nougatine—he noticed that virtually everyone on the street seemed happy. Maybe they weren't truly happy, but they looked happy, some practically sprinting in the warmth of the day, delighted to be comfortable again. He was happy, too. It was almost seventy degrees and, as soon as he dropped Cindy off, he was going to take the car to a garage, pay for parking with his own money, and rush into Central Park to breathe in some fresh air. He'd sit on the grass, read a newspaper, have his lunch by a lake or pond, and—

His cell phone rang.

"Madam, I am so . . . so very sorry, madam," he said to Cindy, realizing he'd forgotten to turn it off. He searched frantically in his jacket pocket, scolding himself as he pulled it out. "I swear I turned it off this morning, madam. I was sure I turned it off right before—"

"You can get it," Cindy said.

"It's okay, madam," he said, looking at the phone and quickly pressing the side button to silence it. "It's only my brother calling me from Cameroon."

"No problem, take it."

"Okay, thank you, madam, thank you," he said, fidgeting with his earpiece to pick up before his brother hung up.

"Tanga, Tanga," he said to his brother, "I beg, I no fit talk right now . . . Madam dey for inside motor . . . Wetin? . . . Eh? . . . No, I no get money . . . I don tell you say things them tight . . . I no get nothing . . . I beg, make I call you back . . . Madam dey for inside motor. I beg, I get for go."

He sighed after hanging up, and shook his head.

"Everything's okay, I hope?" Cindy asked, picking up her phone to start typing.

"Yes, madam, everything is okay. I am sorry I disturbed you with the noise. It will not happen again, I promise you. That was just my brother calling with his own troubles."

"You seem upset. Is he all right?"

"Yes, madam, nothing too big. They drove his children away from school because they have not paid their school fees. They have not gone to school for one week now. That is why he is calling me, to send him the money. He is calling me over and over, every day."

Cindy said nothing. Jende's voice had come out cloaked in such helplessness that she probably thought it best to ask no more questions, figured it would be better to let him ponder how to help his brother. She continued typing a message on her cell phone and, after putting the phone away, looked up at him and said, "That's a shame."

"It is shameful, madam. My brother, he went ahead and had five children when he does not have money to take care of them. Now I have to find a way to send him the money, but I myself, I don't even . . ." He made a right turn, and she asked him no more questions. For the next two minutes they drove in silence, as they did ninety percent of the time when she wasn't on her cell phone with a client or a friend.

"But that's not right," she said, her voice suddenly hollow. "Children should never have to suffer because of their parents."

"No, madam."

"It's never the child's fault."

"Never, madam."

She was silent again as they neared Central Park West. He heard her open her purse, unzip and zip at least one pocket, before taking out her lipstick and compact foundation.

"I'm sure it's going to work out for the kids," she said, reapplying her lipstick and puckering her lips in the compact's mirror as he pulled up in front of the restaurant. "Something's going to work out one way or another."

"Thank you, madam," he said. "I will try my best."

"Of course," she said, as if she didn't believe for a second that he had a best to try.

When he came around to open the door for her, she reminded him to pick her up in two hours and then, without prelude, pulled out a check from the front pocket of her purse and handed it to him.

"Let's keep this between ourselves, okay?" she whispered, moving her mouth close to his ear. "I don't want people thinking I'm in the habit of giving out money to help their families."

"Oh, Papa God, madam!"

"You can go cash it and send it to your brother while I'm eating. I'd hate to see those poor children miss another day of school because of a little money."

"I . . . I do not even know what to say, madam! Thank you so much! I just . . . I'm so . . . I'm just very . . . My brother, my whole family, we thank you so much, madam!"

She smiled and walked away, leaving him on the curb with his mouth half open. After she'd climbed the steps and entered the restaurant, he opened the check and looked at the sum. Five hundred dollars. He reentered the car and looked at the sum again. Five hundred dollars? May God bless Mrs. Edwards! But his brother had asked for three hundred. Was he to send the whole check because Mrs. Edwards had demanded so? He called Neni, to tell her the story and get her opinion, but she didn't pick up—she was probably in her school library with her phone on silent, studying for her finals. He didn't want to wait until he got home to discuss it with her because Mrs. Edwards had asked him to send the money today, and he had to do as he'd been told. His years on earth had taught him that good things happen to those who honor the kindheartedness of others. So, after parking the car, instead of going to Central Park, he half-ran to a Chase branch across from Lincoln Center, cashed the check, and began walking north along Broadway. He stayed on the east side of the street, rushing and sweating under the immaculate sky, forgetting to enjoy his favorite kind of weather because he was too focused on finding a Western Union and getting back to Mrs. Edwards on time. Somewhere in the mid-Seventies, he found one and sent his brother the three hundred dollars the children needed. He'd debated the right thing to do as he filled out the Western Union form, and decided it wouldn't be right to send the full sum Mrs. Edwards had given. He knew his brother too well. He knew Tanga was most likely going to spend the balance on either gifts for a new girlfriend or new pairs of leather shoes for himself, this while his children went to school with rubber shoes held together with twine. Enabling his brother to do such a thing would never be fair to Mrs. Edwards. Besides, it was better he saved the two hundred dollars, because, in another month or two, a brother or cousin or in-law or friend was going to call saying that money was needed for hospital bills or new school uniforms or baptism clothes or private French classes, since every child in Limbe had to be bilingual now that the government had declared that the next generation of Cameroonians had to be fluent in both English and French. Someone back home would always need something from him; a month never went by without at least one phone call asking him for money.

As he sat in the car with the two hundred dollars in his pocket, he fervently hoped Cindy wouldn't ask if he'd sent all the money because he would either have to tell her a half-truth or give her a long explanation of how this business of sending money to relatives back home worked and how some relatives had no consideration for those who sent them money because they thought the streets of America were paved with dollar bills.

Cindy reentered the car twenty minutes later and immediately got on her phone.

"I'm still speechless, Cheri," she said. "Completely speechless . . . My gosh! Mike? Of all people? . . . Oh, God, I feel so awful for her . . . Of course she's in a daze! I'm in a daze. I thought she looked a bit down when I walked in, but to hear this . . . She doesn't deserve it! . . . No! . . . She's been nothing but wonderful to him. Thirty years of marriage, and you wake up one day and say you're in love with someone else? I'd die . . . Yes, I'd die! . . . Okay, maybe I wouldn't die, but I certainly wouldn't be getting out of bed the next day to meet up with you guys for lunch . . . Oh my God! Of course! Oh, gosh, that could be me . . . I feel like it's going to be me one day, Cher. I'll wake up one day and Clark will tell me he's found someone younger and prettier, oh, God! . . . Yeah, out with the old, in with the new . . . I don't care if she's forty-five, she can't be more beautiful than June . . . Me, neither. I've never met even one of those skanks who was anything worth writing home about . . . I mean, some of them . . . It's never about the looks. We went to dinner last night with the Steins, and the waitress, she was definitely not that pretty except for a cute accent from some Eastern European place. But you should have seen how Clark was looking at her . . . Maybe early thirties . . . Every time she came over, Cher . . . No, I'm not kidding you . . . Of course he still does it, right in front of me . . . Subtle? Not last night; I had to go to the bathroom to gather myself . . . Yeah, that's how bad it was. Humiliating . . . Maybe it was all in my head because I didn't want to be there, but the way he was talking to her, smiling at her, curious about her tattoo . . . It was! A big reminder to me, you know . . . I just don't know . . ."

Fourteen

PEOPLE HANGING OUT IN BARS MADE NO SENSE TO NENI. WHY WOULD anyone want to stand in a crowded place for hours, screaming at the top of their voice to chat with a friend, when they could sit comfortably in their own home and talk to their friend in a calm voice? Why would they choose to sit in a dark space, consuming drinks that sold at the grocery store for a quarter of the bar's price? It was an odd way of spending time and money, and a decision like Winston's was even odder. Winston lived alone in a seven-hundred-square-foot one-bedroom apartment in a doorman building, and yet he was going to celebrate his birthday with some friends in a bar at the Hudson Hotel, across the street from his apartment building.

"But your apartment can fit at least thirty people," Neni said to him when he came over and invited her and Jende to join in. "I can come and cook the food for the party."

"And who's going to clean the next morning?" Winston asked her.

"You have a cleaning lady!"

"No, I'm not dealing with all that," he said. "And why are you making all this *sisa* about going to a bar? Didn't you like going to drinking spots in Limbe?"

"Yes, I like drinking spots. So?"

"So, isn't it the same thing?"

"Same thing? Wait, you want to compare American bars to drinking spots in Limbe?"

"Why not? You go to the place, you order your drink, you find somewhere to sit down and enjoy it—"

"Please, don't make me laugh, Winston," Neni said, laughing. "There's no comparison, okay? In Limbe you sit outside, it's warm and sunny. You're enjoying a nice breeze, listening to *makossa* in the background, watching people go up and down the street. That is real enjoyment. Not these places where—"

"How many American bars have you been to?"

"Why do I have to go to any of them? I see them on TV—that's enough for me. People act as if things in America have to be better than things everywhere else. America doesn't have the best of everything, and when it comes to where you can go and enjoy a nice drink, it can never compete with Cameroon. Even if someone wants—"

"Neni, I'm begging, enough with the too many arguments," Jende said. "Let's just go, okay?"

"Maybe," she said, pursing her lips.

"You'll have a good time, and I'll have one of those drinks they call Sex on the Beach," Jende added, winking at her as she rolled her eyes and walked out of the living room.

On the evening of the party, they arrived an hour late, thanks to Neni changing and unchanging her mind on which blouse to wear so she could look equally sexy and respectable. Winston was standing near the counter with a group of friends when they walked in holding hands, Jende in front, Neni behind. Next to Winston and his friends, two men sat on stools, smiling with their faces so close Neni was convinced she was about to witness her first kiss between two men. The sight of the men reminded her of the instructor—thanks to whom she'd gotten an A-minus final grade in precalculus and ended the semester with a 3.7 GPA—and got her wondering what his boyfriend looked like, and where they were in the adoption process, which the instructor had told her on the last day of class they were ready to begin because he didn't want to wait until after his graduation anymore, being that he was about to turn forty.

"What should we do?" Jende whispered in her ear as they stood by the door, unsure of how to navigate the room packed with patrons sipping beer and swirling cocktails. She shrugged—how was she supposed to know what to do in a place like this? With no choice but to wait for Winston to come get them, they remained by the door, waving intermittently at him and hoping he would see them, which he did only after one of his friends waved back at them. Winston put up a finger and mouthed something but seemed unable to extricate himself from his friends, so Jende and Neni continued standing by the exit, hands linked like adjacent trees with interlocked branches, awkwardly shifting their feet and looking at the drinkers despite knowing they wouldn't be seeing a familiar face in the roomful of good-looking, young white people.

"I'm going to the bathroom," Neni whispered in Jende's ear, and rushed for the ladies' room before he had a chance to respond. In front of the mirror, she noticed that her face was getting sweaty, certainly not from the heat in the air-conditioned room. What was she going to do or say to those people out there for two hours? She'd never been invited to a party with mostly white people, and even if she had, she would not have attended. She was only doing this for Winston, but maybe she should have stayed home and cooked him some *fufu and eru* for his birthday gift. This place wasn't her kind of place; the people out there weren't her kind of people. Winston had friends of all races, she knew, but she had no idea he had so many white friends—she didn't have a single non-African friend and hadn't even come close to being friends with a white person. It was one thing to be in the same class with them, work for them, smile at them on the bus; it was a whole other thing to laugh and chat with them for hours, making sure she enunciated every word so they wouldn't say her accent was too difficult to understand. No way could she spend time with a white woman and be herself the way she was with Betty or Fatou. What would they talk about? Laugh about? Besides, she hated it when she said something and they smiled or nodded and she could tell they had no idea what she'd just said. And the people in the bar, they looked like that kind—they were mostly associates at the firm where Winston worked, so she had to be careful not to embarrass him. Nothing shamed her more than black people embarrassing themselves in front of white people by behaving the way white people expect them to behave. That was the one reason why she had such a hard time understanding African-Americans—they embarrassed themselves in front of white people left and right and didn't seem to care.

She pulled a tissue from her purse, dabbed the sweat and oil off her face. She reapplied her dark purple lipstick, which needed no reapplication. This should be a good exercise, she thought as she walked back into the bar, pulling down her red halter blouse to cover the top of her jeans, which was annoyingly bunching up beneath her belt and overlapping belly. She was glad Jende had talked her out of wearing high heels—her legs were shaky enough on the two-inch cowgirl boots into which she'd tucked her jeans. Shaky or not, though, she had to make herself at ease and act as if she went to places like this every night. After she becomes a pharmacist, she might have to attend lots of parties with white people. Hopefully, her accent will no longer be as strong as one of her professors has said it is; maybe she'll learn to speak with an American accent by then. But for tonight she would try to speak as slowly as she could and then smile. No one would ask her to repeat herself three times if she just smiled.

For perhaps a minute after reentering the bar, she couldn't see Jende or Winston, so she stood by herself, looking around the room at friends and co-workers and couples whispering into ears or conversing at the top of voices. Then she saw Jende by the door, chatting with someone, probably one of Winston's friends whom he'd met during the month he lived with Winston when he first came to America.

She was trying to decide whether to join Jende or order a glass of soda on Winston's tab when a young white woman with curly dark hair appeared in front of her, a cocktail glass in hand, smiling as if she'd just seen something incredibly special.

"Oh my God!" the young woman said. "You must be Neni!"

Neni nodded, broadening her smile.

"I'm Jenny. Winston's girlfriend."

Winston's girlfriend?

"So glad to finally meet you!" Jenny said, giving Neni a hug.

"I am glad to meet you, too," Neni said, struggling to enunciate and scream above the hip-hop music blasting into her ears from every direction.

"Are you having a good time?" Jenny shouted, moving closer to her. "Would you like a drink?"

Neni shook her head.

"I'm so glad we finally get to meet!" Jenny shouted again. "I've heard so much about you."

"Thank you. I am happy to meet you, too."

"I've been telling Winston that we need to hang out, all four of us, but it's just so tough with everyone's work schedules. But we've got to. Is Jende here?"

Neni nodded and smiled, still thinking: Winston's girlfriend?

"How do you like New York? Winston tells me you've been here for only two years."

"I love it. Very much. I am very happy to be here."

"I'd love to go to Cameroon!" Jenny said, smiling and looking upward dreamily. "Winston doesn't seem too eager to visit anytime soon but I'm pushing for us to go sometime next year."

Neni looked at Jenny, grinning and sipping her cocktail, and couldn't decide whether to laugh or feel sorry for her. What was she thinking? Winston was never going to marry a white woman. He didn't even bother introducing the ones he slept with to his family, because he changed them the way someone changes underwear. All Neni and Jende knew right now was that he was playing one of the other associates at the firm: Apparently this was her. The poor thing. The way her eyes lit up every time she said his name. She looked no older than twenty-six, but not too young to have noticed that successful Cameroonian men like Winston hardly ever married non-Cameroonian women. They enjoyed every type for as long as they could: white, Filipino, Mexican, Iranian, Chinese, any woman of any color who availed herself out of infatuation or undeniable love or mere curiosity. But when the time came to choose a wife, how many of them married one of those women? Too few. And Winston would never be one of those few. If he couldn't find a good Bakweri girl, he would marry one from another tribe in the Southwest or Northwest regions (but definitely not from the Bangwa tribe, since his mother hated Bangwas, for whatever reason). He would marry his kind because a man like him needed a woman who understood his heart, shared his values and interests, knew how to give him the things he needed, accepted that his children must be raised in the same manner in which his parents had raised him, and only a woman from his homeland could do that.

"There you are," someone said from behind them. Neni turned around to see another young woman with a cocktail glass in hand, probably Jenny's friend. Jenny turned around, too, hugged the other woman, and introduced Neni as Winston's cousin who just came from Africa. Just came from Africa? Neni thought. She didn't *just come from Africa.* She considered correcting Jenny, but, not knowing if it would be polite to do so, instead forced out a smile at Jenny's friend, who nodded but otherwise barely acknowledged her presence. The friend began telling Jenny a story, and the women veered into another conversation, leaving Neni a smiling spectator to their camaraderie. After ten minutes, unsure of what to do besides continue trying to prove to herself that she could be at ease in a bar, she hurriedly excused herself; the two women hardly paused to say goodbye. She pushed through the crowd, which seemed to have tripled since she and Jende arrived, and inadvertently hit a young man's drink with her elbow. The drink did not spill, but the young man gave her a look that she was certain meant: What the hell are you doing here, you stupid African woman?

Jende was standing alone where she'd last seen him, sipping a drink through a straw and slowly moving to the hip-hop music in his bright yellow Madiba shirt.

"I'm ready to go," she said in his ear.

"Why?" he said. "I was wondering where you were. Did you have anything to drink?"

"I don't want a drink."

"Is it your nausea? Won't some Coca-Cola help—?"

"Did I complain to you about my nausea? Let's go."

"Ah, Neni. Just thirty more minutes. I've only had two Sex on the Beach."

"Then stay. I'm leaving."

"You won't even talk to Winston and wish him happy birthday?"

"I'll call him tomorrow."

Outside on Fifty-eighth Street, the air was cool and refreshing, the noise level bearable except for two ambulances rushing to Roosevelt Hospital a block away. Neni turned her face away from the hospital in an attempt to block out the memory of what had happened there a year ago, the afternoon she had rushed with her friend Betty to Labor and Delivery because Betty was cramping heavily. Betty had received an emergency C-section only for the baby to come out stillborn.

"Let's go sit at Columbus Circle for a little bit," Jende said, and she quickly agreed, banishing from her mind the image of the lifeless newborn she wished she hadn't seen. Jende began talking about how great a time he'd had talking to one of Winston's friends, but she was barely listening. She was noticing something for the first time: She was realizing that most people on the street were walking with someone who looked like them. On both sides of the street, going east and west, she saw people walking with their kind: a white man holding hands with a white woman; a black teenager giggling with other black (or Latino) teenagers; a white mother pushing a stroller alongside another white mother; a black woman chatting with a black woman. She saw a quartet of Asian men in tuxedos, and a group of friends who had different skin colors but were dressed in similar elegant chic styles. Most people were sticking to their own kind. Even in New York City, even in a place of many nations and cultures, men and women, young and old, rich and poor, preferred their kind when it came to those they kept closest. And why shouldn't they? It was far easier to do so than to spend one's limited energy trying to blend into a world one was never meant to be a part of. That was what made New York so wonderful: It had a world for everyone. She had her world in Harlem and never again would she try to wriggle her way into a world in midtown, not even for just an hour.

When they got to Columbus Circle, she called Fatou, who told her that Liomi was fine, they could stay out for however long they wanted. So they sat beneath the statue of Christopher Columbus, side by side, hand in hand, surrounded by skateboarders and young lovers and homeless people, looking north as cars came around the circle and went up Central Park West. The spring air was crisper than she would have wished, but not crisp enough to send her rushing into the subway. And even if it had been, she would have stayed in the circle, because it wasn't every night she got a chance to enjoy the sounds of the city and its millions of lights blinking around her, reminding her that she was still living in her dream. Bubakar had assured them that they could be in the country for many years, which meant they could be in the city for many years. A massive smile involuntarily appeared on her face at the thought, and she moved closer to Jende and leaned against him.

"This is the best place in the whole city," he said to her. She did not ask why he thought so, because she knew why.

In his first days in America, it was here he came every night to take in the city. It was here he often sat to call her when he got so lonely and homesick that the only balm that worked was the sound of her voice. During those calls, he would ask her how Liomi was doing, what she was wearing, what her plans for the weekend were, and she would tell him everything, leaving him even more wistful for the beauty of her smile, the hearth in his mother's kitchen, the light breeze at Down Beach, the tightness of Liomi's hugs, the coarse jokes and laughter of his friends as they drank Guinness at a drinking spot; leaving him craving everything he wished he hadn't left behind. During those times, he told her, he often wondered if leaving home in search of something as fleeting as fortune was ever worthwhile.

"You know what I'm realizing now?" he said to her.

"What?" she asked, looking at him adoringly.

"We are sitting in the center of the world."

She laughed. "You're so funny."

"No, think about it," he said. "Columbus Circle is the center of Manhattan. Manhattan is the center of New York. New York is the center of America, and America is the center of the world. So we are sitting in the center of the world, right?"

Fifteen

ON THE WAY TO THE GOLF COURSE IN WESTCHESTER, CLARK COMPLAINED about his stiff neck, grumbled about Phil inviting a bunch of other people to join them and thus making it hard for him to pull out, griped about spending his afternoon doing an activity he didn't care for when he could be in the office. Jende listened and nodded, as always, agreeing with everything he said.

"Golf's not my thing," Clark said. "A lot of people like to pretend it's their thing, but I couldn't care less about going today, if it wasn't for a chance to spend time with the guys outside of work."

"It looks like a very hard game, sir."

"It really isn't. You should try it sometime."

"I will, sir," Jende said, though he had no idea why or where he would ever go to golf.

Halfway to the course in Rye, Clark's mother called to check on him, and he put her on speakerphone, saying he didn't want to stiffen his neck any further. His mother thanked him for the anniversary gift and was about to tell him a funny story about bumping into an old neighbor from Evanston when another call came in. Clark told her he had to go and promised he would call her back after taking the incoming call from his boss.

"You're heading to join Phil and the others?" Tom asked. His voice over the speaker sounded far less powerful than Jende had expected the voice of a CEO to sound. It was genial, but lacked the authority that Clark's possessed.

"Yeah, you're coming, right?"

"No, can't make it. Michelle's not feeling too well."

"Sorry to hear."

"How's Cindy?" Tom said after a few seconds. "She looked great on Thursday."

"Yeah, she knows how to take care of herself."

"Heard a couple of guys at the bar wondering whose trophy she was."

Clark chuckled. "I'll take whatever compliments I can get these days," he said.

Jende cleared his throat, not because it needed clearing but because he could tell Tom wanted to say something important and he wanted to alert Clark of his presence so Clark could switch his phone off speaker mode. He knew enough about Lehman as it was and didn't care to hear anything else, especially something he would be tempted to tell Leah, since she'd been hounding him for details about Clark's conversations so she could know how bad things really were. He always told her he knew nothing, but the woman didn't know how to give up.

"So," Tom said, finally ready to get to his point, "I imagine you know why I'm calling."

"I'm guessing you spoke to Donald," Clark said. "I was hoping to—"

"You have no right to go to a board member behind my back, Clark."

"It wasn't my intention. I bumped into him rushing to get to my son's hockey game, quickly told him that I've been trying to get a meeting with you to talk about—"

"About what?" Tom said, his voice rising. "About your bullshit about coming clean? Changing strategy? What do you think we're doing here? Playing patty-cake?"

"I think we need to rethink our long-term strategy, Tom," Clark said, raising his voice, too. "I've been saying it, and I'll keep on saying it. We're sitting here acting as if we're dealing with forces out of our control when we're not. It's merely a matter of looking at other angles, considering other models. Back in August I came to you when it was crystal-clear that ABS performance was never going to really pick up and the damage was quickly spreading past subprime to Alt-A. Remember we had that talk and I suggested we change course?"

"What's your point?"

"When you and Danny laughed off the Chinese, I pushed for us to take whatever infusion they were throwing at us, get us out of this mess as soon as—"

"And tell the world we're drowning? Sure! Let's become laughing-stocks!"

"BS didn't want to become a laughingstock!"

"We're not BS! We're Lehman, and if you don't know that, if you don't know that we're The Brothers and that we always win, then I really can't help you, Clark! If you don't believe in what we're doing here, then you've been wasting your time for the past twenty-two years."

Jende heard Clark scoff, and imagined he was shaking his head as well.

"Why are you scoffing?" Tom asked.

"All I'm trying to say is that we need to change our approach a bit, maybe get more aggressive on raising capital. Everyone else on the Street's been running around raising capital, and we're sitting here deceiving shareholders that we're strongly capitalized. If we could so much as even—"

"You will not circumvent me and talk to a board member again, do you understand?"

Clark exhaled deeply, but did not respond.

"Do we have an agreement?"

Clark ignored the question.

"As for coming clean—"

"How long do you think before the world finds out about the leverage ratio?" Clark said. "Are you going to sit in front of Congress and say you knew nothing about Repo 105? 'Cause there's just how long we can sustain this, and at some point we're going to have to—"

"So you think airing our dirty laundry is what's going to get us back in the right direction? You think we should listen to you because you decided to grow a damn conscience?"

"This has got nothing to do with a conscience! You know I love the game. You know I love winning as much as the next guy, and I'm all for doing what we need to do to win. But there's a level where we've got to admit that we've gone too far, and if we keep on going at this rate . . ."

"Really?" Tom said derisively. "How far back should we go so we're not too far ahead of the curve? Back to the seventies? Why don't we all jump into a '75 Buick while everyone is passing us by in '08 models? That's what you're asking for, right? Because we've become so ruthless, let's try and be sweet and nice."

"I'm not—"

"I really can't help you, you know?" Tom said almost sympathetically. "Whatever crisis you're going through, I can't do anything to help you, and frankly, this isn't the best time to be dealing with it."

"I'm simply saying that we should show we stand for something better than everyone else, Tom. That could be our salvation. If we quit pulling the tricks, place the blame on someone else if we must— auditors, rogue accountants, whoever—give ourselves a chance to get straight before it gets worse. Because right now we're pulling these tricks and the SEC's playing dumb, but you know as well as I do that if this shit falls apart and the chaos starts spreading they're going to throw us out for the public to crucify by claiming they didn't know a damn thing, and we all know it's a lie."

"And you think the board's going to love your suggestion?"

"Donald wasn't exactly opposed."

"What gives you that idea? Donald thought you'd gone crazy!"

"What's crazy is thinking we're going to survive doing business this way!" Clark shouted, apparently unaware of how much his voice had risen. "We've made a ton of mistakes already. We're in this shit because we haven't shown great foresight! We've got to think far beyond Lehman. We've got to think about the next generation taking over the Street after we're gone, about how they're going to judge us. About how history's going to judge us!"

Another phone rang wherever Tom was. He picked it up, spoke softly to someone he referred to as "honey," and assured the person that he would be there, no way in the world was he going to miss it.

"I'd rather not lose you right now," he said to Clark after hanging up, his voice as soft as if he were still speaking to the other person. "We've survived highs and lows together for eighteen years, and I know, I'm absolutely certain, we'll survive this one, too. But if you think this is all too much for you then I'll sadly accept your resignation."

"I'm not going anywhere," Clark said. "There's a battle going on, and I intend to keep fighting for Lehman."

"Good."

"Yes, good."

"So why don't you get back to work and fight the way I've decided is best? And if someday I'm proven wrong, you can look back at this moment and be damn proud of yourself."

Sixteen

HE HAD BEEN WAITING ON THE CURB FOR THIRTY-FIVE MINUTES WHEN Vince finally came out of his apartment building and hopped into the backseat, a cup of coffee in one hand.

"Jende, my man," Vince said, patting him on the shoulder.

"Good morning, Vince."

"So sorry for making you wait. I wish I had a good excuse."

"It's no problem. I will try to drive fast so we are not late for your appointment."

"No, take your time. I'm never eager to be on time for a dental appointment. I wouldn't even be going all the way to Long Island if my mom didn't insist Dr. Mariano is the world's best dentist."

"It's good to have a dentist," Jende said, imagining how good it would feel to have someone else clean his teeth. He made a right turn onto Broadway and drove from the Nineties to the Fifties and then from west to east, onto I-495. "Would you like me to turn on the radio?" he asked Vince.

"No, I'm good," Vince said distractedly. He was fidgeting and looking around the car. "I think I left my phone at home," he said.

"I can go back," Jende said.

"No, it's fine."

"It is no problem for me, Vince."

"No, it's all good," Vince said, leaning back in his seat and taking a sip of his coffee. "It'll be a good exercise in disconnecting from the world. Besides, I get to talk to you uninterrupted and continue trying to unindoctrinate you on all the lies you've been fed about America."

Jende laughed. "There is nothing you can say, Vince. Nothing you or any man can say to me to make me stop believing that America is the greatest country in the world and Barack Obama will win the election and become one of the greatest presidents in the history of America."

"That's cool. I'm not going to argue too hard with that. But what if I tell you that America killed the African revolutionary Patrice Lumumba in their effort to stop the spread of communism and tighten their grip around the world?"

"Ah, Lumumba! I used to have a T-shirt with his face back in Limbe. Whenever I wore it, people stopped me on the street to look at his face and say, oh, what a great man."

"So, what if I tell you America killed that great man?"

"I will say I am sorry for what happened to him, but I don't know the whole story."

"I'm telling you the whole story."

Jende chuckled. "You are so funny, Vince," he said. "I like how you want to help me see things another way, but maybe the way I see America is good for me."

"That's exactly the problem! People don't want to open their eyes and see the Truth because the illusion suits them. As long as they're fed whatever lies they want to hear they're happy, because the Truth means nothing to them. Look at my parents—they're struggling under the weight of so many pointless pressures, but if they could ever free themselves from this self-inflicted oppression they would find genuine happiness. Instead, they continue to go down a path of achievements and accomplishments and material success and shit that means nothing because that's what America's all about, and now they're trapped. And they don't get it!"

"Your parents are good people, Vince."

"In their own way, sure."

"Your father works so hard. Sometimes he looks so tired I feel bad for him, but it's what we do for our children."

"I don't doubt his sacrifices."

"Even if you don't like America too much, I think you should still thank God that you have a mother and father who give you a good life. And now you can go to law school and become a lawyer and give your children a good life, too."

"Become a lawyer? Who said anything about me becoming a lawyer?"

Jende did not respond. He thought he was mistaken; maybe law school wasn't only for people who wanted to become lawyers.

"This is my last semester at law school," Vince said. "I won't be returning in the fall."

"You're not going to finish school?"

"I'm moving to India."

"You are moving to India!"

"I'd rather you don't tell my parents any of this just yet."

"No, I would never—"

"I'm only telling you this because I enjoy talking to you. And maybe as a parent you can advise me on how I can tell my parents."

Jende nodded and for a brief stretch of time said nothing. The highway was mostly empty and quiet, except for the siren of an ambulance far in the distance. On the side of the westbound lane, billboards displayed advertisements for hotels and hospitals with pictures of good-looking people, the people at the hospitals looking as healthy and happy as the ones at the hotels.

"I just do not know what to say, Vince," Jende finally said. "I only think that you should please finish school and become a lawyer. Then maybe you could visit India for vacation."

"I don't want to be a lawyer. I've never wanted to be a lawyer."

"But why?"

"A lot of lawyers are miserable," Vince said. "I don't want to be miserable."

"My cousin is a lawyer."

"Is he happy?"

"Sometimes he's happy, sometimes he's not. Is there anybody who is happy all the time? A man can be unhappy doing any kind of work."

"Sure."

"Then why can you not just think you will be a happy man no matter what kind of work you do?"

"I can't even stand law school right now. I look at my classmates and I feel terrible—just saddens me to see them spending all those precious hours of their lives being indoctrinated with lies so they can go into the world and perpetuate the lies. They don't know they're about to become pieces of a ruthless machine that specializes in ripping out the innards of innocents. The whole system is a joke! People going around living meaningless lives, because it's what they've been conditioned to think is good for them. Walking around completely mindless of the fact that they're living in a society ruled by a cold-blooded cabal. How long are we going to remain in this bondage? I mean, really, how long?"

Jende shook his head. Vince's rant made no sense to him, but from the manner in which the young man's voice was rising and his tone hardening, he could tell Vince truly hated law school and anything to do with lawyers. And he could tell this wasn't even about law school or lawyers or America; it was more about Vince wanting to leave his world and everything his parents wanted for him; Vince wanting to become a whole new person.

"I am so sorry, Vince," he said.

"You don't have to be sorry for me. I'm living my Truth."

"No, I am sorry . . . I am not sorry for you . . . I am just sorry for how you feel."

Vince chuckled.

"I am not going to lie to you," Jende said. "If my son tells me that he is going to leave law school and move to India, I swear I will bring out my *molongo* and whip his buttocks well."

"What's a *molongo*?"

"The stick our parents use to beat us back home when we behave like bad children. I have one for my son, but he is lucky—I cannot use it here; I don't want any trouble whatsoever."

Vince chuckled again.

"I can't do anything besides shout at him—"

"And in your country you'd beat him even when he's my age?"

"No, man," Jende said, laughing. "I was just joking with you there. Our parents stop whipping our buttocks when we are like nineteen."

"Nineteen!"

"Or twenty, sometimes. But the thing I am trying to say is that if your father and mother are angry when you tell them this news, I hope you will understand."

Vince did not respond, and for a minute he was quiet, staring out the window. "I know it won't be easy for them to understand," he said, "considering I'm nothing like them. Then again, all the hundreds of thousands of dollars they spent at Dalton and summer camps and NYU and Columbia was for me to be what they want me to be. So my mom can tell her friends about her son's new job as a clerk with Judge So-and-So. Total bullshit."

"Oh, Vince," Jende said. "Someday when you have children, you will not talk like this."

"It amazes me, you're so different, and yet you're so like my parents in many ways."

"Maybe that's why me and your father get along very well. In fact, I think that if you could just take it easy on your father, maybe you will see him from another angle and see that he is a very nice man."

"Yeah, well, maybe someday I'll see this super-niceness that you see," Vince said. "We've never been a close family, so I've never been able to see him as much more than an absent provider who's going through the motions for the sake of his family."

"It's not easy," Jende said, shaking his head as he turned onto Elm Street, where the dentist's office was located.

"Who is it not easy for?"

"For you, for your father, for every child, every parent, for everybody. It's just not easy, this life here in this world."

"No," Vince said. "That's why our only choice is to embrace Suffering and surrender to the Truth."

"Embrace suffering?" Jende laughed. "You are talking some funny things here, eh?"

"Well, we can talk about what that means on the way back," Vince said, smiling and sitting up as Jende moved toward a parking spot. "But please, whatever we discussed about law school and India, that's just between me and you for now."

Jende nodded, turned around, and extended his hand, which Vince shook before exiting the car. When Vince returned to the car an hour later, his mouth was heavy from the anesthesia that had been used to numb him before his wisdom tooth extraction, and he could barely talk. He fell asleep within minutes, his right hand holding the ice pack soothing his lightly swollen face. At intervals, Jende looked through the rearview mirror at Vince's face, and every time he imagined Liomi in about eighteen years. He knew he would never permit Liomi to throw away a chance at a successful career and a good life to go walking around India talking about Truth and Suffering, and yet he couldn't fully denounce what Vince was doing. Looking at the young man sleeping, he felt proud of him, even as he worried for him.

Seventeen

THE CITY THAT SUMMER OVERFLOWED WITH THE HOT AND THIRSTY: panting on subway platforms, battling the sun with wide hats and light clothes, rushing to scaffoldings for shade, dashing into department stores not for the sales advertised on windows but for the AC. Those unable to escape to beaches and countrysides congregated in places where the humidity could briefly be forgotten: world music concerts with musicians from far-flung lands like Kazakhstan and Burkina Faso; rooftop revelries where everyone seemed absolutely certain of their good looks and sophistication; street fairs with too much grilled chicken and not enough moving air; sunset cruises with last-minute tickets and mediocre cocktails. There was much to do in the city, and yet the desperation remained among many to be out of it, to be in a place where the mission was pleasure and not endurance, to sit where the air moved without burden and the water went on for thousands of miles, a place like the villages of the Hamptons.

Jende could take a paid vacation in the first two weeks of August, Clark informed him as they drove down Lexington on a mid-June morning. The family would be spending late July and pretty much all of August in Southampton (Cindy and the boys, mostly), as well as random days in early July, so it should be an overall light summer of work.

"I am very grateful, sir," Jende said without a change in his countenance, though inwardly he was grinning wider than the Great Rift Valley. It would be the first time in America he'd be paid to do nothing, though he knew he wasn't going to sit around idle for two weeks—he was going to call the livery cab company he used to work for and get shifts so he could add to the funds he and Neni were saving for his deportation case.

"You should ask Cindy if she needs a housekeeper for that last week in July and the first three weeks in August, when Anna takes her vacation," Clark added minutes later. "She usually gets someone from the agency. Maybe your wife would like to do it and make some extra money?"

"Oh, yes, sir. My wife . . . she would . . . we would be very grateful, sir."

Cindy did need someone, and Neni needed a break from the oft-gloomy task of feeding and bathing incapacitated senior citizens, though it was the prospect of earning more money in four weeks than she made in three months that prompted her and Jende to discuss the offer for only five minutes before agreeing that she would skip the second summer semester (since her student visa allowed her to) and go to Southampton. She called Cindy Edwards that evening—after Jende had coached her on what to say, what not to say, how to say the right things well—introduced herself, and said she would like the job. Cindy offered her the job, though not before telling her what was involved: maintaining a spotless five-bedroom house, grocery shopping for specific items that must be gotten right, daily laundry, cooking specific recipes, serving guests in a dignified manner, babysitting a ten-year-old as needed, twelve-hour workdays with lots of downtime.

"I will do it all very well, madam," Neni said, holding the phone tightly against her ear.

"I trust you will. Jende's a hard worker, and I imagine you're no different."

"Only, madam, it's just one more thing," she said.

"What's that?"

"I'm four months pregnant, madam. It's not going to be a problem for me, but—"

"Then it won't be for me, either," Cindy said, ending the matter, and then telling Neni that in the last week of June she would need to take the Long Island Rail Road with Anna to the Hamptons so she could get acquainted with Cindy's needs and expectations.

"Make sure you only do what they say you do and exactly the way they say you do it," Jende said to Neni just before she descended the steps into the subway to travel to the Hamptons to begin her four-week stint. "No more, no less."

"Ah, you, too," she said, laughing. "What do you think I'm going to do over there?"

"It's not a laughing matter, Neni. Just do your work well. That's all I'm saying. Don't do or say anything that doesn't concern you. These people are our bread and tea."

"Don't worry," she said, still laughing at his serious demeanor, which she found both cute and unnecessary. "I won't disgrace you. It's not like I've never been around rich people."

Which was true—her family used to be rich in the eighties and early nineties. Back then her father was a customs officer at the seaport in Douala, and, thanks to all the gratuities (not bribes—her father swore he never once got his palms greased) he and his colleagues took from merchants bringing goods into the country, he was able to multiply his annual government salary by ten and ensure that his family lacked no good thing. They lived in a brick house with tiled outer walls and floors, and running water. They owned electrical appliances and a working telephone, and her father even owned a car (a dilapidated blue 1970s Peugeot, but still a car and thus a symbol of prosperity in Limbe). They were the first family in their Down Beach neighborhood to own a TV set. Neni still remembered those early days of television in the late eighties, when CRTV broadcasted only from six o'clock to ten o'clock in the evening. By five-forty-five every evening, the neighborhood children would be in their living room, sitting on the floor, waiting for "telleh" to begin. When the TV static, which the children called "rice," slowly disappeared to reveal the Cameroonian flag, the children would giggle with delight, and the adults, packed on the sofa and chairs all around the living room, would tell them to be quiet. Television was on. No one was allowed to make noise when television was on. Children were supposed to watch the news in silence while the adults discussed the atrocities in South Africa every time a picture of Nelson Mandela came up, wondering when those bad white people were going to set that good man free. Children were supposed to watch documentaries in silence; watch fast-talking cartoons, which they called "porkou-porkou," in silence. They had to be quiet during whatever British or French or American series CRTV was broadcasting, soap operas and sitcoms which they barely understood but nonetheless giggled at whenever kissing scenes came on and groaned whenever someone was punched. The only time children were allowed to talk was when a music video came on. Then, they were encouraged by the adults to stand up and dance to Ndedi Eyango, or Charlotte Mbango, or Tom Yoms. And every time they would stand up and bust out their best *makossa* moves, twirling tiny buttocks and moving clenched fists from right to left with all their might, smiling to no end. To be able to see their favorite musicians singing in a black box, what a privilege.

Neni smiled at the memories as she sat in the train. She was a teenager back then, but as a middle child she wasn't allowed to touch the TV—turning it on and off were rights reserved for her father and oldest brother. Nowadays even three-year-olds in Limbe could turn a TV on and off. Every third house in town had CNN, though, funnily, her parents' house didn't.

Her father had stopped working at the seaport in '93, forced out by a Bamileke boss who wanted his tribesman to take Neni's father's job. With no warning, he had been transferred to a far less lucrative position at the Treasury Department in Limbe, and six months after that his widowed sister had died, leaving behind three children he had no choice but to take in and raise alongside his five. With the loss of his prestigious job came the loss of some of the power and respect he'd had as a rich man. Folks still greeted him with both hands, but many stopped coming to his house to visit, knowing that upon leaving they wouldn't receive five or ten thousand CFA francs to "pay taxi." These days he was retired, living on a meager pension, without much to his name besides an ancient blue Peugeot in the garage of his brick house.

Eighteen

THE EDWARDS SUMMER HOUSE WASN'T MADE OF BRICKS, BUT IT DIDN'T need to be; all the brick houses of New Town, Limbe, put together couldn't compete with one of its rooms. When Neni had first gone there with Anna to learn her duties, she had tried not to show Anna how awed she was, but Anna must have seen it on her face: Her eyes couldn't stop roving from the moment they stepped out of the cab in front of the two-story warm gray stone-and-wood-shingled house with meticulously manicured boxwood spheres on both sides of the four-columned portico. It wasn't only the size that astounded her (why did they need such a big house for only a few months a year? why five bedrooms when there were only two children? didn't they understand that no matter how much money a person had, they could sleep on only one bed at a time?) but also the profuse elegance. Even on her third day there she was still flabbergasted by the sumptuousness of her surroundings, especially the living room, with its all-white decor and large windows as if to never lose a view of the sky. She was astonished by its spotlessness, which Anna had told her was because Cindy hated dirt even more than she hated cheap things; its plush white carpets and wool rugs, which she almost feared stepping on; and its black chandelier and glass accents, so delicate-looking she dusted with tenderness, worried she would leave a mark.

The afternoon she arrived, Vince had given her a hug and told her to make herself comfortable, though she couldn't see how she could possibly do so if she was in a constant state of unease about ruining something. She spent all evening of that first day in the kitchen with Mighty, too circumspect to go anywhere besides her bedroom after Vince left for the city (to meditate at Unity; Jende wasn't exaggerating) and Cindy went out to dinner with friends. Even in those first hours in Southampton, she could tell Mighty would be her only true source of joy there—he reminded her of Liomi, thanks to his abundant eyelashes and the way he never seemed to lack something to laugh or smile about.

"Do you like living in Harlem?" he asked her while she was making his dinner, surprising her with his forwardness, a characteristic untypical of children from Limbe.

"It's nice," she said.

"Jende says he doesn't like it too much."

"He said that?" Neni said, turning from the stove. "Why would he say that?"

"Because he's honest," Mighty said with a laugh, "and honesty's the best policy, right?"

Even when she wished he wasn't so inquisitive, she couldn't deny that he was a token of how normal rich children could be. During their first days together, he amused her with questions about African lions and leopards and what kind of animals she had seen roaming around Limbe, questions she was sure he'd already asked Jende at least a dozen times but which delighted her so much that she made up tales about monkeys stealing her lunch when she was a schoolgirl, and a classmate who used to come to school riding on an elephant. I don't believe it, Mighty would say to such stories, and Neni would make up an even more incredible one. Babysitting him was by far the most enjoyable part of her job, and the part she was certain she impressed Cindy the most in executing. Every time Cindy walked into a room to see her and Mighty laughing or playing, Neni could sense Cindy's approval because nothing appeared to matter to the madam more than the happiness of her children, their nonstop possession of every good thing life had to offer. If Mighty was laughing and Vince was smiling, there couldn't be a happier woman on earth than Cindy Edwards. This desire for their happiness (constantly asking if they needed something; always reminding Neni to make their meals and snacks just the way they liked them; giving Mighty three kisses every time either of them left the house) was followed closely only by her obvious need for a sense of belonging, an utterly desperate need she could never seem to quench.

It was a longing that confounded Neni, because on the day they met, Cindy Edwards appeared to be a woman with no desperate needs. From the moment they shook hands in the portico until Cindy left for her dinner, the madam was enveloped in an air of superiority, standing tall and keeping her shoulders back as she walked in long strides, slowly enunciating every word when she spoke, as if she had the right to take as much of the listener's time as she wished. She pointed with slender manicured fingers bearing a sole emerald ring, nodding like an omnipotent empress as she took Neni around the house to give her polite but specific instructions on what she must do every morning and how she must do it; as she told her things that Anna might have said but which she needed to reiterate, things like what she couldn't stand in a housekeeper: dishonesty, poor communication, and not acting with poise when company was around.

And yet, despite this portrait of a self-assured woman, Cindy seemed to have a near obsession with being where everyone was and doing what everyone was doing. Within four days, Neni noticed that she was on the phone with a friend at least once a day, wondering if the friend had gotten an invitation to So-and-So's cocktail party, or This-and-That's dinner party, or that upcoming gala or wedding. On the few occasions when her friends apparently told her they'd gotten their invites and she hadn't gotten hers, she seemed to be in physical pain, her deep sighs and suddenly slumped shoulders and sad voice revealing to Neni that despite the fact that she was telling her friends that it was okay, she wasn't okay because she was probably wondering why she hadn't been invited, what she'd done to not be invited, if her social status was intact. This desperation to always be a part of something, always maintain a sense of specialness thanks to the action of others, baffled Neni, but she didn't call Jende to talk about it because she knew he would say what he always said whenever she said she couldn't understand why people cared about stupid things like the approval of others: Different things are important to different people.

Five days after her arrival, though, she called him to talk about Cindy, terrified.

"I think Mrs. Edwards is very sick," she whispered from her room in the basement.

"What's wrong?" he asked.

There was no one else in the house, and Mrs. Edwards looked sick, she told him.

"What kind of sick, Neni? Fever? Headache? Stomachache?"

"No, no, not that kind of sick," she whispered again.

Where was everybody? he wanted to know. Mr. Edwards was in the city, and Mighty and Vince were at the beach, she informed him. What did it matter where they were? she asked in frustration after replying to the question. Mrs. Edwards did not look well, and she was afraid because she didn't know what to do. The madam looked like she was very sick, but maybe she wasn't sick. She needed advice from her husband, not one question after another.

"But you're saying fifty different things," he said. "Say something that makes sense."

Mrs. Edwards had told her she was going into her bedroom for a nap and asked that she not be disturbed. Neni had stayed in the basement, doing laundry, before remembering that the sheets in the guest bedroom needed to be laundered. She had opened the door to the second-floor guest room without knocking, assuming Mrs. Edwards was asleep in the master bedroom on the first floor. When she entered, she had seen the frightful sight: the always composed and elegant madam splayed against the headboard of the bed, hair strands lying on her sweaty face, her hands limp on her sides, her mouth half open with saliva halfway down her chin.

"I'm afraid," she said to him, panicked and near tears. "She was fine this morning. She told me one hour ago that she was going to nap, and then I go to the guest bedroom and see this."

"Does she look dead?" Jende asked.

"No, I saw her breathing," she whispered. "Oh, Papa God, what should I do?"

Jende was silent for a moment. "Don't do anything," he told his wife. "Just pretend you didn't see anything. If something happens to her, you can say you did not know. You can say you never entered the room."

"But what if something is wrong and I am supposed to do something?"

"Neni, Neni, listen to me," her husband commanded. "Let her husband and her sons find her and decide what to do. Do not touch her, you hear me? Don't even go back to the room. Do not involve yourself in their business, I'm begging you."

"I have to do—"

"You don't have to do anything!"

She hung up and called her friend Betty. Betty was in her seventh year of nursing school—she would know what to do.

"I think it's drugs, oh," Betty screeched above the sound of her children screaming in the background. "Only drugs can make you look like that."

"Betty, please stop joking. I'm talking about something serious which—"

"Who said I'm joking? I'm telling you that it's drugs."

"No . . . not Mrs. Edwards."

"Why are you arguing with me? Rich people like them, they like drugs."

"Not Mrs. Edwards! She's not that kind of person, Betty, I swear to you."

"Where do you know her from? Because she wears nice clothes, you think—"

"What would she do drugs for?"

"Neni, please, if you don't want to believe me, then let me get off the phone."

"Oh, Papa God!" Neni cried, slapping her thigh as the phone beeped and displayed an incoming call from Jende. She ignored his call, knowing what he wanted to reiterate.

"Listen to me," Betty said. "Listen. Go wake her up. Shake her only softly, okay?"

"And what if she doesn't wake up?"

"You move that thing one more time," Betty shouted away from the receiver, "I'll come over there and cause you some serious injuries."

"Betty, I don't know—"

"Hold on," Betty said, and for almost a minute Neni heard nothing but the sound of a toddler screaming. "You don't teach these children how to obey, tomorrow they'll start behaving like American children," Betty said when she returned to the phone.

"You think I should wake her up?"

"Yes, go wake her up."

"*Chai!* Man no die ei rotten."

"You've used your pretty legs to walk right into trouble."

Neni laughed, the kind of mirthless laugh her mother used to emit when life was so strange only a laugh could give one the strength to face it.

"If she's dead," Betty added, "call her husband, not the police."

"Okay, okay, let me go."

"And Neni," Betty said right before she hung up, "please, don't tell the police you called me first. I'm begging, don't even mention my name for any reason whatsoever. I'm afraid of police people."

Neni hung up and ran back upstairs, her grip tight around her cell phone. Cindy was sleeping in the same position. For a minute Neni stood next to the bed, staring at the prescription pill bottle next to the empty glass and half-empty bottle of red wine on the nightstand, before moving closer.

"Mrs. Edwards," she whispered, nudging Cindy in the arm. Jende would kill her for this, but she couldn't leave the woman alone in this state.

Cindy did not respond.

Neni put her cell phone in the pocket of her *kaba*, leaned closer, and spoke directly into Cindy's ear. "Mrs. Edwards."

Immediately, Cindy closed her mouth and began smacking her lips.

"Mrs. Edwards, are you okay?"

Cindy opened her eyes slightly. "What do you want?" she asked in a husky slur.

"Nothing, madam. I just wanted to make sure you're all right."

Cindy sat up, brushed off the hair lying on her face, wiped her chin. She opened her eyes fully and looked at Neni. "What time is it?"

Neni took out her cell phone and looked at the time. "Five o'clock, madam."

"Shit," Cindy said, turning her legs around to get out of the bed. She staggered with her first step, and Neni quickly caught her by the arm. "It's okay," Cindy said, pulling away. "I'm okay."

Still brushing hair off her face, she sat on the armchair next to the closet and asked for a glass of cold water, which Neni hastily ran off to get even before she was done asking. When she finished drinking, Cindy asked for a second glass of water and a plate of salad—plain lettuce with oil and vinegar—which Neni brought on a tray. Carefully, Neni lifted Cindy's legs and placed them on a footstool so the tray could balance with ease on her lap.

"Would you like me to run a bath for you, madam?" Neni asked.

Cindy nodded.

Neni went into the bathroom, scrubbed her hands, and turned on the water in the bathtub. She poured in ten drops of bubble bath, knelt by the tub—her growing belly against its cold skin—and stirred the water in the gentle circular manner that Anna had taught her. When the tub was full, she came out and took Cindy's tray.

"Clark won't be coming tonight anymore," Cindy said as Neni was about to exit the bedroom. "Vince is leaving after he and Mighty get back—he's spending the next couple of days with a friend on Martha's Vineyard. You can serve Mighty his dinner whenever he wants."

"Yes, madam," Neni said, and hurried downstairs.

Around seven o'clock, she heard the Jaguar's engine in the driveway, Cindy leaving for one social engagement or another.

Nineteen

SHE STOOD AT THE DOOR KNOCKING LIGHTLY AND INSISTENTLY, deter-mined to wake her up.

"What is it?" she heard Cindy groan.

"It's me, madam," Neni replied.

"Yes?"

"I was just wondering, madam, about your breakfast. If you would like me to bring it in there or set it out for you by the pool."

"What time is it?"

"Eleven o'clock, madam."

"By the pool," she said after a pause. "Set it in an hour."

When Cindy came out of the bedroom just before noon, after showering and putting on a purple-striped halter-top dress, Neni was at the kitchen counter, slicing up pineapples. "Almost ready, madam," she said. "Good morning."

Cindy nodded and went to the table by the pool. Through the window Neni could see her staring at the pool water, which was blue and still except for a lone leaf causing frail ripples at the center. Neni picked up the tray and hurried outside.

"I am sorry to keep you waiting, madam," she said, placing the tray on the table. "Would you like anything else?"

"Where's Mighty?"

"He went to the water, madam, with the neighbor and the neighbor's son. He said it would be okay with you. I gave him a sandwich and a banana."

Cindy picked up a glass pitcher to pour milk into her coffee. Neni turned around and started walking back to the kitchen.

"Neni?" Cindy called, just as Neni was about to reenter the house.

"Madam."

"Pull up a seat and sit right here."

Neni looked at Cindy, puzzled, but she returned and obeyed.

For the next minute, Cindy took little bites of her egg-white omelet, her sliced pineapples, and her blueberries. Neni sat across from her and stared at the concrete.

"Thank you for helping me yesterday," Cindy began, setting her coffee mug down and dabbing her lips. She picked up her sunglasses and put them on despite the cloudiness of the day.

Neni watched her and smiled, a smile tightly bound by nerves and discomfort. "It was nothing, madam," she said in the slow, delicate manner in which she had been training herself to speak whenever she spoke to non-Africans. "You were a little sick, madam. I am glad I was able to come in and help you."

"But I wasn't sick," Cindy said. "I know you know that."

"I only thought—"

"It's okay," Cindy said, raising her palm to silence her. "You're a grown woman. There's no need to lie. I know you saw everything on the nightstand, and you didn't think I was just napping. You're smart enough to put two and two together. I could see in your eyes how scared you were."

"I did not see anything, madam."

"Yes, you did. And I'd rather you don't try to take me for a fool."

Neni put her hands together on her lap and began rubbing them.

She moved her eyes from Cindy's face to her own widening feet piling out of her blue flip-flops and back to Cindy's face. "I did not, madam, I swear . . . I only thought you were sick, that is why I came this morning to wake you up when you did not wake up at your normal time."

Cindy snickered and shook her head.

"I am truly very sorry, madam," Neni continued, looking pleadingly into Cindy's eyes. "I did not mean to find out anything."

Cindy stirred her coffee with a silver spoon and set it down. The ocean breeze which Neni had enjoyed that morning was no longer relaxing—it'd become a nuisance as it gained force and blew her braids into her face.

Deliberately, Cindy took off her sunglasses, put them on the table, and looked into Neni's eyes. "You probably look at me," she said, "and think I came from a life like this. You probably think I was born into this kind of money, right?"

Neni did not respond.

"Well, I wasn't," Cindy went on. "I came from a poor family. A very, very poor family."

"Me, too, madam—"

Cindy shook her head. "No, you don't understand," she said. "Being poor for you in Africa is fine. Most of you are poor over there. The shame of it, it's not as bad for you."

Neni closed her eyes and nodded as if she completely understood and agreed.

"Over here, it's embarrassing, humiliating, very painful," Cindy continued, looking into the distance beyond the trees. "Waiting in lines with homeless people to enter food pantries. Living in a poorly heated house in the winter. Eating rice and SPAM for almost every dinner. Being laughed at in school. Having people treat you as if you're some sort of . . ." A lone tear dropped down her right cheek. She brushed it off with her index finger. "You have no idea how much I've endured."

"No, madam."

"I won't ever forget the night I told my mother I wanted shrimp and vegetables for dinner. Such a luxury, how dare I ask for it? She slapped me and sent me to bed hungry. That was her thing. A slap or a reminder that I was just a piece of shit."

She cleared her throat.

Neni looked down at her hands, then Cindy's face.

"But I came away from all that, as you can see. I worked my way through college, got a job, my own apartment, learned how to carry myself well and fit effortlessly in this new world so I would never be looked down on again, or seen as a piece of shit. Because I know what I am, and no one can ever take away the things I've achieved for myself."

"It's true, madam."

Cindy picked up her teaspoon, stirred her coffee again. She put down the teaspoon and looked at Neni, whose eyes were now lowered.

"Why am I telling you all this, Neni?" she asked.

"I don't . . . I don't know, madam," Neni replied, her voice low and loaded with fright.

"I'm telling you this because I want you to know where I came from and why I fight hard every day to remain here. To keep my family together. To have all this." She spread her arm and motioned toward the house and the pool and the yard. "I'm telling you this," she said, her eyes fixed on Neni's face, "because I want you to never tell anyone what happened yesterday."

"I swear to you, madam, on my grandmother's grave, that I will never tell anyone."

"You are a woman, Neni. A wife, a mother, like me. I am asking you to make this promise to me not as from an employee to an employer but as from one woman to another, as from one who knows how important it is to protect our families."

"I swear to you, madam. I promise you, from one woman to another."

Cindy laid open her right hand on the table, and Neni put hers in it.

"Thank you," Cindy said, smiling her first smile of the day and squeezing Neni's hand.

Neni smiled back.

"You're a good woman."

Neni bowed her head and nodded. Cindy released her hand. Neni stood up and began walking back to the kitchen.

"By the way," Cindy said, "what size clothes do you wear? When you're not pregnant, that is."

Neni took a few steps back toward Cindy. "Size six, madam," she replied.

"That's bigger than me," Cindy said, the smile still on her face, "but I think you can make do. I have a few things I was going to send over to the thrift store."

"Oh, madam, yes, thank you. I'll take it. I know how to alter clothes. Thank you—"

"They're real designer goods," Cindy said, crossing her legs and picking up her iPhone. "Dresses and stuff. I'm not sure if it's your style, but you can have it all."

"Thank you, madam! I'll take it all. I'll make it my style. Thank you so much."

"I'll have some things for your son, too. Mighty's old clothes and toys. You can take it all when you leave."

"Oh, madam, I am so glad. I don't even know how to thank you."

"And remind me of your bonus before you leave. You'll need some extra money to prepare for the baby."

"We will, madam, I will!" Neni sang, placing her hand on her chest, then over her belly. "Thank you so much, madam. I am just so grateful."

Cindy looked at the gleeful woman and smiled again.

Neni smiled back at her.

They had found a win-win solution.

Twenty

LIOMI SAT NEXT TO HIM IN THE PASSENGER SEAT, SLIDING TO THE FLOOR whenever a police car came in sight. When a white woman pointed out one morning that it was illegal for a child of Liomi's age to sit in the front seat of a car, Jende graciously replied that yes, it was, he knew, thank you so much, madam.

Father and son went to sleep together every night in their bedroom facing a funeral parlor, sometimes to the sounds of curses and scuffles among the grieving. They woke up in the morning with their bodies covered in sweat, the weak fan having brought little relief from the midsummer heat. After bathing, they ate fried ripe plantains and eggs, Jende always forcing Liomi to eat at least a whole plantain and two eggs, and drink a full glass of orange juice. They dressed for the day together, donning jeans and T-shirts, Liomi always making sure he wore the same colors as his father. Their bellies full and lunch bags packed, they walked to the subway station hand in hand and took an uptown subway to pick up the cab in the Bronx. In the subway, they sat close to each other, Liomi's hand always in Jende's. After four hours of picking up and dropping off passengers, they took out their lunch—food Neni had cooked and frozen—and ate in the backseat of the car. For dinners they went every other day to one of the African restaurants on 116th Street, where they ordered *attiéké* with grilled lamb, their favorite meal in all the restaurants there. Sometimes, after they were done eating, they bought ice cream at a shop on 115th Street and walked down Malcolm X Boulevard holding hands and licking ice cream. The days were perfect for Jende, almost heavenly, and even though he missed his wife, he was happy to be alone with his son.

"Papa?" Liomi said to him as they dined at a restaurant adjacent to the 116th Street subway one evening.

"Eh?"

"Is it true that we're going back to Cameroon?"

Jende stopped chewing. He put down the ball of *attiéké* he had in his right hand. "Who told you we're going back to Cameroon?" he said, keeping his voice low so as not to pull attention but widening his eyes to show Liomi how much he had aroused his anger.

"No one, Papa," Liomi replied, averting his eyes.

"Then why are you asking me?"

"Nothing, Papa," he replied. "I only heard Mama saying it on the phone."

"Mama said it, eh? To who?"

"I don't know, Papa."

"When did she say it?"

"Papa, I don't—"

"You don't what? Why were you listening to your mother's conversation?"

The boy went mute, his small mouth covered with the white granules of *attiéké*. Beside them, the bald man eating *thiebou djeun* had paused eating to watch the father, fists clenched on the table, and seven-year-old boy who appeared ready to run in terror.

"We're not going back to Cameroon, you hear me?"

"Yes, Papa."

"You're never going back to Cameroon, do you hear me?"

"I hear you, Papa."

"Finish your food."

Back at the apartment, Jende called Neni and, without asking questions, mercilessly scolded her for exposing Liomi to their pain. "How dare you mention it in front of him?"

"I didn't know he was listening."

"You don't need to know anything, Neni. You don't have to know who is listening to what you're saying. You only need to learn how to shut your mouth sometimes."

"But what if he knows? If the immigration judge decides to send us back home are we going to shut his eyes so he doesn't know we're taking him back to Cameroon?"

Jende slapped the frame of the bed and stood up, unable to believe his wife's words. "Eh, Neni!" he shouted. "Is that what you think? You think we should tell a child his father might be deported? You want Liomi to know what's happening to *me*?"

Neni did not respond. It was the first time he had screamed at her so loudly, the first time in almost twenty years, from when they were teenagers at National Comprehensive.

"Bubakar has promised us that we will be here for years even if things don't end up the way we want them to. You know that! You know we still have many years in this country. Don't you know that?"

"I know what he said."

"Then why are you going around talking as if we're leaving next month?"

"No one knows the future. Anything can happen. You know that."

Jende sat down and closed his eyes, shaking his head. For a moment he didn't know what to say to his wife. "Are you saying this because you think I'll be deported?" he said. His voice was low and woeful, saturated with anguish. "Eh, Neni? Is that why you're talking to me like this?"

"No, *bébé*, please," Neni said, embarrassment at the misery she was mindlessly causing him suddenly obvious in her voice. "That's not what I'm saying."

"Then what are you saying?"

"I'm not saying anything, *bébé*. I'm sorry. I don't even know what I was trying to say."

"Why are you making me feel so bad?"

"I'm really sorry, *bébé*. You know what is best for us. I won't talk about it when Liomi is home anymore."

"Just stop talking about it! There's nothing to talk about. I'll get a green card!"

"You will, *bébé*," Neni responded, her voice cracking. "It's just that I'm so afraid sometimes, and I want to talk about it with my sister. I don't want to go back to Limbe, *bébé*. I don't even want to imagine what is going to happen if . . ."

"I'm afraid, too, Neni. You think I'm not afraid? But what has fear ever done for anyone? We have to be strong and protect Liomi."

"You're right."

"We cannot go around worrying about what the judge is going to decide. We just have to keep living."

"Yes. And we're doing that, aren't we?"

"So what's your problem then?"

"Nothing . . . nothing. I will remember not to talk anymore. We will be fine. I'm sorry I angered you, *bébé*. Please cool your temper and rest. And please, let's not talk about it over the phone. You know what Bubakar said about the government listening."

Jende went to bed that night bitter in spite of Neni's apologies, angry at her for recklessly exposing their child to harmful untruths and angrier at himself for all the failures of his life. He made Liomi sleep alone in his cot that night, wanting nothing of cuddling with a child he might one day disappoint. But the next morning, when he awoke, Liomi was at his side, his small hands on his father's belly. Jende looked at the round sweat-covered face and knew he had no choice but to snuggle close to his child and enjoy the rest of their father-and-son summer.

That evening they attended a classical music concert in St. Nicholas Park and listened as a blind pianist performed a piece so sorrowful it briefly clouded Jende's eyes. The next afternoon, eager to experience more of what a New York City summer had to offer those unable or unwilling to leave the city, he ditched the money he could be making in the Bronx and took his son for a swim at the public pool in East Harlem.

"Papa, show me how you and Uncle Winston used to swim at Down Beach," Liomi said, and Jende did, flaunting the backstroke he and his cousin used to do in the waters behind the Botanic Garden. After completing two laps while a giggling Liomi watched, Jende lifted the boy and positioned his back against the water to teach him the strokes. Watching Liomi laughing and flapping his arms in the water, Jende saw, for perhaps the first time, his son not only as a child but also as a man in the making, a young man watching and learning from his father, a boy who wanted to follow in the footsteps of his papa and become a man like him in disposition, if not in possessions. That night they slept together as usual, Liomi's arm around his father and his head on Jende's chest. Never much of a praying man, Jende said a lengthy prayer for his boy as they lay, that Liomi would live a long happy life.

Twenty-one

HALFWAY INTO HER STAY IN SOUTHAMPTON, VINCE EDWARDS WALKED into his bedroom, jumped on his newly made bed while she was fluffing his pillows, and asked her to take a guess.

"Guess about what?" she asked.

"Today's the day," he said, beaming.

"Day for . . . ?"

"The day I tell them."

Neni looked confusedly at the face exploding with joy. "Tell who what?" she asked, wondering why Vince assumed she had to know his news.

"Jende didn't tell you . . . ?"

"Jende didn't tell me what?"

"Never mind," he said, standing up and walking out of the room.

Hours later, around five in the evening, Vince and Cindy left to meet Clark for dinner at a restaurant in Montauk. The next morning Neni saw nothing of Vince and very little of Cindy, who declined her breakfast and lunch and spent much of the afternoon on her phone, begging someone to please be reasonable and think about the consequences of his/her actions. When Neni called Jende later that evening to ask what he thought might be going on, Jende asked her to please stay out of other people's business.

"If you know something, why won't you tell me?" she asked.

"If I tell you, what will you do with the information besides gossip about it with your friends?"

She hung up determined to find out the story for herself. She couldn't eavesdrop any further on Cindy, who had left the house to go for an evening walk on the beach, and Mighty could only tell her that his parents and Vince were fighting—his mom wasn't telling him why, and Vince was back in the city. When Mighty had called Vince to ask why their mom was so upset, Vince had told him they would talk about it as soon as Mighty returned to the city since it was hard explaining certain things over the phone.

Two nights later, though, Neni wouldn't have to wonder anymore: After making Mighty sautéed salmon and oven fries for dinner—plus *puff-puff*, which Mighty had asked for after she told him it was what she and her siblings ate in the mornings as they walked to school—playing video games with him, and tucking him in bed, she went to her bedroom to read a chapter in the textbook for the social psychology class she'd signed up for in the fall semester. Engrossed in a chapter on persuasion, she initially didn't notice the voices escalating in the kitchen. It was only after perhaps three minutes, after the beseechings and accusations appeared to have reached a crescendo, that she realized it was Mr. and Mrs. Edwards shouting in the kitchen after returning home from a wedding.

She got out of bed, tiptoed up the basement stairs, and leaned on the door with her ear pressed against it.

"No!" she heard Clark shout. "You can go back to her and work on your long list of issues if you must, but I'm not going anywhere."

"You'd rather see your family fall apart?" Cindy shouted back, her voice trembling. "You'd rather that than see a therapist and admit you've got problems that are destroying your family?"

"Yeah, let's focus on my problems, because you don't have any."

"I'm not the reason our son is moving to India!" Cindy cried.

"You think Vince is moving to India because of me?"

"He's moving to India because he's unhappy, Clark! He's miserable—"

"Because of me?"

"Because we haven't succeeded in giving him a happy life! Because all he wants is to feel happy in his own family, and we can't even give him that. Can't you see?"

"Bullshit."

"Bullshit to what?"

"Bullshit to all your crap about feeling responsible for Vince's happiness," Clark shouted, amid the sound of the refrigerator door opening and slamming hard. "He's a grown man. He's responsible for his own happiness. I can't help it if he wants to be an idiot and throw away a perfectly good life. I can't do *anything* about it!"

For many seconds they were silent. Neni closed her eyes and shook her head, unsure which of them to feel more sorry for. She imagined Clark was angrily drinking wine or beer straight from the bottle, while Cindy was silently weeping.

"Do you care?" she heard Cindy say, her trembling voice now lower but sadder. "Do you give a shit about how badly you're hurting us?"

"Right. Sure! Working hard to give my family this life. How awful of me. Doing everything to make sure—"

"You're not doing everything! You've never done everything! Until you understand that family must always come first—"

"There are times when careers must take priority."

"There has never been a time when this marriage took priority for you. There's never been a time when this family took priority for you! Not once! That's why you're afraid of us going back to therapy—you don't want to see how selfish and callous you are!"

"What do you want from me, Cindy?" Clark shouted so loud Neni thought the walls vibrated. "Tell me what you want from me!"

"I just . . . I want," Cindy wept, "I want you . . . I want us . . . I want the boys to be happy, Clark . . . That's all I want . . . for us to be . . . for my family to be . . ."

Neni heard footsteps walking away, and she could tell it was Clark Edwards leaving his wife to cry alone in the kitchen. She heard a thump and a wail, and pictured Cindy slipping from against the counter to the floor. She imagined her sitting alone, crying on the cold kitchen floor.

Neni pulled her head away from the door and leaned against the railing. Should she do something? Would it be appropriate? What could she do besides go to the kitchen and see how she could help Cindy?

She opened the door gently and silently stepped into the kitchen, afraid of startling Cindy, who was sitting where Neni imagined she would be sitting. She was moaning softly with her head bowed, so lost in her misery that she didn't notice Neni walking toward her. Only when Neni stooped close to her did she lift her red tear-stained face, look Neni in her eyes, and begin weeping again.

"I'm sorry, madam," Neni whispered. "I'm just . . . I only want to see what I can do to make you feel better."

Cindy, with her head bowed again, nodded and sniffled. Neni stood up, her hand supporting her belly, and grabbed the box of tissues on the kitchen island. She sat down next to Cindy and offered her a tissue, which Cindy took, blew her nose with, and began crying in.

"I hope you and Mr. Edwards are going to solve everything soon, madam."

"He thinks . . . he thinks he has the right," Cindy whimpered, slightly above a whisper. "Everyone . . . they all think they've got the right to treat me as they wish."

Neni nodded, struggling to ignore the smell of alcohol spilling out of Cindy's mouth alongside her words. Her throat sounded parched, and her words stumbled in a slur, evidence to Neni that the madam had drunk more glasses of wine than she could handle.

"Can I get you some water, madam?" Neni asked.

Cindy shook her head and asked for a glass of wine, which Neni quickly got and returned to her position on the floor.

The madam took a sip, crying as she swallowed. "Every single person . . . they believe they can treat me . . . however . . . anyhow . . ."

Neni nodded again, the box of tissues in her hands.

"First it was my father . . . he thought he had the right, you know?" Cindy said. "Drag my mother into that abandoned house . . . force her . . . do it to her by force . . . don't give a shit about . . . not care for a second about what would happen to the child . . ."

She sniffled, took another sip of the wine, and wept.

"And the government . . . our government," she moaned, slurring, tears running down her cheeks, snot running down her nose. "They had the right, too. Force my mother to carry the child of a stranger. Force her to give birth to the child because . . . because . . . I don't know why!"

Neni's throat tightened at the sight of the devastated woman in pearls, confused, though, as she was about which child Cindy was talking about.

"I hated her . . . but can you blame her? She thought she had the right, too . . . it was her right. To beat me, and curse at me, and call me fat . . . because every time she looked at me, she was reminded . . . I was a reminder . . . of what he'd done to her . . . But why? What did I do? It's never the child's fault . . . never the fault of an innocent . . ."

Neni looked away as Cindy picked up the wineglass from the floor and took a long sip. The realization of who the child was had come on so suddenly that her eyebrows had risen, and her eyes had widened, and she'd had to restrain herself from cupping her mouth. She kept her face turned away, hoping Cindy hadn't seen the look on it, and not wanting to stare too hard at the wet pitiful mess the madam had become. What was she supposed to say to Cindy now? She couldn't give her a hug to express what she wanted to say without words, so she had to say something. But what could she say to a drunken confession about the unbearable yoke of a life conceived in violence? What could she say about things she'd never pondered?

"And now Clark has the right, too," Cindy went on, looking blankly ahead as her voice quivered. "He's got every . . . single right to love me far less than he loves his work. He's got every right to toss me aside, pick me up when it suits him . . . And Vince . . ." She pulled out another tissue, pressed her face into it, and began bawling hysterically. "Now Vince, too! He thinks . . . he's got every right to abandon me even . . . though I've been a perfectly good mother . . . even though I never abandoned my mother . . . even after all those years of . . ."

Her shoulders shook and Neni, uncertain still of the best thing to do, put the tissue box on the floor and warily moved a hand to Cindy's right shoulder and began rubbing it. Cindy's cries grew louder as Neni rubbed gently, simultaneously thinking about what else she could do to help the madam. She had to call someone to come over as soon as possible. But who? Not Clark. Not Vince. Maybe Cheri or June—their numbers were on the refrigerator. But what would she give as a reason for calling at midnight? Tell them that a highly intoxicated Cindy couldn't stop crying? Tell them she didn't know what to say or do to make Cindy feel better?

"I am so sorry, madam," Neni whispered. "I am so sorry for what your father did."

Cindy continued crying, her shoulders quaking in accordance with her sounds.

"Did the police catch him, madam?"

Cindy shook her head.

"Maybe . . . maybe you could search for him, madam? Maybe if—"

"I walk down the street . . . every day I'm looking . . . looking at any man who looks like me . . . I'm wondering, could that be him? My mother told me I must have his hideous face because I don't look anything like her . . . I walk around with this face, the face of a monster . . .

and no one knows. No one knows how much it hurts! Vince has no idea how much it hurts!"

"I am sorry about Vince, too, madam," Neni said.

Cindy picked up her glass of wine and gulped down the remainder. Neni continued rubbing her shoulder as they sat in silence, the only noise in the kitchen the sound of high-end electrical appliances. The kitchen floor had grown warm underneath them.

"I don't want him to move to India," Cindy said, a firmness slowly appearing in her voice. "But supporting him, that's not what's so hard for me to do. I can muster the strength to support my child even if it's not what I want. But his hurtfulness to me . . . how he thinks he's suddenly so righteous because he's found spirituality, that's what hurts me the most. I said to him, if what you care about is people, changing the world, what about getting a job at the Lehman Brothers Foundation? Clark could help him do that, but oh, no, what a ridiculous idea! He asked me, do I really think the goal of the Lehman Foundation is to make the world a better place? Do I know what Lehman Brothers does? Do I care about how corporations are destroying the world? I've tried to understand this anger . . . I can't. What does he have against being wealthy? Why should good hardworking people feel bad about their money just because other people don't have as much money? Once we were friends . . . my son and I, we were good friends. He found the Truth, and now I am naïve, closed-minded, materialistic, lost. The only way I can see the light is to first lose my ego."

Cindy sighed and tilted her head as if trying to stretch out an intolerable pain in her neck. "I told him, fine, go . . . go search for this Truth and Oneness . . . I want you to be happy. But instead of going all the way to India what about a retreat center somewhere in America . . . maybe someplace I heard about in New Mexico? Surely the Truth has to be present in America, too? Maybe go to a grad school somewhere near a retreat center? I just . . . I can't bear the thought of him being so far away. If anything happened to him, it would . . . it would kill me."

Twenty-two

She returned from the Hamptons with far more designer clothes than she'd ever imagined having; shoes and accessories, too. Cindy had told her to take as much as she wanted from the storage space in the attic because whatever she didn't take was going to charity, so Neni had cheerfully obliged, taking an old Louis Vuitton carry-on suitcase with a broken zipper, jam-packing it like roasted peanuts in a liquor bottle, and tying it shut with one of her blouses. Walking through Penn Station and the streets of Harlem, she had needed to stop at least a dozen times to rest from the weight of the Louis Vuitton on her right shoulder, the big brown paper bag full of Liomi's clothes and toys on her left shoulder, her rolling luggage in one hand, and more clothes and toys for Liomi in the other.

"Did you have to suffer like that just for some free clothes?" Jende asked later that night, laughing, after she told him how difficult it had been managing all the bags while the baby kicked nonstop.

"What do you mean, 'just for some free clothes'?" she said. "This is not just any free clothes, *bébé*. You know how much these things cost?"

Jende laughed her off, saying he didn't care. Clothes were clothes, he said, no matter how much they cost or whose name was printed on them. But Betty did not laugh her off—Betty understood that there was an undeniable difference between the styles and auras of Gucci and Tommy Hilfiger; unlike Jende, she knew that all labeled clothes were not created equal, even if they were made from the same fabric by the same machine.

"You walk down the street wearing this Valentino blouse!" Betty exclaimed, looking at the label of a white silk blouse when she visited days after Neni's return.

"Can you imagine?" Neni said.

"But you can't wear this just to walk down the street."

"Never in this lifetime. Something like this? I don't even know where I'll wear it to. Maybe a wedding. Or maybe I'll save it and they'll bury me in it when I die."

"Then let me wear it for you now, eh?" Betty said, laughing and placing the blouse against her chest. "I'll rock it with a leather skirt and high-heel boots and then bring it back as soon as I hear you're dead so you can—"

"I beg, give me back my blouse, crazy woman!" Neni said, laughing and grabbing the blouse from Betty's hands. She stood in front of the full-length mirror on the bedroom door, put the blouse against her chest, and felt its fine silk and delicate buttons.

"That woman must have really liked you, eh?" Betty said.

"Like me why?"

"To give you all these things."

Neni shrugged and knelt down next to the Louis Vuitton suitcase to repack the things they'd taken out to admire. "She didn't like me nothing," she said as she refolded the dresses and blouses. "I did what she wanted me to do, she paid me with money and clothes."

"But still . . ."

"It's not like she's ever going to wear them. You should have seen her closets. I never knew anyone can have that many clothes and shoes in one house."

"I would have taken one or two pairs of shoes."

"No, you wouldn't," Neni retorted, scoffing at Betty's bluff.

"Yes, I would," Betty insisted, widening her eyes and laughing. "Maybe some Calvin Klein and DKNY jeans, too, if I can force this mountain buttocks into it. How would she know she lost it if she has so many things?"

"She wouldn't ever know. How can anyone know if one of their fifty pairs of shoes gets lost? And I'm not just saying fifty. I swear to you, Betty, I stood in the shoe closet and counted. Fifty!"

"Plus another fifty or one hundred in her apartment in Manhattan."

"I'm sure."

"And she's still so unhappy," Betty said with a sigh. "Money truly is nothing."

"She has her own kind of suffering that we can never understand," Neni said, rising from the floor to sit next to Betty on the bed. "And she is trying her best to cover it, which is not easy—"

"Your father was a rapist, you don't know his name, you don't know his face. What kind of money is going to help you with that kind of problem? You don't even know if he is black or white or Spanish."

"Ah, Betty, don't take it too far. Her father has to be a white man."

"You're saying that because you know the man?"

"The woman is a white woman!"

"That's what you think, eh? I can take you to the Internet right now and show you on Google. All these white people, they all thought they were white, and then one day they find out that someone was black; their father, their grandfather—"

"Ah, whatever. I don't think something like that is what's going to bother her the most."

"But it would bother me. If I find out one day that I'm not one hundred percent black . . ." Betty turned her lips downward, shook her head, and Neni laughed.

"You don't have to ever worry about that," Neni said. "With your charcoal skin and mountain buttocks, there's no way there can be anything inside you except African blood."

"Jealousy is going to kill you," Betty shot back, laughing as she leaned sideways and tapped her buttocks to emphasize the beauty of their size. "But seriously," she said, "I don't know what I would do if my father—"

"I don't know what I would do, too. I would be afraid that I'm a curse, because it's a curse, right? You are a bastard, and on top of that, everyone knows your father was some rapist."

"*Kai!* No wonder the woman drinks. Did you see her looking like that again?"

"Like that day? No, thank Papa God. But I saw an empty medicine bottle in the guest bathroom garbage. Same one like the one from that day."

"It was for painkillers, right?"

Neni shrugged. "I don't know."

"It had to be for painkillers. I was reading about it in my pharmacology class—"

"Eh, now that you've taken one little pharmacology class you think you know everything about drugs. Why don't you just go ahead and open a pharmacy?"

"Ah, don't be hating, girl," Betty said in her fake American accent. "You can take the class when you're ready. But I swear, it must have been something like that, some kind of painkiller."

"Because why?"

"What do you mean, 'Because why?' Aren't you the one who told me what she looked like when you found her with the medicine and the wine? I've taken painkillers, I know how those things can—"

"No," Neni said, shaking her head. "I was thinking that, too, that maybe it was bad drugs, but—"

"But what?"

"But what if she was sick?"

"Sick of what? If she was only sick, why was she begging you not to tell anyone?"

"I don't know; the whole thing about that woman just confuses me."

"Then why are you arguing with me? I can show you the chapter in my textbook. She's taking the painkiller, then adding the wine . . . These women, they start taking the pills for some pain in their body, and then it makes them feel good, so they take more, and then more—"

"But I've taken Tylenol," Neni said with a laugh, "and I didn't feel anything special."

"Tylenol is not the same kind of thing, you country woman," Betty said, laughing, too, and then instantly developing a somber tone. "I'm talking about prescription painkillers for some really bad pain, the kind I had when . . . They gave me some last year at Roosevelt. Vicodin and—"

"That was the name on the bottle! Vicodin. Wait, I'm not sure if it was—"

"It must have been," Betty said, standing up to fold the Burberry scarf and Ralph Lauren maxi dress Neni had given her from Cindy's things. "I felt better every time I took it. Even with everything I was feeling . . ."

"But you wouldn't have eaten it like candy, the way it looks like Mrs. Edwards is swallowing them."

"Is that what you think? Don't be so sure, oh. The hospital only let me have a ten-day supply, but if I had a way, I would have gotten more. Maybe for another week. That thing made me feel so much better, but this country, doctors are too afraid of addiction. Mrs. Edwards, she must know someone who is giving it to her, maybe a friend who is a doctor, or a pharmacist. Or sometimes they buy it from other people . . . I just wonder how many she is taking a day."

Twenty-three

EVERY TIME CLARK WAS IN THE CAR — MORNING, AFTERNOON, EVENING — he was shouting at someone, arguing about something, giving orders on what had to be done as soon as possible. He seemed angry, frustrated, confused, resigned. This place is a mess, Leah told Jende whenever they were on the phone. He's going crazy, he's yelling at me and making me crazy, they're all going crazy, I swear it's like some kind of crazy shit is eating everyone up. Jende told her he was truly sorry to hear how bad it was for her and assured her repeatedly that he knew nothing more than what she already knew from the memos Tom was sending to Lehman employees, memos in which he told them that the company was going through a bit of a tough stretch but they should be back on top in no time. Leah's circumstances saddened Jende, the fact that she was clinging to a job that made her miserable because she was still five years away from receiving Social Security. It bothered him that she couldn't quit her job even though her blood pressure was rising and her hair was falling out and she was getting only three hours of sleep a night, but it wasn't his place to tell her anything about what Clark was saying. Or doing. He couldn't tell her that Clark was sometimes sleeping in the office, or going to the Chelsea Hotel some evenings for appointments that often lasted no more than an hour. He couldn't tell her that after these appointments he usually drove the boss back to the office, where Clark probably continued working for more hours, his stress having been eased. His duty, he always reminded himself, was to protect Clark, not Leah.

"Where are we going to, sir?" Jende asked on the last Thursday of August, holding the car door open in front of the Chelsea Hotel. Clark's appointment that day had lasted exactly an hour, but he had returned to the car still seeming weary, his face tightly bound by perpetual exhaustion. It was as if his appointment had been only half-effective.

"Hudson River Park," Clark said.

"Hudson River Park, sir?" Jende asked, surprised the answer wasn't the office.

"Yes."

"Anywhere in the park, sir?"

"Go close to Eleventh and Tenth. Or somewhere near the piers."

"Yes, sir."

Jende dropped Clark off at the end of Christopher Street and watched as he crossed the West Side Highway to the pier, his already slender shoulders sagging under the weight of the heat and the sun.

"Where are you?" he called to ask Jende ten minutes later.

"Around the same area, sir," Jende replied. "I backed up into a good spot that opened up behind me."

"Listen, why don't you come join me? There's no need for you to sit in the car."

"At the pier, sir?"

"Yes, I'm sitting all the way at the front. Come and meet me here."

Jende locked up the car and dashed across the highway toward the pier, where Clark was sitting on a bench, his jacket off, his face turned toward the sky. When Jende got to the bench, he realized Clark's eyes were closed. He seemed to be finding respite in the bountiful breeze blowing toward them; for the first time in months, he looked relaxed as the wind tousled his hair and wiped his brow. Jende looked up at the empty sky, which bore no resemblance to the thick air below. In a couple of days, August would be over, and yet the humidity was still dense, though it felt good to him, the sultriness mingled with the wind blowing over the Atlantic-bound river.

On the bench, Clark breathed in. And out. And in, and out. Again, and again. For five minutes. Jende stood next to him and waited, careful not to move and disturb him.

"You're here," Clark said when he finally opened his eyes. "Have a seat."

Jende sat down beside him, took off his jacket, too.

"Beautiful, huh?" Clark said as they watched the Hudson, nowhere as long, but every inch as purposeful and assured, as the Nile and the Niger and the Limpopo and the Zambezi.

Jende nodded, though confused as to why he was there, sitting on a bench at a pier, gazing at a river with his boss. "It is very nice, sir."

"Thought you might enjoy it, instead of just waiting on the street."

"Thank you, sir, I am enjoying the fresh breeze. I did not even know there was a place like this in New York."

"It's a great park. If I could, I'd come here more often to watch the sunset."

"You watch sunsets, sir?"

"Nothing relaxes me more."

Jende nodded and said nothing, though he thought about how funny it was that both Clark and Vince loved sunsets—the only people he'd ever met who went out of their way to sit by a body of water and stare at the horizon. He wondered if Vince knew this about his father, and what difference it would make if he didn't know and then discovered it by chance; how differently Vince would feel about his father if he realized that they shared a great love for something only a sliver of humans make a deliberate effort to see.

For a few minutes the men sat in silence, watching the river flowing leisurely, in no rush for its meeting with the ocean.

"I'm sure you know by now that Vince will be moving to India in two weeks," Clark said.

"No, sir, I did not know. India?"

Clark nodded. "No more law school for him. He wants to wander the earth."

"He is a good boy, sir. He will come back safely to America when he is ready."

"Or he may not, for a long time. That's fine. I'm not the first father to have a son who defied him and decided he wanted to live his life in an unorthodox manner."

"I hope you are not too angry with him, sir."

"Actually, Cindy thinks I'm not angry enough. And that makes her angry, like somehow I'm giving up on him because I don't love him enough. But the thing is, I almost admire him."

"He is not afraid."

"No, and there's something to be said for that. At his age, all I wanted was the life that I have right now. This exact life, this was what I wanted."

"It is a good life, sir. A very good life."

"Sometimes. But I can understand why Vince doesn't want it. Because these days I don't want it, either. All this shit going on at Lehman, all this stuff we would never have done twenty years ago because we stood for something more, and now really dirty shit is becoming the norm. All over the Street. But try to show good sense, talk of consequences, have a far-long-term outlook, and they look at you as if you've lost your marbles."

Jende nodded.

"And I know Vince has got a point, but the problem is not some system. It is us. Each of us. We've got to fix ourselves before we can fix a whole damn country. That's not happening on the Street. It's not happening in Washington. It's not happening anywhere! It's not like what I'm saying is new, but it's only getting worse, and one man or two men or three men cannot fix it."

"No, sir."

"But everything I have, I worked hard for, and I'm proud of, and I'll fight to the end to preserve it. Because when this life's good, it's very good, and the price I pay, that's just part of it."

"Very true, sir," Jende said, nodding. "When you become a husband and father, you pay a lot of prices."

"It's more than your duty as a husband and father. It's your duty to your parents, too. Your siblings. When I went to Stanford I was going to study physics, become a professor like my dad. Then I saw what was possible on a professor's salary and what was possible on an investment banker's salary and I chose this path. I'm not going to sit here and be one of those self-righteous assholes, because my original reason for choosing this career was never noble. I can't say I didn't fantasize about the sports car and private jets. But it's different now. Now it means the world to me how well I'm taking care of my family. No matter how bad it gets at work I know that at the end of the day I can send my parents on vacations to see the world, pay for every medical bill that comes up, make sure my sister doesn't suffer because her husband's dead, make sure my wife and sons have far more than what they need. That's what Vince doesn't understand. That you don't only do what makes you happy. You think about your parents, too."

"Vince doesn't see this side of you, sir. He sees a father who works at a bank and makes money but I tell him, I say, your parents have other sides you do not see because you are their child. It is only now that I am old that I look at some things that my father did and I understand."

"I told him. I said, I'm not asking you to stay in law school and become a lawyer so you can be like me. I'm asking you because I know what it takes to be successful in this country. You've got to separate yourself from the pack with a good education, a good-paying career. I read about folks who thought it was all fun and games when they were younger and look at them now, barely getting by, because unless you make a certain kind of money in this country, life can be brutal. And I don't ever want that for him, you know? I don't ever want that for my son."

Jende nodded, looking afar.

For several minutes the men were silent, just as the sun was one third of the way below the low-rises of New Jersey. They watched as it went down ever so slowly, bidding them adieu, bidding the city adieu, until it rose again from behind the East River to bring a new day with its promises and heartbreaks.

"Wow," Jende said, mesmerized by what he'd just witnessed. "I know the sun comes up and goes down, but I never knew that it does it so nicely."

"Amazing, isn't it?"

"Sir," Jende said after a brief silence, "I think Vince will stay in India for a few months and run back to law school."

"I won't be surprised," Clark said with a laugh.

"I don't know how India is, Mr. Edwards, but if there is heat and mosquitoes there like we have in Cameroon, I will be picking him up at the airport before New Year."

The men laughed together.

"I will not worry about Vince for one minute, sir. Even if he stays, he will be happy. Look at me, sir. I am in another country, and I am happy."

"That's one way of looking at it."

"A man can find a home anywhere, sir."

"Funny, as I was thinking about Vince today, I wrote a poem about leaving home."

"You write poems, sir?"

"Yeah, but I'm no Shakespeare or Frost."

Jende scratched his head. "I'm sorry, sir," he said. "I have heard a little about Shakespeare, but I don't know the other man. I did not make it that far in school."

"They were both great poets. I'm just saying my poetry is pretty remedial, but it keeps me going on many days."

Jende nodded, and he could see that Clark could tell he didn't quite understand the last point, either. "You learn how to write poems in school, sir?" he asked.

"No, actually, I just started a few years ago. A colleague gave me this little book of poetry, which I thought was a rather odd gift—why would anyone think I could use a book of poetry? Maybe it was just one of those lazy gifts where people pull stuff off their shelves."

"A Christmas gift, sir?"

"Yeah. Anyway, I kept it on my desk, picked it up one day, and loved the poems so much that I decided to try writing one. Feels real good to just write out lines about whatever you're feeling. You should try it sometime."

"It sounds very good, sir."

"I wrote one for Cindy, but she didn't like it much, so I just write for myself now."

"I will be glad to read one, sir."

"Really? I can show you . . . Dammit," Clark said, looking at his watch. "Didn't realize it was getting this late."

"Oh, I'm so sorry, sir, I should have kept my eyes open. I was just talking and talking without paying any attention to the time."

"No, no, I'm glad we talked. Thanks for joining me; I really appreciate it. I hope I didn't put you in an awkward position, throwing out my feelings about work and shit."

"No, sir. Please, Mr. Edwards, thank you so much for inviting me here."

"Well, thank you for listening," Clark said, smiling. "And I'll be glad to recite the poem to you. It's called 'Home,' and if you don't like it, I'd rather you don't say anything."

"Yes, sir," Jende said, smiling, too. "I will not say anything whatsoever."

"Okay, here goes:

Home will never go away
Home will be here when you come back
You may go to bring back fortune
You may go to escape misfortune
You may even go, just because you want to go
But when you come back
We hope you'll come back
Home will still be here."

Twenty-four

THE ONE THING SHE MISSED ABOUT THE HAMPTONS (BESIDES THE BOYS, Mighty especially) was the food—the scrumptious catered food served at the Edwardses' cocktail parties. All her life she'd thought Cameroonians had the best food but, apparently, she was wrong: Rich American people knew something about good food, too. Despite having to work fifteen hours on the days when Cindy hosted the parties around the pool, she looked forward to them because the food was too good, so ridiculously good that she had called Fatou one evening and told her she was sure she'd died and gone to food heaven, to which Fatou had replied, how you gonno be sure the cook no piss inside food to make it good? Neni was sure the cook hadn't done anything to the food, since the three chefs Cindy always hired for the parties prepared most of it in the kitchen, and their three servers, with her assistance, took it directly from the kitchen to the backyard. All kinds of foods were there, things she'd seen in magazines and wished she could taste just by looking at the perfectly lighted pictures, wickedly delectable creations like sesame seared tuna with lemon-wasabi vinaigrette; beef tenderloin and olives on garlic crostini with horseradish sauce; California caviar and chives on melba toast; mushroom caps stuffed with jumbo lump crabmeat; steak tartare with ginger and shallot, which she loved the most and devoured without restraint though she'd never once imagined she'd one day find herself eating raw meat like a beast in the forest.

She was certain she'd gotten her fill, thanks to the ample leftovers at the end of all three parties, but she was nonetheless glad when Anna called and asked if she could come help out at a brunch Cindy and her friends were having in Manhattan.

"Are they going to use the same chefs from the Hamptons?" she asked Anna.

"No," Anna said. "This one is just brunch. Two chefs from here and no servers. So me and you, we going to serve and clean after. The other girl who works for Cindy's friend used to work with me every year, but she quit last week, so Cindy tell me to call you."

"All those people for just the two of us to serve and clean after?"

"No worry, not too many people. Just her and the five friends and their husbands and some children. Cindy says one hundred dollars for you, only three hours. It's fair, no?"

Neni agreed it was beyond fair, and arrived at June's apartment on West End Avenue the next Sunday afternoon. There were no more than six children there, and Mighty, thankfully, was one of them. He ran to her when he saw her entering the apartment and hugged her so tightly that Neni had to remind him he wasn't her only baby, she had another baby growing inside her.

"How were your last days in the Hamptons?" she asked him in the kitchen as she and Anna waited for the chefs to hand them the first appetizers.

"Boring," Mighty said.

"You did not have any fun after I left?"

"Not really."

"But now I feel bad, Mighty," Neni said, inflating her cheeks to make a funny sad face. "Your mom really wanted me to take off my last two days, but next time I will stay if that is what Mr. Mighty demands."

"I'll demand!" Mighty said.

"Yes, sir. Or maybe you'll come with me to Harlem instead. That way we can continue making *puff-puff* for breakfast in the morning and playing soccer on the beach in the evening. Do you want that instead, Mr. Mighty?"

"Really? It'll be so cool to go to Harlem . . . but, hold on, there's no beach in Harlem."

"Then we will . . . I will—"

"We'll watch stupid movies, and I'll beat you at Playstation and arm wrestling every time!" Mighty said, laughing, a twinkle in his hazel eyes.

"You should never be proud that you beat a woman," Neni said, contorting her face to feign indignation as she picked up a tray of appetizers. "Come, everyone is going to start eating."

As she walked the appetizers around the room before setting the leftovers on the table, she smiled and nodded at Cindy's friends, all of whom she'd met in the Hamptons. They had been kind and polite to her: offering her advice on the benefits of prenatal yoga and telling her where the best yoga studios in the city were (thank you so much for the information, madam, she always said); reminding her it was okay for her to call them by their first names (something she could never do, being that it was a mark of disrespect in Limbe); complimenting her smooth skin and lovely smile (your skin is so smooth and beautiful, too, madam; you have a lovely smile, too, madam); wondering how long it took her to get her braids done (only eight hours, madam). Their friendliness had surprised her—she'd expected indifference from them, these kinds of women who walked around with authentic Gucci and Versace bags and talked about spas and vacations and the opera. Based on movies she'd seen, in which rich white people ate and drank and laughed with nary a glance at the maids and servers running around them, she'd imagined that women who owned summer houses in the Hamptons wouldn't have anything to say to her, besides ordering her around, of course. After she'd met no fewer than four of them, all of whom had smiled at her and asked how far along she was in her pregnancy, she'd spoken about this unexpected congeniality with Betty, and she and Betty had agreed that the women's behavior was likely due to the fact that it wasn't every day they met a beautiful pregnant Cameroonian woman from Harlem. Such women couldn't possibly be kind and polite to every housekeeper, they surmised. Cindy, on that Sunday afternoon, was the kindest and politest of them all, reminding Neni to do only the easiest work and make sure she didn't overexert herself. Watching Cindy chatting with her friends and laughing with her head thrown back, Neni had to convince herself that the strange episodes in the Hamptons had indeed happened.

"We have to talk about Cindy," Anna whispered in her ear in the kitchen.

"What?" Neni quickly asked. "What is wrong with her?"

Anna pulled her by the arm to the far end of the kitchen, away from the chefs and the guests entering and exiting with plates of egg-white omelets and glasses of smoothies.

"She got problems," Anna whispered.

"Problems?"

"You don't see no problems in the Hamptons?"

Neni opened her mouth but said nothing.

"You see something in the Hamptons, no?" Anna said, nodding rapidly. "You see it?"

"I don't know . . . ," Neni said, confused by the direction of the conversation.

"I come in the morning for work and she is smelling alcohol," Anna whispered, waving her hand in front of her face as if to disperse an invisible smell.

"Yes," Neni said, "she likes wine."

The housekeeper shook her head. "This is not liking wine. This is problem."

"But—"

"Last week I look in the garbage, three empty bottles of wine.

Mighty do not drink wine. Clark is not home. I see him one, two times every week."

"Maybe—"

"Can someone please refill the punch for the kids and get some more napkins?" one of the chefs called out. Anna gestured for Neni to stay put while she took care of it.

"To be honest," Neni whispered when Anna returned, "I saw it in the Hamptons, too."

"Ah! I know I'm not crazy."

"I didn't know a woman can drink like that."

"This family has problems. Big problems."

"She wasn't like this before?"

"No. Before, she drink like normal person—little here, little there. Twenty-two years I work for them and I see no problems like this. But always they have other problems. They eating dinner, not too much talking. You don't see them fight too many times, you don't see them happy too many times."

"You think he knows?" Neni asked, looking over her shoulder.

Anna shook her head. "He don't know anything. No one knows. See how she looks out there. How can people know if they don't see the bottles?"

Neni sighed. She wanted to tell Anna about the pills but thought it would be no use further upsetting her. The alcohol was bad enough. "Maybe one day she'll just stop," she said.

"One day people don't stop drinking," Anna quickly replied. "They drink and drink and drink."

"But we cannot do anything."

"No, don't talk like that," the housekeeper said, shaking her head so vigorously the two clumps of hair that made up her bangs swung away from her forehead. "We cannot say we cannot do anything, because something happen to her, then what about us? A man in my town, he drink until one day he die. If she die, who will write me check? Or your husband check?"

Neni almost burst out laughing, half at Anna's reasoning and half at the way she was so terribly and unnecessarily afraid. Lots of people in Limbe drank seven days a week and she'd never heard of alcohol killing any of them. One of her uncles was even known as the best drunkard in Bonjo—he serenaded the whole neighborhood to Eboa Lotin tunes on his best drunken days—and yet he was still living on in Limbe.

"You think it's little thing," Anna said, "but I know people lose the job because the family got big problem. My friend with family in Tribeca, she lose her job last month—"

"Oh, Papa God," Neni gasped, moving her hand to her chest. "You're scaring me now."

"I know Cindy for many years," Anna went on. "Ever since her mother die four years—"

"You knew her mother?"

"Yes, I know her. She come to the house four, five times. Bad woman. Bad, bad woman. You see the way she talk to Cindy, angry with her, nothing make her happy."

"No wonder . . ."

"But Cindy's sister, the child of the mother's husband who die long ago, the mother always nice to her. When they come together, everything the bad woman say to the sister is sweetie this, sweetie that. But with Cindy . . ." Anna shook her head.

"I'd cut that kind of person out of my life, if it was me."

"No, Cindy goes to see her for Mother's Day every year, until the bad woman dies."

"Why?"

"Why you ask me? I don't know why. And this Mother's Day, Mighty comes to me, telling me he's sad because his family no longer go to Virginia for Mother's Day, because he wants to see his cousins there. I want to shout at him and say you want to go back to Virginia for what? Cindy's sister, ever since their mother died, I never see her again in the house. Cindy, she has no family now, except for the boys and Clark."

"But she has a lot of friends."

"Friends is family?" Anna said. "Friends is not family."

Out in the living room Cindy was laughing, perhaps amused by a story a friend was telling. How could anyone have so much happiness and unhappiness skillfully wrapped up together? Neni wondered.

"We got to tell Clark about the alcohol," Anna said.

"No, we cannot!"

"Dessert is ready to be served," the second chef called out. Neni hurried to take out the desserts while Anna cleared the entrées.

"We don't have to be the ones to tell him," Neni said after they'd returned to their corner. "He'll find out. Maybe you can leave the empty wine bottles on the table for him to see."

"How he's going to see when he's not home? And she will know that I'm trying to do something if I just go take bottle out of trash can and put on the table. You have to be the one to tell him first."

"Me!"

"We do it together. If I alone I tell him, he will not think it is serious problem. But if you tell him, too, he knows it's serious. Just tell him somebody was drinking too much wine in Hamptons. You don't know who. He is smart man, he will know."

"And he will tell her, and she will know it's me!"

"No man is stupid like that. After you tell him, next week I, too, I'll tell him the same thing about some person drinking the wine in the apartment. Then he'll know it's really true. He can do what he wants to do. We know our hands are clean."

Neni walked to the kitchen island, picked up a bottle of water, and gulped down half of it. Maybe Anna was right, she thought. Maybe they had to do the right thing and warn Clark. But she didn't think it was ever right to get involved in other people's marriages, marriage already being complicated and full of woes as it was. But Anna had made a good point: Clark was working all the time and would never know the extent of what his wife was going through. The whole time Neni was in the Hamptons, she'd seen him in person only on the days of the cocktail parties, where he and Cindy had acted as if they slept in the same bed every night. At the first cocktail party, which was to celebrate Cindy's fiftieth birthday, they had floated around the pool hand in hand, smiling and hugging guests in the warm candlelit evening as a string quartet played on. Cindy, in an orange backless dress and blow-dried hair, looked like Gwyneth Paltrow that night, maybe even more beautiful and certainly not much older. Toward the end of the party, they had stood with their arms around each other, flanked on either side by their handsome sons, as Cindy's friends toasted her, speaking of what a wonderful and selfless friend she was. Cheri tearfully told of the evening she'd called Cindy crying because her mother had fallen at her nursing home in Stamford and needed surgery the next day and Cheri couldn't be there because she was stuck at work in San Francisco. As an only child, Cheri told the guests, it was hard, really hard, but on that day Cindy made it easy for her. Cindy offered to be there for her mother and took a five A.M. train from Grand Central to Stamford. She stayed at the hospital until the three-hour surgery was over and Cheri's mother was comfortably settled in her room. Cindy wasn't just her best friend, Cheri said, choking back tears, Cindy was her sister. The guests, tanned and clad in designer labels, smiled and clapped as Cheri walked over to Cindy and the friends held each other in a prolonged hug. Clark asked everyone to raise their glasses. There wasn't much he could add to what Cindy's friends had said, he said, except that it was all true, Cindy was a gem, and my, was she the hottest thirty-five-year-old or what? Everyone laughed, including Vince, who hadn't been smiling much all evening. To Cindy, they cheered. To Cindy!

Neni couldn't tell if Clark had spent that night there, but she knew that the next morning he was gone, as was Cindy's ceaseless smile from the evening before. When Neni asked Mighty during lunch where his father was, Mighty, without looking up from his plate, had said only one word: work. He had finished his lunch in silence and, as Neni was clearing his plate, muttered, "I hope he loses his job." Neni had shaken her head, unable to decipher Clark Edwards. Why was he always working? How could anyone love work that much? Working nonstop made no sense whatsoever, especially when a man had such a nice family at home. Clark had to know what he was doing to his family and why he was doing it . . . but still, it would be good for him to know how unhappy his wife was, because that had to be the reason she was drinking excessively. Neni's mother had told her that unhappiness was the *only* reason people drank too much, and that it was the reason her uncle drank too much, though no one could understand how he could be so unhappy when he had two wives and eleven children.

"Go talk to him now," Anna whispered to Neni. "After dessert, everyone start to leave."

Neni nodded and began walking toward the living room. She wasn't going to tell Mr. Edwards anything about the pills. That had to be Cindy's deepest secret, and she had to keep the promise she made. She was going to say only what Anna had told her to say. Tell Mr. Edwards about the wine. Nothing more and nothing less.

But then, as she was about to enter the living room, she remembered something: Jende. She turned around and went back to Anna. "Jende will kill me," she said.

"For what?"

"For putting my mouth in their business. He never stops warning me to just do my work and leave, and never say anything that doesn't concern me."

"Then don't tell him nothing. This is only me and you. Go."

Clark was standing alone by the window, looking outside either at traffic on West End or kayakers on the Hudson River.

Neni picked up a tray of scones and walked toward him. "Hi, Mr. Edwards," she said. "Sorry I did not say good morning to you yet."

"Hi, Neni," Clark said. "Thanks for helping out." He looked down at the scones. "I'm going to pass on that, thanks."

"Should I bring you another kind of dessert?"

He shook his head. Two weeks since she'd last seen him and he appeared to be a different man: His hair seemed to have gone thinner, his face was unshaven, and he looked as if he needed a hug, a cozy bed, and at least fifteen hours blocked out to do nothing but sleep. He turned his face back to the window and continued looking outside.

Neni stood with the tray, staring at the blank white wall to the left of the window, unsure of how to say what she wanted to say. Cindy was at the other end of the room, chatting on the sofa with two of her friends; the husbands were thumbing their BlackBerrys and iPhones; the children were in another room—the timing and setting for her to tell Clark was ideal.

"Er . . . Mr. Edwards, I, er . . . ," she began.

"Yeah," Clark said, still looking out the window.

"I was . . . I just needed to ask you a question."

"Sure," he said, without turning around to face her.

"It's just that . . . er . . . I have always wanted to know . . . are you related to John Edwards?"

Clark turned around, chuckling. "No, not that I know of. But that's funny. You're the first person to ask me that."

"I just think that maybe he looks like you a little bit," Neni said, rubbing her elbow against her belly at the spot where the baby was kicking her, perhaps for being so boneheaded.

"That's funny," Clark said, before suggesting that she go offer the scones to others in case they were interested in trying them. Neni nodded and ran back to the kitchen.

"How did it go?" Anna asked her.

Neni shook her head and buried her face against the refrigerator.

"You don't tell him?"

She shook her head again.

"Well," Anna said, "we tried."

Twenty-five

She spent the day cleaning the apartment, shopping for groceries, and preparing a five-course farewell dinner for Vince. All afternoon she stayed in the kitchen, making *egusi* stew with smoked turkey, *garri* and okra soup, fried ripe plantains and beans, *jollof* rice with chicken gizzard, and *ekwang*, which took two hours to make because she had to peel the cocoyams, grate them, tightly and painstakingly wrap teaspoons of the grated cocoyam into spinach leaves, then simmer in a pot with palm oil, dried fish, crayfish, salt, pepper, *maggi*, and bush onions, for an hour. She would have preferred if Jende had given her more time to prepare, but he'd told her only the night before that Vince was coming over. He had asked Clark, while dropping him off at home, if it was okay for him and Neni to have Vince over for a little dinner, just to wish him well and have him eat some Cameroonian food, which he'd said he'd love to try, and Clark had said he had no objection if Vince was interested. He and Cindy were taking Vince and Mighty out to dinner on Sunday but it was unlikely it was going to be a festive farewell dinner, so Vince might as well go somewhere where there would be more merrymaking. When Jende had called Vince to invite him, Vince had said sure, he would actually be free for a couple of hours in the evening, so he would be down for some sweet Cameroonian food, thanks man.

At three o'clock, two hours before Vince was supposed to arrive, Jende's phone rang, and it was Vince.

"I don't know, Vince," Neni heard Jende say in the living room. "Let me first ask my wife what she thinks."

His hands over the mouthpiece, Jende came to Neni in the kitchen. "Vince wants to know if it's okay for him to bring Mighty."

"No!"

"That's what I told him."

"God forbid! You want Mrs. Edwards to kill us? Her baby in Harlem? In the evening? Please, God, oh, I'm not participating. No, no, no. I don't want any trouble whatsoever."

Jende went back into the living room, spoke to Vince for a half minute, and came back. "He says his parents don't have to know. Mr. Edwards is at work and Mrs. Edwards is at a dinner something and they're not going to know anything. He says Mighty had a playdate, but the playdate canceled, so he's just going to spend all evening sitting at home with his nanny."

"Let him do that, then."

Jende turned to walk away but hesitated. "Let the child come, Neni," he said.

"I said no."

"He's never been on the subway, he's never been to Harlem. Let his brother bring him. Vince is leaving next week, and they will not see each other again for who knows how long? And it's only for one hour."

"And you don't think something bad can happen in one hour?" Neni said, sweating over the stove as she scrubbed off the grime from all the cooking and frying.

"If something happens, it'll be on Vince's head. I'll tell him that."

"That's what you're going to say when they try to put us in prison?"

"Don't worry, I'll go to prison alone for both of us," he said, winking at her.

Neni turned her face away and continued scrubbing the stove with greater fervor. Just like him to think he knew the answers. She heard him tell Vince that it was okay, they were all excited to see them at five o'clock, and later tell Liomi that the special guest they'd spoken about was bringing another guest, so he better go change into even nicer clothes. By the time Vince and Mighty arrived, Neni had showered and changed her clothes, too, and her mood was far more excited than fearful.

"Neni!" Mighty said when she opened the door, rushing to hug her.

"What are you guys doing in my house?" she teased them as Vince gave her a hug and stooped to high-five Liomi.

"I can't believe I'm in Harlem!" Mighty said. "Did you make *puff-puff*?"

Neni and Jende laughed. "That's for breakfast," Jende said. "This evening we have food that you will eat and your belly will get so full it will explode."

"Cool!"

If the Edwards boys were fazed by the obvious signs of poverty in the apartment (the worn-out brown carpet; the retro TV sitting on a coffee table across from the sofa; the fan in the corner struggling to do the job of an AC; the fake flowers hanging on the wall and doing nothing to brighten the living room), they did not show it. They acted as if they were in any of the apartments they visited on Park or Madison, as if it were just a different kind of beautiful apartment in a different kind of nice neighborhood. Mighty ran to the bedroom with Liomi to see Liomi's toys and called out to his brother that wow, everyone gets to sleep in the same bedroom here, how cool! Vince sat with Jende on the faded green sofa, drinking Malta and eating roasted peanuts with him, talking about America the good country, America the bad country, America the country that no one could argue was the most powerful country in the world.

When Neni was done putting the food in serving dishes and placing them on the table, Jende announced it was time to eat.

"We are going to eat Cameroon style," he said to Vince and Mighty. "In Cameroon we do not usually sit around the table, like you do in America. Everyone takes their food and sits where they like, on a chair, on the floor. They eat how they like, with a spoon or a fork or with their hands—"

"I wanna sit on the floor and eat with my hands!" Mighty said, and Liomi immediately added that he wanted to do the same thing. So Neni put a tablecloth on the floor, moved the food from the table, and they all sat in a circle on the floor and ate, laughing out loud with full mouths as Jende told them stories from his boyhood, like how he and Winston used to go stealing mangoes when they were eleven and how one time his foot got caught in an animal trap and he had to run all the way back home with a trap stuck to his foot, only to arrive and have his father beat him before going to fetch the man who owned the trap to come take it off. Vince chuckled, and Mighty and Liomi laughed so hard they almost choked, but Neni only rolled her eyes because she'd heard the story before and every time the story had a different ending.

"Papa has the best stories!" Liomi exclaimed.

"I wanna hear more!" Mighty said.

Vince looked at his watch, then at Jende and Neni, and shook his head. "I'm sorry, bud, we've got to leave now."

"Why?"

"I'm sorry, I've got other plans. I've got to take you back home to Stacy."

"But Neni!" Mighty cried, looking at Neni, who averted her gaze. Vince stood up and walked to the kitchen to wash his hands.

"I don't wanna go back just yet," Mighty said to Jende and Neni, looking beseechingly from one to the other. "Please, can I stay a little longer?"

"Your mother and father will not be happy, Mighty," Jende said.

"But they won't even be back home till after midnight. Dad may not even come back till tomorrow, and Mom said she might not be home till after two in the morning. I heard her tell Stacy that. So I can stay till ten or eleven and they won't even know it."

"I'm sorry, bud," Vince said, coming out of the kitchen. "I've got other plans. This was fun, right? I'll pick you up Monday evening and we'll do something fun again, okay?"

Mighty did not respond. He pouted and turned his face away, rubbing his fingers, which were fully covered with palm oil from the *ekwang*.

"Maybe I'll come to your house for a playdate, too," Liomi said to Mighty, perhaps in an attempt to cheer him up or perhaps because Mighty had mentioned that he had the latest and cooler model of some of the toys Liomi had, most of which Cindy had given Neni. Whatever his intention, he said it so sweetly and sincerely that Neni almost laughed but, seeing how upset Mighty was, thought it best not to openly laugh at her child's innocence in believing he would someday get an invite to a playdate at the Edwardses'. But then, she thought, she couldn't be so sure Cindy wouldn't invite Liomi over. Without ever meeting Liomi, Cindy had been sending him toys and clothes, some of them brand-new. When Liomi had come down with a case of pneumonia barely a month after Jende started working for them, Cindy had sent Jende home one evening with a basket of fruits and teas and healthy snacks. She'd written Liomi a letter, after he sent her a hand-made thank-you card, praising his handwriting and saying Jende must be doing a great job raising him.

"Why can't Jende take me home later?" Mighty asked, still pouting and ignoring Vince's pleas to stand up and wash his hands. "I'm going to go home, and it's going to be boring sitting—"

"But you told me you have fun with Stacy," Neni said.

"Yeah, but not this kind. Please, Neni. We didn't even get to make *puff-puff*."

"Maybe I'll come back to the Hamptons next summer," Neni said. "Then we'll get to do everything all over again, right?"

"Yeah, yeah."

Jende stood up and held out his hand to Mighty to help him stand up. "There will be another time, Mighty," he said to the boy. "By the grace of God, there will be many more times."

Mighty stood up and followed Jende to the kitchen sink, where he washed his hands.

After an hour and a half of fun, the Jongas hugged the Edwards boys goodbye and wished Vince a good time in India, and the Edwards boys thanked the Jongas for a really cool dinner party.

As they were about to leave, Mighty remembered something.

"How's there going to be another time like this when Vince is leaving?" he asked Neni. "My mom and dad are never going to bring me here."

Smiling, Neni told him that he was going to have to take the subway and come all by himself then, which made Mighty grin—the idea of taking the subway alone from the Upper East Side to Harlem to have Cameroonian food must have sounded totally awesome.

Twenty-six

IT HAPPENED IN THE MIDDLE OF SEPTEMBER, AROUND THE TIME WHEN the night air begins to ruthlessly wipe out memories of summer and once-happy chimes of ice cream trucks begin to sound like elegies.

Two weeks before it happened, he had a lifelike dream, the kind of dream he would remember in detail even months after. He was back in Limbe, strolling through the market with his friend Bosco, who, oddly, was slender and tall and looked nothing like the tree trunk of a man he was in real life. It was a market day, a Tuesday or a Friday—he could tell from how crowded the market was and how slowly cars moved through it, drivers impatiently honking and pushing their heads out of windows to swear at each other, screaming, *Commot for my front before I cam jambox ya mouth; ya mami ya; ya mami pima!*

As they strolled past the brick store that sold chocolate spread, imported wine, and other luxurious foods, Bosco pointed out that there were no singing gamblers in the market that evening. Jende looked at the spot where the singing gamblers usually gathered, next to the women selling *jaburu* and *strong kanda* and assorted smoked fishes. There was no one there. No men from some unknown place, wearing *agbadas*, beating *djembe* drums, and singing in perfect harmony as they tried to entice passersby to come spend a little bit of money to play games that could win them a whole lot of money.

"I think they moved to another spot," Jende said. "Today is a market day—they cannot miss their chance to come on a day when everyone comes with big purses."

"I've never liked those singing gamblers," Bosco said, "but at least they're not half as bad as money doublers. I hate money doublers."

"You shouldn't hate anyone."

"But I hate them! I really hate money doublers!" Bosco screamed, his face suddenly unpleasantly twisted like that of a child about to descend into a tantrum. "My mother gave them my school fees to double so she could use the second part to pay for my sister's school fees, but they never brought back the money. My mother lost everything! That's why I never finished school. They stole my school fees!"

"But it's your mother's fault for giving them the money."

"No, it's not her fault! It's the doublers' fault. They promised to double the money. They didn't double it! They took it and spent it and left us with nothing."

Bosco sat down on the sidewalk and began wailing. Jende tried to calm him down by rubbing his shoulders but he refused to be consoled, pushing away Jende's hands and hysterically crying and cursing the money doublers over and over. A crowd gathered around him, asking what was wrong. Money doublers, money doublers, he cried. The crowd started laughing. Stupid man, ei di cry like small baby, they said. Money doublers them know how for talk sweet talk. If they want we money, we go give them.

"No!" Bosco begged. "Don't give your money to money doublers. Money doublers are bad people. God will punish them! They will have everlasting diarrhea for what they did to my mother! They will never sleep at night again. Their children will all die horrible deaths!"

Embarrassed, unsure of how to get the crowd to leave his friend alone, Jende began running. He ran through the market, elbowing a girl with a tray of yellow peppers on her head and a burly man carrying yards of fabric on his shoulders. The wind was pushing against him, as if to prevent him from going forward, as if to stop him from deserting his friend and leaving him a carcass for mockers, but he pushed against it, running faster than a man fleeing salivating wildcats, hoping to see the ocean and be relieved by the sight of it. Finally, out of breath, he got to the beach. But there was no water there, only a pile of garbage in its place, foul-smelling and stretching to the horizon.

He woke up sweating.

While showering that morning, he thought about the dream and decided that it was because he hadn't kept his promise to Bosco. Bosco had called him two months earlier, asking for money to take his wife to see a specialist at Bingo Baptist Hospital for pain and swelling in her right breast. The doctor at the government hospital at Mile One hadn't been able to explain what was wrong with the breast, and Bosco's wife had been crying incessantly for days, unable to move her right hand. *The bobbi dey like say ei don already start rotten for inside,* Bosco had said, his voice breaking as his wife screamed in the background. Jende had promised to see what he could do. He had done nothing. The night before his dream, he'd spoken to Sapeur, who'd told him that Death was coming for Bosco's wife any day now. The dream was therefore his guilt manifesting, Jende decided. He thought about calling Bosco to see what he could do, but there was no credit on his calling card. Besides, he didn't think he had any kind of money that could save Bosco's wife. And he had to rush to work.

At work he continued thinking about the dream as he drove Mighty and Stacy to a playdate, about what else it could mean. Maybe one of his friends back home had given money to a money doubler. It wouldn't surprise him if that were the case. People didn't learn, even after all the stories that circulated around Limbe of how money doublers had deceived Ma-this or Pa-that. *Why couldn't people learn?* he asked himself. By all accounts, no one in Limbe had ever given money to a money doubler and gotten the money doubled. No one had ever given money and gotten *any* money back. And yet people continued to give to them, falling into the trap of crafty young men who walked up to them on the street and visited them in their homes, promising quick and high returns on their money through incomprehensible means. One woman at Sapa Road had been so enraptured by the two charming men in suits who visited her at home that she'd given them all of her life's savings for double the money in three months' time. Her hope, the story around Limbe went, was that she would use the doubled money to buy a ticket for her only son to move to America. But the doublers did not return on the appointed day. Or the day after. Or the month after. Destroyed, the woman had eaten rat poison and died, leaving the son to bury her.

By the time Jende woke up on the day Lehman collapsed, he had pushed the dream and Bosco to the hinterland of his mind. He was thinking nothing of money doublers and their unfathomable victims, merely glad he didn't have to go to work on a Monday. Cindy had given him the day off, telling him Clark would be too busy in the office to go anywhere, and assuring him that she and Mighty would be fine in cabs, considering she had only one appointment and Mighty's piano teacher was on vacation.

Jende thankfully accepted Cindy's gift—a weekday off would be great for him. With Liomi at school, he could spend some alone time with Neni and help her around the house: clean the bathroom, do laundry, and, if he had enough time, cook and freeze a couple of meals so Neni wouldn't have to worry about cooking until at least the following week. Her back had been aching unceasingly since she returned from the Hamptons, and he'd asked her to stop working and take only the minimum number of classes needed to retain her student visa. Pregnant women are not supposed to do anything strenuous in their last months, he'd said to her, even though his mother had continued farming till the day she gave birth to each of her five children and had in fact given birth to his youngest brother under a guava tree at their farm behind Mawoh Quarters.

"But I like to work," Neni had protested, berating herself for days after she'd called the agency to say she wouldn't be available to work for a few months. Work will be there for you when you're ready, he assured her. He listened patiently whenever she began a piteous and long-winded rant about how being pregnant and not working made her feel fat and lazy and worthless, told her to remember how much she sometimes hated her job, and guaranteed her that not working was the best decision because her health was the most important thing. I'll go out there and work four jobs before I let you go to work in pain and discomfort, he promised her.

A week after she quit her job, he took his dedication to her a step further and informed her that she was going to take off the upcoming spring and summer semesters and stay home after the baby arrived in December.

"No!" she immediately responded, standing up from the sofa where they'd been cuddling. "I'm not taking off any time from school."

"I've already thought about it and decided," he calmly informed her, leaning back on the sofa and crossing his legs.

"You've decided, eh?" she said, glaring at him, hands akimbo, as he picked up the remote control and turned on the TV. "What do you mean you've decided? When did you decide this? You know I don't like this. I don't like it one bit when you decide something about me without asking me. I'm not your child!"

"You're my wife and you're carrying my child," he said without looking at her, leisurely clicking the remote control as if he and his wife were discussing what to have for dinner. "I want my wife to stay home with my new child for some time."

"Why?"

"I think it's going to be best for you and the baby."

"What about what I think is best?" she retorted, angry at him for making a decision about her life without consulting her and, even worse, for forcing her to add another year to the time it would take her to become a pharmacist. "How can you decide I'm taking off two semesters without asking me if it's going to make me happy?"

"You're going to stay home with the baby for a few months," he said again, the finality of his decision evident in his tone. "Babies need to start their lives in the hands of their mother, and I want you to enjoy the baby while you're recovering from the pregnancy."

"Nobody needs to recover from pregnancy! And I can't take off two whole semesters!"

"I've already decided."

"I don't want to! You know I can't!"

"Yes, you can."

"I can't! You know I'm going to fall out of status and lose my visa, and then what?"

She wasn't going to fall out of status, he told her. He'd already discussed the matter with Bubakar, who was going to help them do what they needed to do so the international students' office at BMCC would approve her for a medical leave of absence.

I can't believe you're doing this to me, she cried as he continued clicking the channel buttons on the remote control, unable to find anything interesting to watch and unmoved by her tears. Why can't I at least take the minimum number of classes I need for my visa, like I'm doing now? Why are you always acting as if you own me?

Having anticipated her reaction, he ignored her, making it clear he'd thought about the matter for days and wasn't going to change his mind. Ultimately, she grew quiet and went to bed defeated, because there was nothing she could do. He had brought her to America. He paid her tuition. He was her protector and advocate. He made decisions for their family. Sometimes he conferred with her about his decisions. Most times he did what he deemed best. Always she had no choice but to obey. That was what he expected of her.

As her feet grew wider and her belly longer, her complaints to her friends about his behavior multiplied—there were too many things he wanted her to do or not do for both her and the child's well-being. He insisted she eat the salmon and sardine dinners he made for her, she said, because he'd read in one of Mrs. Edwards's discarded magazines that they were good for pregnant women and that fetuses whose mothers ate oily fishes grew up to be intelligent adults. He wanted her to please wash her lettuce well before making salad, because what if there were harmful germs on the leaves? She couldn't wear heels anymore for fear he was going to dive into a tirade about how she might hurt herself and the baby, and was it worth risking an unborn child's life just so she could look good? It was as if she had become an egg that might break at any minute. And you gonno complain about that why? Fatou said to her. Betty and Olu, another friend from school, said the same thing. Why are you making noise when he's only looking out for you, they said. You said you suffered the last two times when you were pregnant and gave birth while living in your father's house, Betty reminded her, and now that your husband is treating you like a queen so you don't suffer again, you're grumbling? If you like a hard life so much, come and take my life and I'll take yours for the next few months.

Eventually, shamefully, she decided to defer to his wisdom, knowing that few women (rich women included) had the privilege of being married to an overly protective man who not only did everything he could to ensure his wife's comfort but also spent hours wiping the dust-covered walls of their apartment and killing the roaches that sprinted from one end of the living room to the other like track-and-field athletes, all so he could protect the health of his unborn child. Though she could neither understand nor appreciate his decision about her taking two semesters off, she slowly allowed herself to feel no guilt about being a housewife in a city full of independent women, and not being, at least for a while, a successful career woman like Oprah or Martha Stewart. She decided to enjoy the unwanted privilege of sitting at home all day watching too many hours of talk shows and sitcoms and breaking news, which was what she was doing on the Monday morning the news came up on CNN.

"Jende," she called from the living room. "Jende, oh!"

"Eh?" he replied, running out of the bedroom, where he was folding the clean clothes he'd just brought back from the laundromat. Her panicked voice made him nervous; every time she called his name like that, he feared it had to do with the baby.

"Watch," she said, pointing to the TV. "Something about Lehman Brothers. Is that not where Mr. Edwards works?"

Yes, it was, he said, not yet panicking, not wanting to think that the news had anything to do with what Leah had been dreading. He heard a journalist say that the collapse was a massive earthquake that would reverberate across the world for months to come. He heard another journalist talk about the catastrophic fall in stock prices and the possibility of a recession. A former employee of Lehman Brothers was interviewed. She hadn't seen this coming, she said. People were suspicious but no one thought it was really going to come to this. They'd been told just today that it was over. She had no idea what she was going to do. No one knew what they were going to do now.

Neni placed her hand on her chest. "Does it mean Mr. Edwards has no job now?" she asked.

Neither of them asked the next question—did it mean Jende would have no job, too? The fear within them could not let loose the words. Similar questions would burrow into the minds of many in New York City in the coming weeks. Many would be convinced that the plague that had descended on the homes of former Lehman employees was only a few blocks from theirs. Restaurateurs, artists, private tutors, magazine publishers, foundation directors, limousine drivers, nannies, housekeepers, employment agencies, virtually everyone who stood along the path where money flowed to and from the Street fretted and panicked that day. For some, the fears were justified: Their bread and wine would indeed disappear, along with the billions of dollars that vanished the day Lehman died.

"I have to call Mr. Edwards," Jende said, hurriedly picking up his cell phone from the dinette table.

Clark did not answer his cell phone, but Cindy did when he called the house number. "You still have a job," she said to him.

"Oh, thank you, madam. Thank you so much!"

"Nothing's changing," she said. "Clark's going to call you to let you know when to come back to work," she added, before quickly getting off the phone to take another call.

Jende placed the cell phone on the table and sat down next to Neni. He was dizzy, grateful but stunned. It had just dawned on him how tightly his fate was linked to another man's. What if something ever happened to Mr. Edwards? His work permit was set to expire in March and he might not be able to renew it again, depending on how his court case went. Without working papers, he would never be able to get another job that paid as much. How would he take care of a wife and two children? How many restaurant dishwashing jobs would he have to do for cash?

"Please let's not think like that," Neni said. "You have a job for now, eh? As long as we have Mr. Edwards, we have a job. Are we not better off today than all those people walking out of Lehman? Look at them. I just feel so sorry for them. But then, we don't know what's on the road coming for us, too. We just don't know. So let's only be happy that today we were spared."

Twenty-seven

Neither of them said much to the other on the first day they spent together after Lehman fell. There wasn't much to say and there was certainly too little time to say it, with Clark sighing and hammering on his laptop as if the keys were obstinate. He seemed to have gotten older by ten years in seven days—a deep crease suddenly evident on his forehead—and Jende couldn't stop wondering why the man was doing this to himself, why, with all the money he'd made, he couldn't pick up and go live a quiet stress-free life somewhere far away from New York City. That's what he would do if he were in Mr. Edwards's position. By the time he was close to being a millionaire, he would give suffering a firm handshake and tell it goodbye. Why should a man intentionally live his life with one kind of anxiety followed by another? But men like Clark Edwards did not think like that, it appeared. It didn't seem to be about the money anymore. His life on Wall Street, as suffocating as it was, appeared to be what was giving him air.

"I am very sorry, sir," Jende finally forced himself to say, ten minutes after they'd been in the car together, as they drove to Clark's new workplace at Barclays, the British giant that had swallowed up Lehman after it was declared legally dead.

"Thanks," Clark said without looking up from his laptop.

"I hope everyone will be okay, sir."

"Eventually."

Jende knew what the curt response meant: Stop talking. So he did precisely that. He kept his eyes on the road and drove in silence for the rest of the week—from the Sapphire apartment building on the Upper East Side to Barclays in Midtown East, or the Lehman-turned-Barclays office tower on Seventh Avenue; from a meeting with ex–Lehman executives to a meeting with Barclays executives; from a lunch with Treasury officials in Washington, D.C., to a dinner with lawyers at a Long Island steak house. Clark said little to him except for quick greetings, or orders to hurry up, or reminders to return by a certain time after picking up Cindy or dropping off Mighty. Once, he barked at Jende to cut around another car, but most days he sweated in the backseat, mumbling to himself when he wasn't on the phone, moving from one end of the seat to the other, speaking in rushed, anxious tones to various people, flipping through piles of papers, opening and closing his laptop, opening and closing *The Wall Street Journal*, scribbling on his notepad. Jende understood nothing of what he heard him say—after months of educating himself with the *Journal*, he'd come to understand the concept of buying low and selling high, but the things Clark was talking about these days, things like derivatives and regulations, ratings and overrated junk, were indecipherable. The only things decipherable in his voice were misery and exhaustion.

"You should have seen him the night it happened," Cindy said to Cheri as Jende drove them to Stamford to visit Cheri's mother. "I've never seen him that scared."

"Of course he would be," Cheri said. "Everything he worked for just went down the drain. And Lehman, of all companies? I was speechless!"

"You, me, and the whole world."

"For some reason these things keep happening when I'm out of the country. 9/11, I was out. Oklahoma City, I was out. This one I was out."

"Maybe that's not such a bad thing," Cindy said. "Sometimes it's better to be far away from the center of the madness."

"No," Cheri said. "I'd rather be home. There's nothing pleasant about running across Florence so you can get back to your hotel room and stare at the TV, watching what's happening in your country. I'd rather be home and go to sleep scared in my own bed."

"I guess."

"I tried to call you the moment I landed last night."

"I know. I'm sorry, I wasn't in a talking mood. But I sent you a text. Didn't you see it?"

"No, I didn't see any text. If you hadn't called this morning, I would have taken the train alone. I figured you'd probably changed your mind, with everything that's going on."

"Oh, no, I need this," Cindy said. "I need to get out of the city. It's just too much."

"It is."

"I would have left yesterday for a long weekend alone but Mighty and I have a movie-and-dinner date on Saturday, and I need to help him prepare for his youth orchestra audition. Besides, I promised your mom I was going to come back. I need to get my mind off myself for a little bit. It's just been awful. Clark has been *so* hard to be around."

"He must have looked like crap when it happened," Cheri said, and Cindy nodded.

Clark had returned home early from work two nights before, she told Cheri, around nine o'clock. He took off his shirt and sat on the edge of the bed with his head bowed, his bare back humped like that of a man waiting for a load to descend. He did not move or speak, not even when she came in, said hello, and climbed into bed. She had an early-morning appointment for a mammogram and needed a good rest, so she wasn't in the mood for small talk, which was why she hadn't asked him why he was just sitting there like that, somber and mute and motionless. Instead, she had picked up *The New Yorker*—she hadn't had a chance to read the profile of Obama—and flipped it open.

Lehman is going to file for bankruptcy, he'd said abruptly, his head still bowed. She'd gasped, dropping the magazine and covering her mouth with her hand. She sat up in the bed, staring at the back of his head. You heard me right, he said without turning to face her. They'd done everything. The company couldn't be saved. The announcement would be coming within days. They were still trying to fight it, hold on to it, but . . . He shook his head.

"The poor thing," Cheri said.

"I had no idea what to do or say to him," Cindy went on.

All she could do was gasp again, as it sunk in. She looked at her hands—she hadn't realized they were shivering. A thousand questions were rushing through her mind: How much were they going to lose? What were they going to do if they lost too much? What was going to happen to his career? Was he okay? What was he feeling? How was this possible? Was there a chance the Fed would make a last-minute decision to intervene and prevent the bankruptcy? They intervened with BS, didn't they? She wanted to move close and hold him so they could be together in their fear, but she couldn't be certain he wanted or needed any of it, so she slid to the edge of the bed and sat beside him.

"Did you know any of this?" Cheri asked. "That it was this bad?"

Not really, Cindy said. She had known of the struggles at Lehman but not in detail, certainly not how close it was to its end. He had told her only that the company was treading perilous waters, and asked her to understand when he had to cancel plans in order to work. But how was she to know that the times he did it over the summer were any different from all the other times when she'd had to cancel dinner plans and postpone vacations and attend parties alone because he had to work?

"That's the danger of dealing with workaholics," Cheri said. "It's hard to trust them."

"Welcome to my life," Cindy said mournfully. "Or whatever's left of it."

"Everything's going to be all right, Cindy. We'll be all right. Sean has to constantly remind me, too. He says I have to stop checking our portfolios twenty times a day, but I can't help it. I woke up every morning in Florence panicking about losing everything. Of course, I call Sean to talk and he's sleeping. I have no idea how he still sleeps so peacefully at night. I don't think I've slept more than four hours any night all week."

Cindy did not immediately respond; she seemed lost in a maze of a hundred thoughts. "I wish I had Sean's calmness," she finally said. "Nothing ever seems to unravel him."

"Yeah, but you won't believe what he suggested to me yesterday," Cheri said.

"What?"

"He thinks maybe we should get rid of Rosa for a few months, to save."

"Are you kidding me? Was he serious?"

Cheri laughed. "Incredible," she said. "I didn't even deign to respond when he said it."

"Yeah, that's exactly what we need now, right?" Cindy said. "To be cooking and cleaning and doing laundry while we're losing money and sleep. That would be wonderful!"

The women laughed together.

"But it's scary how bad this could get," Cheri said, her tone turning serious as their laughter ebbed. "When people start talking about flying coach and selling vacation homes . . ."

"It's scary, but Anna's not going anywhere, no matter how bad it gets or what everyone else starts doing to survive. I don't know what I would ever do without her."

"Rosa's not going anywhere, either. I guess we just have to be hopeful that everything's going to be all right, as ugly as it seems."

Cindy agreed. That was what Clark had said, too, she said. When she'd asked him that night if the impending bankruptcy was going to hurt the economy, he'd said that yes, he believed the economy was going to get really bad; everything was about to change, one way or another, for everyone in the country, at least for some time. When a powerful house like Lehman falls, he'd told her, people start questioning if indeed there is power in the other houses. There was going to be panic in the market. Portfolios losing up to half of their values. Lots of crazy stuff that could destroy the investments and livelihood of millions of good, innocent people. It could be very bad. But they were going to be okay. The likes of them were going to lose money in the short term but they were going to be okay, sooner rather than later, unlike those poor devils on the streets.

"I hope he's right," Cheri said. "And I really hope he's going to be okay soon."

"I don't know," Cindy said, after a pause. "We haven't spoken much since that night—he's so stressed out and short-fused I'm almost afraid of saying anything. I went three days without seeing him last week."

"He's got to be very busy transitioning to Barclays."

"I know . . . that's what he says. But . . . you never know. I hope it's only that and not also because . . ."

"Come on, Cindy."

"It's at times like this, Cher," Cindy whispered. "This is when they start turning to those . . ." She cut herself short, perhaps realizing Jende might be listening, which he was, intently.

"You've got to stop doing this to yourself," Cheri said. "Everything's going to be fine. He's not the only one dealing with the crisis. We're not the only ones. There's a long road ahead, but everyone's going to be all right. Clark will be all right."

Jende smiled to himself when Cheri said this, hoping so, too, fervently wishing Mr. Edwards would find his way out of the despondency he'd been enveloped in for months.

The previous night, after work, Clark had called his friend Frank to ponder if it was time for him to get away from the Street. It wasn't worthwhile anymore, he'd said, and he was getting tired of the bullshit that came with everything else. He'd never cared about what people thought of him but, all of a sudden, he did—he was watching those assholes on MSNBC and agreeing with them, and the fact that the whole country had turned against the likes of him was completely justifiable. He couldn't help but feel somewhat responsible for the shit that was happening, he told Frank, not because he had personally done anything to hurt anyone but because he was part of the system, and no matter how much he hated to admit it or how much he wished Lehman hadn't lost its principles or how badly he wished there was more conscience on the Street, he was part of it, and because of his involvement in lots of bullshit he didn't even agree with, however small his involvement had been, this had happened. He wasn't sure about a future at Barclays; it wasn't anything about the bank, it was him. Maybe he was just getting old. Maybe he was beginning to question the meaning of his life. Why was he all of a sudden sounding like Vince?

Hearing Vince's name had made Jende wonder how the young man was faring in India. He thought about Vince whenever he saw a mention of India in the newspaper, but didn't think it right to ask Clark about him and open up whatever wounds were still healing.

He thought about Leah, too, in the days after Lehman fell, but had no way of reaching her besides through the number at Lehman. The thought of calling it left him with an eerie feeling, as if doing so would be akin to calling a dead friend at a cemetery. But he worried about her, about her high blood pressure and her swelling feet, and so a few days after returning to work he had called the work number, hoping for a recorded message that would direct him to her.

"Leah!" he said, shocked and elated when she answered the phone. "What are you doing there? I thought . . . I was afraid . . ."

"Oh yeah, honey," she said. "I was canned, too. My last day's tomorrow. They want me to clean up some things before I leave. Otherwise, I don't need to be here for one more minute."

"I am so sorry, Leah."

"I am, too . . . but what're you going to do? Sometimes it's better when it happens, you know? You spend months losing sleep, fearing for what's ahead. At least now it's happened and it's over and . . . I don't know . . . I can finally sleep well and get the hell out of this shitty place."

"It's the fear that kills us, Leah," Jende said. "Sometimes it happens and it is not even as bad as the fear. That is what I have learned in this life. It is the fear."

Leah agreed but said she couldn't talk much at the moment. She gave Jende her home number to call later, which Jende did that night.

"What are you going to do now?" he asked her.

"Something really great," she said, sounding more upbeat than she had in the morning. "I've got over twenty years of experience, honey. I'm not worried. I'm going to take a month and relax before I start a job search."

"You should do that."

"I will, maybe go see my sister in Florida. That's the good thing about a life with no husband or children—no one to hold me back, make me feel as if I can't go where I want, whenever I want, do what I want. I'm going to enjoy myself in Sarasota, and when I come back, I'll dust off the old résumé."

"You will get a new job very fast when you return," Jende said. "Mr. Edwards will surely tell everyone that you were a good secretary."

"He better."

"When you come back, call me, please? You are going to let me know you are all right?"

Leah promised she would, and Jende wished her a good time in Florida.

The next day, as he drove to drop off and pick up the Edwardses, Jende thought about Leah and the ex–Lehman employees. He thought about the state of the city and the state of the country. He thought about how strange and sad and scary it was that Americans were talking about an "economic crisis," a phrase Cameroonians heard on the radio and TV virtually every day in the late eighties, when the country entered a prolonged financial downturn. Few people in Limbe understood the origin of the slump, or what the government was doing to get the country out of it and prevent a recurrence, but everyone knew that it made buying food and other necessities beyond difficult, thanks to the evaporation of large amounts of money. Now it was happening in America. And it was bad. Very bad. No one could tell how long it would take before this avoidable pandemonium that Lehman's fall had caused would end. It could take years, the experts on TV said. Maybe up to five years, some said, especially now that the crisis was spreading around the world and people were losing secure jobs, losing life's savings, losing families, losing sanities.

But him . . . thank God, he still had a job.

His gratitude overflowed every time he picked up the car from the garage, knowing he could be jobless like many all over the country. He read of job losses daily in Clark's discarded *Journal* and watched news segments about layoffs on CNN after work.

Every night he went to bed hoping it would get better soon, but it would only get worse in the coming weeks.

More jobs would be lost, with no hope of being found in the immediate future. The Dow would drop in titanic percentages. It would rise and fall and rise and fall, over and over, like a demonic wave. 401(k)s would be cut in half, disappear as if stolen by maleficent aliens. Retirements would have to be postponed; visions of lazy days at the beach would vanish or be put on hold for up to a decade. College education funds would be withdrawn; many hands would never know the feel of a desired diploma. Dream homes would not be bought. Dream wedding plans would be reconsidered. Dream vacations would not be taken, no matter how many days had been worked in the past year, no matter how much respite was needed.

In many different ways it would be an unprecedented plague, a calamity like the one that had befallen the Egyptians in the Old Testament. The only difference between the Egyptians then and the Americans now, Jende reasoned, was that the Egyptians had been cursed by their own wickedness. They had called an abomination upon their land by worshipping idols and enslaving their fellow humans, all so they could live in splendor. They had chosen riches over righteousness, rapaciousness over justice. The Americans had done no such thing.

And yet, all through the land, willows would weep for the end of many dreams.

Twenty-eight

THEY DROVE TO THE CHELSEA HOTEL AT LEAST A DOZEN TIMES IN THE first five weeks after Lehman fell. Clark seemed to need those appointments more as hysteria in the market grew and the weight on his weakening shoulders got heavier; he seemed to need them desperately, like a scorched land panting for rain. It was as if they were his sole path to aliveness, his sole means of feeling sane in a demented world—only when he called to confirm each appointment did his tone change from morose to expectant. Always, he confirmed the rendezvous on the way there. Always, he verified with the person on the phone that the girl would do the acts she had promised to do on the website. Always, he nodded, and sometimes smiled, as the person assured him that he would get his money's worth, that the girl would make him very, very happy.

In the driver's seat, Jende pretended not to hear anything. It was his job to drive, not to hear. Before every appointment he pulled up in front of the hotel, dropped Clark off, and searched for a spot on the street. There, he waited until he got a call from Clark to pick him up in five minutes. When Clark reentered the car, Jende saw a man who looked relaxed but, in other ways, was no different from the man who had exited. His hair was combed back, as when he left the car. His blue shirt was without wrinkles, his collar without a dent. No guilt was evident in his demeanor.

Jende drove him wherever he needed to be next and asked no questions. He had no right to ask questions. Sometimes when Clark re-entered the car he made remarks about the weather, the Yankees, the Giants. Jende always responded quickly and agreed with whatever the boss said, as if to say, it's okay, sir, it's perfectly all right, sir, what you're doing. And he could tell Clark felt that way around him; that Clark trusted him and knew that no one would ever know. Without speaking of it, their bond had been firmly established—they were two men bound by this secret, by their dependence on each other to move forward every day and carry each other to the achievement of daily and lifelong goals, by the relationship they had forged after almost a year of cruising on highways and sitting in rush-hour traffic.

Theirs was as solid a bond as could be between a man and his chauffeur, but not solid enough for the chauffeur to venture into a delicate territory. Which was why Jende said no more than was necessary the night Clark returned to the car without his tie on.

On any other day, Jende wouldn't have noticed the tie's disappearance, since he cared little about ties. Winston had given him one—after Jende told him what Clark had said at the job interview, about him getting a real tie if he hoped to further his career—but he'd rejected Winston's offer to teach him how to tie it, believing he still remembered how to do it from the couple of times he'd worn one in Limbe. On the morning of his first day on the job, though, neither he nor Neni could figure out how to tie it. Neni had suggested they Google it but he didn't have the time for that. He'd gone to work with a clip-on, and Clark had complimented his "more professional look," which Jende took as a validation of everything he was wearing. Later that week, Winston had again offered to teach him, but he'd declined because he found it unnecessary and, besides, why did a man have to tie his neck like a goat? Few ties seemed worth the discomfort, but Mr. Edwards's blue tie had gotten his attention that morning, when he picked him up.

It was a tie of many flags, and at a stoplight Jende had looked at it through the rearview mirror and recognized the British Union Jack, the American Stars and Stripes, the *Drapeau Tricolore* of France, *il Tricolore* of Italy—flags he knew from years of watching the World Cup. He had searched for the Cameroonian green, red, and yellow flag with a yellow star on the red, but it wasn't there, though the Malian flag was there, for some reason. While waiting for Clark in front of the Chelsea Hotel that night, he considered making conversation about the tie when the boss reentered the car, partly to diffuse the awkwardness that often sat between them in the first minutes after Clark returned, and partly because if he was going to spend money on a real tie, he wanted it to be something notable, and he was hoping Mr. Edwards could tell him where he could get a cheap version of his tie, since his was probably from one of those rich-people stores on Fifth Avenue.

But Clark had returned to the car without the tie.

Jende had opened his mouth to say something and immediately shut it. He had no right to comment on the boss's appearance. And it wasn't his place to speculate where the tie could be, though he couldn't stop himself from wondering. It couldn't be in Clark's briefcase—he never took the briefcase into the hotel. It couldn't be in his pocket—that would make no sense. And he couldn't have given it to whomever he had just . . .

"Back to the office, sir?" Jende asked as he pulled out of a parking spot in front of the hotel, wondering how much pleasure the man must have received for him to forget his tie.

"No, home."

"Home, sir?"

"That's what I said."

Immediately, Jende could see how this was going to play out. Clark was going to walk into the house, and Cindy, being a woman and being as inquisitive as women couldn't help being, was going to ask him where the tie was. Clark was going to stammer and quickly mutter a lie, which Cindy would not believe. Cindy would start a fight, maybe their third fight of the day, and tomorrow Jende's ears would be subjected to more cringe-inducing details about their marriage. And poor Clark, as if he wasn't suffering enough, would have one more battle to fight.

Or maybe Cindy wouldn't notice.

It was already ten o'clock, and she might be sleeping. Clark would return home, undress, take a shower, and, thankfully, the poor woman wouldn't know a thing.

Twenty-nine

CINDY ASKED HIM TO COME UPSTAIRS ON AN EVENING EARLY IN NOVEMBER, a week after the tie went missing. It was three days after Barack Obama had been elected president and New Yorkers had danced in Times Square, three days after he and Neni had jumped all around the living room and shed euphoric tears that the son of an African now ruled the world. It was a day after Clark had told him that he would be getting a two-thousand-dollar raise for having been an exceptional employee for one full year.

"Please have a seat," Cindy said, pointing to a chair at the kitchen table.

Jende lowered himself onto the black leather dining chair. There was a clear vase of fresh purple calla lilies on the rectangular marble table; a blue notebook sat next to it. Jende glanced at the leather-bound book, and then Cindy. He could tell: She had noticed the tie. She *must* have noticed the tie. They must have fought about it or about something else. It must have been a big fight, maybe a fight like the one Neni had told him they'd had in the Hamptons over Vince moving to India. It was always easy to tell when a married person had had an ugly fight with their spouse—they looked as if the whole world had deserted them, as if they had nothing and no one. That was how Cindy looked that evening.

She no longer looked like the gorgeous Mrs. Edwards from when he started working for them. Her skin was still beautiful, wrinkle-free and spotless, but there was an emptiness in her eyes, which even her well-done mascara and eyeliner could not conceal, and he could see that something had happened to the madam, something was happening to her. Even with the loose waves of her glossy strawberry blond hair lying on one side of her face, her pearls sitting on her chest, her lips painted red, it was clear to Jende how much pain she was in and how badly she needed something to happen to bring her peace.

"How was your day?" she asked him.

"I thank God, madam."

She nodded, picked up her coffee mug from the table, and, holding it with both hands, took a sip. "Your wife and son are well?"

"They are very well, madam. I thank you for asking."

Cindy nodded again. She said nothing for ten seconds, maybe, and bowed her head while her hands remained clasped around the mug.

"I'm going to need you to do me a favor," she said softly, lifting her head to look into Jende's eyes. "A huge favor. I need you to start doing it tomorrow."

"Anything, madam. Anything."

"Good . . . good."

She paused again, nodding with her head bowed. He waited, looking at the collar of her yellow cotton blouse in lieu of her face. She kept her head bowed. He glanced around the kitchen, at the bare countertops and the trio of glass pendant lights above the island. Just when it seemed she was going to remain with her head down for a full minute, she lifted it, pushed back her hair, and looked into his eyes.

"I want you to write in here," she said, pushing the blue notebook toward him, "everywhere that you drive Clark to. Everyone you see him with. I want you to write everything, in here."

Jende shifted in his seat and sat upright.

"You don't have to tell him what I'm asking you to do, okay? This will be between the two of us. Just do as I say. Everything will be all right. You'll be fine."

Her voice was guttural, her nose reddish at the top. She pulled a tissue from a box on the table, wiped her nose, stood up, discarded it in the trash can, and returned to her seat. Jende picked up the notebook and examined it. He flipped through the empty pages, turned it around as if to make sure it really was a book. Carefully, he put the book down, took a deep breath, clasped his hands on his lap, and waited for courage to possess him so he could give her the right response.

"Mrs. Edwards," he said, "what you are asking me to do is very difficult."

"I know."

"What you are asking me is . . . In fact, madam, I can lose my job with Mr. Edwards if I do something like this. Mr. Edwards made it very clear to me—"

"You will not lose your job," she said. "I'll make sure of that. You work for the whole family, not just him. Get me what I want, and I'll make sure you keep your job."

"But madam . . ." His voice trailed off; it had suddenly become too heavy to flow. "Madam," he began again. "Surely you must know that this is a very difficult time for Mr. Edwards. I see how much he is working, madam. I can see how hard this time is for him. He looks tired, he is working so hard, always on his cell phone, always on his computer, one meeting after another."

"I don't need you to tell me what a hardworking man my husband is."

"Yes, madam. Of course, madam."

"There's another woman," Cindy said. She paused and turned her face away, as if ashamed of confessing her fear to a mere chauffeur. "What do you know?" she asked him.

"I know nothing, madam."

"Where have you driven them to?"

"I swear to you, madam—"

"Do not lie to me!"

Her hands were shivering. His were cold; he couldn't recall his hands having ever been this cold indoors. He yearned to reach across the table, steady her hands, tell her not to worry or fear. He couldn't bring himself to do it—he had no right to touch the madam. Still, he had to caution her.

"Madam," he said. "I hope you do not take this the wrong way, madam. But please, do not worry yourself too much."

Cindy shook her head and laughed, a weak derisive laugh.

"I just think, madam, that whatever you think Mr. Edwards is doing or wherever you think he is, he is just working and working all the time. It is not easy for a woman, any woman, madam. It is hard for my wife, too, with me not coming home until late most of the time, and sometimes I have to work weekends. But she understands that I have to do this to take care of the family, just as Mr. Edwards has to."

Cindy nodded. "Your wife is pregnant, right?" she said.

"Yes, madam," he said, pushing out a flimsy smile. "The baby will be coming next month."

"That's nice. You still don't know if it's a boy or a girl?"

"No, madam, we still do not know. We will find out on the baby's birthday."

"Well, Jende," she said. "Think about your pregnant wife and your new baby. Think about your family and your situation. Think very carefully, and let me know if you'd like to have a job to support them."

She stood up, wished him a good night, and walked out of the room.

Thirty

HE RETURNED HOME EARLY THAT EVENING, AROUND EIGHT O'CLOCK, TO find Winston eating *kwacoco* and *banga* soup at the table. Two blue enamel serving bowls were on the table—one bowl containing ten-inch-long sticks of grated and boiled cocoyams, the other holding palm nut soup with pieces of smoked turkey neck peeking from beneath the oil swimming on top. There was a plate of snails, too, fried in tomato, onions, cilantro, and shiitake mushrooms.

"You'll never guess who I'm going to see next weekend," Winston said as Jende washed his hands to join him at the table while Neni set up another plate.

"Maami?" Jende asked.

"How did you guess?"

"As if I only met you today. What other woman will make your eyes sparkle like that?"

Winston smiled. "I found her on Facebook," he said.

"Facebook?" Jende said. "This Facebook thing is something else, eh? Neni, didn't you just find your cousin who moved to Checko, Checkslo . . . some country over there?"

Neni nodded on the sofa, without taking her eyes off her Oprah magazine. "He doesn't call home or send his mother money," she said, "but the *mbutuku* has time to show the whole world pictures of his new shoes and clothes on Facebook."

"I'm telling you it's something else, this Facebook *wahala*," Winston said. "I join the thing for one minute, I see one friend from BHS, connect to another friend, before I know I'm looking at Maami's picture, her *makandi* still as *manyaka ma lambo* as it was in high school. *Kai!*" He clapped his hands and spread them to show the full width of the buttocks. "That same night I call her, we talk till two o'clock in the morning."

"She's not married?"

"She says she has a boyfriend, a little white thing down there in Texas. We'll see about that when she sees me with her two eyes again."

Jende chuckled with his mouth full. "When you see her," he said after he'd swallowed, "just ask her to compare the snakes. Whoever has the longer one that can glide in and out fastest, wins."

"Jende!" Neni said, widening her eyes and motioning with her lips toward Liomi.

"Uncle has a snake?" Liomi asked, turning from the TV.

"Yes," Winston said, laughing, "and you're not allowed to see it."

"But Uncle—"

"Stop asking stupid questions to grown people and go do your homework," Jende yelled.

"Don't shout at him because of that," Neni retorted after Liomi had gone into the bedroom. "You guys are the ones who started it."

"Then he should have closed his ears."

"Why should he close his ears?"

"Because children—"

"Married people!" Winston exclaimed, throwing his oily hands up. "Stop with your bickering before I swear off marriage forever. I'm begging you!"

Neni gave Jende a dirty look and returned to her magazine.

"How *bolo*, Bo?" Winston asked Jende.

"Condition is critical," Jende said, before recounting the story of his meeting with Cindy.

Neni put her magazine down to listen. "You have to tell her what you know," she said after Jende was done telling the story. Her hand was on her belly, her swollen feet on a stool. "I believe it's my right to know everything about you. It's her right to know everything about her husband, too."

Winston nodded as he ripped the skin and meat off a piece of turkey neck.

"Ah, you women," Jende said. "You worry too much. Why do you want to know all of a man's business, eh? I don't want to know all of your business. Sometimes I hear you talking to your friends on the phone and I don't even want to hear what you're saying to them."

"Well, that's you," Neni said. "It doesn't mean it's the same for everyone. I don't want to know where you went and who you saw every day and all that but some wives want to know. Some husbands want to know, too. That is okay by me."

"So you don't mind if I start asking your friends about you?"

"If you want to call my friends right now and ask them something about me, you can call them. My hands are clean. There is nothing my friends are going to tell you that is different from who you think I am."

"Eh, truly?"

"What do you mean, 'Eh, truly'?"

"I mean, if I ask your friends they won't tell me that you've been doing dirty things with one of those African-American men on the street with pants falling down their legs?" he said, winking at her.

Winston laughed.

"New Yorkers, come and hear something!" Neni said, raising her hands. "Why would I ever do that? Why would I take one of the ones with no job and five baby mamas? I beg, oh. If I ever want to try something new, I'll find me a nice old white man with lots of money and an oxygen tank."

"Not a bad idea," Winston said. "We could all split his money when he goes." Neni and Winston cackled together and gave each other an air high-five.

"But seriously," Jende said, "women have to learn to be more trusting. They have to trust their husbands that they know what they're doing."

"I have to agree with Neni, Bo," Winston said. "You have to tell her."

"Have you guys been drinking *kwacha*? I cannot ever say anything about what he does. To anyone! I don't have any business talking about him. I signed a contract when he hired me. You remember?"

"Yes," Neni said, standing up to clear the table. "So?"

"The contract said I cannot discuss anything about him with anybody, even his wife."

"Forget the contract," Winston said.

"Ah, Bo, how can you say that when you're a lawyer? How can you tell me to do something that you know can make me lose my job?"

"But what are you afraid of telling her?" Neni asked, walking back from the kitchen. "Do you know something that he's hiding from her?"

Jende did not reply; he'd wanted to tell her for a long time.

When he first found out about the women, he'd thought it would be nice for her to know so they could gossip about it late at night, laugh about Mr. Edwards booking an appointment with a tall woman or a blond woman. Whenever he dropped Mr. Edwards at the Chelsea Hotel, he would tell her about it and they would laugh, and she would be grateful that he would never do such a thing because he was a good man, an honorable man, a man of integrity. But the more he thought about it, the more he realized how differently it could play out if he told her. She might become suspicious, even anxious. She would think: What if Mr. Edwards offered him a prostitute, too, as some sort of gift or bonus? What if Mr. Edwards indoctrinated him, contaminated him, made him feel as if it was every man's God-given right to satisfy himself as often as he needed to? He could see her becoming needlessly terrified, especially now that her face had grown fat, her legs had grown fat, and her whole body looked like it would be fat for years to come. Which didn't bother him. Didn't bother him at all. But he knew that she thought he cared, which was why she bought all those magazines with skinny women on the cover and made sure she didn't put too much palm oil in the food. Now she was talking about weight loss and calories and cholesterol and sugar-free this and fat-free that and stupid things no one in Limbe talked about. Now she was beginning to worry about nonsense. She was becoming a fearful wife.

He loved her so much (he wouldn't have traded her even for an American passport), but he could understand why she was afraid. He was the only man she'd ever loved, just like her father was the only man her mother had ever loved. And then what happened? Twenty-four years into their marriage, the year after her father lost his job at the seaport, her mother found out that her father had impregnated a teenager who lived in Portor-Portor Quarters. Her mother had been humiliated; Neni had been humiliated more than her mother, if such a thing were possible. Her mother had caught her crying and yelled at her. Wipe those tears, she'd said. Men are ruled by a thing they cannot control. Neni had wanted to yell back at her mother and tell her to stop justifying her husband acting as if his unhappiness was everyone's fault. She'd wanted to scream at her for staying married to an angry man who scolded her in front of her children, but she knew that with only a part-time secretarial job and eight children, her mother would struggle to start a new life. So she had dried her eyes and decided on that day that there was one thing she wanted in a man above all else: loyalty. And that was the one thing Jende was best at, above all other men she'd ever known: keeping his promises.

"Do you know something?" she asked him again.

"Why would he share his secret with me?" he said to her. "I'm his driver, not his friend."

"Then so?" she said. "Tell her. I wouldn't try to anger Mrs. Edwards if I were you."

"I agree with Neni," Winston said. He was now sitting on the sofa with Neni, while Jende sat alone at the table. "The moment Neni told us about the woman and her drugs, I knew something was not right with her."

"That doesn't mean—"

"That means that, Bo, this woman can make you lose your job."

"Rubbish!"

"It's not rubbish, Jends."

"Women can be very determined," Winston said. "If you don't give her what she wants, you could lose your job. He hired you, but she can fire you, I'm telling you."

"But what am I supposed to do about that?" Jende said. "Why can't she ask her own husband what she's concerned about?"

"Who knows what kind of marriage they have? The kinds of marriage people have in this country, Bo, very strange. It's not like back home where a man can do as he sees fit and a woman follows him. Over here it's reversed. Women tell their men what they want and the men do it, because they say happy wife, happy life. This society is funny."

"So what do you think I should do?" Jende asked Winston.

Winston looked at his cousin intently and scowled. "I just thought of something," he said, crossing his legs and folding his arms.

"What?" Jende asked.

Winston uncrossed his legs, stood up, and untucked his shirt. "This house," he said, "it's so hot someone can fry *puff-puff* in the air." He walked over to the window and cracked it open by two inches. "You guys should leave this window—"

"Forget about the window and come tell us something useful!" Neni said.

"Okay, okay, here's what I'm thinking," he said, beaming as he walked back to the sofa and sat next to Neni, loosening his tie in the process. "This is what you should do . . . but you have to do it without *any* worrying about if something goes wrong."

"This one?" Neni said after a scoff. "His worrying is something else. Just tell us. If he cannot do it, I'll do it."

"No, he has to do it himself."

Jende nodded.

Winston sat up and leaned forward.

"This is what you do," he said, looking at Jende. "You go up to the woman. Not tomorrow. Maybe in two days' time, so she knows you've had time to think about it, eh?"

Jende nodded again.

"You see her and you look her right in the eye. Don't do that thing where you're talking and avoiding people's eyes, acting like a *mbutuku*, because you're afraid."

"Can you just tell me the idea already?"

"You say to her, 'Madam, I thought about what you want and I understand. But I'm sorry, madam, I cannot do it.'" Here Winston opened his arms and shrugged. Then he creased his brow. "She's going to say, 'How dare you, this is the end of you, no more job.' And then you look at her right inside her eyes and say, 'Madam, I don't want to hurt you, but you fire me, I tell everyone about the drugs.'"

"What!" Jende exclaimed.

"Mamami eh, Winston!" Neni said, high-fiving Winston.

"Are you guys crazy?"

"You want to keep your job or not?"

"I want to keep my job, but—"

"But what?" Neni said.

"I'm not going to do this to a poor woman who looks like she has so much of her own troubles. I mean, you guys are sitting here talking as if she's just a stranger on the street to me."

"She's nothing to you!" Neni said. "You think tomorrow you lose your job, she'll remember your name?"

"You're just a black man who drives her around," Winston said. "I'm telling you, Bo, if you know the things I know about this kind of white people, you wouldn't worry about her."

"I'm not worried about her!" Jende said. A line of sweat ran down the right side of his face. "You guys think I'm stupid? I know I'm only a chauffeur. But that doesn't mean I shouldn't feel sorry for her. I mean, I was looking at her as she spoke to me today, and tears filled my eyes."

"Eh?" Neni said, raising the left side of her upper lip. "So you're sorry for her, eh? You know what, *bébé*? If she decides you're going to lose your job, guess whose eyes are going to fill up with tears? Mine!"

"Mr. Edwards will never fire me because of his wife."

"I hope so," Winston said, looking at his cell phone.

"He'll never do it. He's not that kind of a man."

"Don't trust another man like that, Bo. People have many different colors."

"Let's leave the topic alone, please. I'll handle it right. I won't lose my job."

Neni pursed her lips, muttered something under her breath, and leaned back with her arms folded.

"Have I showed you guys Maami's picture?" Winston asked. He picked up his iPhone and tapped on it a few times to bring up a picture of his high school girlfriend, a pretty painted face with a long weave and plentiful cleavage. He showed it to Neni, who nodded and passed on the phone to Jende, who, knowing Neni's eyes were on him, carelessly acknowledged that Maami would make a very fine Mrs. Winston Avera.

"You have to do what Winston says," Neni said, her arms still folded over her high belly. "The only way you can escape this is to shut her up, because if you tell her something Mr. Edwards doesn't want her to know, Mr. Edwards will fire you for breaking the contract. If she ever finds out you knew something and didn't tell her, she'll fire you for lying to her. She won't care if you have a family or if—"

"Neni, please! Let me rest, I'm begging you. My head is aching, okay?"

"My head is aching, too, okay? I don't like this situation at all. I know Mrs. Edwards. I know what kind of woman she is. She looks like she is weak, but she gets what she wants from people, one way or another. You cannot make any mistake with your job right now, let me tell you. One little mistake, you lose your job at a time when—"

"You think I don't know that!"

"Everyone calm down," Winston said. "And Bo, please, don't talk to our woman like that. Not especially when she's carrying our fine American baby."

"Maybe a woman carrying a baby should know when to stop talking."

Neni looked at Jende from head to toe, her momentary disdain unconcealed. She sat up and started lifting herself off the sofa. Winston stood up and pulled her to her feet.

"Put some sense into that coconut head of his," she said to Winston. "Because if I say one more thing to him, I swear to you, my mouth will start bleeding like a slaughtered cow's."

Jende and Winston chuckled as Neni bade Winston good night and waddled into the bedroom.

"How did I get myself involved in other people's married business like this?" Jende asked Winston after Neni had closed the bedroom door. "This one is beyond me."

"Women can be very tricky," Winston said. "If you don't give her what she wants, she'll go to him and make up a story about you so that he'll do away with you."

"Then I'll become like Joseph in Egypt."

"Yes, you'll be like Joseph in Egypt. But instead of solving a dream about seven years of plenty and seven years of famine, you'll be living in seven years of hardship."

Thirty-one

ON THE MORNING OF HIS THIRTY-EIGHTH BIRTHDAY, HE STOOD OUTSIDE the car and held the back door open for Clark Edwards, as he did every workday morning. He was dressed in a suit Neni had bought for him at Target as his birthday gift, a gray wool ensemble that he paired with a white shirt and red clip-on tie and completed with a pair of brown dress shoes. Earlier that morning, as he'd stood in front of the mirror admiring himself, Neni had walked into the bedroom and told him he looked more handsome than ever, and he had agreed, giving her a long thank-you kiss.

"Today is my birthday, sir," he told Clark.

"Happy birthday, then," Clark replied without taking his eyes off his laptop, which was booting up. "I won't ask how old you are."

"Thank you, sir," Jende replied, smiling. While they waited for the light to turn green at Park and Seventieth, he pondered how best to bring up the topic.

"I know this is a very busy time for you, sir," he said, "but there is something I wanted to discuss with you."

"Go on," Clark said, still not lifting his eyes from the laptop.

"It is about Mrs. Edwards, sir."

Clark continued looking at his laptop. "What about her?"

"Sir, I think she wants to know where you go to. And who you see. And all those kinds of things, sir. She wants me to tell her about what I see you doing."

Clark looked at Jende in the rearview mirror. "Really?"

Jende nodded. "I do not know what to do, sir. That is why I am asking you."

He wanted to turn around to see the reaction on Clark's face—rage? disappointment? frustration?—but he couldn't; he could only catch a glimpse of the boss's eyes in the mirror.

"Tell her what she wants to know," Clark said.

"I can tell her, sir? Do you want me, sir . . . you want me to—"

"You can answer her questions."

"You mean I can tell her everything, sir?"

"Of course you can tell her everything. Where do you take me to that you can't talk about? Who do you see me with?"

"That is what I told her, sir. I told her I only take you to office buildings in midtown and downtown and sometimes—"

"Never mention Chelsea."

"I have never mentioned Chelsea, sir. I will never."

The car was silent for a minute, the men acknowledging without words what they each knew the other knew. Jende wanted Clark to know more; he wanted to assure him of his loyalty, promise him again that his secret would always be safe. He wanted to tell Mr. Edwards that because he had given him a good job that had changed his life and that was enabling him to take care of his family, send his wife to school, send his father-in-law a cash gift every few months, replace the roof and crumbling wooden walls of his parents' house, and save for the future, he would always protect him every way he could.

He did not say it, but Clark Edwards said "Thank you" nonetheless.

The perspiration running down Jende's back dried off. "Thank you so much, sir, for understanding," he said. "I was not sleeping well. Not knowing what to do. I am glad I can make both you and Mrs. Edwards happy."

"Of course."

"I was so afraid I would lose my job if I did not do the right thing."

"There's nothing to be afraid of. Your job is secure. You've been excellent. Continue doing as I ask you to do, and you won't have to worry about anything."

Both men were silent again as the car crawled through the midtown madness of tourist shoppers and harried commuters and street vendors and city buses and tour buses and yellow cabs and black cars and children in strollers and messengers on bikes, and too much of everything.

"Sir," Jende said, "is Mrs. Edwards doing well?"

"Yeah, she's fine. Why?"

"It looked to me, sir, as if—"

Clark's phone buzzed and he picked it up. "Did you talk to Cindy?" he said to the person on the line. "Great . . . I think she's putting you guys at the Mandarin Oriental, not sure why . . . No, it's fine, if that's what everyone prefers." He listened for a while and then laughed. "Sounds like Mom," he said. "And Dad's visit to New York is never complete without a Central Park walk . . . Yeah, I'll make sure Jende is available to pick everyone up from the airport . . . Me, too, I'm excited; it's going to be great . . . I can't remember the last time, either. Maybe the year Mighty and Keila were born and no one was in the mood to deal with the holiday crowd with babies? . . . Don't worry about bringing anything, and tell Mom not to. Cindy and June are taking care of everything. They've got their menu down . . . I don't think they need help; they've been doing it for years . . . Oh, okay . . . Go ahead then. I didn't know you'd already suggested it to her. I'm glad everyone's on the same page . . . Listen, Cec, I've got to go . . . Sounds good.

"Sorry about that," Clark said to Jende after hanging up. "We're very excited about being together in New York for the first time in so many years."

"I understand the excitement, sir."

"You were saying something about Cindy?"

"Yes, sir," Jende replied. "I was just saying, sir, I don't know if it is the right thing for me to say, but it looked to me like she has lost some weight, so I just wanted to make sure that she is fine. I will be glad to do whatever is needed if she is not well and . . . if you need me to help around the house, sir."

"That won't be necessary, but thank you. She's doing very well."

"I am glad to hear that, sir, because I was a bit worried—"

"The recession is hard on us all, but she's doing good."

"By the grace of God, sir, we will all be okay soon."

Clark picked up the *Wall Street Journal* lying next to him. After a few minutes of reading it, he lifted up his head and looked at Jende. "You should tell her that she lost weight," he said. "She'll be glad to hear that."

Jende smiled. "Maybe I will, sir," he replied. "Mrs. Edwards is a good woman."

"Yeah," Clark said, returning to his newspaper. "She's a good woman."

Thirty-two

TWICE A DAY, DURING HIS LUNCH BREAK AND BEFORE PARKING THE CAR FOR the day, he wrote down everything he thought Cindy would love to read: benign information, banal rundowns. He provided details that were far from necessary; included times, locations, and names that served no purpose; added descriptions of people whose actions and behaviors contributed nothing to the narrative. This was his first chance to write something on a daily basis since his student days at National Comprehensive, so he took the opportunity to employ phrases and expressions he hadn't found a way to use in everyday conversation; throw in words he'd learned from reading the dictionary he'd owned since secondary school; display sentences and tenses he'd picked up from the newspaper and which he hoped would be proof to the madam that he was thinking carefully as he wrote.

On a Tuesday afternoon, he wrote:

Pick Mr. Edwards up at 7:05, but the slow traffic discombobulated Mr. Edwards because he has meeting at 7:45. Drop Mr. Edwards at work at 7:42. Before when we were still in the car, he call his new secretary (I continue to forget her name) and tell her he was going to be late. When I drop him in front of the office, a black woman wearing a suit is outside. It looks like she just comes out of a car too. I see her and Mr. Edwards say hi to one another and then walk into the office together. I have seen this woman before. My brain cells fire around all day and I remember where I saw her. She used to work at Lehman too. It is 2:30 now and I have not seen Mr. Edwards because he demarcate this whole time to be in the office.

On a Friday evening, after driving Clark from the Chelsea Hotel to the office, he wrote:

At 4:00 Mr. Edwards and I leave Washington, D.C. He gets plenty of phone call but nothing sounds chary and fishy. Everything sounds like work. Someone who he says this to, another person who he says that to. Different work things. I do not talk to him all the way back for fear of uttering disturbances to him. When we return to the city, it is after 8:00. I drive him to his gym. He gets out of the gym at 10:00 and then I drive him to work.

As often as he could, he put the gym in place of the Chelsea Hotel, but in the weeks when Clark went to the hotel more than twice, he concocted other reasons, something novel every week. One evening, fearing that Cindy might have tried to reach Clark while he was in the hotel, he wrote about being stuck in bad traffic in the Holland Tunnel, which has "staggeringly deficient phone reception." Another time he wrote that Clark had to hurry to a meeting, "so he jumped quickly into a yellow taxi when I was on my way back from picking up Mighty so I have no way that is indisputably solid to know where he was going to or who he was seeing. But I am unequivocal in my believe that he was going to a very crucial meeting."

He carried the blue notebook with him at all working hours, and presented it to Cindy every morning so she could read it on her way to work. Sometimes she appeared to read every detail, nodding and referencing previous pages. Always, she gave it back to him with no comment besides a quick thanks and a reminder to keep writing.

"I will continue writing, madam," he always said as he held the door open for her to step out of the car. "Have a great day, madam."

And her days did seem to be getting great, right from around when he began submitting the entries to her.

Phone calls with her friends were no longer peppered with teary whispers about "what he's doing to me" and doubts about "how much longer I can go on like this." She was laughing a little more, and by the time Jende gave her three weeks' worth of entries, she was laughing a lot more, and louder. Her looks did not return to where they'd been the year before (her skin, though still supple-looking, had lost some of its glow, and her collarbones were sticking out even higher), and she did not stop talking about Vince, worrying that he hadn't responded to her email in three days, but she found reasons to smile, like the fact that June and Mike had reconciled, and she and Mighty and Clark were going to St. Barths for Christmas. It should be a wonderful time, she told her friends, and Jende fervently wished so, too, because after months of hearing her groan and sigh, and watching her rest her head against the window with her hand on her cheek and her eyes on the blissful world outside, shake her head, and dejectedly say, whatever, Clark, do whatever you want; after seeing too much of the persistent pain she concealed so splendidly when she wasn't around her family and closest friends, he very badly wanted the madam to have a wonderful time.

Which was what she seemed to have had when she and Clark attended a gala at the Waldorf Astoria the Monday after Thanksgiving.

Clark's parents had come for the holiday, along with his sister and nieces, and days later, Mighty had told Jende what an awesome Thanksgiving his family had had. They had celebrated it with June's family, as they always did (the two families alternated hosting duties every year), and his mother and grandmother and aunt had cooked and baked all day, laughing and telling stories in the kitchen. It was the first Thanksgiving his dad's family had spent together in forever, because with his grandparents in California and his aunt and cousins in Seattle, it had been hard to get everyone together, considering work schedules and his dad and aunt's shared hatred of holiday travel. But this year everyone said they had to do it, and it had been so much fun. Jende was surprised to learn that Cindy and her mother-in-law loved each other, because in Limbe mothers-in-law were often the reason wives stayed up at night crying, but Mighty had told him that no, his mom called his grandparents "Mom and Dad" and always made sure to phone them at least once a month as well as on their birthdays and wedding anniversary. She always insisted Mighty and Vince do the same, and whenever they forgot, she scolded them and reminded them that family was everything.

Indeed, Jende could see in Cindy's new joy, days after Thanksgiving, that the security of family was her greatest source of happiness. Thanks to this rediscovered bliss, hers was no longer a marriage limping from day to day but one skipping and kicking up its heels and waltzing from evening to evening to Johann Strauss's "Voices of Spring."

On the day of the Waldorf Astoria gala, she and Clark entered the car beaming, the happiest Jende had ever seen them, apart or together, in over a year of working for them. Maybe the notebook entries had blown her fears away, Jende thought, assured her that her husband was a good man. Or perhaps the family reunion had reminded her of everything worth fighting for. Or perhaps it was due to something else that had happened between her and her husband, something Jende had no way of knowing. Whatever it was, it was more than sufficient to turn them into young lovers, whispering and giggling on the ride to the gala: she, lustrous in a red strapless trumpet gown; he, youthful and suave in a perfect-fitting tuxedo. They reentered the car five hours later in even greater merriment, laughing about things that had transpired on the dance floor.

"I never thought the day would come when I would see Mr. and Mrs. Edwards happy like that," Jende said to Neni when he got home after midnight.

"Were they kissing and doing all kinds of things in the backseat?" Neni asked as she placed his dinner on the table.

"No, God forbid. I would have had an accident in one minute if I'd seen that. They were only leaning against each other and speaking into each other's ears and she was laughing very loud at everything he was saying. He was playing with her hair . . . Anyway, I didn't want to look too much, but the whole thing was really shocking me."

"I wonder what happened. You think maybe she put a few drops of love potion in his food? The really strong one that makes a man fall for you and treat you like a queen?"

"Ah, Neni!" Jende said, laughing. "American women do not use love potions."

"That's what you think?" Neni said, laughing, too. "They use it, oh. They call it lingerie."

Thirty-three

IT WOULD BE NOTHING BUT A BLIP IN A LONG PERIOD OF ENNUI, A BRIEF reprieve from the agony of putrid unions. Two days after the gala at the Waldorf Astoria, a story would appear in a daily tabloid, and the butterfly their marriage was turning into would morph back into a caterpillar.

It was a story that, in ordinary times, would have been dismissed as rubbish. Because, really, no one with a true sense of the world could be naïve enough to think such things didn't happen. If there had been no collective desire to find the presumed architects of the financial crisis despicable, few would have cared to read the story. Its regurgitation in newspapers of record and blogs of repute would have been another reminder why the American society as a whole could never call itself highbrow, why the easy availability of stories on the private lives of others was turning adults, who would otherwise be enriching their minds with worthwhile knowledge, into juveniles who needed the satisfaction of knowing that others were more pathetic than them.

But the story, though it first appeared in an ignoble tabloid, was not dismissed. Rather, it was talked about in barbershops and on playground benches, forwarded to neighbors and classmates. It was a time of anguish in New York City, and those who put the story on the front page knew where they wanted the rage of the downtrodden to flow.

"Did you see it?" Leah said to Jende after he had seen her missed call and called her back during his lunch break.

"See what?" Jende asked.

"The story from the prostitute. It's juicy!"

"Juicy?"

"Poor Clark! I really hope he's not—"

"I don't know what you are talking about, Leah."

"Oh, honey, you obviously haven't read it," Leah said excitedly. "Well, you won't believe it, but this woman, this escort—I hate when they use such fancy words for prostitutes—anyway, she claims she has a lot of clients from Barclays, and, listen to this, her clients are paying for her service with bailout money!"

"Bailout money?"

"Bailout money! Can you believe it?"

Jende shook his head but didn't reply. The bailout thing was in the news every day, but he still didn't understand if it was a good thing or a bad thing.

"And you want to hear the crazy part?" Leah went on, her voice getting pitchier in excitement. "One of the executives she mentions as her frequent clients is Clark!"

"No," Jende immediately said. "It's not true."

"She says it right here."

"It's not true."

"How do you know it's not true?"

"She wrote his name down?"

"No, she only mentions them by title, and I know Clark's title."

Jende chuckled to himself. "Ah, Leah," he said. "You should not believe everything you read in the newspaper. People write all kinds of things—"

"Oh, I believe this one, honey. I know those men, what they do . . . No one's going to make me think this is impossible—"

"There is no way it can be true—Mr. Edwards would never use bailout money for his own things. And even if the other men at Barclays use this prostitute, how does she know which pocket the money came out of? Mr. Edwards has his own money. He would never touch government money."

"Maybe not, but what about touching prostitutes? You think he's never used one or two or a hundred? I bet you've seen him—"

"I've never seen anything."

"Poor Cindy."

"Poor her for what?"

"For when she reads this. She's going to go crazy!"

"She is not going to believe any of this," Jende said, getting upset and wondering if Leah was excited about the downfall of a family or just loving the gossip. "It is funny in this country, how people write lies about other people. It is not right. In my country, we gossip a lot, but no one would ever write it down the way they do in America."

"Oh, Jende," Leah said, laughing. "You really believe in Clark, huh?"

"I don't like it when people make up stories about other people," Jende said, getting increasingly agitated at Leah's glee. "And how does this woman even know what Mr. Edwards's title is?"

"Yeah, that's the one thing that's funny, right? The madams don't give the name of the clients to the girls. The girls are just told the time and place to show up and . . . Please, honey, don't ask me how I know all this." Leah laughed at herself. Jende did not join her.

"But Cindy," Leah went on, "she's not going to care about any of that. That woman is paranoid to a T, and, let me warn you, she's going to be asking you lots of questions. She used to pepper me with questions whenever she had a chance, and I had to tell her, 'Woman, I don't work for you, you can't take twenty minutes of my time—'"

"What is she going to ask me?"

"Oh, tons of stuff, honey," Leah said, and Jende could sense her smiling, perhaps delighting herself with the thought of the entertaining drama that was likely to unfold. "She's going to ask you if you ever took him to a hotel, if you ever saw one of those bimbos. I'd be really careful if I were you, because—"

"Ah, Leah, please stop worrying yourself for me," Jende said, forcing himself to sound nonchalant. "If she has any questions, she'll ask her husband."

"The poor woman. I'd hate to be in her shoes. Any of their shoes. Now you see why I never bothered getting married?"

Actually, Jende thought, you didn't get married because no one wanted to marry you, or you didn't find anyone you loved enough to marry, because no woman with a brain intact will say no to a man she loves if the man wants to marry her. Women enjoy making noise about independence, but every woman, American or not, appreciates a good man. If that wasn't the case why did so many movies end with a woman smiling because she finally got a man?

"I mean, marriage is good, don't get me wrong," Leah went on, as Jende barely listened because he was praying the story was fake and Cindy would be able to tell that someone was out to hurt men like Clark. "They've been through a lot, you know. Clark almost died one time—ruptured his appendix so bad it burst; he had to be rushed into emergency surgery. And I think, if I remember clearly, that was the year Mighty was born a preemie. Apparently, Cindy only wanted one child, and they didn't plan for Mighty—at least that's what I heard. Though I bet Cindy is thanking her lucky stars she had a second child, now that Vince has run off to India and Mighty's the only one left . . . Anyway, the poor thing spent a whole month in the hospital. Clark and Cindy, God bless them, they pulled through together. But that's marriage, right? He tells me to send her calls to voicemail, but when you see them at company parties, you'd think they're the happiest couple in—"

"I'm sorry, Leah—" Jende said, looking at the clock and starting the car.

"Some people are real good at covering up their shit, and these people, if you weren't in my position, you wouldn't know a thing judging from how they're laughing and—"

"I'm sorry, Leah," Jende said again, "I really have to go get Mighty."

"Oh, sorry, honey!" Leah chimed. "Go on, but promise you're going to call me and tell me what happens when Cindy finds out. I'm dying to know!"

Jende dismissively promised to do so and quickly hung up, remembering only minutes later that he hadn't asked her how her job search was going. The last time they'd spoken, Leah had sounded depressed about not getting any calls back after sending out over fifty résumés, but today she'd sounded cheerful, thanks to sordid details about the lives of others. Women and gossip.

But what if Leah wasn't just making up gossip to pass the time? He called Winston as he drove uptown, hoping to ask him to read the story online and advise him on what he needed to do, but Winston didn't pick up. He thought about calling Neni but decided it would be useless—what would she say besides something along the lines of what Leah had said?

He needed to decide what he was going to say to Cindy when he picked her up at five. He had to assume she'd read the story. He had to imagine that she would have questions for him as they drove to Lincoln Center, where she was to meet a friend for dinner and the opera. He had to be prepared to assure her again and again that he had never seen Clark with a prostitute, and that was the truth: He had never seen Mr. Edwards with a prostitute with his own eyes. He had to be ready for Cindy to doubt him, but he had to try as hard as he could to convince her that he knew nothing about it and everything he'd written in the blue notebook was the absolute truth.

"Good evening, madam," he said as he held the car door open for her.

She did not reply. Her countenance was as hard as marble, her eyes covered with sunglasses in the light darkness, her lips pursed so tightly it was unimaginable they had ever broken into a smile.

"Lincoln Center, madam?"

"Take me home."

"Yes, madam."

He waited for her questions, but nothing came—not one word during the forty-minute traffic-laden ride to the Sapphire, not even a word on her phone. He imagined she had turned her phone off, and he couldn't blame her for silencing the world at such a time—her friends were probably trying to reach her to express their shock, tell her how awfully sorry they were, say all manner of things that would do nothing to take away her disgrace. What good would it do her to listen to all that? And if they weren't calling her, they were calling each other to say, can you believe it? Clark of all people? Poor Cindy must be utterly devastated! But how could he? Do you think the story is true? What's she going to do now? And they would go on and on, saying the same kind of things his mother's friends used to say in their kitchen in Limbe when one of their mates' husbands had been caught atop a spread-eagled woman. In New Town, in New York, the women all seemed to agree that the friend had to find a way to move on, forgetting that the wreckage of so devastating a betrayal cannot easily be cleared away.

As they approached the Sapphire, Jende looked at Cindy in the rear-view mirror, hoping she would say something, anything, to open up the opportunity for him to profess his innocence, but she remained silent. He had not anticipated this silence and, even if he had, he wouldn't have imagined it would be more dread-inducing than the questions.

They got within a block of the Sapphire and still she remained silent, her face fully drawn down and turned toward the window and the cold dark world outside.

"I'm taking you to the office at eleven-thirty tomorrow, madam?" he asked as he pulled in front of the building.

She did not respond.

"I have the book with all the entries for the day, madam," he said as he held the car door open for her to exit. "I wrote down everything he—"

"Keep it," she said as she walked away. "I've got no use for it anymore."

Thirty-four

FIRST HE THOUGHT IT WAS JUST A COLD—THE BOY HAD BEEN SNIFFLING ever since they pulled out from in front of the Sapphire. Then he thought Mighty was making playful sounds to amuse himself, so he asked no questions. Most mornings Jende would have asked him how he was feeling, if he was all right, but today his mind was on nothing but the quagmire in which he was wobbling and the adversities that were certain to engulf him if he couldn't extricate himself from the Edwardses' marriage and protect his job. He had to talk to Winston as soon as he was alone in the car, get advice on what to say or do, or not say or not do, when he picked up Cindy later in the morning.

"Do you have any tissues?" Mighty asked him at a traffic light.

Jende pulled one out of the glove compartment and turned to give it to him.

"Mighty," he said, surprised to see a tear running down the boy's left cheek. "What is wrong? What happened?"

"Nothing," Mighty whispered, wiping his eyes.

"Oh, no, Mighty, please tell me. Are you okay?"

Mighty nodded.

Jende pulled to the side of the street. They needed to be at the school in ten minutes to avoid being late, but he wasn't going to let a child go to school crying. His father once did that to him, let him cry all the way to school when he was eight, the day after his grandfather died. He had begged his father to let him stay home for that one day, but his father had refused: Sitting at home and not learning how to read and write is not going to bring your *mbamba* back, Pa Jonga had said to Jende and his brothers as he left the house with other male relatives to go dig a grave. Jende had begged his mother to let him stay home after his father left, but his mother, never one to disobey her husband, had dried her son's eyes and told him to go to school. Even now, thirty years later, he still remembered the despondency of that day: wiping his eyes with the hem of his uniform as he walked up Church Street with his *mukuta* school bag; friends telling him *"ashia ya"* over and over, which made him cry even more; floundering in grief as he watched his classmates excitedly raise their hands to answer arithmetic questions and tell the teacher who discovered Cameroon ("The Portuguese!"); sitting under the cashew tree during recess, thinking of his *mbamba* while other boys played football.

He turned off the car and got into the backseat. "Tell me what is wrong, Mighty," he said. "Please."

Mighty closed his eyes to squeeze out his tears.

"Did someone say something to you? Is someone bothering you at school?"

"We're not going anymore . . . ," Mighty said. "We're not going to St. Barths."

"Oh, I am so very sorry to hear that, Mighty. Your mother just told you that?"

He shook his head. "They didn't tell me. I just . . . I can tell. I heard everything last night."

"You heard what?"

"Everything . . . her screaming . . . she was crying . . ." His face was fully red, his nose flaring and unflaring as he struggled to compose himself and handle his heartache with as much dignity as a ten-year-old could. "I stood outside their door. I heard Mom crying and Dad saying that . . . that maybe it was time to stop everything, that he couldn't play games anymore . . . and Mom, she was just crying and screaming so loud . . ."

Jende took the tissue Mighty had in his hand. "Married people fight all the time, Mighty," he said as he wiped the tears rolling down Mighty's cheeks. "You know that, right? Just the other night me and Neni, we had a fight, but the next morning we were friends again. You know your mommy and daddy are going to be friends again, right?"

Mighty shook his head.

"I will not worry myself too much if I was you. They will become friends again, I promise you. You will go to St. Barths, and I will hear about all the fun—"

"It's going to be the worst Christmas ever!"

"Oh, Mighty," Jende said, pulling the child to his chest. He thought for a moment that someone might see him and call the police—a black man with a white boy against his chest, inside a luxury car, on the side of a street on the Upper East Side—but he hoped no one would, because he wasn't going to push the child away as his tears ran full force. He was going to let Mighty have a good cry, because sometimes all a person needs to feel better is a really good cry.

"Can I come visit you and Neni this weekend?" Mighty asked, wiping his nose with the back of his hand after he'd finished his cry and Jende had dried his eyes again.

"Me and Neni would be so glad to have you, Mighty. That is a very good idea. But your parents, we cannot lie to them."

"Please, Jende, just for a little bit?"

"I am sorry, Mighty. I would really like for you to come, but I cannot do something like that."

"Not even for one hour? Maybe Stacy could come, too?"

Jende shook his head.

Mighty nodded sadly, wiping the last of the fluids on his face.

"But you know what we could do?" Jende said, smiling. "Neni could make you some *puff-puff* and fried ripe plantains, and I will bring it to you tomorrow. Maybe you can eat some in the car going to school and eat the rest coming back home. Will that make you happy?"

The boy looked up at him, nodded, and smiled.

Thirty-five

THEY NAMED HER AMATIMBA MONYENGI, HOPING IT WAS THEIR DEAD daughter who had returned to bring them happiness: Amatimba for "she has returned" and Monyengi for "happiness," both in their native Bakweri. They would call her Timba, for short.

She was born on the tenth of December at Harlem Hospital, two blocks from their apartment. On the twelfth of December they walked home from the hospital, father cradling newborn daughter in a carrier, mother holding firstborn son by the hand. In their apartment were their friends, who had come to celebrate with them. Winston was in Houston for the holidays, to continue wooing Maami back, but nine friends were packed in the boiling living room to eat and rejoice and welcome Timba to earth.

"Take as much time off as you need," Clark said when Jende called to share the news. "Mighty's going to be on his winter break soon, Cindy is taking some time off work. We'll be fine."

"Thank you so much, sir," Jende replied, unsurprised at his employer's generosity. "Merry Christmas to you and to Mrs. Edwards."

Jende called Cindy, too, to personally tell her the news. She did not return his voice message, but Anna stopped by with a box of size-two diapers a couple of days later, which he and Neni assumed was from the Edwardses.

"How can we ever thank Mr. and Mrs. Edwards?" Neni asked him after Anna had cooed to Timba and hurriedly left to avoid missing her train home to Peekskill.

"We can't ever," he said. "Let's just remember to always thank God for them and for everything we have."

"Truly, we have to," she said.

The next day a letter from Immigration arrived for him.

On the basis of being admitted to the United States in August of 2004 with authorization to remain for a period not to exceed three months and staying beyond November 2004 without further authorization, it has been charged that he is subject to removal from the United States, the letter said. He was to appear before an immigration judge to show why he should not be removed from the country.

The date was set for the second week of February.

"There's nothing to worry about, my brother," Bubakar assured him again when Jende called that evening to discuss the letter. "I have handled cases like this before. I know what to do."

"What are you going to do?" Jende asked.

"There's not much to do during this first hearing—it's only a master calendar hearing. The judge just wants to verify your name, your address, ask us to admit or deny the charge against you; different kinds of protocol things like that. Then he's going to schedule another date to see you again for who knows when. Like I told you before, my brother, between the backlog in the court and me filing one appeal after another if we need to, we're going to buy you a whole lot of time in this country."

How much was all this going to cost? Jende wanted to know. If they had to file appeals, one after another to buy time, how much would they each be?

"It's going to cost good money, my brother. Immigration is not cheap. You just have to do what you gotta do and pay it. I know my fee is not as cheap as some of those nincompoops who go out there and stammer in front of the judge, but you stick with me and I'll help you through this, that's my promise. We are in this together, my brother. Step by step, together, eh?"

Jende called Winston after getting off the phone with Bubakar. He did not know what to do, he told his cousin, whether to continue believing in Bubakar or change course.

"I don't know, Bo," Winston said. "I think this man is taking you down a bad road."

"But he says he has handled many cases like mine. And they all got approved in the end."

Winston was incredulous. Bubakar, he had decided, was a useless loudmouthed buffoon. A former colleague of his who had left Dustin, Connors, and Solomon to start an immigration law practice had recently told him that asylum applications could not be won with preposterous tales like that of a man running to America because he was afraid his father-in-law was going to kill him.

Who does he think sits in Immigration offices? the former colleague had asked after Winston told him all the pertinent details about Jende's case. Sure, those folks aren't the smartest cookies in the can of federal employees, but they're very intelligent and they've heard enough false stories of persecution and seen enough beautiful young women proclaim endless love to ninety-year-old men for the sake of green cards that they can tell a contrived story from one that resembles the truth. And sure, the former colleague had added, asylum has been granted to applicants running away from nothing, but for heaven's sake, a made-up story should be much better than the laughable crap Bubakar had given Jende. What was also unfathomable about the case, the man went on, was why Jende's asylum application process took so long. He'd heard of immigration cases disappearing into black holes and applicants waiting months and years for interviews and decisions, but Jende's was quite extreme, which means either he was one unlucky guy or he had a ridiculously lazy lawyer. Could this former colleague take him on as a client? Jende asked when Winston told him all this. No, was the former colleague's reply. His specialty was investor visas—helping foreign billionaires and multimillionaires obtain entrance and legal status in America through investment, business development, and trade; more lucrative stuff, you know? Jende's case, the former colleague had said, was for a much smarter storefront lawyer than Bubakar.

"Why didn't he use a political asylum story?" Winston asked Jende, a question that would have been more useful at their first meeting with Bubakar. "Isn't that what most people seeking asylum use? Langaman's younger brother, the one in Montana, he's claiming he left *pays* because Biya was going to put him in Kondengui for challenging him. That *paysan* never went near a voting booth in *pays* but he's now saying he was a member of SDF and submitting evidence of how his friends were beaten and locked up for months and how he, too, could be if he returns to Cameroon. Anyone entering this country can make up any story about what their life was like back in their country. You can say you were a prince, or someone who ran an orphanage, or a political activist, and the average American will say, oh, wow! Heck, I tell *ngah*s all the time that I was a political activist in Cameroon, when they start asking me things like 'So, how's the political situation in Cameroon?' Instead of thinking up something like that for you, that useless idiot told you to stick to a story about running away from your father-in-law."

"Winston may be right," Neni said after Jende told her about their conversation, "but if a river has carried a load halfway downstream, why not let it take it all the way to the ocean?"

Jende agreed. Their fate was in the hands of others—what use would it be to get another opinion and find themselves weighing bleak option against bleak option? They would stay with Bubakar; it was all going to work out. They encouraged each other to be hopeful, to believe that they would one day realize the dream of becoming Americans. But that night they each had nightmares that they told the other nothing of the next morning. Jende dreamed of knocks on the doors and strange men in uniform taking him away from his fainting wife and crying children. Neni dreamed of returning to a largely deserted Limbe, a town devoid of the young and ambitious, scantily populated with those too old, too young, and too feeble to flee to distant lands for the riches that could not be gotten in Limbe. In one dream, she saw herself at the annual canoe race at Down Beach, dancing alone as empty canoes approached the shore. When she woke up, she pulled her sleeping daughter closer to her bosom and kissed her. Timba was going to enter Limbe one day as a proud Cameroonian-American returning to see the land of her ancestors, she told herself. Not as the child of failed asylees tossed out of the country like food that had turned sour.

And Liomi was going to become a real American one day, she whispered in the darkness. He had taken so well to America, hardly missing anyone or anything in Limbe. He was happy to be in New York, excited to walk on overcrowded streets and be bombarded by endless noise. He spoke like an American and was so knowledgeable in baseball and all the state capitals that no one who came across him would believe he was not an American but a barely legal immigrant child, a mostly illegal one, in fact, whose future in the country rested on a judge believing his father's incredible story of fleeing persecution. They could never take him back to Limbe. If they took him back he might no longer be the happy child he is and was before coming to America. He might become angry, disappointed and hostile, forever resentful toward his parents.

On the second night after they received the letter, Neni spent most of the hours staring into the darkness, unable to stop thinking these things. The next morning, as she ironed her children's clothes, she sang the hymns the churchgoing people of Limbe sang when life gave them no answers to their questions. She sang a song about having a very big God who was always by her side and another about Jesus never failing even though the man of the world would let her down. Singing the songs reminded her of the times she had visited a church in Limbe and left feeling better, happy and unburdened, because for two hours she had been surrounded by joyful people who believed their circumstances were about to change because an omnipotent Being was in control. During Timba's naps, she searched the Internet for a nearby church to visit. There were many to pick from, most professing acceptance of anyone with any kind of belief, all seemingly just eager to fill up their pews. She decided to go downtown to a church in Greenwich Village called Judson Memorial Church, a brown building facing Washington Square Park, because she enjoyed the street music in the Village and loved the fountain at the center of the park, where she'd taken Liomi to play the past June.

The Sunday before Christmas, while Jende was working, she and the children went to the church. Her mother had warned her not to take the baby too far out of the house before she was three months old, but Neni ignored the advice. She bundled Timba in her carrier and took Liomi by the hand, from the 3 subway to the A. When she got to the West Fourth station, she got out and trudged through Greenwich Village. She walked rapidly, breathing out light clouds in the chilly December morning, eager to get to this place of prayer where she could find respite.

When she got there, she was disappointed in what she saw. Instead of a house of worship filled with a youthful diverse crowd of New Yorkers rocking and jiving and saying "Amen!," the vast pewless room was full of middle-aged white people, not rocking and not jiving but rather singing hymns without the slightest attempt to shake their bodies and cast off their cares and sorrows the way the churchgoers of Limbe did every Sunday morning. Avoiding stares, Neni settled in a seat at the back, the baby still in the carrier, Liomi quiet by her side. The pastor was a woman with long gray hair and red-framed glasses who preached about some kind of coming revolution, a message Neni neither understood nor found applicable to her current situation.

After the service, the pastor came to her and introduced herself as Natasha. Other congregants came over, too, to greet her and to admire Timba sleeping in the carrier. One man said he had worked in Cameroon many years before as a Peace Corps volunteer, far up in the northern region of Adamawa. Neni raised her eyebrows and smiled, surprised and excited to meet someone who had been to her country in a place like that. Though she'd never been to the Adamawa region, she felt as if she'd just reconnected with a long-lost childhood friend.

"I can't believe you have been to my country," she said to the man as she handed her completed visitor information card to an usher. "Some people I meet in America don't even know there is a country called Cameroon."

The man laughed. Yeah, he said, Americans were not renowned for their knowledge of African geography. He even knew of Limbe, he added, though he'd never been there. He wished he'd gone there to sit on its black sand beaches.

"Everyone was so happy to welcome us," Neni told Jende that night.

"Maybe because they don't have black people there, and they want to have a black family," Jende retorted. "Those kind of white people are always trying to prove to their friends how much they like black people."

"I don't care," Neni said. "I like the place. I'm going to go back."

"What for? You didn't even go to church in Limbe. You're not baptized in any church."

"So what if I'm not baptized? Didn't I use to come with you to Mizpah for Christmas and Easter? And didn't I sometimes go to the Full Gospel near our house?"

"That doesn't mean you were a church kind of person."

"Then I'm going to become a church kind of person now. I think it's good for us to start going to church at a time like this. I was watching on the news the other day about this family that was supposed to be deported and they ran to a church. The church people let them stay in the church—the government could not touch them there."

Jende shook his head and let out a short derisive laugh. "So you think that's what we're going to do, eh?" he asked. "What kind of stupid idea is that? I'm not going to hide in any church. How long did the people stay in the church?"

"I don't know. How am I supposed to know?"

"You're the one who thinks it's a good idea. Why would I do such a thing? A grown man like me, hiding in a church? For what?"

"For what?" she said. "You want to know for what, Jende? For your children! That's what for. So your children can continue living in America!"

She stood up from the sofa as she spoke and took a seat at the dinette, irritated by his declaration and not wanting to sit next to him anymore. He seemed taken aback by her sudden anger, infuriated that she dare challenge him on the matter.

"You think I don't care about my children?" he asked her. "You think I won't do anything for us to stay in America?"

"No!" she said, jumping up from the chair and pointing her index finger directly at him. "I don't think you will fight till the end for us to remain here. I think when the time comes, you'll give up, because you care too much about your pride. But I'll do whatever I need to do for us to stay in America! I'll go sleep on a church floor, no matter if I have . . ." She ran to the bedroom and sat on the bed, next to her sleeping daughter.

"What are you crying for?" he said, having followed her and looking angrily at her from the bedroom doorway. "What are those stupid tears for, Neni?"

She ignored him.

"You think I don't want to remain in America, too? You think I came to America so that I can leave? I work as a servant to people, driving them all over, the whole day, sometimes the whole week, answering yes sir, yes madam, bowing down even to a little child. For what, Neni? What pride are you talking about? I lower myself more than many men would ever lower themselves. What do you think I do it for? For you, for me. Because I want us to stay in America! But if America says they don't want us in their country, you think I'm going to keep on begging them for the rest of my life? You think I'm going to sleep in a church? Never. Not for one day. You can go and sleep on the church floor all you want. The day you get tired, you can come and meet me and the children in Limbe. Nonsense!"

He slammed the door behind him and left her whimpering in the bedroom.

Alone in the darkness she cried herself to sleep, Timba on her bosom, Liomi in the cot beside the bed. When she woke up early the next morning, Jende was in the living room, sleeping on the sofa.

Thirty-six

CHRISTMAS WAS THREE DAYS AWAY AND THE DARKNESS THAT HAD FALLEN upon the city appeared to be on hiatus, outshone by the radiance of lighted trees at Rockefeller and Lincoln centers and the mesmerizing displays in shops along Fifth Avenue. Throughout the boroughs, there were steady, if faint, glimmers of hope shining through the windows of apartments where people lived with the belief that the good times would soon return. Even the despondent willed themselves to the streets, to hear something or see someone or go someplace that would remind them that Christmastime was here, springtime was ahead, and in no time it would be summer in New York City again.

"Welcome and a very merry Christmas to you," the pastor Natasha wrote in an email to Neni. "I'm so glad you were able to stop by at Judson, and I'd so love to get a chance to know you more. Please schedule a time to come to the office for a little chat."

Neni scheduled the meeting for the next day and told Jende nothing of it.

In the church office, she met the assistant pastor, a redheaded and bearded young man from New Hampshire named Amos. He told Neni he used to be a Buddhist monk before deciding that progressive liberal Christianity was more aligned with his beliefs than Buddhism. Neni was curious about the difference between the two but thought it wise not to ask—asking might lay bare her ignorance about religion and spiritual matters and expose her true motive for coming to the church.

In private, the pastor Natasha was a more subdued woman than the fiery preacher who had stood at the pulpit and spoken about the need for a revolution that would shake the country to its core. Her mid-back-length gray hair was straight and side-parted, and Neni couldn't help admiring her courage in growing her gray hair long, and for leaving it gray in a city where there was no shortage of salons eager to rescue middle-aged women from grayness. There were framed pictures of happy families on the bookshelves in her office, families of all kinds: two fathers and a baby; two mothers and a toddler; an old man and an old woman and a dog; a young man and a young woman and a newborn. Natasha told Neni they were all congregants in the church. She asked Neni about her family and what brought her to Judson. I think I want to become a Christian, Neni responded, to which Natasha replied that she did not need to become a Christian to join the Judson family. Neni was relieved, though she still wanted to become a baptized Christian— what if the people at the Full Gospel Church near her house in Limbe were right about heaven and hell? She wanted to be on the safe side so she could get into heaven if it ended up being real. Her family didn't go to church (except for a brief period after her father lost his seaport job), but she believed there was a God with a son named Jesus, though she had a hard time believing that people speaking in tongues were truly possessed by some Spirit. You can believe whatever you want, and we'll accept you here, Natasha told her. We take everyone. From anywhere. We don't care if you believe in heaven and hell and pearly gates. We don't even care if you believe that the best way to get to heaven is by subway or Metro-North or LIRR, she added, which made Neni laugh.

Over tea, they spoke about motherhood and marriage. So open was their conversation about the sacrifice of dreams in parenthood and the loss of self in marriage that Neni went further than she thought she would and told Natasha about Jende's deportation case. She told her about their argument on Sunday and the shame she would experience if she had to return to Limbe; the sense of failure she might never escape for not having given her children a good life, a life full of opportunities, the kind of life that would be all but impossible for them to have in Cameroon. Natasha listened and nodded, allowing the stricken woman to release months' worth of tears. She offered Neni a tissue and took Timba when—perhaps sensing her mother's distress—the baby began to cry, too.

"The American immigration system can be cruel," she told Neni, rubbing her knee, "but Judson will stand and fight with you. We will stand with you till the end."

Neni Jonga walked out of Judson and into Washington Square Park that afternoon with the lightness of a beautifully crafted kite. There was a man playing a flute on a bench, and a young woman in a black down jacket playing a violin. She smiled as she walked through the park listening to them—she hadn't realized until then how divine classical music was. On the other side of the park, beneath the arch, a group of young people held placards, chanting and protesting the bailout. Bail us out, not our oppressors! Why are you using our taxes to destroy us? Death to Wall Street! Paulson the Antichrist!

Neni stood by the empty fountain and watched them, admiring their passion for their country. One of them in particular was a pleasure to watch, a dreadlocked young white man who was prancing and shaking his fist at their absent foes. Someday, Neni thought, if Judson could help them stay in America, she would be an American citizen and she would be able to protest like that, too. She'd say whatever she wanted to say about powerful people and have no fear of being thrown into prison the way dissidents were being thrown into prisons in some African countries for speaking out against abominable authoritarian regimes. She wanted to skip around the park, rejuvenated by the hope that had been handed to her by a compassionate woman of the cloth, but she couldn't—Timba was waking up from the cold, and she had to pick up Liomi from his last day of school and cook dinner.

When Jende came home from work at close to midnight, she hurriedly dished out his food and sat at the dinette as he took off his jacket, unable to wait any longer to tell him the amazing news of how the people of Judson would help them stay in America.

"I went down to the church in the Village today," she began after he'd had a few bites of his dinner.

"What for?"

"It wasn't for anything. The pastor sent me an email to welcome me and said I should come for a visit, so I went."

"You didn't think you should tell me before going?"

"I'm sorry. You were angry the last time I went. I didn't want you to get angry again."

He glared at her and returned to his potatoes and spinach. She pretended the look wasn't half as nasty as he'd intended it to be. She had to forgive him easily these days or her marriage would be doomed. She just had to, because he hadn't been the same man since the day the letter for the deportation hearing arrived. The weight of the letter was crushing him, she could see; he was now a man permanently at the edge of his breaking point. No longer did he reach over to stroke her hair while she nursed the baby. He did not care to playfully punch Liomi in the ribs. The husband who seldom uttered words like "stupid" and "idiot" was now throwing those words left and right, in moments of rage and frustration, directing them at nameless Immigration officials, his lawyer, his family in Cameroon, his son, and, most of all, his wife. He scolded his mother for asking for money to patch the kitchen wall and barked at Liomi when the child asked if his father could take him to an arcade. He pushed his food away if he thought it didn't have enough salt or pepper, and ignored phone calls from his friends. It was as if the letter of his court appointment had turned him from a happy living man to an outraged dying man intent on showing the world his anger at his impending death.

"The pastor told me that the church will help us stay in the country," Neni said.

"What are you talking about?"

"Our *papier* situation. I told the pastor about it—"

"You did what!" he said, banging the table.

She said nothing.

He pushed his food aside and stood up.

"Are you crazy?" he said, pointing to his temple. "Are you losing your mind, Neni? Have you lost your mind? How dare you discuss my *papier* situation with those people without asking me first? Have you really lost your mind?" He was fuming and breathing heavily. Beneath him, she sat like a lamb before a teeth-baring lion.

"What's wrong with you? What is wrong with you these days? You think you have the right to go about discussing something like that with other people without asking me first? Do you know who these people really are? You think because you go to their church for one day you can tell them my private business? Eh, Neni? Are you crazy?"

She did not offer an excuse. She knew she had gone too far—Bubakar had warned them to guard their immigration story and share it with no one. You tell person say you no get paper, the lawyer had said, the day you get palaver with them, they go call Immigration, report you. "No one except me, you, the Almighty, and the American government should know how you entered this country and how you're trying to stay in it," he had cautioned them repeatedly. He knew of the consequence of their scheme being leaked to the government by a hateful individual: It could spell the end not only for them but for him, too.

Neni had agreed with the lawyer's advice; she believed in the value of keeping certain matters private to protect from negativity and malice. To her, it was not only wise but easy—keeping crucial facts concealed was as effortless to her as singing. Back when she was a teenager, she had told no one besides Jende about her pregnancy with their deceased daughter. She had waited to tell even her parents until she was five months along, tactfully hiding her growing belly with oversize *ka-*

*ba*s and handbags. It was equally easy for her to hide their immigration travails in New York. Except for Betty and Fatou, she told no one. When asked by other friends about her family's legal status, she dodged the question by casually saying that their papers would be arriving very soon.

Despite her shame, she had told Natasha about their plight because she believed there were Americans who wanted to keep good hardworking immigrants in America. She'd seen them on the news, compassionate Americans talking about how the United States should be more welcoming to people who came in peace. She believed these kindhearted people, like Natasha, would never betray them, and she wanted to tell Jende this, that the people of Judson Memorial Church loved immigrants, that their secret was safe with Natasha. But she also knew it would be futile reasoning with a raging man, so she decided to sit quietly with her head bowed as he unleashed a verbal lashing, as he called her a stupid idiot and a bloody fool. The man who had promised to always take care of her was standing above her vomiting a parade of insults, spewing out venom she never thought he had inside him.

For the first time in a long love affair, she was afraid he would beat her. She was almost certain he would beat her. And if he had, she would have known that it was not her Jende who was beating her but a grotesque being created by the sufferings of an American immigrant life.

Thirty-seven

On Christmas morning they ate fried ripe plantains and beans but exchanged no gifts since Jende did not want Liomi believing that the giving and receiving of material gifts had anything to do with love. Anyone can go to the shop and buy anything and give to anyone, he told Liomi when the boy asked him for the umpteenth time why he couldn't get even a little toy truck. The true measure of whether somebody really loves you, he lectured, is what they do for you with their hands and say to you with their mouth and think of you in their heart. Liomi had protested, but on Christmas morning, as on all the previous Christmas mornings of his life, he got no gifts.

In the afternoon they ate rice and chicken stew, like most of the households in Limbe. Neni made *chin-chin* and cake, too, using the cake recipe she'd relied on in Limbe in the days when she baked over a blistering fire in an iron pot filled with sand. The night before, while the whole family was on the sofa watching *It's a Wonderful Life*, Jende had thought about inviting Leah to spend the day with them, since she was probably all alone in her Queens apartment being that she had no husband or children or living parents. He hated to think that Leah would be alone on a day when everyone should be with someone, but he didn't want to ask too much of Neni, because he was certain that if Leah accepted his invitation, Neni would cook seven different dishes for the American coming to her house, and he knew he would feel bad that she was doing it while also taking care of Liomi and the baby. So he merely called Leah in the morning to wish her a merry Christmas. He told her work was going well, then listened as she told him about her plans to go to Rockefeller Center later in the day, speaking excitedly, as if going to stand in the cold and look at a tree was such a wonderful thing.

For the rest of the day he told Liomi stories and rocked Timba to sleep after her feedings. No one came to visit them the way people did in Limbe, going from house to house, saying, "Happy, happy, oh!," and yet it was a happy Christmas for him, far happier than his first Christmas in America.

On that day he had lain on his upper-level bunk bed all morning and afternoon in the basement apartment he shared with the Puerto Ricans in the Bronx, the weather outside too cold for a walk, the people on the streets too unknown to celebrate the specialness of the day with. With Winston gone to Aruba to vacation with a woman he was dating, he had no one to eat and laugh with, and reminisce with about the Christmases of his boyhood, which always involved too much eating, too much drinking, and way too much dancing. Lying in the dark room, he had pictured Liomi in the red suit he'd sent for him to wear to celebrate the day; he'd smiled at the thought of his son strolling around town and proudly telling everyone who asked that his clothes were from his papa in America. He imagined Neni taking Liomi to New Town, to wish a happy Christmas to his mother who must have prepared a meal of chicken stew with yams and a side of *ndolé*, as well as a dish of plantains and *nyama ngowa*. He yearned to hear their voices, but there was no way for him to talk to them—the telephone lines from the Western world to much of Cameroon were overcrowded and bursting with the voices of those like him, the lonely and nostalgic,

calling home to partake in the Christmas merrymaking, if only with
their words. Frustrated, he had flung his calling card away and stayed
in bed until four o'clock in the afternoon, making only one call, to his
friend Arkamo in Phoenix, a call that did nothing to lessen his lone-
someness because Arkamo was having a grand time at a Cameroonian
party, thanks to living in a city with a large close-knit Cameroonian
community. After a shower and a dinner of Chinese leftovers, he had
sat by the window in the common area, wrapped in his twin comforter
and looking outside: at the weather so dull; at the people so colorlessly
dressed; at the happy day slipping away so quickly and crushing him
with longing.

Five days after Christmas, he returned to work, only to find there
wasn't much to do. Clark was at a hotel, Anna told him when he called
to ask her why the boss wasn't picking up his phone; he was going to
do most of his work from there, she added. Cindy was taking time off
from work (probably since the day of the tabloid story, Jende guessed,
since Anna had called him the day after, while he was on his way back
from dropping Mighty off at school, and told him that he didn't need
to come to the Sapphire because Cindy would not be needing a ride
to her office). The only person who needed to get around that day was
Mighty, to his piano lesson and back. All Jende had to do, Anna said,
was take Mighty to his teacher's building on the Upper West Side,
hand him over to Stacy, who was meeting him there, and then bring
Mighty and Stacy back to the Sapphire an hour later, unless Mighty
wanted Stacy to take him to do something else, which was unlikely,
since Mighty wanted to do nothing this winter break except sit alone
in his bedroom. Jende could go home after that and the rest of the
holidays would be equally light because, Anna said, whispering in a
frightened voice, there was no way of knowing how long Clark would
stay at the hotel or how much longer Cindy would keep herself locked
in the apartment now that she wasn't even going out to do things with
friends, being that her drinking was getting worse and poor Mighty

now had two parents who— Anna caught herself before she could say too much and said she had to go.

"Mighty, my good friend," Jende said after Mighty had settled in the backseat. "How was your Christmas?"

"I don't wanna talk about it."

"Okay, okay, there is nothing wrong with that. You do not have to tell me, except for one thing—did you get to Skype with Vince?"

"Yeah, Mom called him."

"How is he?"

Mighty shrugged and did not respond.

"He is having fun over there? Did he tell you some good stories about India?"

"He has dreadlocks."

"Dreadlocks?" Jende asked, almost laughing at his visualization of Vince with dreadlocks. He liked the look of white people with dreadlocks, but Vince Edwards, son of Clark and Cindy Edwards, with dreadlocks? The look on Cindy's face must have been worth taking a picture of.

"Yeah," Mighty said. "He has, like, some funny-looking dreadlocks."

"Really? Did he look good with it? I'm sure he still looks very handsome, right?"

"I don't know."

Jende decided it was best to leave Mighty alone. He clearly did not want to talk, and attempts to cheer him up seemed to be making him only sadder.

"They fought in the kitchen last night," Mighty said suddenly, after minutes of silence.

"Who? Your mommy and daddy?"

Mighty nodded.

"Oh, Mighty, I am so sorry to hear. But remember what I told you about married people fighting? Your mommy and daddy fighting does not mean anything bad. Married people like to fight sometimes. They even shout and scream at each other, but it does not mean anything, okay?"

Mighty did not respond. Jende heard him sniffle and hoped he wasn't crying again—the child had cried enough.

"I heard my mom crying, throwing stuff at the wall . . . I think it was glasses and plates, they were breaking. My dad was shouting for her to please stop it . . . but she was . . ." He pulled a tissue from the pack of tissues Jende was offering him and blew his nose.

"Your parents are going to be friends again soon, Mighty," Jende said, not only to convince Mighty but to convince himself, too.

"She was saying, 'I don't ever wanna see his face again.' She was telling my dad that he had to get rid of him, get rid of him right now, or else . . ."

"Get rid of who?"

"I don't know, but she was screaming it over and over. And my dad was saying, 'I won't do it,' and my mom was screaming that he had to, otherwise she was going to do something . . ."

"I'm so sorry to hear all this, Mighty. But your mommy, she was just angry, right?"

"She was very angry. She was crying and screaming so loud."

Jende inhaled and exhaled.

"I couldn't sleep," Mighty went on. "I covered my head with my pillow but—"

"They did not say the name of this person?"

Mighty shook his head. "But I think it was Vince."

"Vince?"

"Yeah, my mom was really upset about the dreadlocks. She said he looked like a hooligan."

"No, Mighty," Jende said, laughing lightly. "There is no way your mommy will ask your daddy to get rid of Vince. Your mommy loves you and Vince a lot—"

"They're going to get a divorce!"

"No, please don't say that," Jende said, holding the steering wheel with one hand and reaching behind to rub Mighty's leg with the other. "Do not say these kinds of things and make yourself angry. They will be happy again. It is just how grown people are. They will be friends again."

"No, they won't! They're getting divorced!"

"Please do not make yourself sad worrying about things that will never happen," Jende said as he struggled to drive with one hand. "Everything will be all right, Mighty . . . Everything will be all right . . . Everybody will be all right . . . Please wipe your eyes."

When they got to the building on Eighty-ninth Street and Columbus, Stacy came out to get Mighty. Jende watched as the boy forced a smile and told Stacy that yes, he was super-excited about the piece the teacher had planned for the day.

Jende got back in the car after Mighty and Stacy had left, and called Winston, who, thankfully, picked up his phone on the first ring even though he had barely picked it up since the day he went to Houston to visit Maami.

"Ah, Bo, you and your worries," Winston said after Jende told him about Cindy wanting to get rid of someone. "She could be talking about ten different people. Maybe she was talking about—"

"It has to be me," Jende said, shaking his head in disbelief. "There is no other man who works for her. Anna is a woman, Stacy is a woman, her assistant is a woman. Everyone except me."

"Then maybe it wasn't someone who works for her. Women like her, they have all kinds of people who do different kinds of things for them. Doctors who take care of their wrinkles, people who do their hair, people who do their decorations—"

"You really think she would be screaming in the middle of the night to tell her husband to get rid of the person who does her decorations? Ah, Bo . . ."

"Okay, okay, fine. I just don't want you to worry, that's all. You cannot hear a story from a little child and start shaking like a leaf, eh?

Don't do this to yourself. You keep acting like this and tomorrow a heart attack will hit you, let me warn you. You don't know anything. You don't even know if the child heard correctly, eh?"

"Without this job, what will I do? My whole body is shaking. What am I going to do if they—"

"Hey, what is all this *sisa* for? Eh? Listen, if you're so afraid, I can call Frank and ask him. If Cindy wants Clark to fire you, Clark will not hide it from Frank. And I can ask Frank to help you convince Clark."

"Yes, please, that'll be the best idea. He's the one who helped me get the job. And he likes me . . . Please do that. Every time I drive him and Mr. Edwards together, he is nice to me."

"So there's nothing for you to worry about. I'll call him tomorrow, okay?"

"I don't know how to thank you, Bo."

"Give me your firstborn son to be my servant," Winston said, forcing Jende to laugh.

After he got off the phone, Jende leaned his head against the headrest, closed his eyes, and told himself to think of only good things. His father had always told him that: Even when things are bad, think of only good things. And Jende had done that as often as he could during his darkest days—while in prison after impregnating Neni; after his daughter had died late one night and Neni's father had ordered her buried first thing in the morning, denying him the chance to say goodbye; after Neni's father had denied his request to marry her for what seemed like the hundredth time; after he'd gotten a call from one of Neni's sisters, seven months after he arrived in America, telling him that Neni and Liomi had been involved in a bus accident on their way to visit Neni's aunt in Muyuka. In those moments he had done only what was in his power and thought of the countless number of good things that had happened in his past, and the many good things that were highly certain to happen in his future.

He'd done it when he felt powerless, like during those four months he'd spent in prison in Buea, waiting for his father to borrow enough money to convince Neni's father to request his release. Everything about prison had been far more horrendous than he'd imagined: the cold mountain air, which made his skin itch and had him shivering from evening to morning; the inadequate portions of barely palatable food; the dormitories packed end to end with snoring men every night; the easily transmittable diseases, like the dysentery he'd caught, which had lasted two weeks and kept him writhing all day from stomach cramps and a high fever. It was during the nights of his illness that he thought about his life, about what he would do with it once he was released. He couldn't think of anything he wanted more than to leave Cameroon, move to a country where decent young men weren't thrown into prison for minor crimes but were instead given opportunities to make something of their lives. When he finally got out of prison—after his father had given Neni's father enough money to cover Neni's maternity bills and the child's expenses for the first year of life, and after Pa Jonga had promised that Jende would stay away from Neni indefinitely—Jende returned to Limbe, determined to start saving money to leave the country. He got a job at the Limbe Urban Council, thanks to his friend Bosco, who worked there, and began putting away as much as he could every month for a future with Neni. For a year after his release, though, Neni wanted little to do with him, first because of her father's threat to kick her out if she continued wasting her life on Jende, and later because of her grief over the dead baby. Jende finally won her back—thanks to his bimonthly hand-delivered love letters splattered with words like "indefatigable" and "pulchritudinous"—but his dreams of a life for them in America always seemed farther than the nearest star when he compared his savings to the cost of an airline ticket. It was only thanks to Winston's job as a Wall Street lawyer, more than a decade later, that he was able to get the funds to journey to America to start a new life.

Liberating as it was, though, the new life had come with its share of new pains. It had wrought new forms of helplessness he hadn't considered, like the dread and despair he'd experienced when Neni and

Liomi were both in the hospital after the bus accident. Although their injuries were not critical (a black eye and swollen face for Liomi; a sprained neck and broken wrist, plus cuts and bruises, for Neni), he couldn't stop thinking that he might have gotten a different kind of call from Neni's sister, a call not to inform him of their injuries and ask for money for their hospital bills but to tell him that they were dead and ask for money for their funeral expenses. The thought of them dying while he was stuck in America had turned his blood icy, so as often as he could, he had told himself to think of good things and good things only.

Which was what he was now doing in the car with his eyes closed. He thought about Mr. and Mrs. Edwards reconciling and being happy again, the way Vince had told him they were back when they lived in Alexandria, Virginia, before his father began working eighty hours a week at Lehman and traveling four, five times a month, and before his mother stopped smiling as much as she used to, except when she was with her sons or her friends or when she was at an event where she felt compelled to pretend to the world that she was a happy woman in a happy marriage. Jende was not sure the Edwardses' marriage would ever return to those happy days long gone, when there was less money and more togetherness and Vince was an only child, but that was okay, because some marriages did not need to be happy. They needed only to be sufficiently comfortable, and he hoped the Edwardses would at least find that.

He thought of Vince in India and wished him success in his pursuit of Truth and Oneness. He hoped the family would be together again one day and he would continue driving them for years. He loved his job, and if God willed, he would be happy to do it for as long as he lived in New York. There were hard days, but Mr. Edwards was a good man, the boys were good boys, and Mrs. Edwards, even when she acted as if the whole world had let her down, was a good woman.

His phone rang as he was opening his eyes. He looked at his caller ID. It was Mr. Edwards. He smiled. He had just thought of him and now he was calling—that meant Mr. Edwards was going to live a long life.

"How was your Christmas?" Clark asked him.

"Very good, sir. I hope you had a good one, too, sir?"

"Good enough," Clark said. He paused, then cleared his throat. "Are you waiting for Mighty?"

"Yes, sir."

"Right. Listen, do me a favor, will you? After you've dropped off Mighty, can you come down to the office?"

"You are at the office now, sir?"

"Yeah, just got in, I took a cab. I didn't want to take you away from Mighty."

"I understand, sir. I will come down the moment I drop Mighty at home."

"Good, great. And . . . can you park the car and come upstairs? I need . . . we need to talk."

Thirty-eight

HE FOUND HIMSELF IN MIDTOWN NOT KNOWING HOW HE GOT THERE. HE might have run a couple of red lights without realizing, changed lanes without signaling, stayed too close to the car ahead of him. He might have driven on the curb and he wouldn't have noticed, because he certainly didn't notice any of the thousands of people on Broadway. He was that dazed.

When he got to the garage he pulled out his briefcase from beneath his seat and held it on his lap for a full minute. Owning the briefcase and carrying it every day to work—that was one of his greatest career prides. It made him feel accomplished, like he was a sort of big man himself, not just a little man driving a big man around. Two months after he began working for the Edwardses, he had gone shopping for the perfect briefcase and found this one in a store on the Grand Concourse in the Bronx, a black faux-leather rectangular box with a nickel-plated handle. It looked like the ones the white-collar workers at Limbe Urban Council used to take to work, the ones he'd admired as their bearers strode into offices while he remained outside, cleaning streets and emptying garbage cans. With his own briefcase, he'd become a white-collar professional, too. Every morning, before leaving for work, he packed his lunch inside the box, next to his dictionary, a map of the city, a handkerchief, a pack of tissues, pens, and old newspaper and magazine articles he hoped to read. On the downtown subway, dressed in his suit and clip-on tie, he held it firmly, looking no different from the accountants and engineers and financial advisors sitting next to him.

He placed the briefcase on the passenger seat and opened the glove compartment. It was better he remove everything he owned from the car, he told himself. He wasn't being fearful or pessimistic—it was just better a man be prepared for a meeting that could go either way. Mr. Edwards probably just wanted to talk, tell him something he needed to start doing, or stop doing. The meeting was most certainly going to end with him smiling, chiding himself for sweating even before he got out of the car. But what if it didn't end happily? Of course it was going to end happily. It was probably going to . . . most likely going to . . . but it was best he took out everything he owned and tidied up the car. He searched in the glove compartment, but there was nothing of his in it, nothing he'd tossed in there and forgotten to take out. He'd always been diligent about that, keeping everything he owned, even his garbage, in his briefcase; even though he spent hours a day in the car, practically lived in it all day, he was constantly aware that it wasn't his car and it would never be.

He turned around and checked the backseat. It was impeccable, as were the mats, thanks to his visit to a car wash just before Christmas. If he had to leave, he would leave everything in a good condition. But he wasn't leaving. He was just going to have a talk with Mr. Edwards about something. A simple talk. Nothing more.

He put on his gloves and hat, picked up the briefcase, and stepped out of the car.

For the first time in his life he was grateful for winter, for its breath, which was taking away the sweat on his brow. He felt refreshed by the light wind blowing south as he walked toward Barclays in the early evening's darkness, going past men in suits, some with briefcases, some with messenger bags, some with no bags, probably because they'd left them at their desks, certain of their return to work the next day.

In the Barclays lobby, the guard, perhaps ready to leave and start an early celebration of the coming New Year, distractedly nodded when Jende said hello, and did not ask for his ID. He misspelled Jende's name and handed him a visitor pass without glancing at him, his attention on the woman he was chatting and laughing with, a female security guard who was swearing that 2009 would be her year, the year she finally got herself a real good man.

In the elevator he stood next to two men talking about their year-end bonuses. Mr. Edwards had mentioned a raise, but he'd said nothing about a bonus. Could that be what he wanted to talk about? That would be very kind of Mr. Edwards, but he didn't think he needed a bonus on top of a good salary, a raise, and good treatment. If Mr. Edwards offered him a bonus he would have to do that thing American people do when they want something but are somewhat embarrassed to take it—he would protest lightly, saying, oh, no, sir, you don't have to; really, sir, it's not necessary; you really don't need to, sir . . . and then he'd take the money.

"Good evening, sir," he said as the receptionist closed the door behind him. Clark was sitting at his desk, writing on a legal pad. He lifted his head, smiled, and, without words, motioned for Jende to have a seat. He continued writing.

Jende sat down and told himself to breathe, because breathe was all he could do.

If there were lights sparkling outside the window adjacent to Clark's desk, he did not see them. If there were any paintings on the wall, anything worthwhile about this new office, he didn't notice. The only thing he noticed was his breath and his heart beating like the drums he used to play in his boyhood when the moon was full and children danced in the streets of New Town till midnight.

Clark put aside his writing pad, looked up at Jende, and clasped his hands together on the desk. "I hope you know, Jende," he began, "that I think very highly of you."

"Thank you, sir."

"You've been by far my favorite chauffeur . . . there really isn't any comparison, by any stretch of the imagination. You're hardworking, you're respectful, you're a good guy to be around. It's been really great."

Please say what you want to say quickly before I die, Jende pleaded inwardly, even as he nodded, managed a half-smile, and said, "I am so glad you like my work, sir."

Clark ran his fingers through his hair. He exhaled, shook his head, and rubbed his eyes. For a moment Jende wasn't sure what the man wanted to say. Was he sick and wanted him to know what it would be like working for a sick man? Was he moving and wanted Jende to move with him? It seemed as if the discussion was going to be about him, not Jende. But then Clark looked at him, and Jende could see it in his eyes.

"I'm really sorry, Jende," he said, "but I'm going to have to let you go."

Jende bowed his head. So this was happening to him. It *was* happening.

"I'm really sorry," Clark said again.

Jende kept his head bowed. He had been prepared for it, and yet unprepared. A hundred different emotions overcame him but he wasn't sure which to surrender to.

"I know it's a horrible time for something like this to happen, with the new baby—"

"Why, sir?" he asked, looking up.

"Why?"

"Yes, sir!" he said. "I want to know why!"

He couldn't control himself. Anger had defeated the other ninety-nine emotions, and there was no use trying to contain it. The sweat on his palms was no longer of fear but of fury. "Tell me why, sir!" he repeated.

"It's . . . it's complicated."

"Is it Mrs. Edwards, sir?"

Clark did not respond. He looked away to avoid Jende's eyes.

"Is it because of Mrs. Edwards?" Jende asked again. His voice was loud—he couldn't keep it down.

"There's just too much going on now, Jende . . . I'm really sorry. I'm trying to do the best I can . . . I really am, but, apparently, it's not good enough, and it's . . . it's all getting to be a bit too much."

"You still have not told me if it's Mrs. Edwards, sir!"

"I'm just . . . It's a very complicated—"

"Don't lie to me, sir! It's her!" Jende said, standing up and pushing his chair back. He picked up his briefcase from the floor and slammed it on the table so hard Clark jerked backward.

"It's the book, sir!" he said as he flipped open the briefcase and pulled out the blue notebook. He flung the briefcase back on the floor and held the book up in his hand, glaring at Clark as he shook the book vigorously. "It's this stupid book, isn't it, Mr. Edwards?" he shouted, his voice pained, angry, defeated, betrayed. "You told me what to write for her, and I wrote it. I wrote only what you told me to write. That's what I did, sir! So, please tell me, sir! It is this book, isn't it, Mr. Edwards?"

Clark did not reply. He did not ask Jende to lower his voice. He covered his face with his hands, rubbed his eyes again.

"I only did what you told me to do, sir! I do this for you, Mr. Edwards! But she doesn't like it because she believes something else, is that not so, sir? She thinks I am a liar. She thinks I am a liar, right, sir? But I am not a liar! I swear by my grandfather that I would never do anything to cause trouble in another man's house. What I did, I did so you will not have any trouble. And now you will punish me, sir? You will punish me and make my children suffer for doing what you told me to do?"

"I'm so sorry—"

"Don't be sorry for me!" Jende cried, slamming the book on the desk. "I don't want sorry. I want a job! I need this job, Mr. Edwards.

Please don't do this to me! Please, I'm begging you, Mr. Edwards, for the sake of my wife and my children and my parents! For the sake of me and my family, please, please, sir, I'm begging you . . . don't do this to me."

He sat down, sweating and panting. His handkerchief was in his briefcase, but there was no use pulling it out to wipe his sweat.

Clark opened a drawer in his desk, took out a check, and handed it to him. "Your paycheck for the rest of the week," he said. "Plus more."

Jende took the check without looking at him, folded it without looking at the check. He got out of his seat and stooped by his briefcase, picked up his lunch container and his dictionary, which had fallen out when he threw the briefcase on the floor. After slipping the check into the dictionary, he stood up, adjusted his suit, and lifted his briefcase.

Clark Edwards stood up, too, and offered him a hand.

"Thank you for everything, Jende," Clark said, shaking Jende's weak hand.

"Good night, sir."

Thirty-nine

REJOICING WITH OTHERS IN THEIR TIMES OF JOY AND YOUR TIMES OF SORrow is a mark of true love, Natasha preached at Judson. It shows an ability to subjugate the ego and view one's self not as a separate entity but as a vital piece of the Divine Oneness.

Neni wanted to tell Jende about Natasha's message when she returned home from church. She wanted to say that in spite of their circumstances, they should be happy because there was so much happiness in the world and because all of humanity was one. She wanted to say all this and more, but couldn't, because she wasn't sure if she believed it. She was hopeless, and there was nothing anyone else's happiness could do about it.

The Jende who had returned home to her on the night of his firing was a husband pitilessly bowed by life. She had suspected something was wrong that night but she did not deem it right to push an exhausted man to talk, so she let him be. He went to bed without eating, saying nothing to her except that he'd had a bad day and was very tired.

"I won't be working for Mr. Edwards anymore," he told her at five o'clock the next morning, when she woke up to feed Timba.

What happened? she wanted to know. Oh, God. What happened? How were they going to manage? How could this be happening now? With the court date only a couple of months away?

Nothing happened, he told her. Mr. Edwards is a good man and has been very happy with his service. He just did not need him anymore.

"But why!"

"He didn't say why. He just thanked me and said he won't be needing me anymore."

"Oh, Papa God. Why, oh, Papa God, why?"

They would survive, he assured her. Mr. Edwards had given him a nice goodbye check which was equal to two months' salary. By the time the money ran out, he should be back driving a cab in the Bronx. He only had to call Mr. Jones and get his old job back.

"Have we not come this far?" he asked her, holding her by the shoulders and looking into her eyes. "If someone had told us back when we were in Limbe and I was collecting garbage that we would be in New York City, would we have believed it?"

She shook her head and closed her eyes to release her tears. Timba was cooing on the bed next to them, still living in a perfect world.

"It's Mrs. Edwards!" she said.

"It doesn't matter, *bébé*."

"It's her!"

"Come," he said, drawing her to his chest.

Forty

MR. JONES, THE OWNER OF THE LIVERY CABS, HAD NO SHIFTS FOR HIM. "People are lining up around the block to drive a cab," he said. "Too many people. Don't even got enough cars to rent to everyone."

"Not even graveyard shift?" Jende asked. "I'll take anything."

"I only got five cars. Five cars and fourteen people who wanna drive them."

Jende tried to coax him into taking shifts from other drivers to give to him. "But I used to take good care of the car, Mr. Jones, remember? No accidents. No scratches."

"Sorry, bro. Ain't no more shifts. Nothing for the next two months. I'll call ya if someone calls to cancel, promise. Keep you on standby."

Neni came into the bedroom as he was ending the call. His head hung so low it seemed in danger of falling off. She sat beside him on the bed.

"We still have a good amount of money saved," she said, placing her hand on his lap.

"So what?"

"So, let's not worry too much, eh?"

"Yes," he said, standing up. "Let's not worry until all the money is gone."

He went into the living room, sat on the sofa, and turned on the TV. Less than a minute later he turned it off—he couldn't watch. To be sitting at home jobless seemed the worst punishment of all. The idleness. The worthlessness. Watching television when others were at work felt completely profane—it was what little children and old people and sick people did, not able men.

"You want me to make you some fried ripe plantains and eggs?" Neni whispered, stooping beside him with her hands on his knees. She was trying too hard, he could tell. It wasn't for her to save him. He had to save himself.

"No," he said, standing up and walking toward the door. "I need some air."

The next week, after a series of long restless nights, he got a job washing dishes at two restaurants. One of the restaurants he used to work for, when he first came to New York, back before he got a driver's license and started driving a cab. On his first day back a colleague told him about an opening at another restaurant in Hell's Kitchen. He took the subway there right after his shift and got that job, too. With the two jobs, he worked mornings, afternoons, evenings. He worked weekends, too. For six days of the week he left before Liomi woke up and came back after he was in bed. For working all those hours, he got less than half of what he used to make working for Clark Edwards.

Better this than to be like all those people with no jobs in this bad economy, he consoled himself. Still, it was an undignified fall. To be wearing a suit and holding a briefcase every day, driving to important places, eavesdropping on important conversations, only to now find himself scraping leftovers from plates and loading them into a dishwasher. To once have driven a Lexus to executive meetings, only to now stand in a corner cleaning silverware. To once have had hours of free time to sit in the car and catch up on his phone calls, call Neni to check on her day, call his parents to check on their health, call his friends back in Limbe for the latest news, only to now have a mere fifteen minutes here and there to sit and rest his hands or have a free meal from the kitchen.

Three weeks into the jobs, his feet began to ache.

"Maybe it's arthritis," Neni suggested, since his father had the same condition. Pa Jonga's fingers and toes had curled up and out from the disease, and Jende always feared it was inheritable. "You have to go see a doctor," she said after he had spent a whole night groaning, unable to fall asleep.

He agreed, but where was he going to find the time? he asked her. Besides, he didn't think it could be arthritis. He was not yet forty, he was young and strong; the pain would go away. A bit of massaging after work would be good enough. So she rubbed them with coconut oil and bound them up every night. In the morning they felt better, ready for twelve or more hours of dishwashing.

She begged him to let her go back to work.

She could call the agency and get another home health aide job really fast. Two incomes would be better than one at a time like this, she argued. He said no—he wanted her home. She was his wife; he would take care of her. He couldn't imagine her leaving a newborn in a daycare they could barely afford and running off to work all day only to return home tired, overwhelmed, and guilt-ridden. And then, no matter how exhausted she was, she'd still have to cater to an infant, a boy, and a grown man. It was his responsibility to protect her from such a life. If he couldn't then he wasn't fulfilling his duty, which was how he felt on the nights he returned home to find her worried because the baby was running out of diapers and Liomi needed a new pair of shoes and there wasn't enough money to buy beef so she could cook rice and beef stew. Whenever he saw her anxiety, he was tempted to take out some of the money from their savings, but he resisted. They would manage with the little he was making at the restaurants. She had to return to school in the fall. His deportation case wasn't over. The worst might still be ahead.

On the day of his court appearance, he wore the black suit he had worn to work on his first day working for the Edwardses. Neni had washed and ironed it the night before, neatly placing it on the sofa for him to wear in the morning. Neither of them ate dinner that night, their appetites having been vanquished by their fears. He stayed on the phone talking to Winston while she sat at the computer reading stories about individuals who lost their deportation cases and families who found themselves straddling two countries because one of the parents had been deported. Whatever happens, we will take it as it comes, he told her before they went to bed, and she nodded in agreement, her eyes filling up with tears.

"You're sleeping?" he whispered to her in the middle of the night.

"No. I can't sleep."

"What are we going to do?" he asked her, his voice plaintive, clearly desperate to be reminded that they would be okay.

"I don't know what we're going to do . . . I don't even know."

They couldn't move close to each other and fall asleep in a comforting embrace—the baby was sleeping between them—so they held hands around the baby.

In the morning he stood next to Bubakar as the lawyer answered most of the judge's questions, speaking in an unquestionable American accent. Bubakar and the judge and the attorney for ICE took turns saying things Jende did not understand. The judge set a date in June for Jende to appear before him again. Bubakar thanked the judge. The judge called for the next case. The whole exchange had lasted less than ten minutes.

"You see what I told you?" Bubakar said, grinning as they exited the federal building. "I continue doing this and we continue buying you time. For now, you're a free man!"

Jende nodded, though he didn't feel free. It seemed to him a rather pathetic way of being, postponing the inevitable. He would much rather be truly free.

Forty-one

SHE SAT ON THE CROSSTOWN BUS WITH THE GIFT BAG ON HER LAP, WATCH-
ing as shoppers entered and exited clothing stores and corner bodegas,
electronics stores and jewelry boutiques, beauty supply stores and fast-
food joints. Traffic on 125th Street was slow—the M60 bus was moving
and stopping every quarter-minute—but she remained calm, listening
as two men behind her chatted about the Obama inauguration.

I wouldn't have missed it for nothing, the first man said.

My son says to me, I ain't coming to stand for hours in no cold, the
second man said.

Cold?

Can you believe these children? A historic moment and you're
gonna be talking nonsense about no cold weather?

The first man chuckled.

I got bumps all over me still, thinking about when that pastor came
up to say prayers, talking about the miracle, how such a day could even
be possible—

In our lifetime.

In my mama's lifetime.

You know, whatever happens from here, it almost don't matter.

No, don't suppose it does.

'Cause somewhere up there, Dr. King is looking down at Brother Barack and saying, that's my boy.

That's right. Our boy did it.

At Lexington, she got off the bus and took the 5 subway downtown. Again, she held the gift bag on her lap, her grip on its handle tight. When she got off at the Seventy-seventh Street stop, she checked the Edwardses' address and began walking toward Park Avenue. She had never been in this part of town and was awed by its elegance—streets with no dirt; doormen dressed like rich men; a woman in six-inch Louboutin heels strutting as if the world should be hers on a diamond-encrusted platter; everything so close to Harlem and yet ten thousand miles away from Harlem.

"Can I help you?" the doorman at the Sapphire said to her, not moving away from the fiberglass door.

"I am here to see Mrs. Edwards, please," she said.

"She's expecting you?"

Neni nodded, hoping the absence of words would hide her deception.

"Service entrance," the man said, motioning toward the garage on the right.

Her heart pumped faster than usual as she walked down the dim-lighted hall to apartment 25A. What if Mrs. Edwards wasn't home? she thought. What if Anna changed her mind and refused to let her in? Anna had told her that Mrs. Edwards might be in the master bedroom and not want to be disturbed, but Neni could stop by, try her luck.

"You lucky," Anna whispered as she opened the door. "She just came back out to living room."

Neni took off her shoes in the foyer and followed Anna into the kitchen.

"What you want to see her for?" Anna asked, looking at Neni curiously.

"I just want to give her a gift."

"I give it to her for you," Anna said, extending her hand.

"No, I want to give it to her myself," Neni said, putting the bag behind her back. She couldn't share her plan with Anna—Anna would definitely try to discourage her.

Anna had called two days after Jende lost his job to say how sorry she was and how much she feared she would be next, because Cindy was acting like a madwoman these days (barely eating; rarely going out; stumbling around the apartment some mornings with puffy, bloodshot eyes), and Anna couldn't tell Clark anything about the alcohol now because if Cindy suspected she was talking about her, all the years she'd worked for the family would mean nothing. Now, Anna said, she was secretly calling housekeeping agencies to see if she could get a new job, while jumping even higher at every word Cindy uttered so Cindy wouldn't find any reason to fire her, because she badly needed a job, especially now that her daughter was in college and her oldest son's construction business was failing and he and his wife and three children had moved in with her. Neni, still discombobulated and uninterested in talking about someone potentially losing a job when her husband had already lost his, had aloofly assured Anna that Cindy wasn't going to fire her after twenty-two years of service, but Anna had said over and over that you never know, sometimes people do funny things, so you just never know.

"Wait here," Anna said. "I go see if she wants to see you."

For minutes, Neni stood alone in the kitchen, looking around at the stainless steel appliances and the cream-colored cabinetry with brass handles; the ultraclean kitchen island with a bowl of perfect-looking apples and bananas; the black marble table and vase of fresh pink calla lilies; the Wolf stove, with its frantically loud red buttons. The kitchen was more beautiful than the one in Southampton, which Neni had been certain couldn't be surpassed in beauty. She wondered if Cindy cooked here often, or if she used it only occasionally, to make a special recipe for the boys or give detailed directions to the help during party preparations, the way she'd done over the summer.

"Go to living room now," Anna whispered to her. "Do it quick and leave."

Neni stepped into the Edwardses' Upper East Side living room for the first time, and for a lengthy second all she saw was the view of Manhattan beyond the window—a panorama of steel and concrete buildings tightly packed like the brick and *caraboat* houses of New Town, Limbe. The room smelled of the softest, sweetest intermingling of baby powder and perfume, and she realized, like Jende had said, that everything in it was white or gray: the large chandelier (white crystals, gleaming silvery finish); the floor (glossy marble and gray); the plush carpet (snow white); the sofa and love seat (white); the armchairs (gray with white throws); the textured wall coverings (four shades of gray); the glass center table and the silver vases on it; the candlesticks standing in the four corners of the room (silver); the ottoman (striped gray); the twin wall frames behind the sofa, with line-drawn portraits of a naked woman lying on her back and side (white canvas), and the window curtains and valance (silver).

"Anna says you came to give me something?" Cindy said. She did not lift her eyes from the book she was reading.

"Yes, madam," Neni said. "Good morning, madam."

Cindy stretched out her hand to receive the bag.

"It was made by my mother in Cameroon, madam," Neni said, handing it over. "I thought you would like it, because you said you liked when I wore the same kind of dress in the Hamptons."

Cindy peered into the bag and put it aside, on the floor. "Thank you," she said. "Tell Jende I say hello."

Neni stood in the same spot, confounded.

She hadn't imagined the meeting would begin and end this way. Not considering how much Cindy had seemed to like her in her last days in Southampton, and how well they had parted (with a hug, albeit an awkward one, which she'd felt compelled to give the madam as gratitude for the gifts and bonus money). Cindy had asked about Liomi at the brunch in June's apartment, and told Neni that she'd be sending him a couple of Mighty's old winter jackets through Jende, which she did three days later. But the happy Mrs. Edwards of that Sunday was not the same Mrs. Edwards sitting in her living room that Tuesday. Anna had mentioned that Cindy had lost at least ten pounds since Clark moved to the hotel the day after Christmas, and Neni could tell, from how gaunt her face looked even beneath her makeup.

"Anything else?" Cindy asked, looking up at her.

"Yes . . . yes, madam," Neni said. "I also came to talk to you about something, madam."

"Yes?"

Deciding she had to be brave if she was to say what she had come to say, Neni walked to the sofa and sat down next to Cindy. Cindy's eyes widened at her former housekeeper's audacity, but she said nothing.

"I came here, madam, to see if you can help my husband," Neni said. Her head was tilted, her eyes narrowed to implore in ways her words couldn't. "If you could please help my husband . . . if you could help him get his job back with Mr. Edwards."

Cindy turned her face away and looked toward the window. While the thousand different sounds of New York City blended outside, Neni waited for a response.

"You're funny, you know," Cindy said, turning to face Neni. She was not smiling. "You're a very funny girl. You're coming to ask me to help your husband?"

Neni nodded.

"Why? What do you think I can do for him?"

"Anything, madam."

"Your husband lost his job because Clark no longer needs his services. There's nothing I can do about that."

"But madam," Neni said, her head still tilted, her eyes still beseeching, "maybe you can help him get another job? Maybe you know someone, or one of your friends, maybe they need a chauffeur?"

Cindy scoffed. "What do you think I am?" she asked. "An employment agency? Why can't he go out there and get a job like everybody else?"

"It's not that he can't get a job by himself, madam. He found a little something, washing dishes at restaurants, but it is not easy, too many hours, and his feet hurt every night. It's so hard out there, madam. Too . . . very hard to get a good job now, and it is hard for me and the children, too, with him not having a good job that can take care of us well."

"I'm sorry," Cindy said, picking up her book. "It's a tough world."

Neni's throat tightened and she swallowed hard. "But back in the Hamptons, madam," she said, "you told me to help you. Remember how I promised you, madam? As woman to woman. As a mother to a mother. I am asking the same from you today. Please, Mrs. Edwards. To help me any way that you can help me."

Cindy continued reading.

"In any way, madam. Even if it's a job for me. Even if—"

"I'm sorry, okay? I really can't help you. I wish I could, but I can't."

"Please, madam—"

"If you could leave so I can continue my reading, I'll appreciate it."

But she didn't leave. Neni Jonga wasn't going to leave until she got what she wanted. She turned around, picked up her purse from the floor, and pulled out her cell phone. She opened it, and there, in the picture folder, she found what she was looking for. Her moment had arrived.

"That day, madam," she said, her head no longer tilted, "I took a picture."

Cindy looked up from her book.

"That day in the Hamptons," Neni whispered, moving nearer to Cindy and holding her Motorola RAZR close to Cindy's face, "I took this."

Cindy looked at the photo. In an instant her face turned from gaunt to ghostly as she stared at an image of herself in a stupor, her mouth half open, drool running down her chin, her upper body splayed against the headboard, a bottle of pills and a half-empty bottle of wine on the nightstand.

"How dare you!"

Neni pulled back the phone and closed it.

"You think you can blackmail me? Who do you think you are?"

"I'm just a mother like you, madam," Neni said, putting the phone back in her purse. "I'm only trying to do what I have to do for my family."

"Get out of my house right now!"

Neni did not move.

Cindy stood up and repeated the command.

Neni remained seated and silent.

"Is everything okay?" Anna asked, running into the living room with a duster. She was talking to Cindy but looking at Neni, giving her an angry *What the hell are you doing?* look. Neni ignored her. This had nothing to do with her.

"Call 911!" Cindy shouted.

Still Neni did not budge. She chuckled and shook her head.

"Yes," Anna said, rushing to the kitchen before stopping halfway. "What should I say?"

"An intruder! Hurry. Get me the phone! You want to learn a lesson, I'll teach you a lesson!"

Neni remained seated. "I Googled it all, madam," she said, smirking.

"Googled what!"

"Googled how to do this well . . . what to say when the police comes."

"You useless piece of shit!"

"I know what the police will ask me. What I will say. Before the police comes I will delete the picture. When they come, I will say I don't know what you're talking about. Police will think you're a crazy woman and they'll call your husband. Or your friends. Then you will have to tell them. Is that what you want, Mrs. Edwards?"

"Anna! Phone!"

Anna ran to the living room with the kitchen phone and handed it to Cindy.

"Leave us," Cindy said to Anna, who gave Neni another dirty look before hurrying out of the living room.

Cindy held the phone, looking at it as if punching 911 required a strength she couldn't muster.

"Call them," Neni said.

"Shut up!"

"What are you going to tell them, madam? That I have a picture of you doing drugs and drinking? I'm not afraid. You're the one who should be afraid, because if the police takes me away everyone is going to know why."

Cindy remained standing, clutching the phone and breathing heavily, her chest rising and falling like that of a woman sprinting up Mount Cameroon.

"Call them, madam," Neni said again. "Please call them."

If a glare could kill, dismember, and chop a body into fine bits, Neni's body would have ended up a trillion little pieces because that was what Cindy's eyes would have done to her. But a glare could do no such thing, and Neni could see she was halfway to victory.

Cindy threw the phone on the sofa and sat down trembling. "What do you want?" she said to Neni. Even her cheeks were trembling.

"Help, madam. Any kind of help."

"And you think this is how to get it? This is what you had planned all along when I hired you? To blackmail me? To find a way to hurt my family?"

Neni shook her head. "I never took the picture for this reason, madam. I was afraid that day and I took the picture so that if something bad had happened to you, I will show the police what you were looking like when I entered the room and my hands will be clean. I didn't even remember I had the picture till a few days ago when—"

"You must think I'm stupid if you expect me to believe that."

"Believe it or not, it's the truth, Mrs. Edwards."

"Blackmailing . . . blackmailing . . . ," Cindy said, shaking her head and wagging her finger at Neni. "It's a crime . . . you'll pay for this . . . I'll make you pay for this . . ."

For what seemed like a thousand seconds the women stared at each other: brown eyes next to hazel eyes, round cheeks next to hollow cheeks, face of determination next to face of defeat.

Cindy turned her face away first. "What are you going to do with the picture?" she asked, looking at the skyline outside, panic fully taking over her speech for the first time that afternoon.

Neni shrugged. "I don't yet know, madam," she said, smirking again. "But a person I met, he works for a website that writes news about people in the Hamptons. He told me they are always looking for good pictures of women like you."

"You filthy bitch!"

Neni grinned. The lie had worked. This was precisely where she wanted Cindy. "I wish you, too, a good day, madam," she said, picking up her purse. She stood up and straightened her red turtleneck.

"Sit down," Cindy ordered.

"I'm sorry, madam. I need to go cook dinner for my family."

"I said sit down!"

Neni sat down.

"How much do you want?"

Neni looked Cindy straight in her eyes, let out a short laugh, and said nothing.

"I said name your price."

"You should know better than me, madam, how much this kind of thing should cost."

"Wow," Cindy said, shaking her head again. "Wow. I'm very disappointed in you, Neni. I'm appalled, and so, so disappointed."

Neni Jonga would not be fooled again. A courage she never knew she possessed had fully taken root. She shrugged and pulled her purse closer to her chest.

"After all Clark and I have done for you and Jende? This is how you repay us?"

Neni turned her face away and fidgeted as if getting ready to stand up again. Cindy stood up, hurried out of the room, and returned a minute later with a check.

Without looking at the sum on the check, Neni shook her head. "Cash, madam," she said.

"I don't keep large amounts of cash at home."

"That's not what I heard, madam. I heard rich people keep a lot of cash in their houses, in case something bad happens to the banks."

"Don't make assumptions about me based on what you've read."

Neni scoffed and smiled. She was enjoying this more than she'd thought she would. "Then I'll wait for you to go to the bank. Or we can go together."

She saw Cindy's fist clench and for a second thought the woman was going to break her jawbone, or ask Anna to call 911 again. Instead, Cindy turned around and returned minutes later with a paper bag.

"I'm only giving you this," Cindy said as she handed over the bag, "because of the goodness of my heart. Because I know how badly you need it, and I wouldn't want your children to suffer because of you and your husband's stupidity. But if I ever see you again, I promise you, you will end up in jail. You can choose to believe it or not, but I'll make sure you go to jail, and I won't give a shit. Now hand me the picture and get the hell out of my house."

Neni took out the SIM card from her cell phone, handed the phone to Cindy, and walked out of the Edwardses' apartment.

Forty-two

AFTER SHE'D PUT THE CHILDREN TO BED, SHE COUNTED THE MONEY IN the bathroom, looked at herself in the mirror, and smiled: Nothing like starting the day agonizing over money and ending it triumphant beyond her imagination. She opened the medicine cabinet, took out her red lipstick and applied it, puckered her lips, smiled again, sprayed perfume on her neck, and walked out to the living room, where Jende was watching a Nets game.

"What is this?" he asked, after she placed the brown paper bag next to him on the sofa.

"Guess," she said.

"You went shopping again, eh?" he said, still watching the Nets about to lose.

She shook her head and sat down next to him. She couldn't stop smiling. At any other time she would have been happy to play a guessing game, but she couldn't hold back the good news today. She leaned close to him and whispered in his ear, "It's money!"

"Eh?"

"I showed Mrs. Edwards the picture. She gave me ten thousand dollars!"

"You did what!"

"Ten thousand dollars, *bébé*!"

She started laughing, tickled by the look of shock on his face; by the way his mouth, nose, and eyes had all opened up in disbelief.

He did not laugh with her. He opened the bag and peeked into it. He looked at her, and the bag, and her again. "What did you do, Neni?" he asked for the second time.

"Ten thousand dollars, *bébé*!" she said for the third time, incredulous still at how much Cindy had believed the picture to be worth.

"Are you crazy?"

"Wait, is that anger on your face?"

She couldn't believe him. She'd imagined his reaction wouldn't be one of pure joy, but she hadn't thought it would be this bad. He was looking at her as if she was a thief, as if she had done something disgraceful when she'd just gotten them ten thousand dollars. Ten thousand dollars they needed and deserved!

"What exactly did you do?" he asked.

She told him what she'd said to Cindy Edwards.

"How dare you!" he said, pushing her hand away from his knee.

"How dare me?"

"Yes, how dare you! What gives you the right to treat her like that? I mean . . . how could you, Neni? After everything they did for us?"

"What about what we did for them!" she said, grabbing the paper bag and standing up. "Were we not good to them, too? Why is it that they and their problems are more important than us and our problems? I kept her secret, and what does she do for me? She has her husband fire you!"

"You don't know that!"

"You don't know women like her, Jende. You don't know how they think they're better than people like us. How they think they can do anything they want to people like us."

"Mr. Edwards did what he had to do! I don't like what he did to me but he has every right to do what he needs to do!"

"Oh, so you think I don't have that right, too?"

"That doesn't mean you should have done something like this to her," he said. "We're not those kind of people! How could you even have gone there without asking me first?"

"Because I know what you would have said!"

"Yes! I would have said it because I want nothing to do with this kind of wickedness."

"Wickedness, eh?"

"Yes, it's wicked, and I don't like it. No one has any right to be wicked to another person."

"Oh, so now I'm a wicked person? So you married a wicked woman, didn't you?"

He sighed and turned his face away.

"Just tell me what you think of me, Jende. You think I'm a wicked woman, eh? Just because I do something to help us, you think—"

"You didn't have to do something like this!"

"She thought she could use us, stupid African people who don't know how to stand up for themselves. She thinks we're not as smart as she is; she thinks she can—"

"This has nothing to do with being African!"

"Yes, it does! People with money, they think their money can do anything in this world. They can hire you when they like, fire you when they like, it means nothing to them."

"What are you talking about? That woman was good to us!"

"So you don't want the money?" she said, shaking the paper bag.

He turned off the TV and went into the bathroom. She heard water splashing and figured he was washing his face—he sometimes did that when he didn't know what else to say.

She sat down on the sofa, livid and humiliated. How could he see her as one of those kinds of people when all she was doing was trying to help their situation? And now she was wicked? She was a bad person for being a good mother and wife?

He returned to the living room and sat down next to her.

She turned away from him.

"I didn't mean to get so angry," he said, moving closer to her.

"Don't touch me," she said.

"Let's try and calm down and start the conversation all over again, okay?"

"I said, 'Don't touch me.' Don't even dare touch me right now."

He shifted away from her and for a few seconds neither of them spoke.

"I don't like what you did," he said, calmly.

"If you don't want the money, you don't have to take it!" she said, standing up and jiggling the bag in his face. "I'll open up a bank account and use it for myself only."

"Please sit down, Neni."

"Tomorrow morning I'll go to the bank and open a new account and—"

He reached forward and pulled the bag from her hands. She lunged at him to take it back, but he dragged her down to the sofa and made her sit next to him. She tried to stand up and get away from him, but he held her down.

"I'm sorry, *bébé*," he whispered in her ear. "I'm just . . . I'm so shocked. I mean, I still don't even know what to say."

She scoffed and pursed her lips.

"You just did something . . ." He shook his head. "You surprise me all the time, but you just took it to a whole other level today. In short, I didn't know what kind of woman I married till this night."

"Eh, really? What kind of woman is that? A wicked woman, eh?"

"No," he replied. "A strong woman. I never knew you could do the kind of thing you just told me."

She half-rolled her eyes.

"But please, don't ever do it again. I'm begging you, *bébé*. Never, ever again. I don't care why you think you need to do it, don't ever do it."

"You want the money or not?" she said, smiling and enjoying the new look on his face.

"I don't know . . . I'm just not comfortable, Neni."

"You're not comfortable—"

"But ten *kolo* in our hands?" he said.

"So you're getting happy now, eh?"

"Ten thousand dollars!"

She laughed and kissed him.

Together they did a recount of the money, feeling each of the crisp hundred-dollar bills. "We won't spend any of it," he said to her. "We'll add it to the savings and act as if we don't even have it. God forbid, worse comes to worst one day, we'll use it then."

She nodded.

"Wonders shall never end, eh?" he said.

"Wonders shall never end," she said. "Not while the sun goes up and down."

"But were you not afraid? What if she had called the police?"

Neni Jonga shrugged, looked at her husband, and smiled. "That's the difference between me and you," she said. "You would have been thinking about it too much, wondering whether you should do it or not. Me, I knew it's what I had to do."

Forty-three

WITH HER GROCERY BUDGET ONLY TWO THIRDS OF WHAT IT USED TO BE before Jende stopped working for the Edwardses, shopping at Pathmark became a taxing experience, nothing like in the days when she first came to America, the times when she used to rush through the store excitedly, thinking, *Mamami eh*, so much food! So many choices! All in one place! The only thing she hated about grocery shopping back then was the prices—they made no sense. Three plantains for two dollars? Why? Two dollars in Cameroon was approximately 1,000 CFA francs, and for that amount, as recently as in the early 2000s, a woman could buy groceries to feed her family three good meals. She could buy a pile of cocoyams for 400 CFA francs, smoked fish for 250, vegetables for 100, about six ounces of palm oil for 100, crayfish and spices with the rest of the money, go home and make a large pot of *portor-portor coco* that would feed her family of four lunch and dinner, and there'd still be a little left over for the children to eat the following morning before going to school. If the woman was smart she would make the food extra-spicy, so the children would have a sip of water with every bite, get full faster, and the food would last longer.

It seemed illogical to Neni that the same amount of money in America could buy only three plantains, which wasn't enough to feed Jende alone for one day. She hadn't expected the prices in New York to be the same as in Limbe, but she found it difficult not to be bothered whenever she bought a pound of shrimp for the equivalent of 5,000 CFA francs—the monthly rent for a room with a shared outdoor bathroom and toilet for all the residents in a *caraboat* building. You have to stop comparing prices, Jende advised her whenever she brought up the issue. You keep on comparing prices like that, he'd say, you'll never buy anything in America. The best thing to do in this country, whenever you enter a store, is to ignore the exchange rate, ignore the advertisements, ignore what everyone else is eating and drinking and talking about these days, and buy only the things you need. She began doing so and, after perhaps her tenth visit to Pathmark, she stopped thinking about the exchange rate and learned how to plan meals around what was on sale.

In those first weeks in New York, she always walked the thirteen street blocks north and three avenue blocks west to get to the store. Pushing her shopping cart with one hand and holding Liomi with the other—both of them wearing matching floral spring jackets Jende had bought before their arrival—they walked leisurely whenever the weather allowed so she could take in as much of Harlem as possible: the brownstones with black railings; satisfied patrons admiring their hairdos in beauty parlors; friendly old men, nodding hello; happy Harlemites, smiling at her. Jende had warned her to be careful walking northward because there was talk of gangs and shootings in the housing projects around 145th, but because she never saw anyone with a gun, she walked without worries, going past young and old chatting on street corners.

At Pathmark, even after her first visit, she was impressed with the American way of shopping: the queues at checkout, everyone calmly awaiting their turn; the orderly aisles with prices next to products so shoppers could easily do a comparison for the best value; the superfluous transparency of food manufacturers, who not only attractively packaged products from cornflakes to tea to canned meats but also provided information on what was and wasn't in the food, some manufacturers going as far as supplying details on what the product could and couldn't do to a body. No matter what time of day she went, regardless of how many people were in the store, she found the shopping experience fascinating and weirdly serene, almost unlike what a market shopping experience should be, completely unlike the Limbe market. Which was why she missed the exuberance and disorderliness of her hometown's open-air market. As much as she loved Pathmark, shopping there made her wish she could be back in the midst of the spectacle that happened on Tuesdays and Fridays in her hometown. Those were the days when the stalls that were only half full on other days filled up with smoked fish and crayfish on one end, plantains and cocoyams and vegetables on another end, and with secondhand clothes from Douala next to the flesh of cows slaughtered that morning. She missed the early-morning rush to get the freshest produce and the pushing and shoving of married women determined to pick the best *okrika* clothes for their husbands and children. She missed the pleas from traders asking shoppers to choose them over competitors and the cunning bargaining that ensued between buyers and sellers.

How much for this bunch plantains? a buyer would ask.

Give me three thousand, my sister, the seller would say.

Three thousand? Why? I give you seven hundred.

No, my sister, seven hundred no correct; I beg give me one thousand eight hundred.

No, I go give you nine fifty. If you no want, I go leave am.

Okay, okay, take am; I di only give you for this price because I don ready for go house.

Eh, see you, cunning man.

No be cunning, my sister, na true. I no go make any profit today, but how man go do?

Ah, Limbe market. She missed the joy of walking away knowing she had negotiated a good deal for a bag of rice. There was no haggling in Pathmark. The owners stated the prices and no one dared challenge them. It was as if they were a supreme deity, which was a pity, because if she could bargain she would find a way to make her new grocery budget work. Her family now had to eat a lot of chicken gizzards and save drumsticks for special occasions. Liomi would soon have to start eating *puff-puff* for breakfast, instead of Honey Nut Cheerios, and Jende would need to start drinking less Mountain Dew and more water. As for herself, she would have to hold on tightly to the memories of the shrimp she'd had in the Hamptons, because until good money started coming in again, there would be no shrimp dinners, not even on Sundays and holidays.

Thinking of shrimp as she walked through the store made her think of Anna and the brunch they had worked together. Cindy had told them that they could take home the leftovers, and Anna had let her take all the food, including the bacon-wrapped shrimp, which she, Jende, and Liomi had rapturously finished off that evening. It was also thanks to Anna that she'd had such a successful experience working for the Edwardses—Anna had called her back every time she'd left a message saying she didn't know how to execute an order Cindy had given. Thinking of all this made Neni wish she and Anna had become friends, but she knew it was no longer possible—any chance of a friendship blossoming had ended the last time they spoke.

"What you do to Cindy last night?" Anna had said without prelude when she called just before six o'clock the morning after Neni left the Edwards apartment. She appeared to be on the train, on her way to work.

"Anna?" Neni whispered groggily, rising from the bed to go to the living room so as not to awaken her children.

"I say, what you do to Cindy yesterday?" Anna repeated. "I want to know."

Neni sat on the sofa, her hands on her left breast, which was heavy and painful from too much milk, thanks to Timba starting to sleep through the night at two months old. "I don't understand what you want to know," she said to Anna.

"I want to know why you come to the house yesterday, what you say to Cindy, why she scream for me to call 911. I try to call you after you leave, but I only get your voice message."

"I had to get home to my children," Neni said.

"Okay, you with your children now. So tell me what happen with you and Cindy."

Neni took a deep breath and shook her head. The audacity of Anna, calling at six in the morning to interrogate her. "You know what, Anna?" she said, looking at the bedroom door to make sure it was closed. "I don't like to say this to people, because I don't like it when other people say it to me, but it is not your business."

"Yes, it is my business," Anna quickly replied.

"How is it your business what happens between me and Mrs. Edwards? I have my relationship with her, you have your own relationship—"

"If someone come to this house and do something to any of this people, it concern me. I work for them, I make sure I do everything I can so they happy. You come here last night, you leave, you know what happen after?"

"What?"

"I want to know what you do to her," Anna said again.

"We had an agreement about something, and I only went to remind her of the agreement."

"Agreement for what?"

"Anna, please—"

"You leave this house and the woman lock herself in bathroom and cry alone for two hours!" Anna said, her voice rising slightly in the train. "I try to go to her, she shout at me to leave her alone. She say the F-word to me! Over and over she say F to me, F to we all. Leave her alone. What I do? Maybe she thinks what you did to her was me and you who did it together?"

"I don't—"

"I call Stacy, beg her to take Mighty somewhere after hockey so he don't see his mother like this. I don't want him to hear Cindy crying in the bathroom because you do something to her."

"Please don't make it as if it's my fault, okay?"

"Oh, so it's not your fault?"

"It's not anyone's fault!"

"You know she got problems," Anna said, each word coming out angrier than the preceding one. "You know how many problems she got—"

"Wait, you think I don't have problems, too? Do you know how many problems I have?"

"So you come yesterday for Cindy to solve your problems? That why I see you smile as you leave? Because you make the woman cry after she solve—"

"I did not come for anyone to solve my problems! If I have things that I'm not happy with, I find a way to make them better. I solve my own problems!"

"You think because—"

"I don't think anything!" Neni said. "If Mrs. Edwards is not happy with her life, let her solve her own problems. I am tired of people wanting me to care about them more than I care about myself and my family."

"Nobody asks you to not care for yourself!"

"Yes, you and Mrs. Edwards do. That is what you called me this morning to say. To make me feel bad because Mrs. Edwards has big problems and I should worry about her."

"I only want to know—"

"I'm sorry, Anna, but if Mrs. Edwards wants to change her life then let her go find a way to be happy. And I hope she finds a way to be happy very soon, because I feel really sorry for her."

Forty-four

AT THE CENTER OF THE PLATFORM, BETWEEN TWO FULL BENCHES, A MAN in a wheelchair was singing for dollars and cents. *The answer, oh babe,* he sang in a raspy voice, *is gonna be blowin' in the wind, the answer be blowin' in the wind, oh yeah, eh eh eh, the answer, sweet babe, it's gonna be blowin' in the wind* . . . No one appeared to be listening or watching as he moved his harmonica to his mouth and blew into it with his eyes closed, nodding to the splendor of his own music. At least two people were looking up the tracks, murmuring to themselves, one asking when the damn train was ever going to arrive. Amen, ma brother, someone said when the song ended. A to the men indeed, another voice added, making it clear that more than one person had been listening. Many on Neni's side of the platform nodded; some applauded. Neni applauded, too, and put fifty cents in the man's cup, in appreciation of his ability to compose such a beautiful original song.

When she arrived at the church office, the assistant pastor ushered her into a conference room where a box of letters and envelopes was sitting on the table.

"I can't thank you enough for stopping by," he said as he showed her how to fold the fundraising letters and stuff them into the envelopes. "We're badly in need of volunteers."

"I am glad I can help," Neni said. "I did not know if you needed any help when I called this morning."

"No, it's perfect timing. Where's the baby?"

"I left her at home with my friend. I just wanted to go out alone for a little bit."

"Understandable. I'm not sure I can handle the monotony of being home with a baby every day."

"Is Natasha in today?"

"She's at an interfaith conference, but she should be back in about an hour. I'll let her know you're in here when she comes back."

Forty-five minutes later, Natasha peeked in from the hallway. "Neni, how sweet of you to come out to help!" she said.

"Hi, Natasha."

"I need to get some work done right now but drop by before you leave, let's catch up, okay?"

Alone in the conference room, Neni folded the letters twice and slid them into the yellow preaddressed envelopes, trying not to think about her conversation with Anna the previous morning. The woman had upset her so much she was still fuming a day later.

"What have you been up to?" Natasha asked, motioning to a chair at her desk when Neni entered her office to say goodbye.

"Everything is good," Neni said.

"Kids are good? Your husband?"

Neni nodded.

"You're enjoying the new year so far?"

"I'm okay."

Natasha looked at her dubiously, stood up and closed the door. "How are you, *really*?" she asked. "What's the situation with your husband's papers?"

"I'm trying not to worry about it, but it's not easy."

"Any new developments?"

"We are still just waiting and hoping . . . But one of my friends, she told me about a solution that can help us."

"That's wonderful. What's the solution?"

"I don't know if you will like it."

"It's not for me to like, Neni," Natasha said with a smile. "It's for me to listen to you and help you listen to your heart."

"I haven't even told my husband . . ."

"I understand. You don't have to tell me if you don't feel comfortable."

Neni looked at Natasha's reassuring smile and decided she might as well. "My friend," she said quietly, "she has a cousin."

"Mmm-hmm."

"I can marry him."

"Marry him?"

Neni nodded. "I can get a green card through him if I marry him."

"Hmm, I see."

"I just . . . I have to divorce my husband for a few years. Then I can marry my friend's cousin and he will file papers for me."

Natasha nodded, pulling a scrunchy from her wrist to put her hair in a ponytail. She stood up and walked to a water cooler by the door. "You want a cup of water?" she asked Neni. Neni shook her head and watched as Natasha filled a disposable cup and downed the water in one gulp. "Refreshing," the pastor said with a broad smile as she tossed the cup into a garbage can and retook her seat.

Neni waited, the beating of her heart suddenly noticeable to her.

"You're thinking of marrying another man for a few years," Natasha said.

"It's my friend's idea. Only, I don't know if it is right or wrong."

"Oh, I think we're *way* past the point of right and wrong," Natasha said, chuckling.

"Someone I know used to say that to me a lot."

"Rumi."

"Who?"

"Jalaluddin Rumi, the Sufi mystic. He's the one who said, 'Out beyond ideas of wrongdoing and rightdoing, there is a field. I'll meet you there.' Which was his own way of saying, 'Let's not dwell too much on labeling things as right or wrong.'"

"But everything in life is either right or wrong."

"Is it?"

"It's not?"

"Why would you want to divorce your husband and risk your marriage for papers, Neni? Why? Is America that important to you? Is it more important to you than your family?"

Neni lowered her eyes and stared at the floor. She could hear pedestrians on Thompson Street, chatting as they walked past Natasha's office window.

"So much could go wrong with this plan," Natasha said.

"That's what I told my friend when she suggested it to me. Because I have another friend from work, and her sister did the same thing. She left her husband and children back in their country and came to America and married a Jamaican man for papers so she could bring her husband and children here. But when everything was finished, the Jamaican man refused to give her divorce unless she gave him more money. He wants fifty thousand dollars."

"That's awful."

"Yes, because now she cannot go back to her country and marry her husband back and bring her family here. She's over here and they are still over there and the woman is just praying that the Jamaican man will stop being so greedy because she really wants to be with her husband and children."

"And knowing a story like this, you're still willing to take the risk?"

"My friend's cousin is a nice man."

"Oh, I bet! And the Jamaican man is in all likelihood a wonderful man."

"I just don't know what to do," Neni said.

"Sometimes the best thing to do is nothing."

Neni feigned a smile. Doing nothing was not an option, but it wouldn't be respectful to contradict Natasha. Besides, it was best she stopped talking about their *papier* situation lest she say something Jende wouldn't want revealed. "The guy who used to talk to me about right and wrong," she said, attempting to change the topic, "he has a little brother who hated doing nothing."

"We don't like doing nothing in this country."

Neni and Natasha laughed together.

"I used to work for the boys' family and I was always doing something with the younger one, but I liked it—he was very funny. One time I took him to a playdate with his friend and his friend's mother offered him some food and he said, no thanks, he was not going to eat anything because he preferred to eat my food when we got home. He thought I was the best cook."

"I bet he's right," Natasha said, to which Neni smiled.

That night, while Liomi was counting and tickling Timba's toes, Neni sent Mighty an email. Within seconds a response came back:

**Sorry, we were unable to deliver your message to the following
address
<mightythemightyone@yahoo.com>
This user doesn't have a yahoo.com account
(mightythemightyone@yahoo.com)
Below this line is a copy of the message.**

**Hi Mighty,
How are you? How is school?
I hope you are being a good boy and obeying your father
and your mother. I heard your mother is not feeling very well.
Remember what I told you that mothers are the most special
things in the world so be nice to your mother.
Take care, Neni**

Forty-five

Cindy Eliza Edwards died on a cold afternoon in March 2009, alone in her marital bed, five weeks after Neni Jonga walked out of her apartment. Her husband was in London, on a business trip, as she lay dying. Her firstborn son was in India, walking the Path to Enlightenment. Her younger son was at the Dalton School, being groomed to become a man like his father. Her father, whose identity neither she nor her mother ever knew, had been dead for two decades. Her mother, who she believed loved her too little, had been gone for four years. Her half-sister, completely out of her life since the death of their mother, was still in Falls Church, Virginia, living a life of material comfort better than the one they had lived together as children but far less comfortable than the one Cindy had been living in New York City. Her friends were all over Manhattan, shopping at Saks and Barneys, lunching and drinking fine wine, planning dinner parties and galas, attending meetings for charities, looking forward to their next vacation to an exotic locale.

"But I don't understand!" Neni said over and over as Winston recounted to her and Jende everything he knew based on the story Frank had told him that evening, a day after the passing.

Asphyxiation due to vomit, Frank had said, according to the medical examiner. High levels of opioid and alcohol had been found in her body, leading the examiner to believe she had swallowed multiple Vicodin pills, drunk at least two bottles of wine, fallen asleep, and accidentally drowned in her own vomit.

Anna had discovered her lying flat on the bed, her arms flung wide and hanging stiff off the bed, her eyes and mouth open, dried vomit crusted on her chin, neck, and the neckline of her silk nightgown. With Clark out of town, Anna had immediately called Frank, screaming and crying. Frank couldn't get out of an important meeting at work, so he had asked his wife, Mimi, to hurry to the Edwards apartment. Mimi had gone there and found their friend dead.

"Oh, Papa God!" Neni cried.

"But how could she die that kind of useless death?" Jende asked.

"Why didn't she go to the doctor? She had all that money and she died in her own bed! Why didn't one of her friends try to force her? Why didn't anyone see that there was something wrong with her? What kind of country is this?"

According to Frank, Winston said, Cindy had closed the blinds on the world. Even Mimi, who was one of her good friends, had not seen her in months. Mimi had to show up at the Edwards apartment unannounced after weeks of her calls and emails not being returned, and after having almost a dozen three-way phone conversations with Cheri and June, who were restless and increasingly apprehensive because they couldn't understand why Cindy wouldn't tell them what was going on. The women had agreed that Cindy needed an intervention, and Mimi, three days before Cindy's death, had walked into Cindy's bedroom with Anna's encouragement. There, she had seen her friend ashen and limp, near broken, in a white silk nightgown, sitting on her bed and staring at nothing in particular. Cindy had told her she was living in a dark-

ness she couldn't get out of, and Mimi had begged her to please go see
a psychiatrist because she appeared to be dealing with a severe case of
depression. Cindy had refused, saying she wasn't depressed, but Mimi
had pleaded for her to at least do it for the sake of her children. Think
about Mighty, Mimi had said. Think about how it must feel for him to
see his mother like this. Cindy had cried and, for her sons' sake, agreed
to go to a treatment center outside Boston, because with the end of her
marriage seeming inevitable, her son in India not returning her calls
and emails, her whole life beginning to seem more and more meaningless, she needed to do something now if she ever hoped to taste happiness again. She made Mimi promise not to tell anyone what they'd
discussed, not even Frank, not even Cheri or June. She was going to
apologize to everyone for ignoring their calls and emails and tell them
everything as soon as she felt better.

Neni's hand remained on her chest throughout the story, her mouth
agape. When Winston was done recounting it, she wiped the tears that
had been running down her cheeks with the hem of her skirt.

"Should I call Mr. Edwards tonight?" Jende asked.

"No," Winston said. "Maybe in a few weeks or months. Too much
is happening for them right now. Frank only told me all this because
I saw him when he stopped by the office on his way to pick Clark up
from the airport. He'll let me know when the date for the memorial
service is, and I'll let you know."

Jende shook his head sadly. "But how is Mr. Edwards going to manage?"

"Frank said the man was crying so hard over the phone," Winston
said. "It sounds like no matter what happened between them, he truly
loved his wife."

Forty-six

Mighty Edwards wore a gray suit and played a beautifully imper-fect Claude Debussy's "Clair de Lune" at the memorial service, which took place a week later. In the front pew, Clark sat with his sunglasses on. The mourners, all two hundred or so of them, sat glum under the hundred-foot-high roof of the Church of St. Paul the Apostle on the corner of Sixtieth Street and Columbus Avenue. Around them were depictions of the Savior and the Holy Mother, above them two rows of pendant lighting, and to their right, on a little table, a prayer book where all who were burdened, all who were weary, all who were bro-kenhearted, could leave prayer requests and pleas for blessings.

The priest thanked God for loving Cindy Edwards and calling her to spend eternity with Him. What a great rejoicing must be happening in heaven, he said. After the congregation had sung "Nearer, My God, to Thee" and a soloist had sung "Peace, Perfect Peace," Frank and Mimi's daughter, Nora Dawson, in a black body-fitting long-sleeved mini dress, her blond hair blow-dried straight like that of her deceased godmother on some of the best days of her life, walked to the altar and read from John, chapter fourteen, verses one to three: Jesus' promise to his disciples.

" 'Do not let your hearts be troubled,' " she read. " 'Believe in God; believe also in me. My father's house has many rooms. If that were not so, would I have told you that I am going there to prepare a place for you? And if I go and prepare a place for you, I will come back and take you to be with me so that wherever I am, there you will be also.' Amen."

When the moment for eulogy arrived—after the priest had assured the mourners in his message that indeed, Jesus had prepared a special room for Cindy in heaven; after communion had been served; after Cheri had read a poem she'd commissioned titled "No one warned me loving you would leave me this broken"—Vince Edwards stood up and walked to the front.

He had no sheet from which he read. He spoke in anecdotes. Of the mother who roughhoused with him with her pearls on, back when he was a little boy. Of the mother who took him hiking in the Adirondacks just so she could lose her last ten ounces of belly fat. Cindy's clients, models and actresses who had filled a pew in the center of the church, giggled. He spoke of his mother's passion for healthy living, her commitment to her clients to help them eat better, have better lives, look better, and be better because they looked better. He spoke of her love for her friends, her love for those who needed her. He spoke of her love of the arts—the forced trips to the Met, her failed attempt to get him to learn the violin, her successful attempt to get Mighty to play the piano so he could one day show the world his talent at Carnegie Hall. Someone in the front clapped. Others joined.

Vince bowed his head and cleared his throat. He looked up and smiled at the congregation. He spoke about the mother whom he had been so blessed to have. "She was imperfect," he said. "Flawed, yes. But beautiful. So beautiful. Like we all are."

In the last pew, Jende closed his eyes and prayed for Cindy's soul to rest in peace.

From where he sat, a somber black face surrounded by somber white faces, he could see the red vase holding the ashes of the woman who, until some weeks before, used to hand him a check to buy his daily bread; the woman who had given his nieces and nephews a year of education and his son a suit from Brooks Brothers. He could see half of the back of Clark's head and the top of the white mop of hair belonging to Clark's mother. He couldn't see Mighty's head, but his eyes had welled up with tears as he watched the boy ascend the steps to sit at the piano. He'd felt sorry not only for the woman in the vase but also for the young boy, the cheerful child he'd spent many mornings driving to school, a child who now had to live with the shame brought on by the nature of his mother's death.

"I looked at him and I thought, what is this poor child going to do?" he said to Neni as they lay in bed facing each other that night.

Neni did not respond.

"It's not your fault," he said. "I keep on telling you that. It was Mrs. Edwards's time to go."

"You think you're helping someone by keeping their secret . . ."

"You helped her—"

"I didn't help her."

She sat up, her breast pads peeking out of her nursing bra. "Let's give the money to the church," she said in a tearful voice.

He turned from his side to his back, looking at the ceiling.

"I think we should give the money away," she said again.

"You women are something else, eh?" he said, chuckling and shaking his head.

"It's not a woman thing," she snapped.

"Your guilt will soon go away."

"If I had known she was dying . . ."

"She would have died either way, okay?" he said, his eyes closed, his voice trailing off. "Whether or not she gave you the money, she would have died."

Forty-seven

Though she'd heard of honor societies, she didn't know what they did, so when she received a letter from Phi Theta Kappa inviting her to become a member, she immediately called Betty.

"It means you are smart, oh," Betty said.

"Really?"

"Yes, madam, really! They only invite people who have good grades. Why are you acting surprised as if you don't know there's a good brain inside that oblong head of yours?"

"Jealousy will kill you, Betty," Neni said, laughing.

"Right after it kills you."

When Jende came home that night, she showed him the letter, concerned about what he would say about the hundred-dollar application fee but excited for him to see the validation of her academic prowess, thanks to him working hard to send her to school.

"I don't even know if I should bother trying to join," she said, feigning disinterest.

"But this is good, *bébé*," he said. "The letter says you are one of the top students in your college. Why didn't you tell me that? Even with you not going to school this semester they're still thinking of you."

"So I can spend the one hundred dollars to join?"

"Spend three hundred," he said, wrapping his arms around her waist and kissing her. "If there ever was a reason to pinch out a little something from the savings, this is it. If you can join and get one of these scholarships that they say they give to their members . . ."

"That's the same thing I was thinking, the scholarships. Imagine, *bébé*! If I could get a scholarship to help us pay for September, or even January, wouldn't that be something?"

"Maybe I'll finally know again what it's like to have a good night's sleep."

The next day she submitted her membership application online and, days later, received an envelope welcoming her to the society and telling her about all the benefits. She immediately went to the website the letter directed her to and, there, she saw the scholarships—dozens of scholarships for students with her grade point average, and students with her level of progress, and students with her major and career interest. For most of the scholarships, though, the deadline had passed. For the ones whose deadlines were still open, she needed to be nominated by a dean.

"Then go see the dean and beg him to nominate you," Jende said after she told him what she'd discovered.

"But I don't know any dean," she said, trying not to get upset at his patronizing tone.

"You go to your school, Neni, and ask someone who this dean who nominates people is. You go to the man and tell him your situation, okay? You tell the man that you have to return to school in September to remain legal in the country. Tell him you are very smart and you want to be a pharmacist but your husband doesn't make good money anymore. Let him know how bad you want to be a pharmacist, and how bad your husband wants you to be a pharmacist. You have to say anything you can, because you don't know if the man is going to have a soft heart."

She listened, nodded, and, an hour later, emailed her former precalculus instructor, who wrote back the next morning with the name and office number of the nominator, Dean Flipkens. The instructor told her she didn't need an appointment to see the dean, she could go there anytime. That afternoon she took Timba to Betty's, hoping to see the dean so she could get her scholarship as soon as possible.

On the walk from the subway to the school she imagined the dean as a kindly old white man with a head of sparse gray hair, but when she got there she realized she had visualized incorrectly: He was a white man, but young—with a head of thick brown hair—and within a minute of being in his office, she could tell his heart wasn't nearly as soft as Jende had hoped it would be.

"I'm sorry to disappoint you, Ms. Jonga," he said to her, "but I don't nominate by request. I nominate students with stellar grades who are making a contribution to the college and their community."

"I understand, Dean," Neni said collectedly, trying not to sound as desperate as she was. "But you can see, I have very good grades, which is why I came here to see you today."

"I see your grades all right. But what about your involvement in the college and the community?"

"I—"

"Are you a member of any organization on campus? Have you done anything to enrich the lives of other students at BMCC?"

"Dean, I have—"

"Do you volunteer at any organization in the city? In your neighborhood?"

Neni shook her head. "I volunteered at my church one time, but . . . I really would like to volunteer more, Dean," she said, suddenly feeling ashamed, as if she'd been caught stealing. "It's just that I have no time, Dean."

"No one has time, Ms. Jonga," the dean said.

"I have two children, and before my second child was born I was also working. If I had any time, I would be so glad to do something for BMCC because I like the school. But without the time, Dean, I just cannot do anything."

"I'm not sure what to tell you."

"I need any kind of help, Dean Flipkens. I only have two more semesters before I can transfer to four-year college. But my husband, he lost his job that pays good money. I really don't know how I can come back to school in September if someone doesn't help me with a scholarship. If there's anything you can do to help me . . ."

The dean stared at her through his geek-chic black-framed glasses, then turned toward his computer. He couldn't be less than her age, Neni estimated, though he looked much younger, quite like the flawless-skinned and neatly coiffed young men in the billboards that floated over Times Square. Neni couldn't help thinking he was sitting in that office only because he had to, not because he wanted to, and that was enough to make her believe the man wouldn't care if she had to drop out of BMCC.

As he moved his mouse around the pad, she watched his hands, well manicured and soft-looking, the hands of someone who'd never known a day of hard labor.

"I would send you over to financial aid," he said, turning his attention back to her, "but I see here you're an international student. I'm sure you know that pretty much every scholarship or grant we offer is for citizens or permanent residents, so there really isn't much they can do for you."

Neni nodded, buttoning her jacket and reaching down for her purse lying on the floor.

"Though I must ask you, Ms. Jonga," he went on, ignoring Neni's attempt to end the meeting, "I see here that your plan after graduation is to apply to pharmacy school. Is that still the case?"

Neni nodded, not wanting to waste any more words with him.

"May I ask why pharmacy?"

"I like pharmacy," she briskly replied.

"I understand. But why?"

"Because I want to give people medicine to feel better. When I came to America my husband's cousin advised me to do it, that it's a very good thing to study. And everyone tells me that it's a good job. Is there a problem with me trying to become a pharmacist, Dean?"

The dean smiled, and Neni imagined he was derisively laughing at her inwardly, at the impassioned manner in which she'd just defended her career choice.

"Everyone who told you pharmacy is a great career is right," he said, still smiling haughtily, "but I wonder—and I hate saying this to students, because I don't want anyone to think I'm asking them to dream small—have you wondered if it is the right career path for someone in your circumstances?"

"I don't understand what you mean."

"I'm simply wondering, Ms. Jonga, if perhaps another career path may be better suited for someone like you."

"I want to be a pharmacist," Neni said, no longer trying to disguise her anger.

"That's great, and I commend you for that. But you came here today because you are desperate for money to finish school. You have two children, your husband doesn't make enough money, and, by all accounts, you're having a hard time making ends meet. Pharmacy school is very expensive, Ms. Jonga, and you're an international student. Unless you change your legal status it's going to be hard for you to get loans to get the degree, if you can find a way to get your associate's from BMCC in the first place."

"So you are telling me you think I should not try to be a pharmacist?"

The dean took off his glasses, placed them on the desk.

"One of my duties as associate dean of students," he said, "is to offer our students career counseling. And my aim when I counsel students like you, Ms. Jonga, is to guide them toward achievable goals. Do you understand what that means, for a goal to be achievable?"

Neni glared on without a word.

"There are lots of other great careers in the healthcare field, and we can help you get into those. Licensed practical nurse, ultrasound technician, medical billing and coding, lots of great careers which . . . you know, which will be more achievable—"

"I don't want achievable."

"It would be a shame for you to spend years pursuing a goal which you have such little chance of achieving, don't you think? I'm just . . . I just want us to talk it out and see what the odds are of you, you know, graduating from BMCC, getting into pharmacy school, and becoming a licensed pharmacist while dealing with financial stress, raising two children, and living in the country on a temporary visa. Don't you think it would be a shame to start something, spend time and money, only to give it up later because you realize it's too much for you? And before you think I'm trying to rain on your parade, please know that I'm only saying this from years of experience. You won't believe how often I see this happen, and what a shame I think it is that we didn't give the student the best counsel. Because for every student in your situation who does become a pharmacist or doctor, there are four or five more who never make it into pharmacy or medical school and then they have to turn around and start trying to become a nurse."

Neni laughed and shook her head. The situation wasn't funny, but in a way it was.

"I don't think I said anything funny," the dean said.

"Did you grow up dreaming of having this job you have right now, Dean Flipkens?" Neni asked, the funniness of the situation gone, replaced by a rage bubbling so ferociously within her that she was afraid it would spill out through her nose.

"Actually, I had other dreams, but you know . . . in life you have to—"

"That's why you don't want me to be a pharmacist?" she said, standing up and slinging her purse over her shoulder. "Because you are sitting in this office and not somewhere else?"

"Please have a seat, Ms. Jonga," the young man said, motioning to the chair. "There's no need to get—"

"I want to become a pharmacist!" Neni said. "And I will become a pharmacist."

When Jende came home from work that night she told him nothing of the conversation, except that she was likely not going to get any kind of scholarship. Then why are we still planning to go to the ceremony for this honor society thing? he asked in a tone that made her feel as if she'd sorely disappointed him. Because it would be good to celebrate how far I've come, she responded, but he was unconvinced. He wasn't going to take off work and lose money just to go watch her join an organization that wasn't going to help them. Go with one of your friends, he said to her. Or ask Winston.

Winston told her he would be delighted to attend, when she called to invite him. He teased her about the accomplishment, saying she'd better make sure she was joining an honor society and not a secret society because sometimes they looked the same, and she teased him back, saying the only secret society she would ever consider joining was the one he'd joined, which had taken him from Chicago grocery store cashier to Wall Street lawyer. Winston laughed, told her how proud he was of her, and on the day of the induction ceremony, he left work early to join her and Fatou and the kids in front of the auditorium. While Fatou stayed with Timba in the hallway, Winston and Liomi clapped and cheered as Neni, alongside twenty-eight other students, was formally inducted as a member of Phi Theta Kappa. After the ceremony, Winston took everyone to a sushi restaurant where he ordered a platter of eel and avocado rolls, California rolls, and shrimp and cucumber rolls. He encouraged Fatou to have as much sake as she wanted, laughing with her as she downed it and slammed the cup on the table every time.

"We enjoy lika this when she join *société*," Fatou said, giggling at her silly self for acting like the girls she'd seen on MTV, "what you gonno do when she become pharmacist?"

"He will take us to a restaurant in the Trump Hotel," Neni said, laughing, a spoonful of miso soup in one hand. "He will hire Donald Trump himself to cook steak for us."

Winston shook his head. "No," he said, smiling at the fun the women were having at his expense. "The day this our special girl becomes a pharmacist, I will take everyone to a place called the Four Seasons."

Forty-eight

The rainy season in Limbe begins in April. The rain comes every few days for an hour or two, not too heavy to stop the townsfolk from going outside but heavy enough to force them to put on their *chang* shoes before braving the muddy streets. By May, the rains are heavier and times between downpours are cooler, though not so cool that the townsfolk have to put on sweaters just yet. The May rains tend to come at night, drumming so loudly on zinc roofs that some folks fear they will awaken to find their roofs lying on top of them.

The night Pa Jonga died was one such rainy May night.

His wife and children had spent all evening and the early part of the night rushing out in the unabating rain to the backyard kitchen, to boil *masepo* and fever grass for him. They made him drink it, along with the paracetamol and nivaquine the pharmacist at Half Mile had prescribed. The pharmacist had diagnosed Pa Jonga with either malaria or typhoid fever, and had asked that Pa Jonga be given the meds on a full stomach three times a day. Ma Jonga and her sons did everything the pharmacist said, but neither the white man's medicine nor the native medicine worked: Pa Ikola Jonga died at four in the morning, around the time of the neighborhood mosque's first call to prayers.

Jende had two hours left before the end of his shift at the Hell's Kitchen restaurant when his middle brother, Moto, called him on his cell phone within an hour of the death. The old man's body was still lying warm on his bed. "Papa, don die, oh," Moto cried. "Papa don die."

The chef excused Jende for the rest of the night. "I am so sorry for your loss," he said. "Please extend my condolences to the rest of your family in Africa."

Jende sat with his head down for the entire subway ride home, too stunned to cry. He found Neni wailing on her cell phone when he entered the apartment. Upon seeing him, she dropped the phone and ran into his arms to hold him. It was then the dam behind his eyelids broke.

Papa, oh, Papa, he cried, how could you not give me one last chance to see you again? Eh, Papa, how could you do this to me? His nose, eyes, and mouth were spewing out liquid in all directions. Why did you not wait for me, Papa? Eh? Why you do me so?

Winston and his girlfriend, Maami, came over just after midnight. Winston took off the day from work, and Maami—who had recently moved to New York from Houston after Winston had successfully wooed her back and immediately impregnated her—brought her laptop to do her accounting job in the bedroom. Many friends came over in the evening, the same friends who had come to dance when Timba was born. None of them asked if Jende would be going back home. They figured he would tell them if he was going, and if he wasn't going, well, no grown man should be made to tell anyone that he couldn't go home to bury his father.

Pa Jonga was placed in the Limbe Provincial Mortuary and buried two weeks later. Jende sent the money for the funeral, a two-day extravaganza of food and drinks, speeches and libations, dancing and singing and crying. It was an event that cost more money than Pa Jonga had made in the last ten years of his life. His body, adorned in a white suit, was placed on a bed of bricks covered with a brand-new white bedspread. All night, Ma Jonga sat on the floor beside the bed, dressed in a black *kaba*, nodding as sympathizers filed through the room to view the remains and encourage her to be strong.

Ashia, mama, they said. Tie heart, na so life dey, oh. How man go do?

The next day the remains were blessed by the pastor of Mizpah Baptist Church, even though Pa Jonga had not been to church in decades. Ma Jonga had always wanted him to be baptized just like Jende and her other sons had been; she had envisioned the pastor dipping him into the little stream that flowed through the Botanic Garden and then raising him out of the water as the congregation sang, *Ring the bells of heaven! There is joy today, for a soul returning from the wild!* But Pa Jonga wanted none of that church palaver. When I die, he told his wife, I go follow Jesus if I see ei with my own two eyes.

"Which church is going to agree to bless him now?" Jende had asked Moto as they talked about how they could give Pa Jonga one of the best funerals New Town had ever seen (no one with a grown child in America should have an ordinary funeral, the belief in Limbe went).

"Any church that likes money will bless him," Moto had replied. "I know you've already sent all the money you can, but if you could send a little more so we can give a nice envelope to a church, they'll be glad to send their pastor to bless him and send him straight to heaven."

For the first time in many days, Jende had laughed.

He sent the money and learned the next day that Mizpah Baptist Church had agreed to bless his father. Ma Jonga was still a staunch card-carrying parishioner of the church as well as a member of its Kakane women's group. It was for her sake that the pastor agreed to come to the house and bless Pa Jonga on his journey to Paradise. The money Jende had sent was not to pay the church, after all, but as a thanksgiving offering for his father's long happy life.

After the funeral service, the Kakane women's group, dressed in their *social wrappers*, led the mourners in a march from the house to the graveyard. A hired marching band followed the women, and then came the rented Land Rover bearing Pa Jonga's brass-handled casket. Behind the Land Rover, a two-mile-long cluster of family and friends marched, some with framed portraits of Pa Jonga lifted high above their heads. They marched and they danced and they wailed all through New Town and through the market, crying and singing, *Yondo, yondo, yondo, yondo suelele.*

Jende watched it all on the video he had asked Moto to have made.

He watched the six-hour DVD collection in one sitting. He saw his mother collapse in grief when the casket opened to reveal his father's body after it had been brought home for the wake. He listened to the speeches about what a good man Pa Jonga was, and what a fine farmer and draughts player, too. He watched the dances that went on from late Friday night to early Saturday morning. He listened to the pastor's sermon in the house, a sermon about how neither death nor life, neither angels nor demons, neither the present nor the future, nor any powers, neither height nor depth, nor anything else in all creation, can separate God's children from His love. Jende watched the moment when his father was lowered into the ground and the pastor bellowed, Ikola Jonga, from dust you came, to dust you will return.

His sorrow at not being able to bury his father was as heavy as his grief at the death. Every scene in the grainy video made him cry, except the ones where he was too astonished at the weight gained or gray hair developed or teeth lost by certain friends and family members, people he hadn't seen in almost five years.

The day after he watched the video his back began to ache. He had to leave one job early one afternoon and call off the other job in the evening. The pain in his feet seemed to have traveled to his back, only with more ferocity. He spent many mornings before work lying on the floor, writhing in pain, swallowing as many as five Tylenol capsules at a time. A colleague referred him to a cash-only doctor in Jamaica, Queens, who charged him sixty dollars for a twenty-minute consultation, after informing him that the accident health insurance plan

Neni had bought for them online—after her eligibility for the state's free Prenatal Care Assistance Program ended—was pretty much useless (the children were both receiving insurance through Child Health Plus, at no cost, thankfully).

In a windowless basement office, the doctor examined him and told him his pains might be stress-induced. "Are you dealing with any major stressors in your life?" he asked Jende.

Am I dealing with any major stressors in my life, Jende wanted to say. Yes, Doctor, turns out I am. In a few weeks I am due to stand in front of an immigration judge to continue begging him to please not deport me. My father just died and I could not bury him. What could be a bigger shame for a firstborn son? My mother is getting too old to be breeding pigs and farming and selling in the market, so I have to start sending her money more frequently. I have a wife and two children who I need to feed and clothe and shelter every day. My wife is supposed to return to school to keep her student visa, and I don't know if I'll be able to afford her international student tuition by washing dishes at restaurants. She may have to drop out of school and live without any kind of papers. Maybe she'll end up in front of an immigration judge, too, begging to please be allowed to remain in the country so she can find a way to finish her school. Forget about school, we don't even have enough to cook a good meal with chicken some days. I am holding on tightly to my savings so that I'll be ready for the day when worse comes to worst, but now I ask myself what am I saving it for? The worse has come to the worst, and my back is breaking. So, yes, Doctor, I have many major stressors in my life.

Forty-nine

HE KNEW IT WAS OVER THE MOMENT HE WALKED OUT OF THE DOCTOR'S office.

That night, after work, he asked Neni to sit down at the dinette. He took her hand and looked deep into her eyes. "Neni," he began.

"What's wrong? What did the doctor say?"

"Neni," he called her name again.

"Jende, please—"

"I'm ready to go back home," he said.

"Home where? What do you mean by 'go back home'?"

He took a deep breath and was silent for several seconds. "Home to Limbe," he said to his wife. "I want to go back to Limbe."

She pulled her hand from his and shifted backward in her chair, as if he'd just revealed that he had a vile contagious disease. "What's the meaning of all this?" she asked. Her voice was angry.

"I don't want to stay in this country anymore."

"You want us to pack up our things and go back to Limbe? Is that what you're saying?"

He nodded, looking at her sorrowfully, like a child pleading for mercy.

She peered into his eyes, bloodshot and heavy eyes that seemed to belong to a sick, broken man. When he tried to take her hand into his again, she shifted farther away from him and put them behind her back.

"You want to return to Limbe?"

"Yes."

"Why? Why are you talking like this, Jende? What's the meaning of all this?"

"I don't like what my life has become in this country. I don't know how long I can continue living like this, Neni. The suffering in Limbe was bad, but this one here, right now . . . it's more than I can take."

Neni Jonga stared at her husband as if wanting to feel sympathy but capable of feeling only irritation. "Is it something the doctor said?" she asked. "Is it because of your back?"

"No . . . I mean, it's not only because of my back. It's everything, Neni. Have you not seen how unhappy I've been?"

"Of course, *bébé*. I've seen how you've been unhappy. But your father died, and you have been in mourning. Anyone who loves their father the way you loved your father would be unhappy."

"But it's not only my father's death. It's everything that's happened. I lost my job. My *papier* situation. This work, work, work, all the time. For what? For a little money? How much suffering can a man take in this world, eh? How much longer . . ." His voice broke at the end of his question, but he cleared his throat to push it out.

"You know we can get through anything, Jends," Neni said, taking his hand. "We've been through so much. You know we'll be okay, right?"

He shook his head. "No," he said. "I don't know if I'll be okay. I'm trying really hard, but I don't know if my life will get better in this country. How long will I keep on washing dishes?"

"Only until you get your *papier*."

"That's not true," he said with a sad shake of his head. "*Papier* is not everything. In America today, having documents is not enough. Look at how many people with papers are struggling. Look at how even some Americans are suffering. They were born in this country. They have American passports, and yet they are sleeping on the street, going to bed hungry, losing their jobs and houses every day in this . . . this economic crisis."

Timba started whimpering in the bedroom. They stopped talking, looking past each other as they waited for her to put herself back to sleep. She did.

"Having papers in this country is not everything," Jende continued. "What do you think is going to change with my life if I get papers tomorrow?"

"You will get a better job, won't you?"

"What better job? I have no education that anyone can call a real education. What will I do? Go to work at Pathmark? Spend ten years weighing shrimp like Tunde?"

"But *bébé*, working at Pathmark is a good job. You know that. Tunde has a very good job. He has benefits, all kind of insurance. He even has a retirement plan—that's what Olu told me. And on top of that he buys food for his family on a discount. How is that not a good job?"

Jende looked at Neni and chuckled, a cheerless chuckle followed by another shake of his head. Maybe she thought it was such a good life her friend Olu had because her husband worked at the Pathmark seafood counter, but he didn't think Tunde was so happy with his life. How could he possibly be, spending all those days of the week around seafood, coming home at the end of the day smelling like fish.

"So you think Tunde and Olu have such a good life, eh?"

"I think they manage well, and we can, too, if you get your *papier* and get a job like that."

"And how long do you think I can take care of my family with the kind of money Pathmark will pay me? Eh, Neni? How am I going to send you to pharmacy school with that kind of money? How are we going to send Liomi to college? Or be able to ever move out of this place full of cockroaches?"

"Then we'll go to Phoenix. That's what you've always wanted, right?"

"I'm not moving to Phoenix! You think Phoenix is going to have something better for us? I was sitting here feeling jealous of Arkamo because he has that nice four-bedroom house over there, only to find out two days ago that he lost his house. The department store where he was working closed down, he doesn't have a job, he cannot pay the bank, the bank takes back the house. You know where he and his family are living now? In his sister's basement, which has no windows! Is that what you want for us, Neni? To end up in a basement in Phoenix?"

Neni sighed and shook her head. "Okay, *bébé*," she said. "Then we'll stay in New York. Maybe you could go back to working as a driver. Maybe we can find you another job like the one you had with Mr. Edwards?"

"You're talking nonsense."

"I'm only saying that—"

"You think it's easy to get a job like that? You think it's easy for someone like me to get a good job like that? Were you not here when I sent out one hundred résumés for all those chauffeur jobs on the Internet and no one called me back? You know I only got the job with Mr. Edwards because Mr. Dawson likes Winston very much and he trusted Winston to recommend someone good. I got the job only because of Winston, not because of myself. Okay? So stop talking like someone who has no sense."

She could tell she had incensed him. She tried to rub his shoulder to atone for whatever she had said to infuriate him, but he pulled away and stood up.

"Please, *bébé*," she said, looking up at him. "We're going to be fine, right?"

He walked out of the room without responding and went into the kitchen. When she went to join him, she found him opening and shutting drawers and cabinets.

"*Bébé*, what are you looking for?"

"You need to know something, Neni," he said, turning to face her. "You need to know that much of what has happened to get us here is because of Winston. You understand? If Winston didn't offer to pay the rest of Bubakar's fees, you know we would not have as much money saved right now. We will have nothing if it wasn't for my cousin paying for almost all of Bubakar and my immigration fees, helping me find a good job, helping me find this apartment! But if things start to get too bad for us in this country, you have a student visa, I have the government trying to deport me, you need to stay in school to keep your student visa, we start running out of money, one of us gets seriously sick, who are we going to turn to? Winston is going to have a child. He's going to get married. Have more children. His little sisters are finishing Buea University next year and then he has to bring them over here. We will no longer have Winston to turn to left and right. And even if we could, I am a man! I cannot continue waiting for my cousin to rescue me all the time."

"But no one knows how God works. Maybe, one way or another, you can get another job driving someone else, eh?"

"You're not listening to me, Neni. You're not listening! Forget about how God works, okay? Because even if I try again to look for a job as a driver, do you really think a big man on Wall Street will hire some African man from the street just like that? With this kind of economy, all kinds of people are looking for a job like that. Even some of those people who used to wear suits to work on Wall Street are now looking for jobs as drivers. Nothing is easy anymore. How do you think I'm ever going to get another job that pays thirty-five thousand dollars?"

"Maybe you can—"

"Maybe I can do what?"

"There are other things—"

"Why are you arguing with me? Is it that you don't believe me? You should have been with me last week when I saw this man who used to drive another executive at Lehman Brothers. We used to sit together outside the building sometimes; he was a fresh round man. I saw him downtown: The man looked like he had his last good meal a year ago. He has not been able to find another job. He says too many people want to be chauffeurs now. Even people who used to be police and people with fine college degrees, they want to be chauffeurs. Everyone is losing jobs everywhere and looking for new jobs, anything to pay bills. So you tell me—if he, an American, a white man with papers, cannot get a new chauffeur job then what about me? They say the country will get better, but you know what? I don't know if I can stay here until that happens. I don't know if I can continue suffering like this just because I want to live in America."

Fifty

SHE WOULD NOT BE LEAVING. NEVER. SHE WOULD NOT BE RETURNING TO Limbe.

For years she had stayed in her father's house doing nothing but housework, first too grief-stricken and shamed to return to school after dropping out and then losing her daughter; later—when she was ready to return, four years after the baby's death—unable to do so because her father didn't think it was worthwhile paying for an almost-twenty-year-old to attend secondary school. He had suggested she apprentice as a seamstress, which she was opposed to because, she told him, she'd never imagined herself sitting at a sewing machine five days a week. Fine then, he'd said to her, stay at home and imagine yourself doing nothing for the rest of your life. It was only when Liomi was one year old that he finally agreed to pay for her to attend evening computer classes, after she'd convinced him that acquiring basic computer skills might help her get an office job. After the year of classes, though, she'd been unable to get a job because there were too few jobs in Limbe, never mind one for a young woman who hadn't made it as far as high school. She had been bored and frustrated at home, unable to have any sort of independence because she was financially dependent on her parents, unable to marry Jende because her father wouldn't let her marry a council laborer and unable to do anything about it because both she and Jende believed it wrong to defy a parent and marry against his or her wishes.

By her late twenties, all she could think about was America.

It wasn't that she thought life in America had no ills—she'd watched enough episodes of *Dallas* and *Dynasty* to know that the country had its share of vicious people—but, rather, because shows like *The Fresh Prince of Bel Air* and *The Cosby Show* had shown her that there was a place in the world where blacks had the same chance at prosperity as whites. The African-Americans she saw on TV in Cameroon were happy and successful, well educated and respectable, and she'd come to believe that if they could flourish in America, surely she could, too. America gave everyone, black or white, an equal opportunity to be whatever they wished to be. Even after she'd seen the movies *Boyz n the Hood* and *Do the Right Thing*, she couldn't be swayed or convinced that the kind of black life depicted represented anything but a very small percentage of black life, just like Americans probably understood that the images they saw of war and starvation in Africa were but a very small percentage of African life. None of the folks from Limbe who had emigrated to America sent home pictures of a life like the ones in those movies. Every picture she'd seen of Cameroonians in America was a portrait of bliss: children laughing in snow; couples smiling at a mall; families posing in front of a nice house with a nice car nearby. America, to her, was synonymous with happiness.

Which was why, on the day Jende shared with her Winston's offer to buy him a ticket so he could move to America and eventually bring her and Liomi over, she had wept as she composed a five-paragraph email of gratitude to Winston. She began watching American movies like *Stepmom* and *Mrs. Doubtfire* not only for leisure but also as advance preparation, envisioning a future in New York where she would finish her education, own a home, raise a happy family. Though she'd been surprised to learn upon arrival that not many blacks lived like the ones in the sitcoms, and virtually no one, black or white, had a butler like the family in *The Fresh Prince*, the realization had done little to change her impression of what was possible in America. America might be flawed, but it was still a beautiful country. She could still become far more than she would have become in Limbe. In spite of her daily hardships, she could still send pictures to her friends in Limbe and say, look at me, look at me and my children, we're finally on our way.

But now, after coming so far for so long, with only two semesters left at BMCC before she could transfer to a pharmacy school, Jende wanted her to return home. He wanted to drag her back to Limbe. Never.

"But what you gonno do?" Fatou asked as she braided Neni's hair.

"I don't know," Neni said. "I really don't know."

Fatou turned Neni around by the shoulders and pressed her head down so she could finish a cornrow. "Marriage," Fatou said, "is a thing you want. But when you gonno get it, it bring you all the thing you no want."

Neni scoffed. Fatou couldn't stop herself from making up a new proverb on the spot; she could never prevent herself from being a one-woman book of odd opinions.

"No matter what woman in this country do," she went on, "we African woman musto stand behind the husband and be following them and say yes, yes. That what we African woman musto do. We no gonno say to husband, no, I no gonno do it."

"So you do everything Ousmane asks you to do, eh?"

"Yes. I do. Everything he want, I do. Why you think we got seven childrens?"

"Because Ousmane said so?"

"What you think? What woman no crazy wanno suffer like that seven time in one life?"

Neni laughed, but the afternoon would be one of the few times she would laugh about her plight with a friend. Most times she would shake her head in bewilderment, which was what she did two days later, when Betty stopped by to drop off her children before heading to her second job at a Lower East Side nursing home.

"Tell him you're not going," Betty said in the kitchen while the children fought over the remote control in the living room. "What does he mean life is too hard here? If life was not hard for us back home why did we leave our countries and come here?"

"He thinks it's better for a person to suffer in their own country than to suffer somewhere else."

"Ha! Please, don't make me laugh. He really thinks suffering in Cameroon is better than suffering in America?"

Neni shrugged.

"You'll regret it if you go back home, I'm telling you right now," Betty said. "Why are you guys acting like little children? Life is hard everywhere. You know that maybe it will get better one day. Maybe it will not get better. Nobody knows tomorrow. But we keep on trying."

"You know how hard things have been. Ever since he lost his—"

"What about the money you got from Mrs. Edwards?"

"Ssshh," Neni said. She looked out of the kitchen to make sure Liomi wasn't nearby. "Jende says we cannot use the money," she whispered. "He's hidden it in a separate bank account and says we'll only touch it when worse comes to worst."

"Why does he get to decide how to spend the money?"

"Ah, Betty, there's no need for you to put it like that."

With her mouth half open and her nose flared, Betty looked at Neni, moving her eyes slowly up Neni's face, from chin to forehead and back down, twice.

"Neni?" she said, cocking her head.

"Eh?"

"Did you march to that woman's house that day and earn that money for yourself?"

Neni nodded.

"Is that money Jende's money or both of your money?"

"It's both—"

"Then tell your husband it's your money, too, and you want to use it to stay!"

"What kind of talk is that?" Neni said. "You think I'm an American woman? I cannot just tell my husband how I want something to be."

"Why not?"

"You don't know what kind of man Jende is. He's a good man, but he's still a man."

"So you're going to go back to Cameroon?"

"I don't want to go!"

"Then don't go! Tell him you want to stay in America and keep trying. There are one million things you have to do before you start thinking about packing your things—you get your papers first and you go from there. I've told you if you need to borrow money for your tuition I know people who can help you out. I'll make some calls tomorrow, maybe even tonight I'll start calling people. Just . . . don't even think about this going home nonsense anymore. Tell Jende you're not going anywhere. That you want to stay here and keep trying!"

Neni looked at Betty and her gap tooth that divided her mouth into two equally beautiful halves. The woman knew all about trying. Thirty-one years in this country and Betty was still trying, and Neni couldn't understand why. Betty had come here as a child with her parents and gotten her papers through them. She had been a citizen for over a decade, and yet here she was, in her early forties, working two jobs as a certified nursing assistant at nursing homes, stuck in nursing school. Neni couldn't understand how that was possible. If she were a citizen, she would be a pharmacist in no more than five years. A pharmacist with a nice SUV and a home in Yonkers or Mount Vernon or maybe even New Rochelle.

That evening she sat at the desktop for almost two hours, searching for advice on Google. "How to convince husband." "How to get what you want." "Husband wants to move back home." She found no advice remotely relevant to her situation.

Later, as she stood in front of the mirror staring at her face before applying her exfoliating mask, she promised herself she would fight Jende till the end. She had to.

It wasn't only that she loved New York City and the times it had given her and the times it held in store for her. It wasn't just because she was hopeful that she would one day become a pharmacist, and a successful one at that. It was hardly only about what she would leave behind, things she could never find in her hometown, things like horse-drawn carriages on city streets, and gigantic lighted Christmas trees in squares and plazas, and pretty parks where musicians played for free beside polychromatic foliage. It wasn't merely for what she was leaving behind. No. It was mostly for what her children would be deprived of, and for where they would all be returning to: Limbe. It was for the boundless opportunities they would be denied, the kind of future she was almost denied in her father's house. She was going to fight for her children, and for herself, because no one journeyed far away from home to return without a fortune amassed or dream achieved. She needed to fight so she and her children would never become objects of ridicule the way she'd been when she'd gotten pregnant and dropped out of school.

"How are all those people in town going to look at us?" she said to Jende a few days later, before he left for work. "Look at them, they will say. America don pass them."

"So that's what's bothering you, eh?" was his response. "You want to spend the rest of your life living like this because you're afraid people will laugh at you?"

"No!" she replied, pointing in his face as he put on his jacket. "That's not what's bothering me. You're what's bothering me!"

Betty called minutes after he left. "Now I understand why some women choose to marry other women," she said before Neni had a chance to talk about her own morning.

"What happened?" Neni asked disinterestedly, wishing she hadn't picked up the phone.

"I go to Macy's and buy one dress on sale, and Alphonse acts as if all I do is shop."

"What has that got to do with marrying a woman?"

"What woman is going to make another woman feel bad for buying a dress that makes her feel good? I'm not going to wear an old dress to go to a wedding where people are going to take my picture and put it on Facebook. Next thing you know people will be commenting on my picture 'Betty looks so old, she looks so fat.' These days you have to be careful about—"

"Betty, please, I have to go to the store—"

"What's wrong?"

"Nothing."

"What do you mean, nothing?"

Neni ignored the question.

"Is it Jende?"

"Who else?" Neni said. "I don't know what else I can say to him."

Betty grunted disapprovingly once, then twice. "You know," she said, "I've heard a lot of crazy things in my life, but I've never heard of anyone leaving America to go back to their poor country."

"He thinks he knows something the rest of us don't know."

"What did he say when you mentioned the divorce?"

"I haven't spoken to him about it."

"You still haven't said anything! This whole time—"

"Please, I don't need you to make me feel bad, too, okay? I'm begging you. I've been thinking about it . . ."

"You cannot just sit there thinking about it."

"I'm not *just* sitting there thinking about it! I'll talk to him about it; not today—he's coming back home from work too late."

"When are you going to ask him then? You know the longer you wait—"

"Nothing is going to change in a few days."

"So you're going to wait till next year?"

"I said I'll talk to him."

Fifty-one

A TOPIC LIKE THIS HAD TO BE APPROACHED WITH UTMOST CARE. NOT TOO seriously. Not too lightly. It had to be brought up with just enough finesse so it wouldn't become a fight. Which was why she waited until he was in the bathroom, brushing his teeth. She entered while he was lining his toothbrush with Colgate, from one end of the bristles to the other, the way he always did it, even back in Limbe where a tube of toothpaste sometimes cost as much as a pile of cocoyams.

She sat on the toilet seat and watched him turn on the faucet and wet the toothbrush. "I was thinking," she began, looking at his face in the mirror.

He put the toothbrush in his mouth and began brushing, intensely scrubbing his molars.

"It's just that, I was . . . Betty, she has a cousin . . . she says he can . . . he has citizenship."

He spat out the white foam. "So?" he said, not bothering to turn around.

"He can help us, *bébé*. With *papier*."

He put the toothbrush back in his mouth and continued brushing: up, left, right, down. His eyes in the mirror were the reddest she'd ever seen them. "If you're trying to say what I think you're about to say," he said, his mouth half full of foam, "shut up right now."

"But . . . please hear me out, *bébé*. Please. Betty asked him and he said he can do it for us."

With his mouth half-open, a thin trail of foam pouring out, he turned around to look at her. She turned her face away.

"The money from Mrs. Edwards," she said, "we should use it to pay him."

He lifted the faucet handle, scooped water into his mouth and swished, then spat out the foamy water and began washing his face, splashing as far as the mirror above and the trash can below. When he was done, he pulled the towel hanging on the shower door and covered his face, breathing in and out through it.

"We divorce, I marry him. I get *papier* through him, then me and him divorce and me and you marry back, but the whole time we continue living . . ."

As if he'd heard something unbelievably stunning, he abruptly pulled the towel off his face, which seemed to have grown blacker than his hair. He turned around to face her. "Those screws in your head holding your brain together," he said, poking his temple with his index finger, "they've gotten loose, right?"

"We don't have to go back to Cameroon, Jends," she said, her voice so laden with despair it sank with every word.

He dropped the towel on the floor and opened the door. "If you ever open your mouth and suggest this kind of nonsense to me again—"

"But *bébé*—"

"I said, if you ever say this kind of foolish talk to me again, Neni, I swear to God—"

"The money from Mrs. Edwards, it's my money, too!"

He stood at the door, looking down at her looking up at him. "If you dare open your mouth and say one more thing, Neni!"

"You'll do what?"

He slammed the door in her face and left her frozen on the toilet seat.

Fifty-two

BUBAKAR AGREED TO DO AS JENDE WANTED. HE WOULD PETITION THE judge to close the deportation case in exchange for Jende leaving the country on his own.

"Voluntary departure is what they call it," Bubakar said. "You leave quietly within ninety days. The government will be happy. They don't have to pay for your airfare back to Cameroon."

"And I can come back to America?" Jende asked.

"Of course," the lawyer said. "If the embassy gives you a visa again. But will they? I cannot tell you the answer. You will not be banned from returning to the country like you would be if you had just overstayed your visa and left. You can still come back, but will you be able to get another visa after what you did with the last one? Only the embassy in Cameroon can decide that."

What about his wife and children? Jende wanted to know. Would they be able to come back? The baby could always come back because she was American, Bubakar told him. As for Neni, she should be fine if she formally withdrew from BMCC and left by a certain date after the international students office terminated her record in SEVIS. The embassy would probably give her another visa in the future because they wouldn't hold it against her that she once came in on a student visa and was unable to finish her studies because she had a baby.

"But your son, Liomi," Bubakar said. "He will be in the same hot soup as you."

"Why? He is only a child. They cannot punish him if his parents brought him here. I am the one who made him overstay his visa. It's my fault, Mr. Bubakar. It's not his fault."

"Eh? Na so you think, *abi*?" The lawyer laughed his usual two-note laugh. "Let me tell you something, my brother," he said. "American government does not care whether you are a one-day-old baby who was brought here and ended up illegal or whether you were blindfolded and tossed into a shipping container and woke up to find yourself in Kansas City. You hear me? American government doesn't give the tiniest piece of shit whose fault it is. Once you are here illegally, you are here illegally. You will pay the price."

"But—"

"That's why you have to think *very carefully* about this decision to take your family back home," he said. "You say this country don pass you, eh? I believe you. Sometimes this country pass me, too. America can be hell, I know. Man nova see suffer until the day ei enter America, make I tell you."

He laughed again, the kind of laughter released only at the remembrance of awful things past. "I mean," he went on, "I've been here for twenty-nine years. For the first three years, I spent hours every month searching for a one-way ticket back to Nigeria. But you know what, my brother? Patience. Perseverance. That is the key. Persevere it like a man. Look at me today, eh? I have a house in Canarsie. My one daughter is in medical school. My son is a civil engineer in New Jersey. Another daughter is in Brooklyn College. Hopefully, she'll get into Fordham Law and become a lawyer like me. I'm very proud of them.

When I look at them, I do not one bit regret all my suffering. I can say without feeling any shame that life is good for me. I persevered, and look at me now. I'm not going to sit here and lie to you that life is going to get easy for you next month or next year, because it might not. It's a long, hard journey from struggling immigrant to successful American. But you know what, my brother? Anyone can do it. I am an example that with hard work and perseverance, anyone can do it."

"Rubbish," Winston said when Jende told him what Bubakar had said. Of course he did not want Jende to return home. Cameroon did not have opportunities like America, but that did not mean one should stay in America if doing so no longer made sense. "Why does everyone make it sound as if being in America is everything?" he said.

"All this stress," Jende said. "For what?"

"For you to die and leave bills for your children to pay," Winston replied.

Even if Jende got papers, Winston went on, without a good education, and being a black African immigrant male, he might never be able to make enough money to afford to live the way he'd like to live, never mind having enough to own a home or pay for his wife and children to go to college. He might never be able to have a really good sleep at night.

"Whenever I talk to someone in *pays* who is trying to leave their good job and run to America, I tell them, 'Look out, oh. Look out. Make man no say I no be warn ei say America no easy.'"

"But you didn't warn me seriously enough," Jende said, laughing.

"No," Winston said, laughing back. "I didn't warn you. I just bought you a ticket so you could come see it for yourself."

"That is not a lie."

"But if someone asks me right now if they should leave their job at home and come to America, I swear, Bo, I will beg them to forget about America for now."

"Maybe wait until after this recession thing finishes."

"What finish? Is it ever going to finish?"

"One day, surely, the country is going to get better."

"I don't know about that, Bo. I just don't know. In short, even some people who went to law school like me cannot expect a good life in this country anymore. I read stories about Mexicans who crossed the border to enter America, and now they're trying to cross the border to go back to their country. Why? Because there's nothing left here for them to come and get."

"It's people like you who are lucky," Jende said. "To have a good job and money."

"You think I'm lucky?"

"Are you not luckier than the rest of us? If you don't think you're lucky, you can come live in this Harlem dumpster and I'll live near Columbus Circle."

"I guess I'm lucky," Winston said after a chuckle. "I work like a donkey from morning to night for the people who are taking everything and leaving only a little for everyone else. But at the end of the day, I go home with piles of their dirty money, so—"

"But how man go do?"

"How man go do? I cannot do anything. And even if I could I probably wouldn't, because I like the money, even if I hate how I make it."

"As the Americans would say, 'Gotta do wha ya gotta do.'"

"I'm just sorry for people like you, Bo," Winston went on. "This country—" He sighed. "One day, I'm telling you, there will be no more Mexicans crossing the border to come to America. Just wait and see."

"Maybe it will be Americans running to Mexico," Jende said.

"I won't be surprised if that happens one day," Winston agreed, and they both burst into laughter at the image of a multitude of Americans surging across the Rio Grande.

Jende got off the phone thankful that Winston had supported his decision. He needed the validation—he'd found it nowhere else, not even from his mother. When he had told her of his plan to return home, she had wondered why he was coming back when others were running out of Limbe, when many in his age group were fleeing to Bahrain and Qatar, or trekking and taking a succession of crowded buses to get from Cameroon to Libya so they could cross to Italy on leaky boats and arrive there with dreams of a happier life if the Mediterranean didn't swallow them alive.

Fifty-three

THE DAY LIOMI WAS BORN SHE HELD HIM AND CRIED FOR OVER AN HOUR. It had been a long pregnancy, almost forty-two weeks of nearly every awful pregnancy symptom imaginable: ghastly morning sickness and vomiting for four months; virtually nonstop headaches for the next two months; back pain that had her unable to roll over in bed and stand up without groaning; swollen feet that couldn't fit in the size ten shoes Jende had bought for her; a brutal thirty-hour labor. During the last month, she had used a cane to run errands and get around town, not wanting to spend all day in bed and have her siblings and friends laugh at her for acting as if pregnancy were an illness. Stop behaving like an old woman, they surely would have said, lovingly poking fun at her awkward gait and large belly. What would you do if you were pregnant and had five other children to look after? her father had said to her, angrily, when she said she wouldn't be carrying bags of groceries on her head anymore since pregnant women shouldn't carry anything too heavy. She hated his snide comments but, without a husband to protect her, she had to remain in his house and be subdued by them. When Liomi finally came out—after two midwives had maneuvered and pressed on her belly for over an hour while her mother and aunt held her legs up and shouted, push, push, if you know how to enjoy the sweet part then you must know how to suffer the bitter part, too—she hugged his bloodied and puffy body and cried so hard she feared she would use up all the water and strength in her body. It's over, the women in the room said to her, what are you still crying for? But she knew it wasn't over, and the women knew that, too. It was only the beginning of far more pains, but it would all be worth it as long as at the end of the day her baby was alive and well and she could look into his eyes and see what a wonderful, wonderful gift she'd been given.

"Why then would you want to give him up for adoption?" Natasha asked her.

Neni leaned forward on the couch, pulled a tissue from the box on Natasha's coffee table, and looked away as she patted her face dry. Five feet away, on Natasha's desk, the computer had gone to screen-saver mode and was displaying picture after picture of Natasha and her husband, children, and grandchildren. They looked like a happy family.

"I completely understand that you want the best future for your son," Natasha said. "No one can fault you for wanting what every mother wants. But you have to ask yourself, is this the best way? What are you willing to give in exchange for what you want? And what do you know about this man who you want to talk to?"

"He was my precalculus professor last year," Neni said quietly, her voice wrapped in distress.

"Mmm-hmm, and what else? Is he a good friend of yours?"

Neni shook her head. "Not a good friend like we talk all the time. But we had coffee on the last day of the semester and promised to stay in touch. He is a very nice man. He was nice to me and when he met my son he was nice to him, too."

"How much have you been in touch?"

"We email each other a few times, nothing too special. He included me in his email list when he sent pictures of his fortieth birthday celebration with his boyfriend in Paris. I included him in my email also, when I emailed everyone to say that Timba had been born. He emailed me back congratulations and said he cannot wait for the day he has a child, too. Things like that."

"I see."

Neni nodded. "He told me that he and his boyfriend, they want to adopt very much, that is why two nights ago, when I was up thinking about my son, this idea just came to me like a lightning. I woke up in the morning and I could not think of anything else."

"You haven't told anybody yet, have you?"

"Who can I tell, Natasha? My friends will think I have become a madwoman, and my husband, I don't even know how I will . . . That's why I called you first, if you could help me talk to my husband, let him understand it will be the best thing for our son."

"Do you really think that, Neni?"

Neni did not respond.

"You really believe that giving your son to this professor, who you barely know, and his partner will make your son happy? Make you happy? Because you're going to have to—"

"If it means that my son can remain in America and become a citizen by being adopted by an American couple, I will be happy. I will tell him it is for the best for him and he will be happy, too. And I don't care that they are gay, if they promise to treat him well."

"But will your husband care that they're gay? How does he feel about gays?"

"He's not afraid of them."

"Yes, but is he . . . never mind that. My bigger concern is not about them being gay. I think it's wonderful that they're gay, just like it's wonderful that I'm not. What I care about is how this is all going to play out. Assuming you email the professor and meet and he tells you, sure, if you have to go back to Cameroon, my partner and I would love to adopt your boy. Assuming your son is happy with the arrangements, you kiss him goodbye at the airport and get on the plane, how do you think you're going to feel the moment that plane gets in the air, knowing you might not see him for years?"

"I don't know how I will feel . . . I will be worried for him, but . . . I don't like to live my life thinking too much about how I'm going to feel. I just have to . . ."

Natasha leaned forward and pushed the box of tissues closer to Neni, who sniffled, but didn't reach for a tissue.

"I know you came to see me," the pastor said, "because you want me to validate you, tell you that you're making a tough decision but it's the right one. But I can't do that . . . I really can't, because I believe you will regret it. I don't believe for a second that you'll go through with it, knowing how much you love your son. But if you do . . . I'm sorry, Neni, but regret, especially when it comes to your child, it's not something you want to live with."

"I will not regret it," Neni said. "I will not regret leaving him behind so he can become a citizen, grow up and be—"

"Are you even certain he can become a citizen if they adopt him?"

"I Googled it, and it says American citizens can adopt an illegal child and file for green card for him, and after a few years the child can become a citizen."

"I've never heard of that. I would consult an adoption lawyer first, especially since the couple you have in mind is gay and there's DOMA to worry about."

"But I cannot take money to pay for a lawyer without telling my husband first!" Neni said, throwing her hands in the air. "And if I try to talk to him about this . . . I cannot even say *anything* to him these days without him . . ."

"Don't worry about the money for now—I could always get you a free consultation somewhere or talk to the church board about helping you guys pay for a lawyer."

"Oh, thank you so much, Natasha! From the bottom of my heart, I thank you so much!"

"But before we go ahead and start spending money on lawyers," Natasha said, "I'll ask you to please spend more time thinking—"

"Thinking about what?"

"Think about if this really is the best solution. Spend some more time—"

"I don't have more time!" Neni cried. "My husband is ready to go back home right now, and I don't know what else to do! I'm so angry at him, I cannot eat, I cannot sleep . . ."

"But there has to be another way to get your family out of this situation."

"There are other ways but my husband says no!" Neni cried again, pulling tissues from the box and bawling into them. "He wants what he wants and I cannot do anything about it!"

Natasha leaned back in her seat and for almost a minute she said nothing, looking on as Neni finished her cry, wiped her eyes, and blew her nose. When Neni was done, Natasha stood up, picked up Neni's used tissues from the floor, and brought her a new box of tissues.

"Oh, Natasha, what am I going to do?" Neni said as Natasha retook her seat. "Sometimes I feel as if I am in a movie about a crazy African woman."

"We just have to trust God that the movie will have a happy ending, don't we? And Neni and her family lived happily ever after!"

Neni burst out laughing, then she was crying, then she was laughing and crying all at once. Natasha watched as she went through the full range, dried her eyes, and then laughed again and cried again, unable to believe this was where life had dumped her.

"I can't imagine how difficult this is for you, but you have to look at the things you're willing to do. You're willing to divorce your husband and marry a man you barely know. You're willing to give up your child for adoption knowing you might not see him for many years." Natasha paused, looking at Neni intently. "I think you ought to step back a little bit, ask yourself why you're—"

"I have to do what I need to do."

"I'm not disagreeing."

"I don't like how people say to a woman, oh you want so many things, why do you want so many things? When I was young my father said to me, one day you're going to learn that you're a woman and you should not want too many things; like I should just be happy with my life even if it's not the kind of life I want."

"Mmm-mmm," Natasha said, shaking her head.

"I'm not ashamed of wanting many things in life. Tomorrow when my daughter grows up I will tell her to want whatever she wants, the same thing I will tell my son."

Someone knocked on Natasha's office door and said her next appointment had arrived. Natasha said she'd be ready in five minutes. She stood up, came around the coffee table, sat down next to Neni, and took her hands. "I will support you," she said. "Whatever you decide to do, you will have my full support."

Neni nodded, and bowed her head.

"You don't have to ever worry about me judging you."

For a moment Neni sat in silence, her head still bowed. "A lot of mothers where I come from," she said softly, raising her head, "they send their children to live with other people. They want them to be raised by relatives who have more money."

"Hmm."

"Sometimes these mothers and fathers are poor and other times they are married and living together and have enough to feed their children, but they want their children to grow up in the house of rich people."

"Does this usually work out well?"

"The relatives treat the children well sometimes; other times they treat them badly, but the mothers let their children remain there. I did not understand why." She took a deep breath and leaned back on the couch, her hands crossed over her belly, her eyes on the floor.

"What are you thinking?" Natasha asked her.

"Maybe I'm becoming another person."

"Mmm-hmm. And what do you think of this new person you're becoming?"

"I don't know."

"Let me put this another way: Are you happy with who you're becoming?"

Neni's eyes welled up with tears, but she didn't cry. She looked toward the window and blinked back her tears.

Fifty-four

GONE WERE THE MOMENTS OF TENDER EMBRACES IN THE KITCHEN, MIN-utes of stolen passion in the bathroom while the children slept. They were now in two separate universes, each certain of his or her rightness and the other's senselessness. Unwilling to fully embrace the new person she was becoming—it seemed so futile, considering the final decision wasn't hers to make—she could do nothing but engage in fraught conversations about their future, which ended in accusations from her and rage from him. We're going back home, he would say, and that is the end of that. How can you do this to us? she would screech. How can you be *so* selfish? If she spoke while he was eating, he would push away his food and jump into a rant about how she had been sold the stupid nonsense about America being the greatest country in the world. Guess what, he would say to her in mock instruction, America is not all that; this country is full of lies and people who like to hear lies. If you want to know the truth I'll tell you the truth: This country no longer has room for people like us. Anyone who has no sense can believe the lies and stay here forever, hoping that things will get better for them one day and they will be happy. As for me, I won't live my life in the hope that someday I will magically become happy. I refuse to!

Their worst fight happened four days before his court appearance, after she said to him, while he was groaning in pain on the living room floor, that his best chance at getting his back pain healed was to stay in New York, where the doctors were better than the ones in Limbe. She had spoken mindlessly as she massaged his back, thinking nothing of how a man in pain and four days away from standing before an immigration judge would react.

"Shut up," he said to her between his groans.

A day later, she would look back and realize that she should have said nothing after this warning. But she did not consider doing so then: Her battle to help her husband recognize the folly of his conviction had not yet been won.

"Why are you so stubborn?" she said. "You know the doctors here can find a cure—"

He pushed her off his back and stood up, glaring at her as he tried to massage his own shoulders.

"I'm just saying—"

"Did you hear me say you should shut up?"

"This pain is never going to go away if—"

She didn't see the slap coming. She merely found herself stumbling backward and falling on the floor from the force and shock of it, her cheek burning as if someone had rubbed hot tar on it. He was standing over her, his fists clenched, screaming in the ugliest voice she'd ever heard. He was calling her useless and idiot and stupid and a selfish woman who would be happy to see her husband die in pain all so she could live in New York. She jumped up, her cheek still throbbing.

"Did you just hit me?" she shrieked, her hand on her left cheek. "Did you hit me?"

"Yes," he said, his eyes wide open. "And you dare open your mouth one more time, I'll hit you again!"

"Then hit me again!"

He turned around to walk away but she pulled him back by his shirt. He tried to shove her away but she wouldn't let him go, standing in his way and shouting in his face as her tears came down. "That's why you brought me to America, eh? To kill me and send my corpse back to Limbe. Go ahead and hit me, Jende . . . I'm begging you, hit me again!"

She pushed him with her palms, squealing like one of Ma Jonga's pigs moments before its slaughter. Why don't you just go ahead and kill me, she demanded. Why not? Hit me and kill me right now!

"Don't you make me hit you again," he growled as he pushed her hands away and clenched his fist. "I'm warning you."

"Oh, no, please hit me," she said. "Raise your hand and hit me again! America has beaten you and you don't know what to do and now you think hitting me will make it better. Please, go ahead and hit—"

So he did. He hit her hard. One vicious slap on her cheek. Then another. And another. And a deafening one right over her ear. They landed on her face even before she was done asking for them. She squealed, stunned and pained; she fell on the ground wailing.

"I'm dying, oh! I'm dead, oh!"

Liomi ran out of the bedroom. He saw his mother balled in a corner and his father standing over her, his hand raised and about to descend.

"Go back to the bedroom right now," his father barked.

The boy stood speechless, motionless, powerless.

"I say get back in the room right now before I box your face into pieces!" his father barked again.

"Mama . . ."

"If you don't—!"

Liomi burst into tears and ran back to the bedroom.

Someone knocked on the door.

"Is everything all right?" a man asked from outside.

Neni quieted her sobs.

Jende opened the door.

"Yes, sir," Jende told the elderly neighbor, pushing his sweaty face through a small crack in the door. "Everything is all right, thank you, sir."

"What about the woman?" the neighbor asked. "I thought I heard her screaming."

"I'm okay," Neni answered from the floor, her voice as counterfeit as a dollar bill made on checkered paper.

The man left.

Jende put on his shoes and left, too, slamming the door behind him. No other neighbors came. If they heard something, they did nothing. No police came to the apartment to question Jende about domestic abuse or encourage Neni to file charges. The thought of filing charges against him received no deliberation in her mind, even though she knew it was something wives in America did when their husbands beat them. Such a thing was unimaginable to her; she could never do anything like that to her husband. If he beat her a second time she was going to ask Winston to talk to him. If he did it a third time she was going to call Ma Jonga. Between his cousin and his mother he would be brought back to his senses. A marital dispute wasn't something to get the police involved in—it was a private family matter.

After twenty minutes of crying on the floor she stood up and went into the bedroom, wiping her tears with the hem of her dress. Liomi was sitting on their bed, whimpering. She hugged him and cried with him, both of them too scared to talk. They slept together on the big bed, Liomi taking the place of his father, Timba in the middle. Neni Jonga fell asleep with tears running into her pillow, convinced her husband had beaten her not because he didn't love her but because he was lost and could find no way out of the misery that had become his life.

Jende slept alone on the living room floor, partly in rage, partly for his back.

The next morning she woke up before him, as she often did, and made his breakfast, which he ate before heading off to work.

When he returned fourteen hours later he had a bouquet of red roses for her and a new video game for Liomi, who took it and thanked him without looking in his eyes because he was still scared of his father after what he'd seen him do to his mother.

"I will do everything I can to make you happy in Cameroon," Jende promised Neni. "We will have a very good life there."

Neni turned her face away.

He tried to pull her into his arms.

She resisted.

He went down on his knees and held her feet. "Please," he said, looking up at her face, "forgive me."

She forgave him. What else was she supposed to do?

Three days later, he stood before the immigration judge.

"My client would like to request voluntary departure, Your Honor," Bubakar said to the judge.

"Does your client understand what rights he is forfeiting?"

"Yes, Your Honor."

The judge flipped through the papers in front of him and looked up at Jende. "Mr. Jonga, you understand that if I grant your request for voluntary departure, you have to leave the country before one hundred and twenty days?"

"I do, Your Honor," Jende responded.

The judge asked the attorney for ICE if she had any objection to his granting voluntary departure to the defendant. She said no.

"Very well," the judge announced. "I'll review the case and make a decision. My clerk will notify you, at which point you'll have to leave the country before your time runs out."

Jende nodded, but the relief he'd thought he would feel did not come immediately. It did not come when he walked out of the court knowing that, in all likelihood, he would never have to walk into it again. It did not come when he arrived at work and changed from his suit to his work clothes, knowing he most likely would never again have to wash dishes to feed his children. The relief came only later that night, when Neni looked at him and, with tears in her eyes, said how glad she was that his ordeal might soon be over.

Fifty-five

IT WAS AN INTERNATIONAL CALL BUT SHE KNEW IT WASN'T FROM CAMeroon because the first three digits on her caller ID weren't 237. For a moment she considered picking it up, but she and the children were running late for Olu's mother-in-law's seventieth birthday party in Flatbush, so she ignored the call and the voicemail notification. She threw the phone into her purse, hoping she would get a chance to check the message on her way to the party, but Olu's sister, who was giving them a ride, chatted nonstop about the five-hundred-guest wedding she and her fiancé were planning in Lagos in December. It will be beyond fantastic, oh, the woman said at least five times, to which Neni was tempted to say, yes, enjoy the fantastic wedding because when the dancing is over and it's time to get to the business of being married, you will forget the definition of fantastic. But she didn't need to say it—the woman would find out soon enough; she merely listened and nodded as if she cared. It was only the next morning, after a seemingly endless night of dancing to hits by musicians from Fela to P-Square with a roomful of Yoruba women in the most elaborate *gele* styles she'd ever seen, that she thought about the voicemail and drowsily reached over a worn-out Jende to get her phone.

Hey, Neni, it's Vince, the caller said. Hey, how are you guys? Hope everyone's doing great. I know, you're probably surprised to hear from me, but don't panic, it's all good. I'm doing good; great, actually. Just calling because I have a quick question for you. Actually, something I'd like to discuss with you. I wouldn't wanna be a pain 'cause I know it's a major imposition, but . . . you think you could call me back when you get this message? You could just call me for a second, let me know you're free and I'll call you right back. I wouldn't want you to spend your money calling me in India but if you could get in touch, I'd appreciate it. Okay, peace and love to my man Jende, and to Liomi. Thanks and . . . well, hope we can talk soon. It's Vince Edwards, by the way. Ha, ha. Just in case you know a couple of Vinces in India. Namaste.

She saved the voicemail and lay back on the bed. Outside, two men shouted at each other in drunken voices; beside her Jende snored befittingly for a man who had just finished a sixteen-hour shift at work. She closed her eyes, trying to resume her sleep, but Jende's snoring and the pile of laundry on the floor and Vince's out-of-the-blue voicemail had all combined to wipe off the last drop of sleep left in her eyes, so she climbed over Timba and Jende and went to the living room. There was only one thing Vince would want to know from her, she thought as she listened to the voicemail again: what had transpired between her and his mother. Anna must have told him. He must have been perplexed that someone he'd thought was a good person wasn't such a good person after all. He must have told himself he needed to know the truth, since he was all about Truth. If we do not live in Truth, he always said, we do not live. Good thing she had a phone card. She was going to call him, and if he really wanted to hear her side of the story, she was going to tell him.

"Wow, I wasn't sure you were going to call me back," Vince said delightedly when he picked up the phone.

"Why would I not call you back?"

"I don't know, everyone's got so much going on you can't expect them to return your calls just because you ask them to."

"I'm not like everyone."

"No, you're not, Neni. No one is like everyone, and you haven't changed a bit," Vince said with a laugh. "How are you guys? How's Jende, and Liomi? You've got a new baby, right?"

"Everyone is fine. How are Mighty and your dad?"

They were doing well, Vince told her, though he was a bit concerned about them now that it was just the two of them at home. Neni nodded as he spoke, but she said nothing. She was interested in knowing how the Edwards family was doing, though not at the expense of immediately learning the reason for Vince's call. With any other person, she would have asked within thirty seconds because she hated being kept in suspense by unexpected callers—especially if she suspected the call might be about a matter that would make for an uncomfortable conversation—but with Vince that morning, she had to be kinder and gentler. So she started asking him question after question, and, seemingly eager to share, he proceeded to tell her far more than she thought she needed to know, all while leaving her wondering the reason for his call.

His dad was doing pretty well, he told her, but he'd become such a worrier ever since his wife died. He couldn't stop checking in on everyone all the time. He called his parents at least three times a week, far more than the weekly calls they'd become accustomed to. He emailed Vince at least every other day, to learn about the latest places Vince had visited and to make sure he hadn't run out of money. He called multiple times a day to check on Mighty, though Anna and Stacy and the part-time chauffeur repeatedly assured him that Mighty was fine and promised him that nothing bad was going to happen on their watch.

"It's hard as a parent not to think about your child all the time," Neni said.

Sure, Vince said, but it was really strange how his dad had suddenly become a man who made his life revolve around family. It would even be funny if it wasn't so sad. He appeared to hold nothing dearer than Mighty's well-being, rescheduling meetings to attend Mighty's hockey practices, turning down invitations to parties and dinners so he could stay home and play video games with Mighty, writing poems for Mighty while the boy slept.

"I called him the other day and he's coming back from taking a cooking class," Vince said with a laugh. "He wants to learn how to cook the meals my mom used to make for Mighty."

"I'm so happy to hear this, for Mighty's sake," Neni said. "I'm sure you know more than me, but that child wanted nothing more than to spend time with his father."

"Yeah, I'm glad for Mighty. But it's pretty sad whenever I talk to my dad about his day . . . he seems to be learning quickly and holding it together well, but the Universe has thrown him this heavy curveball, and he's struggling to carry it and walk on his path. And at his age, he still hasn't figured out his path, which is what happens when you go off pursuing illusions."

"For a man to raise a child alone, it's not easy. Us women, it's in our blood."

"It's definitely not in his blood, I'll tell you that. But I'm proud of him, how he's coping and doing his best."

"You should tell him that, Vince. It will make him happy. What would make a parent happier than to hear their child say 'I'm proud of you'?"

"I've told him how grateful I am that Mighty's doing well, and it's all thanks to him."

Neni nodded but said nothing.

"It's going to be a long road for him," Vince continued, "but he seems to have learned the importance of balance and recognizing that—"

"But Mighty," Neni said, "he must still be struggling to understand."

"Yeah. The good days are good, and once in a while he has a bad day when he doesn't want to do anything and poor Dad has no clue what to do. But overall, I'll say he's much happier than I thought he would be, and he gets to have something I never had. I was very worried for him when I left after the funeral."

"You left right after the funeral?"

"No, I stayed for over a month, but when I came back here I thought about returning home a lot."

"You? Returning? Don't you hate America?"

Vince laughed. "I don't love America," he said, "but my family's there, so I have to find a way to at least be able to stomach it."

"I still don't understand what is hard for you to stomach."

"All the bullshit the masses are blind to . . . so much mindlessness. People sit on their couches and watch garbage interrupted by messages to buy garbage which will create a desire for more garbage. They go to their computers and order from incredibly horrible corporations that are enslaving their fellow humans and pretty much destroying any chance of children growing up in a world where they can be truly free. But hey, we have our material comforts and we're saving money and corporations are creating sixty-hour-a-week jobs with sick leave so what does it matter if we're complicit? Let's just carry on with our lives while our country continues to commit atrocities all over the world."

"You want to give me your American citizenship and take my Cameroonian citizenship?" Neni said, laughing.

Vince did not laugh. "Anyway," he said, "now that Mighty and my dad are mostly okay I'm probably never coming back for good. Maybe I'll visit once a year, I don't know."

"Once or twice a year will be good for all of you."

"Maybe. I had a really hard time saying goodbye to them after the funeral."

"I cannot even imagine," Neni said. "I am so sorry about everything that happened, Vince. Truly sorry. I wanted to email to tell you that the news made me very sad, but . . . I couldn't even—"

"Don't worry about it. I know it wouldn't have been an easy email to write."

"No, it wasn't only that. I know how much you and your mother used to be really tight—Mighty told me that one time the two of you went on a vacation without him."

"It's true," Vince said with a laugh. "We went to Fiji the summer before I started college."

"I have heard of Fiji. Was it nice?"

"We had a blast—snorkeling and scuba diving every day and feasting on some crazy delicious seafood at night; pretty much living right in the ocean."

"That sounds like a very nice vacation."

"It was awesome. I remember one morning, this guy on the beach tried to hit on my mom and I came over and pretended she was my girlfriend. It was hilarious." He chuckled. "My mom used to be pretty cool."

For a moment neither of them said anything.

"But what really happened between the two of you?" Neni asked.

Vince did not immediately respond. "She stayed the same and I became a different person," he said. "I guess that's the long and short of it."

"You miss her."

"Yeah, but what can we do in life but accept?"

"I don't know, Vince. You like to talk about this acceptance thing, but it's just not easy to accept when bad things happen, I don't care what anyone says. All those people who walk around saying they accept their life as it is, I don't know how they do it."

"I can't even believe how much I think about home these days. Obviously, it has to do with my mom not being around, but when I came back here, that first week, I called home way more than I promised myself I ever would."

"Because you felt sorry for Mighty?"

"Yeah. I couldn't imagine what his life would be like, you know? My mom gone, my dad working all the time. Even if Mighty has my mom's friends and Stacy and Anna, I knew it wouldn't be the same."

"Only your mother can love you a certain way."

"Maybe. But the Universe gives us different sources of Love to unite us all as One. Who are we to decide what the source of our Love should be at any given time? Love is Love, and at any given point we have everything we need. Though, I must admit, Mighty does not like spending time with my mom's friends as much as he did with you and Jende."

"Maybe if they give him fried ripe plantains and *puff-puff*, he will like them more," Neni said, and they both laughed.

"Actually," Vince said, his voice turning serious, "that's what I'm calling you about."

"About fried ripe plantains and *puff-puff*?"

"No," he replied with a little laugh. "About Mighty."

"You know I'll do anything that I can do for you two, so please ask me."

"Thing is," Vince said, "Stacy is moving to Portland, and we need a new nanny for Mighty."

"Okay?"

"I spoke to my dad a couple of days ago about it. He was going to call an agency to find someone else, but I thought about you, and we both agreed you'd be ideal for the job."

"But I'm not looking for a job," Neni hastily replied.

"I know—we're not asking you to take a full-time job. It would be awesome if you could do it full-time, but I imagine with two kids, you don't want to work full-time right now."

"I don't."

"I get it. It's totally cool. If you can't do it full-time we can make it work another way: We'll get Mighty someone else full-time and you'll only need to spend time with him a few hours a week."

"Like how many hours?"

"Whatever works for you and my dad and Mighty."

"I'm still confused. You don't think one nanny is enough for Mighty?"

"No, that's not the thing. Okay, here's the thing. We think it'll be good for him to have some kind of constant, nurturing mother figure in his life."

Neni said nothing.

"His grief counselor agrees it might help him with his healing. He's a kid, he needs it. Not someone to replace my mom—no one can do that, of course—just a woman he loves and who he knows loves him very much, too."

"But what about your father's sister?" Neni asked. "Or your mother's friends?"

"My aunt's in Seattle, and my mom's friends, don't get me wrong, they have their virtues, but it's not the same thing. It just isn't. You two had a special connection, and my dad and I . . . we really wouldn't mind paying you even if it's just to take Mighty and Liomi to dinner every so often or bring him up to Harlem and give him an evening like the one we had that night."

"You told your dad about that night?"

"I did. Only recently, though."

"And he wasn't angry."

"No. Funny, but he was really glad we got to have the experience."

Neni nodded, but did not say anything.

"You don't have to decide right now," Vince said. "Maybe think about it for a couple of days, talk it over with Jende, and I'll call you next week. Does that sound good?"

Neni shook her head.

She couldn't tell Vince it sounded good because she didn't need a couple of days to decide. Even before Vince was done explaining, she knew what her answer would be: no. She couldn't do it. The judge's decision was coming any day now, which meant that her days in America were most likely numbered. Jende was confident the judge would grant the request—so confident, in fact, that he had started searching for airline tickets and had asked her two nights ago how much she thought their bed would go for on Craigslist. Even if the judge denied the request, or Jende decided to withdraw the petition for whatever reason, she still wouldn't take the job, because she couldn't do such a thing to a dead woman. Mighty was Cindy's baby, and Cindy had gone to her grave hating her. How could she in good conscience look Mighty in the eye after what she'd done to his mother? How would Vince feel if Anna ever told him what she had witnessed? She hadn't killed Cindy, but maybe she had, and it wouldn't ever be right to walk back into Cindy's home, no matter how much she cared about Mighty.

She knew that when she died, her soul would never find peace if her enemy shamelessly walked into her home and took over her place in her children's life.

Fifty-six

HE FOUND OUT ON A FRIDAY AFTERNOON: THE JUDGE HAD GRANTED HIS request for voluntary departure.

"You've got to leave by the end of September," Bubakar told him. "September thirtieth, he says. He was going to give you one hundred and twenty days to leave but—"

"It's no problem, Mr. Bubakar," Jende said, grinning his Great Rift Valley–wide grin. "I am ready."

"I don't know what happened. He changed his mind. You only got ninety days now."

Jende moved to the edge of the park bench to make room for a man in a purple suit. "Ninety days is fine, Mr. Bubakar," he said. "Truly, I don't need any more time."

"Good. I know it's too fast but I can't do anything about it, my brother. I'm sorry."

"No, please don't worry for me, Mr. Bubakar. I saw an advertisement for good tickets on Air Maroc. The price was so good, I bought our tickets for the day they gave me the cheapest price. We are leaving in August."

"Ah? You're really ready to leave, eh?"

"When you told me last week that you were ninety-nine point nine nine percent sure the judge was going to approve my request, I just started looking for tickets. I even bought a new suitcase yesterday." He laughed.

"I'm happy to hear you sound so happy, my brother," Bubakar said. "Some people, when they buy the ticket, they cry until the day they enter the plane."

"But what can I do, Mr. Bubakar? My people say if God cuts off your fingers, He will teach you how to eat with your toes."

"*Abi*, if I was a Christian, I would say amen to that. And how is the madam? Is she as happy to go back home as you are?"

Jende chuckled. "She is not happy," he said, "but she is packing up."

"Just make sure she doesn't spend all your money buying things," Bubakar warned. "Because women, you have to be careful with them and all the things they say they must have before they go back home. Anything that makes them look good is a necessity."

"Too late, oh, Mr. Bubakar," Jende said, laughing. "It's already too late."

He'd given Neni more money for shopping than he'd intended; doing so was the only thing that had made her smile in days—him telling her she could spend five hundred dollars buying whatever she wanted to buy. She'd ended up spending eight hundred, buying things not easily found back in Limbe: dollar-store toys for the children so they wouldn't have to play with mud and sticks; foods in jars and all the sweet cereals Liomi had become accustomed to; clothes for as many years into the future as they would need in order to preserve their American aura.

For herself, she bought beauty creams and anti-aging moisturizers in Chinatown—concoctions she hoped would preserve her beauty and youth for a long time and keep her elevated in looks among the women back home. News had reached her that loose young women were now aplenty in Limbe, good-looking and shameless *wolowose* women who made wives nervous. Sure, Jende was a man of little lust, never once looking at even the largest cleavage (not in her presence, at least) in all their married life, but she'd also never had to worry about another woman trying to steal him. Why would any woman try to lure him away when there were thousands of men in New York City with more money? But in Limbe, it would no longer be so. The loose young women there would be eager to pounce on him. He would no longer be a poor boy from a *caraboat* house in New Town but a man who had returned from America with a lot of dollars. Those *wolowose* girls would be all over him, giggling and exposing their teeth, saying things like *Mr. Jende, how noh? You look good, oh!* She would have to give him no reason to move his eyes sideways, especially now that she didn't have the assets those young women had. She would never look like them again, because motherhood had squeezed out the appeal from her breasts and drawn lines of exhaustion on her belly. Her body was no longer a marvel, thus her best weapon in the battle for her husband's eyes wouldn't be her nakedness but her glowing spot-and-wrinkle-free face and the clothes and accessories she would put on the body from which she planned to lose five pounds in the coming month.

She had to return to Limbe prepared.

"Don't forget the girls in you country, they gonno rub fine America cream, too," Fatou said when Neni went across the street to her apartment to give her a purse she'd bought for her as a belated birthday gift and told her how prepared she was to fight to keep her marriage strong. "They know how to buy cream and spray perfume, too, and look lika America woman."

"They go near him," Neni said, "I'll kill them."

Fatou looked at Neni's wide determined eyes and laughed. "I no gonno ever get that kinda problem," she said. "No woman gonno try to steal my Ousmane. Who want Ousmane, with his leg lika broomstick? No woman. So I keep him."

Neni laughed. For a minute, in a good friend's presence, she forgot how fearful she was about her future and laughed. Having a man other women wanted was a curse masquerading as a blessing, she told herself. But it was a source of pride, nonetheless. Jende was going to be somebody in Limbe when they returned. He was going to be a businessman. He would get a nice brick house for them in Sokolo or Batoke or Mile Four, and she would have a maid. Over dinner at Red Lobster on a Sunday evening, while Winston and Maami watched the kids, he had told her all that. "I promise you with all my heart and soul, *bébé*," he had said to her. "You will live like a queen in Limbe."

She had fidgeted with her food, unwilling to look into his eyes. "What can I do now?" she said to him. "We have to go whether I want it or not."

"Yes, *bébé*, but I want you to come back happy. I don't want you to come back crying the way you've been crying. I don't like to see you cry like this, eh? I don't like it at all." He pursed his lips and made a childish sad face, which made her laugh.

"I love New York so much, Jends," she said. "I'm so happy here. I just don't . . . I don't even know how to . . ."

He took her hands and kissed them the way he had seen the leading men do in movies. After paying for their food they walked to Times Square, one of his favorite places in the city. Before Neni came to America, Times Square was his second substitute best friend—after Columbus Circle—a place that never failed to remind him of what he'd left behind. Being there was like being at Half Mile Junction in Limbe, where billboards for Ovaltine and Guinness towered above dusty streets; cabdrivers honked and swore at impudent pedestrians; drinking spots stayed open virtually all night, every weekend; voluptuous prostitutes cursed loudly at tightfisted patrons; and the noise never died.

At the center of the square, right at the corner of Broadway and Forty-second, Jende and Neni stood side by side and held on to the moment. There would be no Times Square in Limbe, Neni thought. No billboards flashing things she wished she had the money to buy. There'd be no McDonald's where she could enjoy her beloved McNuggets. No people of too many colors, speaking too many languages, running around to thousands of fun places. There would be no pharmacy career. No condo in Yonkers or Mount Vernon or New Rochelle.

She buried her face in his shoulder and begged herself to be happy.

Fifty-seven

IN LIMBE, THE TEN THOUSAND DOLLARS NENI HAD TAKEN FROM CINDY, plus the eight thousand dollars they'd saved (five thousand from diligently putting away approximately three hundred and fifty dollars every month during the fourteen months Jende had worked for the Edwardses; three thousand from the four weeks Neni had worked for Cindy), would make them millionaires many times over. Even after buying their airline tickets and making all the necessary purchases, they would have enough money for Jende to become one of the richest men in New Town.

With the new exchange rate at six hundred CFA francs to a dollar, he would be returning home with close to ten million CFA francs, enough to restart their life in a beautiful rental with a garage for his car and a maid so his wife could feel like a queen. He would have enough to start a business, which would enable him to someday build a spacious brick house and send Liomi to Baptist High School, Buea, the boarding school Winston had attended because his late father came from a wealthy Banso clan, the school Jende could not attend because Pa Jonga could not afford it.

Without any treatment, his back stopped aching.

A month before he was to leave, Winston called with an idea: Would Jende be willing to manage the construction of a new hotel Winston and one of his friends were building at Seme Beach and then become the hotel manager when it was completed?

"We'll talk about salary, Bo," Winston said. "We'll pay you good money, more than what you used to make as a laborer at Limbe Urban Council."

Jende laughed and promised to think about it. Two days later, when Winston stopped by for a visit, Jende declined the offer. He was appreciative of his cousin's help, but he wanted to run his own business, get to know what it was like to answer to no man. All his life it had been yes sir, yes madam. A time had to come for him to stand above others and hear yes, Mr. Jonga.

Upon his return to Limbe, he would start his own business: Jonga Enterprises. His slogan would be "Jonga Enterprises: Bringing the Wisdom of Wall Street to Limbe." He would diversify and conglomerate and acquire as many competitors as possible. But he'd have to start small. Maybe he'd own a couple of taxis or *benskins*. Or hire people to farm the eight acres of land his father had left for him in Bimbia. He could sell the food in the Limbe market and ship some of it abroad. Winston encouraged him to move forward with the farming idea first. There were enough taxis in Limbe, and *benskins*—with their high accident rates which had left many swearing that motorcycles were the devil's creations—were bound to fall out of favor with the public soon enough. But food, Winston said, would always be needed.

"Food," Jende agreed, "and drinking spots."

"Will people in Limbe ever get tired of drinking?" Winston said. "I hear drinking spots are opening all over town like no man's business. They say there's even a spot that sells Heineken and Budweiser. Heineken and Budweiser? In Cameroon?"

Jende leaned forward on the sofa to rock the bassinet in which

Timba was lying belly up and on the verge of fussing. Winston stood up and peered at the baby. He smiled at her, tickled her belly, cooed in response to her toothless grin, and returned to the sofa.

"That's how you know this American domination has gone too far, Bo," Winston said. "*Paysan*s have gone from wanting Guinness and 33 Export to wanting Budweiser and Heineken."

"And Motorola RAZR," Jende said. "My mother asked me to bring back a RAZR for her so she can have the nicest phone among all her friends who she goes to farm with. Don't ask me why she takes her cell phone to the farm. There's no network there. She saw a RAZR in a Nigerian movie, she wants it."

"Why should she be left behind in the twentieth century?"

"I told Neni," Jende went on. "I said, 'Maybe you won't even miss New York too much because Limbe now has so many things New York has.' But no, she doesn't listen. She continues walking around the house with a long face like something whose name I can't even remember right now."

"Ah, Bo. Please, have a bit of sympathy for her. It's not easy for her to be—"

"But isn't it true? Everything she sees here, she's going to see in Limbe. The girls in Limbe now, I hear they all look like Beyoncé. And no one wants to drink *country mimbo* anymore. Palm wine is falling out of fashion. Everyone is American or European now. Emmanu told me a club in West End even sells Cristal glass by glass."

"You're serious?"

"I'm serious. Victor owns the club. You remember Victor?"

"Which Victor?" Winston asked. "The one we used to play football against in the inter-quarter league? The one who lives behind the Catholic church and has those buttocks like a woman's?"

"That one," Jende said. "Emmanu swears the club is *helele*."

"How did he come up with the capital?"

"You didn't hear the story? The boy went to Bulgaria. Bulgaria or Russia or Australia—somewhere over there. Boy comes back with some serious *kolo*. Rumor all over town is that he was a dancer. Who knows what kind of dance he did? From the kind of money he brought back, he must have done it very well."

"A black man shaking it for white women," Winston said. "Isn't that what they want? And Victor could shake it, let me tell you. I'll never forget the time I was dancing toward this fine *ngah* at Black and White. I think it was a Christmas Day. The music was booming, man, I was moving it, ready to pounce and make my move." He stood up and gyrated his hips to show the *makossa* moves of his younger days.

Jende watched him, smiling.

"Then," Winston said, and paused, his hands spread out, "out of nowhere Victor comes out and does this Michael Jackson move, and the *ngah* starts laughing. I think it was 'Thriller,' because that boy was doing some serious vibrations. The *ngah* is laughing and laughing, and next thing I know, wait, where is she? The bastard stole the *ngah* with his Michael Jackson moves, right in front of me! I stood there in the middle of that nightclub, high and dry!"

Jende laughed until he fully doubled over, gasping for air. "Ah, Limbe," he said. "I cannot believe I will be there again."

"Just don't become an American Wonder when you go back," Winston said, laughing as he sat down. "Play it mature, please. That's all I ask of you."

Jende shook his head.

He would never become an American Wonder, one of those *mbutuku*s who went to America and upon their return home spoke with laughable American accents, spraying "wannas" and "gonnas" all over sentences. They strutted around town wearing suits and cowboy boots and baseball caps, claiming to understand very little of Cameroonian culture because they were now too American. *Come and see American Wonder*, the song about them went. *Come* *and see American Wonder. Do you know American Wonder? Come and see American Wonder.*

He would never be laughable. He would be respectable.

Later that evening, after Neni and Liomi had returned home from buying Liomi new sneakers, Jende told Neni the idea of wholesaling food. She kept her head down, saying nothing as she unpacked the sneakers and put them inside a Ghana Must Go bag.

"Maybe we can even find a way to export some of the food over here, eh?" he said. "Maybe sell in African stores here?"

"What do you need my opinion for?" she said, lifting her head to look at him as if he disgusted her. "Aren't you the knower of everything?" Her eyes seemed ready to tear through him like a sharp knife slicing pork belly. It had been less than a week since their moment in Times Square and she was back to despising him for taking her and her children away from America.

"But *bébé*," he said, "I just thought you'd like to know—"

"Why? No, please, don't ask me anything. Just do whatever you want to do, okay? Whatever you want, however you want it, just do it. You don't need to ask me."

Thankfully, Liomi was back to wanting to grow up to be like him, so after Neni shut the bedroom door saying she wanted to finish her work in peace and quiet, Jende went into the living room, where he and his son roughhoused on the floor and tickled each other so hard they both gasped for air.

He called his brother Moto the next day and asked him to begin the search for men to till the land in Bimbia and plant plantains, *egusi*, and yams. He also asked him to be on the lookout for a three-bedroom brick house with a garage, as well as a maid and a temporary car he would drive until the used Hyundai he had purchased at a New Jersey state auction arrived in a shipping container. Three days later, his brother texted to say he had found a house for rent in Coconut Island, as well as a car, a 1998 Pajero.

He would have the house furnished with basic necessities and a housemaid hired by the time the family arrived.

"Look you," Fatou said when Neni told her about the house and the maid. "You gonno leave small one-room and go stay for mansion? Why Ousmane not do this for me, too?"

"So ask Ousmane to take you back home then," Neni retorted.

"Ousmane no want go back home," Fatou said. She paused and looked at the empty luggage lying on the living room floor. "If only me, I go back. I go to my village, build house near my mother and my father. I live quiet life, die quiet die. If only me, I go home *très bientôt.*"

Neni watched the perpetual sparkle in Fatou's eyes dim as she said this, and she knew her friend was serious; for the first time that afternoon, she did not mean what she was saying as a joke. Fatou missed her parents, especially now that they were in their eighties and needed her and her two brothers to take care of them. She and her brothers worried about them, but there wasn't much they could do from far away—one of her brothers was in France, the other in Oklahoma. Her parents had to depend on distant relatives to take care of them using the money transfers Fatou and her brothers sent every few months. They had to live like people who had never borne children, which shamed Fatou every time she got a call from a relative saying one of them had fallen sick and money was needed to take them to a hospital. Fatou always sent the money within a day, even when she had a bill due: What else could she do?

After twenty-six years, she was ready to stop braiding hair for a living and go back home, but the decision wasn't hers alone to make. And even if Ousmane wanted to go back home, her children were Americans who had never been to their parents' homeland. All seven of them, the three in their twenties and four teenagers, wanted nothing of living in West Africa. Some of them didn't even consider themselves African. When people asked where they were from, they often said, oh, we're from right here, New York, America. They said it with pride, believing it. Only when prodded did they reluctantly admit that well, actually, our parents are Africans. But we're Americans, they always added. Which hurt Fatou and made her wonder, was it possible her children thought they were better than her because they were Americans and she was African?

Fifty-eight

THE BAKWERI PEOPLE OF LIMBE BELIEVE AUGUST IS A CURSED MONTH. The rain falls too hard and for too long; rivers rise up too high and too fast. Dry days are few; chilly nights are many. The month is long, dreary, and hostile, and it is for this reason that many in the tribe do not marry, build houses, or start businesses in August. They wait for it to go away, along with its curses.

Jende Jonga, a Bakweri man, believed nothing in curses.

August or no August, it was time for him to go back home, and that was that. Walking through the streets of New York during his last days in America, he couldn't bring himself to feel sad about leaving or wish his experience were ending differently. Enough was enough. He wanted no more of life in a roach-filled apartment in a Harlem neighborhood of fried chicken joints, storefront churches, and funeral homes where young men in cornrows and saggy pants perpetually lingered outside, mourning one of their own and carelessly spitting in his direction. He wanted no more of climbing five flights of stairs to share a bed with his daughter while his son slept in a cot inches away. He wanted no more of smiling for appearances as he stacked dishes and polished silverware, and he certainly wanted no more of riding the subway from work late at night, arriving home sweaty, greasy, and drained.

To him, living such a life for another year would have been the curse. Not recognizing when to go back home would have been a curse. Not realizing that he would be happier sleeping in a bedroom separate from his children, going to visit his mother and his brothers whenever he wanted, meeting his friends at a *boucarou* in Down Beach for roasted fish and beer by the ocean, riding around in his own car and sweating outside in January . . . that would have been the curse.

You're really sure you're not going to miss America? his friends at work asked him repeatedly. Not even the football? He laughed every time they asked. Maybe a bit of football, he would reply. And cheesecake.

Neni, for her part, could summon no joy as the date of their departure drew close. Her tears flowed without provocation on the subway, at Pathmark, in Central Park, in the apartment in the middle of mundane chores. She felt no excitement at the thought of being reunited with her family and old friends, only apprehension at the notion that she might never be happy in Limbe as she'd been in New York. She worried that she might have too little in common with her friends, being that she was now so different from them, being that she had tasted a different kind of life and been transformed positively and negatively in so many different ways, being that life had expanded and contracted her in ways they could never imagine.

Though she looked forward to seeing her mother and siblings, she dreaded seeing her father, whom she'd last spoken to in May, when he'd called to tell her that his illegitimate son who lived in Portor-Portor Quarters was in the hospital and money was needed for medicine. Neni had said they had no money to give and her father had yelled at her. How can you say you have no money when your brother is dying in the hospital? he'd said. But he's not my brother, Neni had yelled back. Her father had hung up when she said that and she hadn't bothered to call back to find out how the boy was faring. The boy wasn't her brother and he was never going to be her brother. She couldn't bring herself to care if he lived or died.

For her children, Neni wavered between joy and sorrow—joy for the beautiful things Cameroon would give them; sorrow for the things it wouldn't. They would grow up in a spacious house in Limbe, learn to speak French, master how to dance to *makossa* music. They would live near doting grandparents and too many uncles and aunts and cousins. They would dress up in their finest outfits on Christmas and New Year's and walk around town with their friends, laughing and eating *chin-chin* and cake. They'd never wonder why their mother preferred to shop at the dollar store or why their father seemed to always be working. Liomi would go to BHS Buea with the children of the elite; he could still become a lawyer like his uncle Winston. Timba would spend her girlhood dancing under the moonlight with her friends, singing *Gombe gombe mukele mukele* on nights when clouds made way for the stars to shine. She would learn to chant, *Iyo cow oh, njama njama cow oh, your mami go for Ngaoundéré for saka belle cow oh, oh chei!* She would go to boarding school at the prestigious all-girls Saker Baptist College, where for eight months a year she would be locked behind iron gates, hidden from boys and made to study alongside girls destined to become doctors and engineers.

In Limbe, Liomi and Timba would have many things they would not have had in America, but they would lose far too many things.

They would lose the opportunity to grow up in a magnificent land of uninhibited dreamers. They would lose the chance to be awed and inspired by amazing things happening in the country, incredible inventions and accomplishments by men and women who look like them. They would be deprived of freedoms, rights, and privileges that Cameroon could not give its children. They would lose unquantifiable benefits by leaving New York City, because while there existed great towns and cities all over the world, there was a certain kind of pleasure, a certain type of adventurous and audacious childhood, that only New York City could offer a child.

Fifty-nine

BETTY HOSTED A FAREWELL PARTY FOR THEM IN THE BRONX. MOST OF their friends, who had been with them from their arrival in the city through Timba's birth and Pa Jonga's death, were there. Winston and Maami were there, as well as Olu and Tunde, the instructor—who stopped by with his equally fine Asian boyfriend on the way to another party, to hug Neni goodbye—and Fatou and Ousmane, whose broomstick legs Neni at once thought of the moment he walked through the door wearing faded mom jeans; imagining what they looked like forced her to smile her first real smile of the evening.

Everyone came with something to eat: fried ripe plantains, bitter leaf soup, *egusi* stew, cow feet and beans, *poulet* DG, grilled tilapia, *attiéké, moi moi, soya, jollof* rice, curry chicken, pounded yams. Winston brought drinks, along with his laptop and speakers.

In Betty's sparsely furnished living room, they ate and they danced, to Petit-Pays and Koffi Olomidé, to Brenda Fassie and Papa Wemba. Then Meiway's "200% Zoblazo" came over the speakers. Trumpets and keyboards sounded, calling all celebrators to the dance floor. The rhythm—fierce, pulsating, resolute—demanded that everyone get on their feet. Those who were eating put down their food. Those who were drinking put down their bottles. *Ting, ting, ting, ding, ding.* Neni moved to the center of the room—her hips couldn't help swaying to music this good. Her feet couldn't stand still even if she wasn't having the happiest day of her life. Everyone was up, packed in the eight-by-twelve space at the center of the room. Arms raised in the air, the women rotated their buttocks, going harder and harder toward the floor, faster and faster as they rose up. Behind them, one arm around their waists, the men worked their crotches: up, down, left and right, forward, backward, side to side. All around, buttocks and crotches moved in one accord, pressed against each other as the music soared. Then, the chorus arrived. They jumped and skipped as they pumped their fists, singing together as loud as they could, *Blazo, blazo, zoblazo, on a gagné! On a gagné!* When one of Jende's non-African friends from work asked him what the song meant, he shouted, without pausing to catch his breath, it means we have won, man. It means we have won!

Judson Memorial Church bade them farewell, too.

Natasha asked Neni if Jende could come with her to church on the second Sunday of August. Jende agreed—it seemed a good time to visit an American church and see if Americans interpreted the Bible the same way as Cameroonians.

The Scripture that morning was from Genesis 18, the story of the weary visitors who visited Abraham and Abraham, not knowing they were angels, treated them with kindness. Natasha preached about the treatment of weary strangers in America. She decried the contemporary American definition of weary stranger as illegal alien. Remember when we welcomed our visitors at Ellis Island with lunch boxes? she asked to loud applause. And a free doctor's checkup! someone in the back shouted. The church roared. Natasha smiled as she watched her congregants whispering among themselves. Sad, she said, shaking her head. Treating our friends in need of help the way we treat our enemies. Forgetting that we could find ourselves in search of a home someday, too. This bears no resemblance to the love the Bible speaks of, the love Jesus Christ preached about when he said we should love our neighbor as ourselves.

Before ending the sermon, Natasha called the Jongas to the front of the church. This is the Jonga family, she told the congregation. In about a week, they'll be returning home to their native Cameroon. They came to America to stay but we won't let them. They're returning home because they cannot get papers to remain in our country and create a better life for themselves and their children. They're returning because we as a country have forgotten how to welcome all kinds of strangers to our home. She paused and looked around, giving the congregation time to digest her words. She then turned to Neni and Jende, hugged them, and thanked them for sharing their story. Father, mother, son, and daughter returned to their seats with the eyes of the congregation following them.

The assistant pastor, Amos, rose to speak after the sermon. You've heard Natasha's sermon and you've met the Jongas, he said. They're not strangers. They're our neighbors, but they cannot make their home among us. So I encourage you all to give generously to help them create a new home in their country. And while we give, he continued, let's remember that there are many more out there like this couple. Worse still, there are many out there who do not have a warm, peaceful country to return to. There are many for whom the only chance at ever having a home again is in America.

Neni and Jende looked at each other when Amos mentioned the money. Natasha had told them nothing about it and this unexpected and kind gesture briefly misted Neni's eyes, the thought that she would be leaving behind a country abounding in institutions of tolerance and compassion.

After the service, a line of congregants stood in front of them, taking turns to greet them. One woman wanted to know where Cameroon was on the map, and another wanted to know if Jende needed help finding a lawyer to continue his immigration case. He told the first woman that Cameroon was right next to Nigeria. To the second, he said no, he did not need a lawyer, his case was closed.

Most congregants simply wanted to shake hands or wish them well or tell them how glad they were that the Jongas had shared their story. A teenage girl choked up while telling Jende of a friend's father who was deported to Guatemala even though he knew no one there. Her friend was very sad now, the young woman said. Jende gave her a hug and told her that, thankfully, they still had many family and friends in Cameroon.

Sixty

THE EMAIL RESPONSE CAME WITHIN TWO HOURS OF JENDE HITTING THE send button. Nice hearing from you, Jende, Clark wrote. I'm surprised to hear you're returning home but I understand. Sometimes a man just has to go back home. You can certainly stop by to say goodbye. Talk to my secretary.

Jende went to visit Clark wearing the same black suit he'd worn for his first day of work as Clark's chauffeur. Neni had told him the suit was unnecessary but he had insisted on wearing it. I'm going to be around people wearing suits, he reminded her. Why should I look like a nobody?

When he walked in, Clark stood from behind his desk to greet him. "It's very nice of you to come say goodbye," he said, smiling as he offered a hand.

"It's me who has to thank you for making the time, sir," Jende replied, taking Clark's hand into both of his.

Clark seemed beyond pleased to see him, smiling more broadly than Jende had ever seen him smile, his eyes brighter than they had been in all the months Jende drove him around, his face younger looking. Jende could tell that Mr. Edwards's happiness was not merely from seeing him—his former boss finally seemed a genuinely happy man.

"I wanted to give my condolences for the death of Mrs. Edwards, sir," Jende said after they were seated. "I was at the memorial service, sir, but I could not get an opportunity to get near you to tell you how sorry I was."

Clark nodded. Jende looked around at the office he'd moved to since they last saw each other. It had neither a sofa nor a view of Central Park, but the view of Queens was special in its own inferior way.

"How's your family?" Clark asked. "Are they happy to be going back home?"

"They are fine, sir, thank you. My wife is angry, but she is not going to stay angry forever. My son is happy because I tell him about all the fun things I will take him to do back at home. The baby does not know anything, so that makes me happy."

"Are you happy?"

"I am, but the more the day comes closer, the more I feel a little bit of sadness that I might never see this city again. New York is a wonderful city. It will be hard to not live here."

"Yeah, I'll have to learn to adjust, too. I'll be leaving next month."

"Oh? You mean you are moving also, sir?"

Clark nodded. "Mighty and I are moving to Virginia."

"Virginia?"

"I found a new job in Washington, D.C. We're actually going to look at houses this weekend. I'm hoping we can find something close to Arlington and Falls Church."

"Falls Church? I remember, sir . . . that is where Mrs. Edwards came from?"

"You've got a good memory. And my family lived in Arlington for a bit before we moved to Illinois. My parents will be moving from California so they can be close to us."

"That will be very good for you, sir."

"Family's everything," Clark said. "I'm sure you know that already."

"It is everything, sir."

"I've got some cousins in the area, and Cindy has a half-sister there. Cindy wasn't close to her before the end, but she came to the funeral and Mighty and I have been in touch with her lately."

"That is good, sir."

"Yeah, we had a great time visiting her a couple of months ago. Mighty's really looking forward to growing up with his cousins. It's important for him to know he has family, now that . . . well, now that so much has changed."

"It is very true, sir," Jende said, nodding. "Very true. And how is Vince?"

"He's good; I spoke to him this morning. He's thinking about opening a retreat center for American execs visiting Mumbai so they can attain peace and quiet between running around pursuing opportunities." Clark laughed. "It sounded funny, but he might be on to something."

"He is a very smart boy, sir," Jende said.

The executive smiled, his pride undisguised. "Yeah, it's just hard for anyone to know where he's going to end up."

"Maybe he'll end up in Limbe," Jende said, laughing.

"Maybe," Clark said, laughing with him. "You never know. He could go to Limbe and teach folks there how to be one with the Universe and free themselves from their egos. Or he could have them walk around talking about rejecting the illusion."

"Or maybe, sir," Jende said, laughing hard now, "he could take them to the beach in the evening and they could watch the sun going down. The fishermen will be returning with their canoes on one side of the beach, and Vince and his followers will be sitting on the sand on the other side with their legs crossed, doing that chanting and meditation thing."

"I can almost picture that!" Clark said, guffawing and slapping the table. "I can completely see that happening."

"He can stay with me and my wife until he gets tired of being in one place."

"Oh, I'm sure he won't have a hard time finding a new place to go to. He told me if his business idea doesn't work out in India, he might head to Bolivia. Don't ask me what's in Bolivia."

"Maybe a lot of mindful people, sir?"

"Maybe a lot of mindful people!" Clark said, and they laughed together.

"The boy is a very special young man, sir," Jende said as their laughter died down.

"Yeah, special is a good word."

"If there were ten thousand more young men like him in this world, or even just one thousand, I swear, sir, there will be more happiness in the world."

Clark smiled.

Jende shifted in his seat. He was enjoying his time with his old boss, but the new secretary had warned him that Clark had only thirty minutes for the meeting. He glanced at his watch. Not much time left. He had to quickly say what he'd come to say.

"Sir," he began, "I came here not only to say goodbye but also to personally thank you for the job you gave me. You may not understand how it changed my life, but because of that job I was able to save money and now I can go back home to live well. Even though I would have liked to continue working for you and stay in America longer, I am happy that I can now go home and live a better life than the life I lived before I came to America. So I am just very thankful, sir."

Clark shifted in his seat and rubbed his eyes with his palms. "Wow," he said. It was apparent no one had ever traveled so far to thank him for doing nothing more than pay for a service. His desk phone rang, but he didn't pick it up.

"I hear all these things that people are saying about Wall Street people, sir, about how they are bad people. But I don't agree with them. Because it was you, a Wall Street man, who gave me a job that helped me to take care of my family. And you were very nice to me. I think you are a good man, Mr. Edwards, and that is why I came to thank you."

Clark Edwards stared at his former chauffeur, clearly thinking of the best words to convey his surprise at what he was hearing. "I'm very touched, Jende," he said. "Really, and I thank you, too. It was a great experience for me, having you. Quite a thrill many times, actually. And if I never said it, I hope you know how much I appreciated your loyalty and dedication."

"Thank you, sir."

"And I'm sorry, Jende . . ."

"No, please, Mr. Edwards, don't be sorry. For what?"

"That our time together had to end. I'm not sure how to put it, but . . . It's a pity, you know?"

Jende shook his head. "Our people say no condition is permanent, Mr. Edwards. Good times must come to an end, just like bad times, whether we want it or not."

"Indeed," Clark said. "I'm just glad we can part as friends."

"I'm also glad, sir," Jende said, nodding as he pushed his chair back and stood up.

Clark stood up, too, and the men shook hands, the streets of New York on which they once drove together visible through the window beside them.

"Do pass on my regards to Neni," Clark said.

"I will, sir. Please tell Mighty that me and Neni send him special greetings."

"Will do. He was very fond of you guys. You may not have realized it but your presence in his life really did impact him a great deal. He still tells me, Jende said this, Neni did that."

"We think about him also, especially after Mrs. Edwards died. I thought sometimes about maybe I should call you and try to see him, but . . . me and my wife, we had so many troubles going on that I did not even have time to do a lot of things I wanted to. But we don't forget him. He is a good boy."

"He is. I'm glad he's looking forward to moving to Virginia. If he didn't want to go, I would have passed on the opportunity, even though it's something I've wanted to do for a long time."

"Barclays is transferring you to work in another office in D.C., sir?"

"No, I'll be starting a whole new job. Heading a lobbying firm."

Jende moved his hand to scratch his head.

"It's a firm that lobbies to protect the interest of organizations," Clark said. "I'll be heading one that lobbies for credit unions. The work's going to be very important in this economic climate. Very exciting opportunity for me."

"It sounds like it is a different kind of work, sir."

"It is. Wall Street's been good to me, but I don't think there's room for the likes of me here anymore. Besides, with everything that's happened, I'm ready for a change."

"I am very glad, sir," Jende said, smiling. "I hope you have success with the lobbying."

"Thank you," Clark said, smiling back. "I hope so, too.

"By the way, Jende," Clark called as Jende began walking toward the door. "I forgot to ask you. Why are you going back home?"

Jende did not need time to think about the best answer. He immediately turned around, walked back to the desk, and told the truth. "My application for asylum was not approved, sir."

"Asylum? I had no idea you were applying for asylum."

"I never mentioned it to you, sir. It is something which I kept between me and my wife and my lawyer. I did not think I should bother you with something like that."

"No, of course, I understand. I'm just surprised. What does it mean it was not approved? Are you being deported?"

"No, sir, I'm not being deported. But I cannot get a green card unless I am granted asylum, and for that to happen I will have to spend many years and a lot of money going to immigration court. And then maybe the judge will still decide to not give me asylum, which means the government will deport me in the end. It's not how I want to live my life, sir, especially when you add the fact that it's just not easy for a man to enjoy his life in this country if he is poor."

"But isn't there some other way you can try to get a green card?" Clark said after picking up his ringing phone and telling the person on the line he would call back. "I know how badly you wanted to raise your children here."

"I did what I could, sir, but—"

"Surely there has to be a way to keep a decent hardworking man like you in America."

Jende shook his head. "There are laws, sir," he said.

"Listen," Clark said, sitting up. "I've got a good friend from Stanford who's an associate director at Immigration. If you had told me you had a case, I would have contacted him for you to get advice, or at least ask for a recommendation for an excellent lawyer. I had no idea."

Jende looked down and shook his head, a rueful smile on his face.

"It might not be too late," Clark went on. "Maybe you could reschedule your flight, give me some time to contact my friend and see if we can still help you?"

"I think it's too late, sir."

"But there's no harm in trying, is there?"

"The judge will not allow it, sir, and even if he did . . ."

"You're ready to leave."

Jende smiled. "The truth, sir," he said, "is that my body may still be here, but my heart has already gone back home. It is true I came here to escape a hard life and I did not want to go back. But when I had no choice but to go back, I found myself happy thinking about home, sir. I will miss America, but it will be good to live in my own country again. I already picture myself going to visit my father's grave to show him my daughter. I see myself walking around Limbe with my friends, getting a drink, taking my son to the stadium. I am no longer afraid of my country the way I used to be."

"But what about the children?"

"They will be fine, sir. We already have my daughter's American passport. She will come back here when she is ready and maybe one day she will file petition for her brother. If not, my son will go to Canada and my wife can go visit America and Canada every few years."

Clark nodded, smiling.

Jende looked at his watch and made for the door again, but Clark asked him to wait a second. He went over to his briefcase, which was lying on a chair to the right of his desk, sat down for a minute as he wrote something, and returned with a white envelope, which he handed to Jende. "Take this," he said, "and take care of your family."

"Oh, sir . . . oh, thank you so much," Jende said, taking the envelope with both hands, his head bowed. "Thank you so much, Mr. Edwards."

"Don't mention it. Have a safe journey."

"Oh, I was just wondering, sir," Jende said as Clark took a step toward the door, "have you heard anything from Leah? Me and my wife, we wanted to invite her to our go-away party, but her house phone has been disconnected."

"Yeah, I heard from her a couple of months ago," Clark replied. "She sent me her résumé to help her get a job here, but I don't think anything came out of me forwarding it to HR, what with the hiring freeze and all."

"So maybe she is still not working?"

"I think so. Tough job market out there, especially for someone her age. My guess is that she's probably picked up and moved out of the city so she wouldn't run out of money."

Jende shook his head, surprised. Leah hadn't mentioned a plan to move away the last time they spoke, on Christmas Day. She had sounded fine, but she must have been downcast about her future—no job prospect, diminishing savings, her Social Security income still a few years away. She must have been scared, though she hadn't given that impression. Could that have been why she was so happy about going to see the Christmas tree at Rockefeller Center? Could it be because she was about to immerse herself in a spirit of hope and, for just a few hours, forget about her circumstances?

"If you ever see her, sir," Jende said, "can you please tell her I say goodbye and that I am sorry for not saying goodbye to her directly? Please tell her I have gone back to Cameroon but maybe one day, by the grace of God, I will come to visit America and we will meet again."

"Let's hope I can remember all that."

"I feel so bad, sir, when I think about her," Jende said.

"The economy's getting better," Clark replied, turning toward the door.

"That's what they say, sir, but . . . I hope she will be okay soon."

"I'm sure she'll be fine," Clark said as the men arrived at the door, where they wished each other the very best and shook hands for the last time.

Sixty-one

SHE GAVE HER POTS AND COOKING UTENSILS TO BETTY, HER DINNERWARE and silverware to Fatou. Winston and Maami took her spices and the food in the pantry: the *garri*, palm oil, crayfish, *fufu*, *egusi*, pounded yams, and smoked fish. Olu came for her old textbooks and the desktop—a nephew of her husband's would soon be arriving from Nigeria to study nursing at Hunter.

Natasha was happy to receive her unworn *kabas*. They weren't worth the space they would take up, she told the pastor, who was excited about adding the colorful dresses to her wardrobe. The dinette set she sold on Craigslist, as well as the dresser in the bedroom, the TV, the microwave, and Liomi's cot. Their winter clothes, old summer clothes, and worn-out shoes she took to Goodwill; the old sofa she had Jende put out on the curb for anyone in need of an old sofa.

By the night before their departure, the apartment was empty except for their luggage in a corner of the bedroom. Whatever they hadn't given away was in the garbage except for the bed, which they would be leaving for the new tenants.

The new tenants had arrived with Mr. Charles to see the apartment and while there they had asked Neni at least a dozen questions: How much of a pain was it dealing with five flights of stairs every day? Any weird neighbors? Where was the best place to order Thai or Chinese takeout late at night? Was Harlem really better these days like everyone was saying? They were a young couple—early to mid-twenties, pretty, giddy, white, with matching long hair—fleeing Detroit and in pursuit of a life as successful musicians. When Neni asked what kind of music they sang, they smiled and said it was hard to label, some combination of techno, hip-hop, and the blues. They called themselves the Love Stucks.

She was tempted to resent them but then they offered to buy the bed for twice what someone else was offering on Craigslist. They paid her cash right away, then shared a kiss in her bedroom. As they were leaving she heard Mr. Charles reminding them to never mention the arrangement to anyone because if he lost the subsidized apartment everyone would lose out on a great deal. The woman promised they would never say a word; she couldn't believe they'd just landed an affordable apartment in New York City.

Less than eighteen hours before their flight and Neni was now alone in the living room. Timba was asleep in the bedroom; Jende had taken Liomi to dinner at a restaurant on 116th Street, for one last meal of *attiéké* and grilled lamb. After dinner they planned to have their last scoop of American ice cream on 115th Street; maybe a slice of cheesecake, too.

With all the bags packed, all the travel clothes laid out, all the itineraries printed out, there was little left to do. Neni sat on the floor, her back against the wall, looking around the living room. It seemed smaller and darker. It felt strange, like being in a faraway cave in a forest in a country she'd never been to. It felt as if she was in a dream about a home that had never been hers.

She looked toward the window, thinking of something she might have forgotten to do. There was nothing. Perhaps a goodbye she hadn't said? There was none. Her friends had offered to come spend this last night with her, reminisce and laugh, because who knew if/when they'd ever see each other again? She had thanked them but said no. She had said her last goodbye, to Fatou, the day before. They had shared a long hug, and Fatou had said, how you gonna make me cry lika baby? She didn't want to say any more goodbyes. Not to Fatou, or Betty, or Olu, or Winston, or any other friend.

She wanted to go to sleep, wake up, shower, get the children ready, pick up her luggage, and leave.

Sixty-two

THEY BADE NEW YORK CITY GOODBYE ON ONE OF THE HOTTEST DAYS OF the year. Late August, around the same time he had arrived five years before. They boarded an Air Maroc flight from JFK to Douala via Casablanca. On the cab ride to the airport, she stared out the window in silence. It was all passing her by. America was passing her by. New York City was passing her by. Bridges and billboards bearing smiling people were passing her by. Skyscrapers and brownstones were rushing by. Fast. Too fast. Forever.

He felt nothing.

He forced himself to feel nothing.

He sat in the front seat with the seed money for his new life packed in a red JanSport backpack, twenty-one little bundles of cash tied with brown rubber bands. Each bundle contained a thousand dollars of his fortune: eighteen thousand from Cindy Edwards and their savings; fourteen hundred dollars from the people at Judson; two thousand from Clark Edwards.

"Why don't you just send it through Western Union and pick it up when you arrive?" Winston had asked him.

"Never," he had said. "You want Cameroon government to know I have this kind of money and come after me?"

"You and your fears," Winston had said, laughing. "What will they do if they know? They can't tax money you transfer."

"That's what you think, eh? Wait until Biya decides to change the law. Then the government is going to start asking for ten percent of all Western Union transfers."

"Ah, Bo! The government can never do such a thing."

"How do you know?"

"I don't know. But, now that you say it, I don't blame you for being cautious. One can never trust any government—I don't trust the American government and I definitely don't trust the Cameroon government."

"No, but it's our government and it's our country. We love it, we hate it, it's still our country. How man go do?"

"It's our country," Winston agreed. "We can never disown it."

At four in the morning of the day after they left New York, they arrived in Cameroon. And as they had been warned, the country was no different from the one they had left.

Douala International Airport was still steamy and overcrowded. Customs officers there still demanded bribes that weary travelers gave for lack of energy to fight a devious system. Men and women in bright African fabrics still crowded the exit from customs, calling out to their recently arrived loved ones, shouting in English, French, pidgin English, and any of the two hundred indigenous languages of the country, saying, I'm over here, we're all over here. Overjoyed parents, and sometimes what seemed like whole extended families, still waited outside the arrival terminal to welcome sons and daughters who had traveled overseas and returned to bring them pride, pushing and shoving to get to a long-awaited hug. Young boys dressed in rags still lingered around the airport parking lot, seeking gullible arrivals who would believe their claims of hunger and homelessness and spare them a dollar or euro. The drive from Douala to Limbe was still arduous, with drivers and pedestrians swearing at each other, young and old alike fighting for space on the dusty and congested streets of Bonaberi.

Jende's brother Moto met them at the airport with a borrowed Ford pickup truck for the two-hour drive to Limbe. The Ford was the only vehicle he could find that could fit the family and their seven suitcases bearing clothes and shoes. More of their possessions would be arriving months later in a shipping container: the old Hyundai; four large boxes of discount store clothes and shoes; three boxes of preserved food, all bought in dollar stores; two suitcases containing Liomi's toys and games and books; a car seat, stroller, and Pack 'n Play bought from Craigslist for Timba. There were also three suitcases containing the clothes Cindy had given Neni and the things Neni had purchased in Chinatown: fake Chanel, Gucci, and Versace purses; cheap jewelry, sunglasses, and shoes; human-hair wigs and weaves; creams, perfumes, and makeup. These purchases were what she would use to prove to the loose women of Limbe that she was not at their level. Cindy's things she planned to reserve for special occasions. She would wear them to weddings and anniversaries to show those girls that even though she had returned home and was living among them, she was not one of them—she was now a woman of class, with real designer items, and none of them could compete with her.

Just after seven o'clock, while Neni and the children slept, the pickup went under the red and white sign above the highway that said "Welcome to Limbe, The Town of Friendship." Memories of the sign had given Jende comfort during his first days in America, a comfort meshed with the belief that he would one day be driving toward it in circumstances different from when he'd driven away from it.

"Welcome indeed," he said to himself, as the lights of his hometown appeared in the distance. Moto moved one hand from the steering wheel and gave him a congratulatory tap on the shoulder.

"What did you say, Papa?" a drowsy and awakening Liomi asked.

Jende turned from the front seat and looked at his son. "Guess where we are," he whispered.

"Where?" Liomi asked, struggling to open his eyes.

"Guess," Jende whispered again.

The boy opened his eyes and said, "Home?"

Acknowledgments

The author is grateful to her wonderful agent, Susan Golomb, for opening up mighty gates for her, and Susan's former and current assistants (Krista Ingebretson, Scott Cohen, Soumeya Bendimerad Roberts), for all the hard work they've done, and continue to do, for her. Profound gratitude to David Ebershoff, for being not only a magnificent editor but also a kind human; and to Caitlin McKenna, his diligent assistant. The author thanks her publisher, Susan Kamil, for giving her an incredibly humbling opportunity, and Susan's entire team at Random House, for their dedication and enthusiasm. Special thanks to Molly Schulman, Hanna Pylväinen, and Christopher Cervelloni, for reading early drafts of this story and providing wisdom and encouragement. Finally, the author will be eternally grateful for her (marvelous!) husband and (beautiful!) children; the unconditional love of her mother; the unwavering support of her sister and brother-in-law; the kindness and benevolence of so many good people in her extended family; strangers and acquaintances whose stories and generosity inspired this novel; and her utterly awesome friends, who ran to her rescue far too many times and kept her laughing during this most extraordinary journey.

Behold the Dreamers

Imbolo Mbue

A Reader's Guide

A Conversation with Imbolo Mbue

Did you know you wanted to be a writer from a young age?

No, I never considered becoming a writer as a young girl. I didn't even know that being a writer was a career choice because I'd never met anyone who was a writer until I moved to New York City in my twenties. I knew there were people who wrote books because I read a lot of books, but I never thought about who these people were and how they came to write books. Even after I read Toni Morrison's *Song of Solomon* and became inspired to start writing, it wasn't so much to become a writer as it was to enjoy writing the same way I enjoyed reading. I'd been writing for twelve years before my first short story was published, and then about two years later this novel was published. So it basically took fourteen years from the time I started writing fiction to when my first novel came out. And in that period, I wrote hundreds of pages that are still sitting in my computer.

What did you think of America before emigrating here?

Much of what I knew while growing up was based on TV shows—shows like *Dallas* and *Santa Barbara*, which depicted characters living in material comfort. I got the impression that there was very little poverty in America and that it was a place where with hard work anyone could succeed. And I can't blame this on the shows—it was simply my way of analyzing the world. My understanding of America was also shaped by people from my town who'd emigrated to America and returned home to visit with nice clothes and shoes and an air of affluence that I attributed to the fact that they were living materially comfortable lives similar to the ones I'd seen on TV.

How did your first impressions match up with what you'd imagined?

I had quite an awakening the very first day I arrived, when I was in a car passing through an inner-city neighborhood. That was the first time it dawned on me that widespread poverty exists in America, and it's tough. And poverty is tough no matter where a person lives. But I'd never considered that this country, which I'd imagined wonderful things about, had people sleeping on the street, unable to afford college or basic healthcare, working long hours to barely make enough money to live on. Over time I would experience some of these challenges myself. One of the things I learned and saw around me is that the sense of failure at living in poverty can be very acute, especially for immigrants who purposely came here searching for a better life. I know many people who can't escape this shame—they work hard but barely get by; they feel like they have nothing to show for all their hard work; they wonder what they didn't do right, how come their American dreams haven't come true.

Your novel strikes a balance in addressing the pitfalls of the "American dream" without moralizing these failings. How did you craft that balance?

I wanted to tell a story about people like myself living in the America I had experienced—a wonderful country, and yet flawed in its own way. While the novel certainly highlights issues of class and income inequality, my goal wasn't to moralize but to tell the story, as truthfully and completely as I could.

Why did you choose to set the story during the Great Recession?

I was interested in exploring how the recession had affected the lives of New Yorkers from different backgrounds. The story starts in the fall of 2007, when the country seemed pretty stable and we were watching the rise of Barack Obama, which I thought was apt, considering that both the Obamas and the Jongas were dreamers— different kinds of dreamers, but still dreamers. The time frame allowed me to present the Great Recession from Jende and Neni's perspective, and being that Clark Edwards is employed at Lehman Brothers, it also allowed me to imagine what it might have been like for employees at Lehman Brothers in the days surrounding the collapse of the bank.

You must be interested in how economic breakdowns affect people's lives.

I'm very interested in the stories behind numbers, especially at a time like the financial crisis, when there were lots of dismal statistics. I remember, in the heat of the crisis, sometimes when I heard of a company laying off X number of employees, I wondered who the employees were and how long they'd been at the company and how that job loss would affect their lives. I had lost my job at the end of 2009 and I was struggling to find a new job when I started writing this story, so mine was one of thousands of stories of how challenging it was to be unemployed during the crisis. The crisis affected the two families in the novel in different ways, but ultimately they both had to deal with it opening and widening up existing cracks. It was a tense time for countless people worldwide—marriages were tested

and careers were derailed and dreams were reevaluated, and sometimes abandoned.

What kind of research did you do to write this novel?

Mostly I relied on my experience of having lived in New York City
for years as an immigrant from Cameroon—Jende and Neni are
from my hometown of Limbe, Cameroon, and they live in a Harlem neighborhood where I used to live. Much of their story, however, was inspired by other immigrants I'd met and with whom I'd
discussed the joys and woes of an American immigrant experience.
As for Clark and Cindy, I mined the brief encounters I'd had with
people who seemed to be from their world, as well as conversations I
had in parks with nannies and housekeepers who worked for people
like them. To better understand what went on at Lehman Brothers,
I read excerpts of the report prepared by the court-appointed examiner who investigated the firm's collapse.

**Clark and Cindy Edwards represent the privileged one percent,
yet they're undoubtedly human, relatable in their struggles and
sadness, and a reader can't help but sympathize with them. It
isn't often we see novelists portraying the uber-wealthy with
empathy, but that is precisely what you did. How were you able
to craft a sense of empathy for these characters and why?**

Oh, it was a long journey for me to develop empathy for Clark and
Cindy Edwards. I wish I could say that from the moment I met
them I understood them and valued them and felt for them, but that
wouldn't be the truth. Writing this novel was a lesson in empathy—
when I started writing it, I had a lot of judgment toward the Clarks
and Cindys of the world. But to tell this story honestly and completely, I had to learn to see them as humans—imperfect humans,
yes, but still humans like the rest of us, with virtues and vices and
joys and despairs and a long list of dreams. Developing empathy for

Jende and Neni wasn't difficult—they're from my town, I know the struggles of being a black, working-class immigrant—but someone like Cindy Edwards, on the surface she couldn't be any more different from me. I had to learn that showing empathy doesn't really have anything to do with having similar demographics or backgrounds or lifestyles. It's about a shared humanity.

Though on the surface the Edwardses and the Jongas seem completely different, many themes and issues unite them, one of which is the desire for wealth—striving to acquire more money. Was it your intention to write about money?

I wasn't exactly aiming to write about money, but it is very much at the center of the American dream, and because of this I ended up writing about how money, or the lack thereof, can make or break families. For the Edwardses, money isn't in short supply, but the price they had to pay to acquire that money has created fractures in the family. The Jongas, on the other hand, have very little money, and that comes with its own share of problems. To borrow from Tolstoy, both of these families are unhappy in their own way.

One of the remarkable things about the Jongas is that they represent the older generation of immigrants who came here, worked hard, got by on as little as they could so they could save for a better life. How do younger immigrants, coming of age in a consumerist culture, differ from the older generation?

The Jongas are indeed good savers, a trait I've noticed among older immigrants. Saving is great, but it's just not easy being a saver in a culture where one is constantly being bombarded with seductive messages about things to buy—things that will supposedly bring happiness. Considering how loud and prevalent these messages are, it is understandable that the younger generation might not value saving as much as their parents. That notwithstanding, I believe it's not only a consumerist culture that makes it hard for the younger generation to save but also the challenges of making ends meet. There are millions of hardworking young people who'd love to save and live a debt-free life, but they can't because low salaries, massive student loans, the high cost of housing, and the concentration of most of the country's wealth in the hands of a tiny minority make it difficult for them to have any money left at the end of the month.

Questions and Topics for Discussion

1. Immigration plays a huge role in this novel. For the Jongas, America is a place of hope and promise, a place where you can "become somebody," but the machine and policies are anything but welcoming and clear, and the road to citizenship is jagged. Discuss the portrayal of American immigration in this novel. How does this shift the traditional representation of America?

2. In Jende's job as a driver for the Edwards family, he often transcends the boundaries between their public personas and their private lives. Behind the safety of a closed car door, the Edwardses show their truest selves, and Jende is often a silent witness to much of what they would not show to the world: marital issues, the crumbling of Lehman Brothers, infidelity, family arguments. How does this affect Jende's understanding of this family? How does it inform our interpretations?

3. Though both the Edwardses and the Jongas have their own individual worries, so much of what concerns both of these couples is the well-being and success of their children. Discuss the parenting styles that the Edwardses and the Jongas utilize. How are they similar?

How do they differ? How can our own pathways in life inform the way we direct our children? How do our parents affect our futures and our view of the world?

4. On the surface, it would seem that Cindy and Neni are two extremely different women. Cindy, in particular, is a conflicted person, sometimes ignorant, conniving, and self-centered. However, it soon becomes clear that, in their own ways, Cindy and Neni are bonded, both women struggling to understand their roles as wives and women, and as the novel progresses, their identities seem to merge. How else are they similar? How are they different? What do they gain from each other?

5. Discuss the character of Vince Edwards. What do you make of his relationship to his family and his thoughts about his country? How do his opinions play a larger role in the novel? What do you think is in store for him in India?

6. Though they moved to America to find a better life as a couple and as a family, both Jende and Neni are inevitably affected by the way America shapes their personal identities. What are some of the ways they change as individuals over the course of the novel? How does their marriage change? Do you feel this is for the better or worse? How does it speak largely to the way America's ideals affect the members of its society?

7. Discuss the role of dreams in the novel. How do dreams drive the plot of the novel? What kinds of dreams do these characters wish to achieve? What dreams are deferred?

8. Though external forces drive the plot of the novel, the marriages of both the Edwardses and the Jongas fuel a lot of the drama as well. How do these marriages differ? How are they similar? How do both of these relationships influence the events of the story?

9. Though Jende and Neni are outsiders in American society, they also seem to have the clearest observations and insight into American culture. What are some examples of this? How does the role of an outsider provide a unique vantage point?

10. The Jendes often reflect on their home of Cameroon with both nostalgia and negativity; though they have left their homeland for a better country, Cameroon still remains in their hearts and minds. However, it is clear that even for Clark and Cindy, who are American citizens, it is very difficult to forget where you came from, the history that made you who you are. Discuss the concept of home in this novel. How does it affect the central characters?

11. Perhaps one of the saddest moments of the novel is the Jongas' return to Cameroon. What do you think of this decision? How do you envision their lives if they had tried to stay in America?

12. Consider the theme of power in the novel. How do some of the characters hold power over others? How do they yield this power?

13. Discuss the choice to set this novel in an America on the brink of recession and the Wall Street collapse. How would this story have looked different without this moment in American history? What would these characters' journeys have looked like?

14. Discuss the character of Clark Edwards, a man who seems to have many different sides. What is his culpability in the collapse of Lehman Brothers? What type of husband and father is he? Would you consider him a good or a bad man?

15. Consider the role of the American dream in the novel. How is this ideal defined in the story? In what ways is it manifested in the central men and women of this story? How does it fail them?

About the Author

IMBOLO MBUE is a native of Limbe, Cameroon. She holds a BS from Rutgers University and an MA from Columbia University. A resident of the United States for more than a decade, she lives in New York City. This is her first novel.

imbolombue.com
Facebook.com/imbolombue

To inquire about booking Imbolo Mbue for a speaking engagement, please contact the Penguin Random House Speakers Bureau at speakers@penguinrandomhouse.com.